D0346590

THE
SWITCH

JUSTINA ROBSON

GOLLANCZ

LONDON

First published in Great Britain in 2017 by Gollancz
an imprint of the Orion Publishing Group Ltd
Carmelite House, 50 Victoria Embankment
London EC4Y 0DZ

An Hachette UK Company

1 3 5 7 9 10 8 6 4 2

Copyright © Justina Robson, 2017

The moral right of Justina Robson to be identified as
the author of this work has been asserted in accordance
with the Copyright, Designs and Patents Act of 1988.

All rights reserved. No part of this publication may be
reproduced, stored in a retrieval system, or transmitted
in any form or by any means, electronic, mechanical,
photocopying, recording, or otherwise, without the
prior permission of both the copyright owner and the
above publisher of this book.

All the characters in this book are fictitious, and any resemblance
to actual persons, living or dead, is purely coincidental.

A CIP catalogue record for this book is
available from the British Library.

ISBN 978 0 575 13406 5

Typeset at The Spartan Press Ltd,
Lymington, Hants

Printed and bound in Great Britain by Clays Ltd,
St Ives plc

MIX
Paper from
responsible sources
FSC
www.fsc.org   FSC® C104740

Tower Hamlets Libraries	
91000008019212	
Askews & Holts	
AF FSF	
THISCH	TH17000105/0117

For Isylon

'Nature, nurture, heaven and home,
Sum of all and by them driven—'

The Humbling River, Puscifer

One: is the loneliest number

The Inquisition Judge glared at me.

A prickle of fear spiked down my back.

My lawyer looked at me through the toughened smart-glass shields that separated us. Her forehead was shining with perspiration.

The Judge's expression said that the battery acid of my trial was eating at her insides and she was glad it was over.

I stared at her robes as she carried on talking, taking in all the details to distract myself. The sun and moon in the planetary emblem of Harmony gleamed softly with their perfectly balanced light. The stars in orbit around them had that cupcake-frosting look the state animations had adopted lately.

'Nico Perseid, you have been found guilty of the murder of Dashain VanSant in the first degree. The sentence for this crime is death. You will be taken directly from this courtroom to the autoclave at Khor's Gyrus and there be terminated without delay. Born of the Sun, so we return to fire and light. Az, Lord of Light, and Muz, Lady of Contrite Reflection, guide your path to the next life.'

The prickle of fear became a trickle of sweat. I closed my throat against the sudden urge to vomit and glanced at my lawyer. She'd promised that the contraband wetware I'd had fitted was too golden to fry, hot or not. It didn't matter what happened in court, I just had to act my part so it looked like I was going the normal route to certain doom and then...

Actually there was no detail about the 'and then'.

What if there was no 'and then'?

The compulsion to vomit reversed polarity. I had to concentrate on not shitting myself. It amused me, that in spite of everything it had faced my body figured it was this empty, dry moment which was something worth fleeing. Then again, it's always been on the money. Dying in a street fight is an ordinary thing, a fair thing. The state killing you, that gets the fires of injustice burning at maximum heat.

As the observed minute of silence following my sentence expired the Judge added her signature to my execution order. You live your life in the Cloud, everything virtual and nothing real, but they do death old-school, on vellum, with black blood running out of a dead bird's feather. I don't know who the fuck that's meant to impress. An Alchemist could tell you, if they were high up enough in the ranks; they'd say that every choice and action has power and that even on those without psionic or magical abilities symbolism gets the voodoo working. It can alter reality through suggestion alone.

I'm a sceptic so I say that its purpose is to legitimise state murder with a ceremony of apparent worldly significance – or that it's a ton of bullshit that gets everyone's juices going so they can better enjoy it. Vellum, feathers, ink. Time to die.

I tried to slow down time by staring harder at those frosted fucking stars but the Judge kept on signing sheets.

'All rise.' The court burst into small movement.

Spots danced in front of my vision. I took a breath. Breathing. That seemed like a good thing. Breathe in, no fear. Breathe out...

I wished I'd killed VanSant. Both he and I would have deserved it. The loss of his death was a sudden deep stab of grief. I didn't even have the memory of murdering him to comfort me in my last hour. And there we were, in bitterness and rage – a

2

poisonous, sour combo that never fails to close down the gut into a pressure cooker. I know I should let it go; I'm the only one hurt by it and I'm the injured party here. Things are as bad as they can get already. But it's so fucking hard to let it go. Hating him and shaking with the need to crush his neck in my hands makes me feel so alive. This is how I know I can't have shot him. I'd never have let a gun come between us in our most intimate moment. I'd never have forgotten it. It might be me on the video, my hand and my gun, but I hadn't been in the driving seat.

I looked at my lawyer as she stood up. She felt around in her pocket and drew out a smoothly squared handkerchief which she folded and refolded with meticulous accuracy before patting her brow. She met my gaze but I couldn't read anything into her expression other than a professional glaze of sorrow which anyone could've practised for a moment like this as they watched their career tank.

My guts which had been sour mash a second ago turned to cold iron.

Abandoned. It figured. Well, good. Anger beats terror on the negative vibe scale. It's a whole vibrational upgrade for me. Yippee ki-yay. At this rate I'll be Enlightened before I get vaporised.

A guard nudged me, 'Time to go.'

I stood up with a heavy forward lean because of the weighted shackle that bound my hands in front of me. The second guard came close behind me as I started walking. I could feel his gun trained on me as sure as if a finger pressed between the ribs behind my heart.

Shit, what if this wasn't the setup I'd been sold? I did get illegal wetware implants and they were hacked into shape by my best friend, the most trustworthy person in existence, but neither she nor I were high on the food chain. I could've already fulfilled the only purpose the wetware had ever had, which was to get me to off VanSant. I mean, he'd been the one to get the gear for me in the first place. He said it was for driving starships and maybe it was, but maybe it had another function which had been exploited by someone – just not him and certainly not the hacker I knew. What had seemed so watertight before any of this happened looked like a big pile of shit from this end of the verdict. Now VanSant was dead I saw another version of events unfolding to the one that was planned. They said I'd go through a show trial and get saved at a point where the authorities would consider me safely slaughtered. Then go become some kind of resistance agent.

But seriously, how fucking likely was that? VanSant had a billion powerful enemies and the resistance to date has been as effective as wet toilet paper in a blizzard. So, who was laughing now? Starships. That was a kid's dream. If I had wetware it was garbage disposal bot brains or enforcement droid parts more likely.

It's not like I'd know the difference. Never could follow technical stuff, but everyone knows that if you see an enforcement droid in Harmony it's the last thing you'll see. They were made to kill first and ask questions – well, they never ask.

But what if it was worse than that and there wasn't even any fucking wetware? What if it was the drugs that made me get up from my bed and shoot VanSant with his own gun, just because he was there and all the hate I'd bottled up over the years had turned into a djinn that took over when the rest of me couldn't stop it? There were people in Harmony who claimed major psionic ability. The stars of Tecmaten's developmental program were the Inquisitors, Confessors – people who could do the cleaning by thinking about it. And others that could heal with a thought. But even if they existed and had any power worth pissing on I can't believe any of it was aimed at mediocre shit like VanSant. They had other brains to fry and I had my own dark god but, like I said, even he wouldn't use a gun. If he'd done it we'd've been found with my face in VanSant's chest eating his still-beating heart.

No, Nico, get a grip. There *was* something because Twostar hacked something, she didn't hack an imaginary object. She'd have noticed if it was an empty box and not the real deal.

So there really was wetware, but it could still have been swapped at the last minute for something else. Suppose it was Frackware – real-time psych vivisection. Sometimes for science. Mostly for profits. VanSant had talked about it once. He'd toyed with the idea of me getting some fitted so people could jack in and fight 'with' me, as me, whenever I went into the ring, or when I was training, or whatever. Adjust the tariff to suit the activity. It'd be a gold mine and sell offworld too, in the recordings market.

If it was Frackware, people could be on death row with me right now, cruising along inside my gibber while they ate popcorn and cracked open a beer. Wouldn't that have a fancy price tag, with me giving my own commentary and all? Look at that loser, thinking all this shit too late. That's fucking hilarious! But come on, let's get to the good part already.

Well, fuckers, looks like it isn't gonna be a long wait.

I walked with my head down and watched the robes of the guard in front. The heavily stitched fabric panels fell in straight, swinging blades as we walked. Their hypnotic sway was impressive. I'd always admired ceremonial tailoring. It had a certain badass defiance to it that spat on pragmatism. That amount of cloth around your legs, even in split panels, is crap for fighting in.

Then again, if you have plasma guns it really doesn't matter. You could wear a mermaid suit and still get the job done. No more triumph of the fittest or the most cunning. Given a gun, a bomb, any oxygen-waster could play dress-up Emperor, just like Tecmaten behind his army of Inquisitors.

Really the detailing on the sigils of the planetary emblems

was incredible. Virtue women made it all by hand, praying over every stitch.

Ain't no fucking prayers going to save you, bud, I thought. They turned off the direct channel to god when his service provider fell over under the load of all the queers asking Why Me, You Bastard? Now all your whining goes into Tecmaten's junk mail to give him something to laugh at while he's counting his money. It's that image of the old git cackling that sold me on the revolution, that and my entire life to date, give or take a day.

I didn't used to know that it was about money. When I grew up, like everyone else, I believed the Alchemy was the truth and that it was essential to keep the world turning by erasing mistakes and keeping all balances in check. Thanks to my position as the dumb friend of a tech genius who showed me news from beyond Harmony's reach I later understood that this world isn't the only safe harbour for humans in the universe, as it claimed. No. It's just one of hundreds of places and most of those weren't made by an incomprehensibly bigoted god with his mind on evolving a species to a perfect vision of himself – more or less Harmony's entire visionary mandate right there. Things were not this way everywhere. Being a deviant from the hallowed norm wasn't a ticket to death in other corners of the galaxy. Major news for me. Huge.

But we were still on Harmony with no prospect of getting out and I didn't change that much as a result of this revelation other than to become more focused in my anger. I still hated the system and everyone in it for being clueless fucktards. That was always going to be reliably safe. That was in the bank. It was only that my understanding of the evil altered. I now lived in a new kind of hell where I could see an outside to the prison but there was still no escape. My rejection was endorsed by reality. Harmony was a minor speck in a vast sky. But I was an even smaller speck of no consequence, until someone suggested that this might all be rearranged. Perhaps. Maybe. A bit. It's a dodgy plan but it might just work. Nico, you're our only hope. We can take it down. So I started to hope. Rookie error. I have to ask again.

Who falls for shit like this?

We walked down the exit ramp. It had worn carpet panels, rucked at the corners. I had to tread carefully so I didn't trip over them. I heard the guard behind me grunt as he stumbled over one and his gun jabbed me hard in the back just to the left of my spine. I recovered without breaking stride. He swore under his breath. I envied that carpet.

You know you're losing your mind when you start wishing you were a piece of cheap underlay so you weren't going to die, even when you thought you wouldn't care about dying now, or ever – but let's yank our shit back into shape again with some good old rage. Screw the carpet and fuck faith and its bastardised abortion the Alchemy, because it had fucked my life.

If it wasn't for the Alchemy I wouldn't be here. Hard to say who I hated most: Tecmaten's priesthood for screwing up my genes and giving me a comedic cocktail of errors, or me for failing to beat the odds. I mean, it had to be pure carelessness or active spite when someone so skilled turns out a creation that carries a socially fatal flaw – homosexuality in my case. Surely that's avoidable, given the level of engineering available. Coffee machine inadvertently filled with decaff the day I was cooked up, I assume. Or possibly dropped into the machinery, causing a short-circuit. And then, having discovered my place in things, there were all those years spent silently playing for time, thinking I'd best the bastards and fate itself if I waited long enough for an opportunity. But instead here I am alone on the short march.

Do not dream. Do not pass go. You're not the player, you're only a piece of a game you can't even see.

We walked under a skylight. The sun's sudden brilliance turned everything to gold.

Even the universe wants to say the joke's on me. Look, Nico, the Alchemy is everywhere proved true!

The sun is male; everything it does is over-powered and incinerative, flashy as a conman's smile. It's balanced by the moon and her never-ending rainy panoply of depressed girls drowning the evenings in beery tears and flop sweat. According to the Alchemy we're all made from a pair of these divine archetypes because everything is twofold, everything is divided and struggling to reunite. It's the eternal round of fire and ice, light and dark, all that binary balancing shit that seems so attractive with its promises that somewhere some fucker's going to pay for whatever crap you're in today. You know. Not now, or in a way that would satisfy you, but Cosmically, and probably after you're dead.

Regular people who go to live in Harmony proper are one sun and one moon (say that they're half and half and you'll end up doing community service for blasphemy). Regular people are exactly as the Alchemy intends. The Alchemy explains everything in terms of twinned energy flows. One of each, nice and tidy. I ended up with two suns, the golden double bullet which is how they look at male homosexuality at an energetic level. Too much sun. And then, if you get it on with someone, that's four suns which is enough to burn a hole in the local vibrational fabric. I forget what happens at that point. Might be it's a hole to another universe and creatures from the id start coming through to eat the souls of children. Something like that. I'm to understand it wasn't deliberate. It's never deliberate. These things are delicate operations. The Alchemists did their best but there's no sense crying over every mistake, just be glad they only execute the ones they find flaunting themselves in Harmony, singeing the warp and weft of reality with their filthy selfishness. (Not you girls, you plunge everyone into a cold, dank depression-pit. You're the drowning pool to our scorched earth. It's wet, it's dark, but it's still not an antidote to the solar burn so you are also fucked and we won't talk about the controversial horrors of bisexuality and every other variation on the theme). Anyway, thanks to this developmental misfortune I never got to live in Harmony itself, I was to be flushed straight down the sluice into its sister dark-side city, Chaontium, fishbowl of the damned.

Harmony purists don't kill you right off, that'd ruin their karma. And in any case it works out because they need a dark soul of degradation to balance the light perfection of Harmony's divinity, so it was all great in the end. Everything in its place. Some souls are just destined for Chaontium. Their existence proves the cosmic truth of the Alchemy's every principle. Where there's light there must be dark, and it must exist in equality. These principles underlie everything in Harmony from sleeping and eating to the most minute creation of variance in genes – not science alone, but science as art, as esoteric wisdom made manifest to the glory of scrod. I mean god. Whatever.

And everyone on both sides believes this hocus pocus like there's no tomorrow. From childhood it's in every cereal bowl and in every idea, every minute, every action. And people like me walk the plank to keep the ship straight.

Probably they just don't want to say to your face that you're the necessary sacrifice that saves the world, but only because some of the people in Chaontium are really dangerous and would turn their guns on the priesthood before they'd take an insult like that. Of course they'll take it up the ass in the dark all day long, and they do, but not to the face, dudes, not to the face when everyone's looking – you can't exploit people openly, what kind of uncivilised behaviour is *that*?

I think you could definitely sell the martyrdom line to the Chaos crew if it wasn't for the cartel bosses and their hair-trigger egos. No, though, because that'd make the bad boys good, right?

See, I never could get the hang of it. Even in my favourite teacher Masen's classes, where she was telling us how it worked with the greatest detail, in laborious, turgid afternoons that passed like stool through an impacted gut – even there the only thing I could pick up was the blissful confirmation that she knew, as I suspected, that it was all bullshit. Very beautifully worked out genius-level bullshit, but still, the end product is the same. I'd loved her double-crossing ways and now I felt like her most disappointing student, because I'd had some kind of chance most of us don't get but I was still following her to the same red exit light.

I wondered if she'd had to walk a long way too, knowing she'd made a mistake and that they were going to have the last laugh now. Twenty metres felt like twenty k in the hallway. I'd gone through a lifetime of lessons in two strides.

In the sun's glare every shining dust mote sparkling on the guard's shoulders was an angel of inexpressible beauty and I wanted to rip their wings right off. One more step and a shadow saved me the bother, wiping them out of existence. Back to reality, Nico.

The entire story I'd been spun about wetware was probably hocus. I was just another mob guy framed for some bigger-ass mob guy's business. That was a far more likely explanation. The wetware story just some soap to get me through the system without kicking up a fuss. They'd sell you any old shit to make their lives easier. It happened every day. What a sap.

We passed through the security doors and down a steeper ramp into the grey, unmarked corridors of the undercourt. The air was dry and crackly, arid, as if it hadn't been outside in years. It caught at the back of my throat and I coughed and stumbled with the surprise of it. I heard the guard behind me swear softly as something clicked on his gun and wondered if he'd come close to shooting me. That would've been funny.

His mate turned and made a grab to steady me or stop me. His hand on my arm was like a vice and I felt it flex once, surprise in it, testing the dense rocky structure he'd grabbed.

That's right, fucker. That's what'd hit you in the ring if we were there. I'd be breaking your bones if we were hand to hand.

He steadied me carefully, like I was his date.

What if my lawyer was wrong about the secret deal? Or suppose she was right but I sneezed and the jumpy bastards shot me anyway? My nervous giggle at this thought became another cough but it was too late to stop, the laugh-demon was out of its cage now and a bubbly kind of hysteria had me cough-laughing all the way through the long maze of corridors to the waiting hovercar.

It had black windows, black paintwork, state police strips all down the sides glowing like crusted lava. The guard put his hand on my head and shoved down hard so I'd clear the door frame. I jerked away from him automatically, cracking my skull on the rim and dazing myself. I'd been in too many fucking cars that creaked with wash-clean synthetic leather and carried the slight tang of vomit.

At least I'd stopped laughing but I kept my head up. I smiled. Never let them see they've got to you. My skin was the wet, red hood over someone else's nonstop scream. I watched from a distance, wary and amused by my own antics. I'd have to shut that crap down if I was going to get anything done.

The flight to Khor's Gyrus took a while. Thanks to the blacked-out windows there were no last views of Harmony City, no great vistas stretching from the cloud-scraping beauties of the priestly inner sanctums to the sprawling mess of levels beneath where Chaontium lay in its ugly roadkill sprawl, but I didn't have to see it to know it was there. I could feel it pulling. Sucking might be more accurate. Shit has its own gravity if there's enough of it.

The car dutifully replayed the solemn Final Rites service for me on a flat-screen. The recording jumped every few seconds and gave the priest a nervous stammer. Hu-hu-hu-holy. Like he was laughing.

The guard on my right kicked the dashboard. It didn't improve, so I lifted my left knee and put my booted foot through the screen. It shivered into a hundred or so jagged shards, half of which kept stubbornly displaying the ceremony in tiny sharp-edged fragments while the rest lay all around in flat plastic triangles like cartoon monster teeth.

'I liked your fights,' said the kicking guard as all three of us looked at the destruction. Almost at the same instant the other said, 'The damage will be paid for out of your legal costs,' in a way that suggested he'd had to say it many times before; these guys went through screens like whores went through tissues.

'I mean, I liked to watch you, you know, kick the other guy's head in. I won money on you a few times.' There was apology in the tone and a vague recrimination.

Well, awkward, but I'm nothing if not an obliging bastard. 'How d'you fancy a bout?' I held up my wrists, joints aching with the grip of the manacles. 'You can leave these on.'

I'd wondered sometimes what it would be like to have just half an hour left. Would I fall to bits and get that Final Moments Montage with its big reveal about the meaning of my life that made it into more than it had been? And here was the answer. No. Screw spiritual shit and all that yap about energy and signs and angels and crap, there was nothing. I was stuck with me right to the motherfucking end. Talk about an anticlimax.

I looked at kicking guard. 'Well? I'll give you an autograph. I could give you a scar. Two scars. Something to talk about down at the bar. How about it? Come on, as a last request?'

'I uh...' His uniform creaked as he looked around. His eye movements were twitchy as he accessed his networks. 'I didn't mean any offence. I guess you must've got a lot of girls. Right?'

'What?'

'You and the other fighters. Even the ugly ones. Ring girls all over the place. Drink, stims, all that stuff, you know. Like a vidstar. I heard they have a tent in the green room for that. Do they?'

I turned away from Number One Fan and looked at the other guard, Jobsworth.

He made an unhappy grunting noise that hinted he didn't approve of this breach in protocol from his partner but, like a buffalo gut-deep in mud, he wasn't about to stir himself over it. I got it.

'They do,' I said, returning to Fan. I smiled at him, batted my eyelashes. 'Would you like to try that instead?'

There was an eerie quiet, broken only by the insentient whirr of the car's drive fan coming dumbly through the bodywork insulation. A lifetime of hiding my sexuality as a deadly double sun in order to survive the Purges and now this. It was just one damn disappointment after another.

We wobbled through some hot air coming up off the stone playa to the city's western edge. I closed my eyes and leaned back, trying to clear my head and use reason to convince myself help might be on the way.

The thing about the wetware implants is they are a notoriously unreliable offworld tech. When they don't work they're a two-billion-credit waste of money that leaves you with a head full of inert metals and synthoids more valuable than your useless, brain-damaged life. When they do work they're a one-way pass to all the credits you can eat, if you happen to live in the free solar market. On a good piece of work you can pump them for twenty-five years and by the end of that you could reasonably assume better gear will long since have come your way. There are too many drawbacks to mention: the disclaimer list on the real thing takes a day to read, beginning with insanity. This explains the lack of people willing to give wetware a shot and the value of those that survive.

So, I was really valuable right now. Must be. Super duper valuable. But I couldn't find quite enough belief in that. My

13

need for it to be true was in a last stand against the battering of the past which had led me here. We were in the last round with the final sucker punch coming right up.

I sat in the car and tried my hardest one more time for the faith thing: I focused on remembering every piece of evidence in favour of it being true. I did have special wetware. I really had become the link to an offworld machine that was much too valuable to risk losing. It was real. The cavalry was coming for me.

The car tilted into descent.

Come on, be there. Prove me wrong. Come and screw up my life, but let me live.

Two Stars: technically this should be minus numbers as we're measuring time from when I got in the car but I don't do negatives so suck it

Twostar was more than the geek genius from the block who refused guild work to remain independent, relying on her too-good-to-kill talent for making machines do what she wanted. Twostar was the kid I used to feed out of dustbins when we lived on the Chaontium streets together, before gangs, before cartels. I'd trust her with my life. I'd even trust her with my money. What she touched was bound to be OK for me.

We met at the state orphanage. For me she'd always been there, so met is the wrong word. There was never a world that didn't have her in it. They called her Fae and her cot was next to mine. The beds got larger as the years passed but the relative positions didn't change. Other kids came and went in our lives and some of them were OK, but from the start she and I were together and we never needed anybody else. We instinctively shared a certainty that one day we'd be leaving together for better things. I don't know what I'd have done without her. Did she save me, or me her? Did we damn each other? Those questions only come at the end, don't they? But fuck them. I don't do end-times shit.

She was the brains of the outfit. Top of every class, the silent do-good girl with the hand that was held up enough to be polite but not so much it made everyone else feel bad. We all knew she knew every answer. I surfed by on the lowest possible effort and achievement, except for Physical Development. I slaughtered everyone at that.

Give me a ball and I'd dunk it. Give me a bat and I'd skyrocket whatever out of the park. Give me a pair of gloves and I'd get banned from boxing for going berserk. Two weeks in isolation – and by isolation I mean the works: Alchemical Isolation where you're so alone you start talking to the furniture and creating imaginary friends and enemies. That's what it's for. To give you enough space to go batshit and destroy yourself. Sweet punishment which is so typical of the Alchemy; they never lift a fucking finger if letting you do it yourself will get the job done.

Obviously I wasn't gonna give them the satisfaction. It was no punishment to me because it was a chance to stick two fingers in their eyes. It was a gift.

I got a room three metres square. It had a bed pad. There was a toilet and shower through a door in one corner that was partitioned off with a sliding screen. Food was lowered from a hole in the roof that opened and closed irregularly. They dressed me in white overalls. Projection covered every surface with the images of a sand desert. During the day the sun went up, around and down. At night the moon made its circles and the stars turned without interruption. It was completely silent and windless.

I saw the minotaur standing in the heat haze on the fourth day, late afternoon.

The sun was lowering, the light at its most golden and the shadows their most distinct. I'd been sleeping a lot, but by this time I was slept out and tired of the bizarre dreams which had become incredibly vivid in the absence of reality. I'd started to dream about the room too, so there were moments when it was hard to be sure whether I was awake or not. So when I saw him I figured he was only part of a mirage, his hooves hidden from the fetlock down beneath the silver sheen of the nonexistent water.

Then he was with me. His breath on my face, his hair, rough and stinking, against my cheek, the unmistakable touch of a horn against my forehead that knocked on the bone. I could feel the rough edge of it where it had slammed into walls and been splintered, then sanded down by endless dust storms. His hands were massive, callused, fingernails like megaliths. Dirt flaked off them as he flexed. He was taller than a human, and much bigger. There was a hellish heat to him. It radiated off him in waves that singed the hair on my arms, stung my cheeks. His skin and fur had a red cast as though he existed in a furnace of his own where red metal under stress was the only source of light. This red light glinted off the massive, planet-sized surface of his eyeball. The white edge was the crescent of the sun eclipsed. The black pupil was a black lozenge, widescreen format. I saw myself reflected in it: small, pale, a boy made out of sand.

I stared at a single eyelash of his and it was a black claw of vast scale, the prow of a spaceship, shuddering with the gravitational forces of his gaze. The mites crawling on it were the size of bears.

My attention snapped back to his eye. Then he was gone in a mirage shimmer. He became a series of stripes on a distant film, blurred with the speed of rising heat. The strips danced on the horizon and a flicker of anger in my guts matched the frequency.

I blinked and he was back. Full size, a behemoth, bigger than the world, bigger than the sun. I wasn't even a dust mote in his eye this time. His heat was intense. I was burning. The stink of crisping hair was everywhere. His attention was focused on me and I was falling into the strip of blackness at the centre of his eye. I felt with absolute conviction that one false move of any kind and he'd kill me.

We were in that orphanage to die. Not physically, that would have gone against the beautiful ethics of the Alchemy, against the rules of the world that said rejects must be treated with mercy, as long as they're grateful and stay within the laws. But in being born we'd already broken those. One false move and prison and death were sure to follow. It was only a matter of time. Two and I weren't up to requirements. Whatever we were, we weren't meant to do anything but exist to display the congenial mercy of the priesthood to all its monsters.

I already knew where all the monsters were. There's only one way to deal with them. You become a better monster. Every moment of my life was dedicated to that supremacy even if I had to wait and grow for another forty years. I'd burn *myself* to bits before I'd submit to any pretenders to that fucking throne. Even here and now I couldn't fall without a fight. Even if he turned me into ash.

I felt an incredible surge of power and strength as I lifted my fists.

Another blink. We stood opposite one another on the desert floor. His hands hung at his sides. His huge horns reflected the dying light of the sun. His skin shivered to shake off a fly. I lowered my hands. We were equals. But I wasn't sure that we were even separate. I recognised him. He was part of me. He was my ally, my power. He was my monstrous anger, my beloved, come to visit me in prison.

But also, he was himself. He stood, his massive muscles relaxed, his long tail swishing like a cat that's getting ready to act in annoyance. I felt the razor's edge on which we stood with each other. He could kill me. But I wouldn't stop if he tried it until one of us was dead, and that was the end of it. I thought he'd come with the intention to eat me – there can't be two kings in one land – but now that we were face to face he'd become uncertain. He and I suspected that if he went ahead with his plan then neither of us was going to survive.

He snorted. Flies and dirt showered out of his thick mane. He shook his head, eyes closed. The image of the desert shook with him. Then he turned and walked away. I watched his hooves kick up tiny dust devils until he vanished into the mirage.

I saw him a few more times after that meeting. I discovered that I could find him if I was half asleep but able to be wakeful enough to keep my attention on the desert. He'd be there in the distance, on the wall, in my mind. He was always there, but sometimes he couldn't be seen.

Hunting him kept me occupied through the endless, unchanging time. We never spoke. He couldn't speak; he had no words. He handled the sand, picking it up in fistfuls and then watching it run through his fingers. He couldn't hold on to any of it, not a single grain. I felt at peace when he did this. I could sleep, and feel that everything was going to be OK.

When the teacher came to get me out he had a curious look on his face. I knew it was because I was supposed to crack in there but instead I'd sat it out. Probably they made a lot of notes. He looked a bit afraid. I gave him the hairy eyeball. Mucho practised at that by now. It calmed him, because it was one of my usual reactions and he could rebuke me for it; it put us back on normal footings. I don't know what he'd been expecting. I should've worked on something special.

He handed over my regular clothes. I changed.

When I got back I was greeted at the dorm door by a hail of filthy balled socks. Other bits of dorm debris fell short or hit the walls above and beside me. I smiled.

Two looked up at me from her desk full of books. 'Did you really not hear them?'

Telling me to stop, she meant, as if the question wasn't separated from the incident by weeks.

'Yeah, I heard them,' I said.

She nodded. 'You looked happy.'

Punching the bag. Hitting it so the shock ran up my arm. Hitting it so no shock went up it. Learning the infinite grades between the shove and the strike, watching the swing, gloves to my face, glued to my cheekbones, snapping back into place, stepping in to find that a short sharp bang could split the seams

19

of the thing and have sand suddenly trickling to the floor. I was alive. I was on fire. It was perfect. I was a god.

'I was.' So happy.

'Did they lecture you on self control?'

I shook my head.

She narrowed her eyes. Around us the rest of the kids were already bored by my normality and had gone off to do other things. 'What then?'

I shrugged. 'Nothing.'

Two nodded. 'They came for Masen.'

'What?'

The dorm fell silent and still like someone'd blasted everything with a freeze gun. I didn't need more to know what had happened but she'd tell me anyway.

'It was on Thursday.' Meaning they had executed her on Thursday. Two days ago.

Immediately I felt it was my fault. They couldn't get me, so they'd got her instead. It was stupid, but it lanced through me just the same. 'Why?' As if I had to ask.

'Someone leaked a picture of her holding hands with a woman she knew outside school. Inquisition. The usual.' We shared a look and I glanced around, making that same connection with everyone else. The recognition of the truth was in everyone's eyes. Masen had delivered her teaching on the Alchemy perfectly. You would never have known if you hadn't closely watched her face that she was always telling us it wasn't true. That came with the brow movement, the lip curl, the gestures, all small, which barely altered her tone of voice but did enough to communicate almost the exact opposite of what she was saying. One lesson and you knew she was one of us and she was doing everything she could to tell us that it was OK to disagree, to think, to know the doctrine was wrong and to survive any way you could, only not openly. Nobody was dumb enough for that.

My brief elation at coming back safely evaporated. I hadn't

given Masen a thought as a human before. For all her badass attitude and the sense of her being on our side I knew she was a risk and I felt her as a weakness that I had to guard against. Because all that rebellion that made her so good as a mentor or a hero made her deadly to get close to. You don't befriend a risk because the system destroys all threats and silences all disagreement. If there is friendship it's secret. Even now I was schooling my face out of any reaction as inside my chest something broke and wet, watery weakness ran out. Who says I have no moon?

Someone had leaked a picture...

Footsteps in the corridor had everyone rushing back into whatever they'd been doing before. I had nothing so I looked at Two. She shrugged. Masen had been her favourite and Two was no danger-dog like me; she loved fiercely and with exacting loyalty. She brushed her arm across her eyes, cleared her throat. Her face was a mask of indifference as she opened up the files she'd been studying and went back to them.

'So, you're back, Perseid.' The footsteps had been Colian, who didn't bother to conceal his dislike of everything. I don't think there was a thing in existence that he didn't feel a special spite for. He was the kind of guy who lovingly cherished every little whisper of his hatreds, spent long evenings polishing them into sparkling gems with razor edges. He was due to cycle back into the echelon in a year and get a post in the Inquisition's finest. The waiting was getting on his nerves. 'Kitchen duty all week for you: bins, garbage, composting, pig-feed. Holiday's over. Snap to it. Haven't got all day.' He was carrying a pair of grey overalls and threw them at me so they hit me around the shoulders. The sleeves and legs wrapped themselves partially around my head like a bag. He was already turning and out the door before they'd fallen to sag in a loop around my neck.

The minotaur looked at me.

I flexed my hands. I needed to be much, much stronger.

I put the overalls on and went to work.

21

Getting out of the orphanage was nothing more than dumb luck but it took another few years for that luck to arrive and when it did there was no warning.

Our tutor left the room in a hurry at the sound of the class bell. The door behind him was blocked as students tried to exit and were slowed by a class filing out of the cloister at the same moment. To my left one of the windows was open thanks to the air conditioning failing for the third time that week. At that same instant there was a fight starting in the corridor: one of those where you knew some older kid had finally snapped and wasn't going down without taking someone with them. No more corrections. No more marks. Enough. A klaxon went off to summon a security drone. Jeers and yells said the fight was getting bigger.

I trod on Two's foot as she tried to get up from her place next to me. I looked at her and then at the window. Her eyes widened and she swallowed visibly, but nodded and that was all it took. I gave her a leg-up over the sill and she jumped out as I got up behind her. We were on the second level of the building.

I fell into the strange heat and muggy air, crashing through wet green masses of foliage so I was drenched before I hit the mud at the bottom. I was winded and lay gasping, unable to breathe. We'd landed at the road's edge. Above me the coal-black face of the building stood like a blunt cliff, the window empty.

We ran as soon as we could breathe, leaving a slugtrail you'd have to be as dumb as shit to miss but nobody was following and in the minutes that passed it came clear nobody would. We were relieved and terrified, but as Two pointed out, we'd crossed the state line into Chaontium after only fifty metres. All the runaways go that way, as god intended they would eventually, after they reached eighteen, heading from the patriarchal care of the pure state to the impure destiny that genetics dictated for us. We were beyond the reach of Harmony. We could never go back. We were unclean and nobody would come to claim us. It was thrilling and a disappointment at the same time.

A short while later a grey car cruised up beside us. We genuinely were dumb as soup so we were still walking along the actual roadside as if we belonged there. We didn't even run as the door slid open.

The interior was well lit so we could see the men and woman sitting inside. The sun shone in on their feet, turning their boots, stockings and laces all to gold. It never occurred to us that it was odd for some tub of rich scum to barge up against us so fast. 'Want a ride? You must be lost.'

Back then those weren't even lines. The car wasn't even a plateless cartel cruiser. These people weren't chancers. We weren't commodities. That was how little we knew.

I looked along the street to where we'd been headed. It might as well have been another planet for all I recognised. A glance up showed the stacks of the buildings rising into vast skies, one cake-layer of ziggurat at a time. Paths strung between them were covered in lanterns. Forty storeys up the second aerial car deck carried quick little pods and steady schooners through the air on invisible rails. Near the clouds at the peaks barques with flotillas of accompanying service vehicles drifted at loose sky anchor; stateless palaces that could take off into the deserts on a whim. I looked back into the car before us. The woman had old, sad eyes in a young face. I tugged Two's hand silently but she was frozen, staring into the soft cool of the interior. She didn't know what to do.

'Isn't your home right over there?' the woman said, indicating the orphanage through the car's window. She made a languid movement with her arm and hand, an underwater gesture that matched her odd tone. She was smiling.

I hauled and got another few steps out of Two. The car slid along to join us.

I knew they'd take us somewhere bad. There was money in it

for them. I could feel it coming off them in waves. The woman's too-casual way and focused eyes, the men's bulging jacket-fronts. They'd get money any way they could. They'd have licked cat shit if someone paid them. And nobody would miss us.

I pretended to stop and consider. 'No, we live the other way.' I pointed up-street, towards the ziggurats. 'Really.' I didn't need to fake the desperation.

'Then we'll take you there. Get in.' The man speaking was a greyleopard, one whose genetic anomalies were written all over his mottled skin. It made his expression unreadable and his features indistinct. His voice expected obedience. His contempt won out over obedience though: he couldn't wait for it, even if it was coming.

At the sound of his impatience Two broke and ran away from the ziggurats and back the way we'd come, across a strip of waste ground filled with weeds and broken bot carapaces. On the other side of the strip a diner and a store looked like they might be open. The street itself was empty. I stood my ground to hold them fast in the car.

'If you get her you can let me go, yeah?' I said.

'Sure,' the woman agreed easily while an arm snaked out of the door towards my shirtfront.

I ran, shouting, 'I'll get her back!' As if.

There were a few moments when it seemed we'd both make it. Then the car's rear flank fishtailed into my back, caught me and sent me flying forwards. I saw the diner wall rushing up to meet me and it was so bad I just relaxed and let myself go with the irresistible power. That had a kind of deliciousness to it: an effortless deep serenity in which there was nothing I could do. I felt successful at escaping, though the opposite was true.

The rest of this story was told me later by Two, as I had no memory of it at all. My memory ended at the wall.

In the end they'd left us. They thought I was dead, and Two

is fast. She made the diner door just as a patrol drone descended from the higher decks to make some regulation street sweep. I guess the cruiser had hot plates because it shot off with the drone in pursuit and then Two ran back out for me. Only she thought I was dead too. She was sure. No heartbeat.

'Your eyes were open,' she said. 'Like glass.'

Her screaming brought people out of the diner. They looked and left, except for one, a woman in grey, wrapped up in scarves, only her face showing. Two said she was fifty or so, not exactly ugly but something like it. She had pale grey eyes, dark skin. She told Two to stand back, then knelt over me and laid her hands on me. Two said there was nothing to see but a minute later I got up, not even blood on my face. She was so happy to see me alive and I was so dazed that we lost track of the rag woman. By the time Two had told me what happened there was no sign she'd ever been there, except a footprint Two swore was hers. Some cheap work boot. Could've been anybody's.

Though we looked, we never found her again. People with that kind of power are never outside the Citadel. Never. It sat badly with me. Much as I hated the world, I hated it more when it didn't fit together right. After a while of pondering the impossibilities I figured that hitting the wall had felt just a bit harder than falling out of the window, and it hadn't hurt that much. The woman must have come just as I was waking up anyway. Two was wrong. I wasn't dead, only stunned. That made a lot more sense.

I never mentioned this to Two. Her brown eyes burned with tears whenever she remembered it and it lit her face up with fierceness I didn't want to take away. It had given her something.

'She was an Exalted,' she said, with absolute certainty, lip quivering.

Exalted are a fable. Tecmaten's pinnacle of human development that justifies all he does and everything that the Alchemy was created to produce. But Harmony grinds on and there's no sign of it stopping in a grand finale, so he can't have made one, can he?

No, I'm not a believer.

At thirteen we were still living on the street.

I hated it most when it rained an hour before dawn in the winter, like this. It was so cold even the rats had buggered off. Twostar and I gripped each other like we were mountain climbing. I couldn't see her in the dark under the layers of rags and old clothes, only feel her bones digging into me and the beat of her heart against my chest. It was faster than mine because she'd woken up first, like always.

I heard the patter of the drops and then the change to a steady burr. Our rags were damp from days and days of rain and we regularly woke up shivering. The smell of the heap was fucking awful, thick with mildew and rot, and it was giving us both a cough.

After a minute or two I stopped feeling her heart. First time it happened I thought she'd died but it was only that it'd synced up with mine so I couldn't tell them apart any more. She was making a soft 'Zhh, zhh' sound through her teeth as she breathed, in the effort not to let her jaw chatter. My hip and shoulder hurt from the ground so hard they were fit to crack.

'Hey,' I said, to fill the silence, but real quiet, in case something was out there to hear us.

'Nng,' she said. She didn't like to taste the air. And she was afraid of rats, though in the daytime she'd trap them to use as bait for garbage-bots.

We were already clutched so tight it wasn't possible to get closer or do anything but let go and neither of us did that. Between us there was a trace of warmth. It would get better at dawn. It would get better later, when we could move. It would be all right in the first half of each night before our clothes ran out of power. It'd be better in fifteen hours or so when I could get food for us. I'd become an expert clock. I knew right where every second of those fifteen hours was. This was the worst part, right at the start, when there was still so much of it yet to go. But it was still better than waking up at the orphanage in the warm, knowing everything that would or could ever happen between one minute and the next.

I coughed first and then Two joined in, both of us trying to keep it as quiet as possible, which wasn't really possible but we had to try because nothing must find us.

Eventually we got warm enough to move. I was the first to burrow out of the mats and rags. I took it slow. The weight of the soaking rubbish was difficult to move. I left props behind me every night, so in the morning I could create a tunnel that would allow a quicker way in and out for daytime access. The best props were the wings of delivery drones. They were big and strong enough to force stuff up and over them and they were some metal alloy that didn't care about the wet. Once the tunnel was done I emerged into the cover of some old bushes and started my checks.

First the sky. It was always busy over the city, day or night, but out here in the wasteland the only regular visitors were surveillance droids and cargo drones using the cheap airzones that took long, slow routes around the city outskirts. Today a weather droid was making its characteristic step by step progress, sampling the air at fixed points before moving on. The survey wasn't due yet and there was nothing else to see. I tapped out the all clear signal and after a few minutes Two squeezed out of the heap and came to crouch beside me. Her wrists were so thin that the veins stood out over the bones. She shivered constantly.

I looked across the spoil heaps for any signs of life. Somewhere out there, not too far away, some little snitch would be holed up watching for us. The rain made it difficult, but also difficult for them. Every day I took us a different route out of the yards and we always had a different plan, random, to help keep us safe, but lately there'd been spies on a lot of points. The gang which had only ever kept an eye on us before was hunting us now. It didn't matter, though, because we had to eat today, so we were going to grab a maintenance droid and get its memory cores and battery packs. They sold for a lot at the right kind of store. But I was worried. We'd done this a week ago and I think that's what had changed the gang activity. They must have found out about it and now they'd be waiting for us to do it again. And we had no choice, because since the gang had moved onto this patch they'd taken up every other source of food and income. We were so tired and hungry, we had to make a decision.

I looked at Two, gripped her hand, 'Still want to do this?' I meant not only the droid theft but the whole thing. Stay here, surviving in the lowest way, in order to be free. She was terrified of the gangs and equally terrified that we'd be swept up and carted off once we entered the city streets. Without a gang we were easy meat.

She nodded, jaw clenched, squeezed back. Fine. We were going. I picked my route and we set off, hand in hand, crouched over, scurrying from stack to stack of sorted recycling as the rain soaked through our clothes and ran out of our shoes. There was mud. It was impossible not to leave a track. On the other hand the rain blurred all the sightlines.

First we had to check the traps. Two had rigged up ten of them at points where composted waste was sorted and graded, because rats searched there for scraps. But today the first trap was open, empty, and the rest had been tampered with. After the third Two sat down on her heels and swore. 'Someone's ruined them.'

In the puddles a variety of footprints of small and large sizes said there were at least three of them. No rats. My stomach growled and hurt. I wanted to exact a large dose of pain on someone. Why? They were rats for the love of Amalgamation. But I knew the answer – my gut knew it – even rats have a value and anything on this turf was now theirs. We were finished.

Two's shoulders shook. I thought she was crying but it was hard to tell.

'We can still get one,' I said, without any notion of how.

'How?' She flicked the broken wire of the trap away from her into the mud.

'Come on.' I pulled at her hand. She didn't budge. 'Now. Come on. They'll be watching.' That got her moving, and it was true. If I was hunting us, I'd know I only had to hang here for long enough and we'd show. I took her where we'd planned to go anyway, as if we had bait, only when she realised she started to lag.

'What's the point, Nic?'

'We're getting one,' I said, towing harder, wishing we had somewhere to run. But there wasn't a stretch of ground left anywhere that wasn't somebody's business. We'd been lucky for a few years and now it had run out. But if we were going to do something then we had to have money, which meant having droid guts to trade.

'And then what?' She was actively trying to stop and give up now. My hand slipped in hers as she let it go limp. I gripped harder but I had to pull less. We stopped.

'We eat,' I said. 'Dry clothes. New ones.' That would cost us nearly everything we had.

'And?'

'We leave.'

'Where to?' She always had a reply for everything.

I shrugged. 'Does it matter? We can't stay here.'

She dashed rain off her face with the back of her hand. I saw her struggling with her thoughts. She was so smart, she could think us through anything, but sometimes she thought us into nothing. I saw her accept it. It took her longer than me, that was all. 'How are we going to get a droid?'

29

The droid. How indeed. Especially when I was sure they'd be waiting for us. I looked around. The rain was slowing, the leaden grey skies lighter. You could see to the third skydecks. I realised where we were standing – at a crossing where one of the many snaking tracks through the spoil heaps transected the major transport lane. I looked up at the sky again.

'What time is it?'

Two looked at the watch she'd made, sewn into the flap of her jacket. 'Ten-oh-five.' She looked back at me, her eyes whiter. 'We can't take that one.'

At ten-ten every day a city security drone, bigger, tougher and faster than any of the others around here, would descend from the fifth skydeck and make a sweep of the recycling plants to collect data from the reprocessors. It would be carrying information from everywhere in the city it had visited that day, including all the parts of the High City where the population of Chaontium wasn't permitted. That drone would be worth a lot. Though there was the small issue of its defences to consider.

'Give me your wrench,' I said, holding out my hand.

'Nic—'

But I always had more strength of will than she did. 'Give me it!'

She reached into her inner pocket and took out the precious metal object, holding it lovingly, before reluctantly passing it to me. 'It has hardly any charge.'

'That's OK,' I said. 'Wait over there.' I pointed to a spot where a tall power relay planted its feet and cast deep shadows, but more importantly provided a hefty reinforced concrete pile.

'What're you going to do?'

I pointed to the largest and highest of the mounds of recovered metal. It was high enough to rise above the droid's typical flight path. It was scarcely a plan, I knew that, but I was making it up as I went along and this was all I could think of. I was sure it was possible. '*Go.*'

30

'You'll get killed,' she wailed, but there was not much fight in her – we were too tired for that and our situation too obviously hopeless.

'No, I won't.' I grinned and shrugged at her. 'I can't die, remember?'

She stared at me, her eyes so large and serious, full of emotions, some of which weren't nice. 'If you die I'll kill you.' She tried to smile but she couldn't do it.

'OK,' I said. 'Deal.' I turned and ran up the heap. My heart was juddering like crazy, like it couldn't settle and didn't know if it was going to run itself out of beats entirely or only panic and skip a few. High above us the droid was already signalling its way out of the airstream and starting its descent. I watched it as I reached near the top, figured that as long as it followed the usual path then it would get close and low enough that a running jump would land me on it. The heap was a treacherous pile of crap but the droid was close enough I didn't need so much of a leap, maybe more of a calculated drop. I picked out a small, loose metal strut from near my feet and gripped it hard. I put the wrench away.

The droid became my entire world. Its fins and curves gleamed silver grey, rain pearling on it, dancing. It had a flat, broad back between its twin fans. The air shimmered around it with the force of its vibrations and the heat of its burners. It came down like a monstrous fairy, ignorant of danger, slowing as it drew close to make its visual sweep. I sprang onto it with the rain, starfished. The wrench was a breathtaking agony against my chest, where I'd stuffed it in my vest.

The droid dropped with the sudden downforce and struggled, whining and tipping, to stabilise itself. I slithered across it, much faster than I'd expected, and fell off the front of it. On my way past, just before it and I parted company, I threw the strut at its left intake vent as hard as I could. Then I hit the edge of the heap and went tumbling down the flank of it.

When I stopped everything hurt but I knew it wasn't fatal. Overhead the droid spun wildly, circling, tipped over. Smoke and black fumes poured from the vent. It made a sputtering noise and its free engine whined suddenly. Correction jets came on and off, leaving puffs of white here and there stabbing into the mouldering, wet air. It veered off course, falling quickly, and passed over my head with a few metres to spare before ditching on the ground and sliding through the mud, engine howling until it hit the upright post of the power pole and wedged fast there. Pretty much exactly where I'd told Two to stand but I saw her running towards me instead, splashing through the filthy runoff.

If that didn't bring the gang out to play then nothing would. We had to get it first. Had to. I felt despair as I realised how long it could take.

As the droid ground and clanked and suddenly whirred into a shutdown mode Two reached me. 'Nico?' She grabbed my shirt but I was already getting up. Bright red was dashing in little rivulets down my hands and off the ends of my fingers.

'Get it, get it!' I shoved her off me, recovered the spanner with my better hand and thrust it at her. I couldn't let all this pain and stupidity be for nothing. I could feel the minotaur wring his hands. 'Go, go, go!'

She took the wrench, bewildered as its lights came on dimly to her touch. 'But what was this for?'

'Luck,' I said, despite it having ripped into my side. I made myself run. It hurt an incredible amount, though different places of me were fighting to pain me the most and so it seemed to flicker all over, like electric clothing. It felt good to spite it and move. Fuck you, death, fuck you all, I'm still alive! I knew I was high as a kite but the rush was too much. I couldn't remember what I was meant to be doing. *Look around you, moron,* I thought, but I was watching Two as she reached the downed machine and started her delicate work. Crouched on her haunches, ragged and black with muck, she looked like a

32

scrawny carrion harpy. The droid sighed and whirred under the touch of the wrench and gave itself up with a soft hiss of vacuum releases.

And then we weren't alone.

They came from every direction in ones and twos, rising up like smoke and coming out of their camouflage in an eerie silence of common purpose – fifteen kids, skinny and wild looking, but none as bad as us. Each of them held some kind of weapon in their hands, ranging from bits of junk all the way up to what looked like an automatic rifle from a police drone, the stump of its mountings trailing the feather and bone rags of the gang colours. I didn't want to risk that thing working, though where they'd get the fucking ammo from I don't know.

I was furious, like I should have seen them and stopped them, but suddenly found myself sitting down, splat, in the heavy mud and water. My legs had decided things for me. My back hurt so bad I hoped one of them was going to hit me with something heavy and not draw it out.

Yeah, said the minotaur, *but fuck that, buddy. Fuck that.*

I got to my hands and knees. I got up.

Then I got up again.

They stopped a respectful kind of speculating distance away, watching Two, eyes round, watching me, eyes narrowed.

I crossed the million miles to Two's side. She hadn't noticed them yet. She didn't notice me. She was in the machine's guts, telling it to quiet down, not to tell on us, to give up its power and its secrets quick and easy. At last she turned, her arms full of slender lozenges, trailing wires and flopping connectors.

She stopped dead, frozen against me. The rain had stopped. The air was full of the sound of dripping.

The kid with the rifle gestured with the tip of it – *give that to us.* He lifted his chin. Cocky. Certain he was in for a killing.

'Nic?' Two whispered, shaking as she clutched the tech.

I couldn't fight them. I couldn't do anything about that gun.

'Come and get it,' I said. I was glad the dead droid was behind me. I leaned on its still-warm body.

There was a moment's silence, then the leader pushed his lieutenant – a short stocky kid with stubble starting on his face – hard on the shoulder. They didn't speak, but the message was clear enough.

He had a piece of rebar in his hand and as he came he lifted it, flexing his hand to grip it better. I watched him cross the slurry of the droid's death track, slipping a bit. He got slower as he neared. Scared. Other members of his gang had had run-ins with me over the last couple of weeks. Now I was the one in ribbons. He'd seen me on the ground, he knew I was slow.

Two was starting to whimper next to me but she didn't have any illusions that handing over the tech would be our ticket out either. She kept hold.

The blow came fast and hard, but aimed badly – his eyes were closing, his face turning away even as the bar was closing in on my head, and it met my forearm and hand instead. Grind my feet into the filth, brace against the droid, grab and twist hard, pull in the same direction as the force is moving and he's right there tumbling into me, one foot in the air, arm out. He's heading face first into the ground and I'm sitting on top of his back and shoulders with the bar in my hands looking at Rifle. He looks at Rifle too as he spits and swears and I bring the bar down and cave in the back of his head. He goes limp under me and the air goes out of him and he deflates. I'm surprised by how you can feel the difference between alive and dead so clearly but it's night and day. Dead is empty.

Rifle stared at me.

I reached around the dead guy's neck and took off his necklace with its signature ganghammered drinks can sign from a brand of orange that had a tiger as its mascot. The meaning was clear to me, and to Rifle by the way he watched me, a glint of greedy approval in his eyes – one out, one in. I put the sign on and then I used the bar as a stick to help me get up and stand. I beckoned to Two and she was at my side, helping me, all the gear cradled in her arms like a baby. We had declared our allegiance.

After about a thousand years Rifle just nodded, once, and slung the gun onto his back. I felt a surge of relief and a sweetness. The others came rushing up to help us, surrounding us, lifting, carrying, arms around shoulders. From nought to family in ten seconds. And then it all went black.

After we'd recovered, our places in the Silent Hands were assured and the huge money Rifle got for the tech didn't hurt. We stuck with them a while, but all they wanted was to hunt droids and spend the profits on weapons or getting high. After a few months Two was restless and unhappy. Every hunt was risky and she felt it pressing on her much harder than the others. Rifle insisted on a hunt every other week, then every week. Two looked at me sadly and I knew we had to go. Getting out was probably harder than getting in. I promised her I'd do something and I went walking on the streets, doing my rounds, wondering how I was going to manage this feat.

There really weren't many ways out of poverty, especially once you'd got consumed by the ganglife. Two got by because she could slice and fry all kinds of gadgets. People like that are worth a lot right from the get-go. Tech is easy for them to steal, easy to process, always sells for a lot. Gangs snap up slicers as soon as look at them, hoard them like gold. I was just her guard dog. I'd shepherd her into the back of a stolen car, run her onto construction sites and watch while she hacked bits of their droids, even whole droids... looking out for rival gangs who wanted to steal her from us, fighting them off with whatever. Sometimes it was guns or knives, sometimes just fists. Cop drones kept an eye on us but they rarely got involved. It was all very small-time, not worth the public money to crack down on.

But Rifle's ambitions grew steadily. It was only a matter of time before he tried for a cop drone.

And then it came to me. Two's slicing and writing abilities were pushing her reputation and it was getting out of hand. Suddenly I saw the way out. Her rep attracted too many hits on the gang from rival outfits. Eventually one of them would get lucky.

A bit of suggestion soon had Rifle's profit-orientation heading in a new direction: he sold her to one of the most prestigious syndicated crime rings. I went with her, because otherwise she wouldn't go. Once it was clear we'd rather be shot than parted things went smoother. Thus I saved her and she saved me on step one of the ladder out of Scum City; otherwise I'd still be there, or more likely be dead. I wished the people that had thrown her into the orphanage could know about it, the fuckers, see the look on their faces if they knew what they'd lost.

The second thing that changed was that my childhood puppy-fat dropped off, my bones grew and my combat training conspired with my genes to transform me from a little thug with attitude into an actual man. There was a hefty surge in attention that came my way and it became much harder to conceal the twin sun factor. Two said maybe it wasn't worth the bother, Chaontium was more than half bent anyway and as long as you pretended and kept quiet you weren't going to get ratted out, but the shadow of the Citadel stretched far into the soul even of those who hated it. Yeah, Masen had played fast and loose with things and that's what happened to her. I didn't want an Open Season ticket stuck to my back and I didn't have time for the complications.

A pair bond of male and female put sun and moon together in cosmic harmony. A gay pair was two suns or two moons: burn or drown, but either way meant destruction, literal and figurative. It was the greatest curse with a power strong enough to ruin lineages, thwart dynasties, and overthrow leaders. The priests even claimed it had some kind of real energy, like magic – a bad kind which would topple the natural order of things if it were not repressed. But the chinless motherfuckers would say that. Once you've got a convenient set of scapegoats for your problems why spoil it?

Of course the insurgents of various rebellious parties and movements challenged this but they were inevitably throttled, infiltrated, poisoned or shot by the success of the ruling zealotry. You could watch the executions on Newsnet. They were always presided over by serious, sad-faced Inquisitors, so very downcast at the tragic horror of their righteous duty in terminating otherwise healthy stock. Then the depression of the anaesthesia, the eyes slowly closing, the swelling music, the grim intonations and all that sick shit that followed before the autoclave burned up the remains and tidily deposited them into little pots.

I wondered where they'd put Masen's little pot. Had anyone even wanted it?

Meanwhile the sun didn't burn brighter. The moon didn't go out. Apparently you could have the technology to travel to either and stand on the arid, cold rocks or photograph the incandescence of gigatonnes of fusion, but you couldn't recognise a fucking metaphor when one was thrust into your face every damn day of your life. Magic my ass, it was hate that the world ran on.

So anyway. Don't be queer. Rule number one of survival. From day one this knowledge had given me a righteous fury that was the burning core of my power. I was, inside, a crusader and I wasn't about to dim that light by doing what Two suggested and finding a boyfriend. Even thinking about it made me feel my passion drain and I wasn't giving up my endless minotaur battery pack for a kiss and a tumble. The rising tides of lust in me burned with a near physical pain and I hoarded them and fed them to my monster.

*

37

Twostar and I could have saved each other, to some degree, by pretending we were in a relationship. But we'd already agreed to stick to friends only and our street brotherhood was seen as bond enough. There were some weird consequences.

As glorified Queen of Hacks within the cartels, Two was high status in a male-dominated world that prided itself on being as generous to every loyal servitor as it was ruthless to every disloyal one. Men as high up as Two were sent escort girls as part of the standard perks so she got sent men, and then later some women after her preferences got known. And Two was not unmoved by the gift; she was moved to homicidal rage at the idea of exploiting more choiceless people. She greeted their arrival with a locked door, leaving me in my capacity as bodyguard and general gofer to serve snacks and make small talk. We spent the time watching movies and playing games.

I learned to be damn entertaining damn fast because none of them owed us a thing. As soon as they figured out I wasn't going to take advantage of Two's disinterest, which they rightly found insulting even if they were relieved, they started to check me out – figure out if I was going to double the pain and give them a bad report, which would make it tough for them to keep eating and breathing. They arrowed in like lightning. What was my deal? Was it drugs? Was it a girlfriend? Was it a vow? Why wasn't Two up for anything?

For Two I told the truth – she was happy for them to say whatever they had to say but she wasn't going to be part of an exploitation ring. They thought it was hilarious, but she signed them off so they didn't care if she was frigid or clueless, idealist or crazy. Crazy kind of went with the territory.

For me, I decided it was a vow. A nice big devotional act of purity of the kind that superstitious types love to swallow. Everyone was superstitious, doubly so in Chaontium where you really needed all the mojo to be working for you. So I acquired a sudden, miraculous faith that rendered me virginal and untouchable. My celibacy was a sacrifice to the god of war and in return I was invulnerable in battle: it was pretty close to how I felt anyway. I could sell it to myself easy. And so I became Two's 'mystic monk', because in Harmony if you're praying nobody can hear you scream.

The Girls adopted me as their little project, perfecting their grooming skills on making me cute while the Guys made every effort to sleep, game or drink their way through the hours, eyeing me with wary caution or contempt as I was turned from bodyguard into dress-up doll. I got to practise my poker face as their beauty paraded itself up and down within reach, idling over my games, drinking my liquor and ignoring my low-status ass. The Girls stained my skin tone to a fashionable darkness and lightened my hair to the lightest blond, nearly paper white, in an effort to make me resemble the hero of their favoured animated soap opera, which I couldn't stand. Pretty Flower was a guy with absolutely no muscle tone and the face of a sixteen-year-old brat who miraculously showed up to kick ass with 'fury of the whirlwind!' whenever his mistress the moon goddess had had enough of whatever idiotic mortal bullshit she'd landed herself in that week. All the gym rats had a good laugh over it whenever I went to train while among the cartel hench-grunts it acted as the bait for a lot of fights, so it had its upside.

The silly transformation became a perfect cover. Combined with the vow and the hours I put in at the dojo in training everyone assumed I was the real deal and I didn't get any hassle. And though the tag itself started as a bit of fun my dedication to the martial art was sincere – I'd been committed since the Master had let me watch her teach through the cut screens of the dojo walls when I was back in the rubbish tips with Two. After dark she'd leave soup out on the porch, which I thought I was stealing at first. When I'd eaten it I moved the screen door aside to look in. Nobody was there. The mats were awry, though, and I rolled them up and put them away. The next night the same thing happened. The night after I saw there was a broom lying on the floor, so I swept up before trying out a few moves in the empty dark.

From then on every night I'd sweep the rooms, roll the mats and clean the pads. Mysteriously the materials for doing this were always waiting outside the office door. One day the Master came out as I was sweeping and feigned surprise. She pointed out a few bits I'd missed. A month later she paused in the middle of the room to practise a form before she went back to her office. I practised it for eight weeks straight before I saw her again. I don't know how long it would have gone on if the Silent Hands hadn't cut us off from the city, but I don't think I'd have managed that move on the droid without her training.

When Two and I graduated to cartels and became employees with actual means I went to join up for real and the Master made no sign she knew who I was. That night I went back and passed the porch, concealed behind the black windows of the huge cartel car that was driving me and Two to see our boss. The Master was sitting out on the railing, eating the soup herself.

Two didn't like me learning fighting properly, even though I told her there was no feeling to beat the one you got when you were getting a pasting from your mates in the ring. She couldn't see how getting kicked across a room was a comparable thrill to flying. It didn't hurt – or maybe my assessment of pain was different to other people's, but I never got seriously injured. It didn't hurt compared to falling off that droid onto the heap. I couldn't seem to find the words to tell her that those minutes were the ones in which I felt real, and all the rest was only the waiting time for those minutes to come round again. She saw it in my face, though, so she supported me by shutting up and never telling me not to go, even though she was afraid for me.

It never occurred to me to be afraid of what would happen to her if we got separated. That was like the car that hit me – something I only saw coming in retrospect.

40

About six months into our new lives as criminals of note we were at home. The Girls – Sulin and Jayda – were visiting and doing my hair. A third woman, Nosheed, who I was reasonably sure was double moon but had no time for them or their fussing, was there as a joint friend of ours – she kept accounts for the crew and liked to play war games with me.

During the hairdressing Nosheed and the Girls kept a distance of mutual professional disgust with me as barricade in the middle, shooting each other with glances over the top of my head. Sulin and Jayda hated Nosheed for having a desk job. They suspected it entitled her to more respect and privilege for the use of her brain than they'd ever get for the use of their bodies, no matter how much brainpower they put into that. They were right. The kind of men who ran the porn element of the cartel weren't interested in them as human beings, and they had no skill with accounts so anyone who did was some kind of witch doctor.

But to be fair, the business side didn't care about Nosheed either, only her ability to keep score and interpret the law in their favour. In the skewed terms that passed for moral hierarchy in Harmony Nosheed won for not being a whore. Esoterically, however, Sulin and Jayda beat her clear since their mopping up all that overly fiery Yang energy from the cartel's male power base meant they were doing the better service for everyone: men, business and state. In Alchemical terms they were gold, so it was OK for the less mystically fortunate to treat them like dirt. Because being so important wasn't fair on the rest. Balance, y'all.

After they'd exchanged verbal daggers across my head the sainted Sulin gave my hair a final brush and packed up her things. Jayda kissed my cheek and whispered filth in my ear about everything she could give me on the day I gave up my vows and then they waved goodbye to Two and left. My submission to beauty treatments meant they got paid to sit around and having a chat so they always gave us the kind of pillow reports that ensured we got the greatest respect from the other assholes at the top of the tree.

Twostar was leaning in the doorway as I set up a fresh game for myself and Nosheed. She was using my phone to cue the payment of the girls' weekly tip. 'You know there's still time to enrol for college this cycle, Nic.'

I looked up from passing Nosheed her controller set. I wasn't sure I'd heard right. 'College?'

Even Nosheed stared, her mouth half open.

'Yes. It's not like you have a lot to do these days. Things are quiet and you're not learning anything new at the dojo.'

I sat back on my heels, almost pouting, although she was right. Aside from keeping up with training my so-called 'duty of care' had dwindled to escorting her to the shops and back. Her work kept her inside. Nobody had made a serious attempt on her person for months now. Our organisation was too big, its reach too vast. She was still essential. I was ... redundant. There was time for home study, if not a full-time college attendance.

It had always been in the Plan. One day, when we had money, when we were old (meaning grown up), we'd get as educated as it took to get our asses forever out of trouble. It was what we talked about on long cold nights in the heap. I'd been able to agree to it because I never thought it'd get that far, so I wouldn't have to worry about it. The notion of it now set every part of me to 'No!'

'Actually I was thinking of entering the Arena,' I said, more defensively than I wanted to. I wasn't sure I had been thinking about it, but there was money in it and we'd need a lot of that whatever we did. The idea of Arena fighting actually irritated me, because the commercial angle made it feel dirty, but it was hardly like I was pure as driven snow. If you could guarantee the level of success by the litres of sweat poured out on those mats then I was the stuff champions were made of.

Two glared at the fading black eye I was sporting and stalked to the sofa to pick up her controller. She knew very well I was bailing out and pretending not to. 'It's illegal,' she said, her dark hair flopping over her eyes and covering their real expression.

Nosheed and I shared a glance of dumbfounded silence at this. Everything we did was illegal. Every credit we had was laundered or blood-soaked. What kind of objection was legality? Two's slumped, sulking posture said she knew it was no kind of objection too, but I felt sick to my stomach from her dis-approval. It seemed to come out of nowhere – I didn't get it. I knew she'd never meant for it to be like this. She only did her work here as part of the Plan and that wasn't finished until we were out and free. She felt dirty every day. But I didn't think this was sharing the crapload. I felt insulted.

Part of my sickness was the realisation that she'd nearly finished her end of things. Two was nobody's idiot. Unlike a lot of other slicers she played every game, including the politics of the cartel we were slaved to. She bragged and she delivered and she cut off anyone in her way with me picking up the rear when folk didn't take her hints. It wasn't her nature to do it. She did it because the Plan said to and she was following it. Her sullen button-mashing as she tanked a battalion of armoured insects prowling across our kitchen table said clearly that I was way behind and failing. I wasn't pulling my weight. Kickboxing and gangland hoodlum-ing weren't her idea of holding up an end, and we weren't going anywhere on cartel money, which paid the bills but always kept you needing more. To break out of them meant becoming a cartel of your own.

Which only made my resolve stronger. I'd never be an A student, but I could win a buttload of money. 'I'm gonna do it. Give me five fights,' I said, focusing on covering fire while Nosheed pumped our avatars both full of stims and antitoxins. 'If I don't win them all then I'll go to college.'

'Wasting your brain,' she said, unable to keep the contempt

out of her voice, or maybe she didn't want to. She waded through carapaces, her lightblades slicing left, right, everywhere, with faultless precision. She was smoking hot, angrier than I'd ever seen her. I didn't know what had got into her. She spat, 'Five fights will take another cycle out of the schedule. We'll have to stay here an extra year.'

'But even if I become an Alchemist we're stuck here.' We'd be working for someone. We'd be on-world. Nothing would really change. 'Anyway, what do you care? I thought you were happy here, especially now you're hanging out with that new woman, what's her name – Tashin – in your net group all the time. It's not like you're here that much any more.'

Two's face turned stony. 'You're wasting your brains, wasting everything, sitting on your ass.'

I felt like I'd scored a direct hit but I didn't know what the hit was. Wasn't she happy? She'd had a glow lately that had made me think everything was going well for her. And she was often out, coming back in the early hours. I'd heard her singing in the shower. She'd bought clothes that actually fitted her. Meanwhile I'd been left to the Girls and teaching classes at the dojo. So where was this college crap coming from?

Nosheed was smart enough not to say anything. Nobody left the cartel except in a bodybag. Either Two wasn't serious or she was so serious Nosheed would be wiser silent. She looked at me for a cue but I was busy dropping bombs and spraying fire so I didn't have to feel Two's defensive super-assault. I was really helped out at moments like this by one of many character flaws – competitiveness. I could tune out the distress because I had to beat the other ten players we were netted up with. I had to. Even though I suspected it made me a total prick, I couldn't stop. Besides, who was there to impress with any kind of restraint?

I didn't remind Two that this was the most stable life we'd ever had. To be honest it was like a holiday. After all we'd been through I felt we deserved some of that. It wasn't even as if once we got to the fabled state of home-and-clear that my life would improve all that much. In fact I thought it would get a lot worse. I didn't know what waited for us outside in the wider solar system on the day we got ourselves out of Harmony. We could be back in the rubbish heap somewhere else. Might as well be hung for a sheep as a lamb.

My bad temper took up too much of my attention as this rushed through my head. I misjudged my position on the battle-ground and got shot by an incoming artillery shell. Wipeout.

Nosheed tried to shock me back to life, called me six types of asshat loser.

I looked across at Two balefully because she'd ruined my concentration and...

'All right,' she said, changed from anger to guilt. A wretched expression contorted her face as if she hated every option in her mind. 'Five fights. Only five. You promise.' *You're going to get killed,* her voice said, *and I don't want to be there to see it.*

I didn't fall for that. Seemed we were committed now, though, even though neither of us entirely wanted to be. How had we got here? But I don't bluff.

'Five,' I agreed, chugging back biopotions and getting myself airborne again.

'You fucking noob,' Nosheed muttered at me, reaching across my lap to steal my beer and drink it herself.

She didn't know how right she was.

In the end it didn't take five fights, only three.

My master rolled her eyes at me when I told her my plan.

'You want to fight in that pit? You're crazy. Think it's a way out? Only for the winner. Only for a short time. Anything else – you lose. Guy like you could do much better. Good-looking. Easier money. Easier way. Yeah? I'm just saying. They'll punch that face in good, rip out that hair. Your fanclub want that after

45

so much effort, heh? They'll cry and leave you, send photo of you looking like week-old cheesecake to their friends. Also, you suck.'

I'd spent more than five hours a day at the dojo since I first walked in the front door. This was pretty high praise from her. Usually she just made noises of disgust because words were all too much like validation. Sometimes, if I did something that was OK, she'd mutter, 'Is not so shit like usual.'

She went to the back of the dojo and stood before the shrine of little holos where great fighters posed over and over with their trophies. I heard her praying under her breath, frowning at everything. She lit incense, possibly by staring at the end of the sticks with the laser focus of her disapproval. People fought to be her students, not in the ring, but in every way, with their hard work, devotion, hours, sweat, blood . . . everything they had. She was the disciple of a great master who was in prison now – the martial arts had been outlawed except for use in the armed services. Everything was underground, for the poor, for desperate people in Chaontium. Our highest victories could only ever rise to the top of that world, not the one above it. When she said Way Out she meant only as far as that invisible limit.

'I'm serious,' I said, and I meant over the limit.

'You will fight for yourself or for the cartel?'

'For me,' I said, thinking that must be the right answer.

'Get in the ring,' she replied, and picked up her sparring gloves and helmet.

I lasted about fifteen seconds before she slammed me so hard in the side of the head I saw stars.

'Lazy guard,' she said. 'Thank the sun you don't have to face Jimmy Vlad.'

Vlad was a third-rate slugger, the one everyone paid to fall spectacularly out of the ring. Little kids jeered at him and he spent most of his fight nights picking rotten fruit out of his pants. His pratfalls were legendary but I barely heard his name

46

because in the middle of her line she landed a knee in my ribs that punched all the breath out of me for a painful minute during which I dared not do more than try to see her over my gloves and dance away, praying I'd breathe again one day. She let me recover.

After that there was no more mercy chatting.

When I got home Twostar took one look at me and went into her room. I tiptoed across and put my ear to the door. I thought I heard her sob, but then she was calling someone and talking in a low, urgent voice like she used to talk to me on nights when we were scared and alone. I couldn't hear the words. I guessed who she was talking to. Tashin. Tashin who was looking better than me.

I went into the kitchen and took a bag of ice chips out of the freezer, sat weakly at the table holding it against my face with one hand. I felt no pain, only a faint bewilderment. When I went back a short while later Two's voice had changed, she was calm. I sat up watching some fight movies and later she came out and cooked me rice and beans. We sat together and fell asleep there.

I saw the minotaur in my dreams. He stood sadly on his own looking at the stars.

I learned very fast from then on. Our cartel boss, Kasha Dann, heard about my shift of interest and came in wanting to sponsor me. She wasn't a fight fan but it was something the cartel made a lot of money on through gambling and she fancied a new angle as the owner of a winning stable. They assigned another guard for Two to give me more time off and put me in for a match against a small-time local champion. Even Dann hesitated, however, scowling at me somewhat.

'I heard you're some kind of cult spirit warrior,' she said. 'The Girls like your face. Sure you wouldn't rather work with them? You've got the body for it, I'm guessing. I mean ... shit, well. You know.' She meant porn. Funny how she couldn't even say the word.

I looked at her, imagining she was in the ring, and she paled and muttered and looked away. 'Guess not.' It was never suggested again.

She entered me into the tournament and told me to get tattooed. All fighters of Faith had tats, and what they chose was important. It was an outward expression of the spirit and a symbol for the banner of the fans and the bookies. Most kept in line with the Alchemical vision of the Solar and had priests draw up their astrological charts and make up designs filled with every kind of luck and charm, but others liked to show their rebellion and spite. They made their own designs.

Twostar listened to me explain this over dinner the night before I was due to get mine. I felt dumb for not getting one sooner, but I'd told Dann that the stars were out of line for it and she bought that.

'Stupid disfigurement,' Two said, pushing the food around her plate. The scowl that had lived on her face for the last few months was firmly in place. She'd get permanent lines soon. 'What are you going to get?'

I felt oddly childish and silly now in front of her, as if none of it were real. I was angered but humbled, a hard combination to deal with. I wanted her to approve. I needed her to be behind me. I put my fork down. 'I want you to choose. It would mean a lot to me.'

She looked at me and I could see the old days in her eyes; just the two of us, running, scrapping, dirty, hungry, always together under the bridge. Crew of two. She looked at her plate and that sulky line from the week before turned her mouth down at the corners. All this over college. Fucksake, really? 'I don't know.'

'Excuse,' I said, pushing my plate away. I glared at her.

She closed her eyes for a moment and then nodded. 'I don't want you to get hurt. And now this. It's like I'm deciding your fate. What the hell for?'

'It's important to me,' I said, still thinking she was making a huge deal over it for nothing.

'Why? More macho games? Everyone knows you're hard as nails. Droid killer. Lunatic. What's the matter?' She stopped as she said it and we shared a long look that said we both knew what the matter was. Something had come between us, but I was damned if I'd name it. I'd thought this would mend it, to show her that I wasn't just in it for me. I was still a good bet. I was the real deal.

She broke first and stared at the table. I saw her resistance waver, fail, and then she decided just to accept me, like she always did. 'All right . . . let me think.'

It was hard to imagine ever loving anyone as much as I loved her. It hurt in my chest.

She held up a finger, as she did when she wanted to show she was working on something in her head, then silently got up and left, heading to her cradle. I guessed she was going to search for some image files.

A patient wait proved me right. She returned with a print and put it down in front of me. 'Just don't put it on your face.'

A white lotus on a background of green leaves, and hiding in the white petals were two golden stars.

'Stars are also suns,' she said.

I looked at it a minute more and then got up, scraping my chair back, and hugged her tight.

'I'll stick it on my ass,' I said, letting go.

'You do that,' she replied and gave me the finger, picking up her coat and sliding out of the room without a backward look. 'I'm gonna see Tashin for coffee. Don't wait up.'

The door closed as I got it. Two was in love with Tashin. That was what was between us, because she couldn't admit it to me. All the joy of the moment before faded away.

I cleared the dishes and told myself I was being an ass. I didn't own her.

I got the tattoo the next day, on the middle of my right thigh, so everyone would see it when I fought. I paid for the most expensive artist, the best photo-reactive inks. It hurt in a good way and it was beautiful when it was done.

My master was pleased with it. She looked at it that night as I peeled back the haemo-strips and nodded. 'For once you do something right. Cover it up. I don't kick you there today.' She kept her word and made all the other students spar with other partners.

The weeks to the first fight ground by in a blur of sweat, food, sleep and pain. The Girls complained when I fell asleep in the middle of *Forge of War* and I woke up with my hair dyed pink and my nails varnished glitter blue. Fortunately the dye was temporary but it was tough stuff and when I got braids done it was still like candyfloss. Jayda decided she wasn't done with her style revenge and rid me of every body hair she could find, even part of my eyebrows. It was fashionable for men to look as if grooming was the pinnacle of life's possible achievements.

'You're destroying my rep,' I told her, fending her off as she brought out tweezers.

'You always look a mess,' she said, pouting, kicking at the sweats I'd discarded so she could strip my skin. She was right: they were holed, worn, baggy. I made an effort to walk the streets looking unobtrusive and always entirely covered up in hats, scarves, old clothes. When I was on duty I wore guard's uniform black, blaster pistols in holsters, looked as sharp as I could. The grooming helped there. The kind of people Two went to see these days were always impressed by a sharp-looking man, even if he did have pink hair. But I felt like myself only when I looked one step up from homeless and passed unnoticed.

When my master saw me after this pre-Arena makeover she took one look and instead of getting the pads out just beckoned me into her office at the back of the dojo.

I sat in *seiza* on her mats as she made tea for both of us – a ceremonial affair, incense and prayers involved – and then drank with her quietly, waiting for her to speak. Finally she did.

'These fights, sometimes they pay for a win, sometimes a loss. Stick with the rules whatever happens. Nobody from this gym slips on the rules. Take no bribes.'

I nodded, feeling she just said this to get it out of the way. The honour of the dojo was mine too. Rival dojos had more famous fighters but this one had a pristine record on sticking to their own dharma.

'Later when the official rounds are done I heard they drive some out to private fights.' Her eyes slid away from mine.

We knew very well what went on. The Arena had a kind of underworld legitimacy, honour, rules; it was a spiritual, sacred place. Nobody fucked with it, that was important to the fans. But there was a high-roller section to the audience who wanted to see people beaten into bloody bits and were prepared to pay for it. For them fighters went out into the underground desert grounds, to the Pit. The only question was ever who was in charge and how much it was going to cost – death and money always told.

'If you get taken there and they tell you take your gloves off then there are no more rules. You will kill there. Or you will die there. This is why I don't want you to go.' Her expression was terrible; shame and loathing warred in it for supremacy, but sadness won. 'I know I say you are a bad student, shame to the grandmaster. All of us are shame. We are dogs, bite for food. It's wrong. Fighting is the path to self-knowledge, is for defence only if nothing left. Is inside, not outside, not this farce. I bring shame on the master. On the power. Because I am here and don't have the courage to say no to cartels. I fear for my family. Nobody can be master who is prisoner to fear. I am no master.'

I faltered, tea halfway to my mouth. I didn't know if she was throwing me out or ... I didn't understand at all. I groped around in her words.

She sat and then picked up her cup and poured her tea onto the floor.

'Master?' I didn't know her real name.

'No,' she said. 'I never meant to lead you here. You're better than that. But this is the only place it leads.'

I realised, too late, that she was lost. For so long she'd been such a rock I couldn't even think of questioning her. I was useless. She was the one who knew, who was right, who told me how, who let me in.

'I will cast fortunes for you all night,' she said, running her finger through the spilled tea, looking at the curl of its steam with grim deliberation. 'Until they work out.'

I thought of Twostar's cradle where she let me ride her connections beyond Harmony into the other worlds at night. I'd found there all manner of things that told me these superstitions were nonsense. In other worlds they laughed at this, did what they wanted, without a care. On other worlds you could be and do anything and there was nobody to come and take it away. I felt a strange sensation in my skull, as if it was heavy with horns.

'It's OK,' I said. I reached over to her and took her hands and put my tea cup into them, closed her fingers on it. 'I chose. I'm not a believer.'

Her head snapped up and she looked at me, her dark brown eyes staring for a moment. 'Yes, you are,' she said before she bowed to me and then went to get a cloth to clean up the tea. We didn't speak again but when she was done the cups were back on the table with the photographs of the dead parents, the missing masters, the little plastic trinkets of the sacred animals.

Three Fights

The first fight was the support bout to the main act, a pretty big entrance fight for an unknown like me. With my tattoo on show and causing a stir of laughs from commentators – flowers, is this guy crazy? – I had to go through all the rituals and prayers, offerings and the presentation of myself to the altar of the religion I'd come to hate as deeply as an animal hates the trap on its leg: it's killing you, it hurts you, you're starting to rot with it, but you can't make it let you go. The two of you are become one. My hate bound me. Every time I thought I'd let it go there it was again, one word, one breath away. In the moment of bowing I vowed freedom and in that vow I felt the old force catch me and blossom.

The two stars were too subtle to see in the petals of the flower, but if anyone was going to ask about it I had a whole story to say they were for Two herself. Nobody asked.

If I could've I would've deleted all religious associations from my mind but for all my efforts it doesn't work that way when you've grown up with the stuff. It fouled up everything like quantum glue. Tacky, heavy, on everything. In spite of myself I felt the power of it alongside the tawdriness of this dusty altar, these burning rings of incense. If I must be here, if I must be me, then let's feel the ancestral power and take it, who cares?

The priest in residence at the pit-fighting arena was about

as low as you could go on the official ladder and still hold an office. I vaguely recognised him as one of a number of disgraced cantors who had been done for sexually exploiting the young women on his staff a few years back in the name of 'rebalancing their excessive lunar energy', or Yinsucking as it was more commonly called.

Priests are supposed to be celibate after a certain level of induction, to retain all their energy for contemplative use in a form unpolluted by contact with others. Although his pathetic excuse was accepted as a plea of honourable Alchemical intent he was still kicked to the outer limits. He'd be pushing paperwork in this dead-end parish and serving the mafia cartels their daily hypocrisy for the rest of his life. I couldn't see the punishment angle. A gig like this would be good pay and probably a fresh chance at some unofficial skirt for him. It was like an upgrade. Maybe some boss would take a fancy to becoming respectable and hire him to cast good fortunes for his family.

By the way he looked at me I knew he saw someone who didn't have anything to offer and was of no interest. He blessed me, chanted, tossed salt over my head, summoned the elements in a businesslike manner and dismissed me without eye contact before moving on to my rival. Everywhere was cheers, jeers, noise, the smell of cheap snacks and fried sausage.

I walked through a narrow valley between the packed stands, feet slipping on fruit peel and discarded cartons, the hem of my badly fitting cape dragging some of the crap behind me and acting like a mop so I left a slugtrail. The overhanging cowl that hid my face made it nearly impossible to see, but to either side of me two of my buddies from the guard strode in suited, groomed splendour, the colours of our cartel blazoned on their sashes, arms in that half-a-gorilla stance you get when you're packing so much heat under your jacket you can barely breathe without rupturing the lining. They were close enough that our sleeves brushed together so I could follow them along the torturous walk-in to the dais where I was to be unveiled in glory.

The previous fighters had gone and the staff were sweeping bloodied sand away and sprinkling fresh down, raking it over. Music was playing. On the sides of the arena half-naked girls were dancing and high-kicking. Lights swept around, jolly in their colours. The air was hot and humid, like a second skin. I could smell every kind of human in it, sharp, acrid, distinct. Adrenaline ran through me. I felt myself on the edge of control.

I tried to focus and think of Two. This was our ticket out. This was my chance to do something for her after all she'd done for me. I knew she wasn't watching but she'd hear about it. And it was my chance to say *Fuck You* to the state. I had a lifetime to be angry about and I was ready to use that for a good cause. I wanted to win, to put to rest all the evil credos inside me that said Twin Suns were bad for everything by smashing all the Sun Moon fighters into the ground.

So I told myself, trying not to notice I was like that cantor, fuelling up on my own special brand of completely orthodox bullshit. Beneath that layer the basic truth of my existence, the animal, lay smug, knowing it was about to be satisfied: I just wanted to fight and smell blood that wasn't mine. It's what had saved me and Two so many times.

I mean: college. What the hell would someone like me do there?

The promoter strode into the circle and did his introductions. He was as hyper as a snort of kandy could make him. As a tease to the audience my boss, Kasha Dann, had decided she would name me after my controversially 'soft' tattoo and animé character. Well, she thought it was her idea although the whole thing was laid out for her already – but who's counting when the boss is congratulating herself on her own cleverness?

They announced my opponent first – Black Dragon, a fierce

brawler known for his fast knees and his resilience. He had some signature moves that were deadly if they landed. Reputation and watching his fights had given me a healthy respect for him and I wasn't under any illusions that his experience wasn't going to be a decisive factor. I was hoping that my bloodlust was going to make up for it and that I'd remember never to let him near my ribs.

My master wasn't there. She'd never deign to show at a dump like this, but the cartel had provided me with a 'trainer' who checked my gloves and foot bandaging. He whisked my heavy robe off with an illusionist's flourish. And so I made my first appearance as Pretty Flower, to much jeering and scorn, whistling and leering. Camera drones zoomed in and around, trying to avoid each other. The trainer leaned in to hiss to me:

'Save your face. Dann's got a big wad o' money ridin' on it. You can go down if you gotta, but don't get broke.'

So inspiring. All I could see was the previously unreal figure of my opponent, sweat standing out on his oiled skin. His toothguard was a scarlet snarl between his lips, although his eyes watched me with a cold, canny knowing that cut all the theatrics like a knife. The gaze wanted to tell me I was his dead meat. I've always loved seeing that in a man's eyes; it means I don't have to hold anything back.

The bell went and I don't remember much more. I was jittery and hot to start with, careless because I was so wired I could hardly see, but without fail the fight switch inside me flicked from *Off* to *On* and after that everything was simple.

He landed some shots that jolted me up – more forceful than I expected but also strangely pain-free. We played a bit of shin tag, just to show we were hard enough. He tried to hammer me for the rest of the round, practising his best moves just out of my reach to make his point that all he had to do was wait for me to tire. I was vigilant, on my guard so nothing got through to my head. But he did slam a knee into my right side. I felt something crack and there was weakness after that. I landed a hook on his ear that rattled him enough to make him blink. Then, feeling it was time for the bell I saw him start to back off and relax so I relaxed too, for a microsecond I thought, but one that allowed him to land one of the slowest moves in creation. He kicked me in the side of the head.

Of all the things not to avoid, a fucking head kick. You can see them coming for years, like comets, you've got forever to get out of the way. But *bam!* Like I was actually already in a coma.

I heard the bell from a distance, kept my feet somehow although the world spun and was shot with light. People made me sit, threw water on me; a doctor came and stared into my eyes. As I was regaining my bearings I saw Dragon across the pit floor, looking at me with contempt: too easy. He gestured at my tattoo and then his own, which was of course a huge black dragon, coiled and fiery, fangs dripping blood, its cyber-ports lit with red and yellow. Sometimes I don't know why they don't just have a metal cock and balls put there instead. He made one of those signs that are rife in gangland: a slow lick of his upper lip that said I was his bitch now.

I wanted to laugh because my stupidity and his arrogance were so funny but it would've hurt too much. I was so used to doing my own share of shit-talking that his efforts made me comfortable rather than the opposite. I put my fingers to my mouth and slithered my tongue between them, looking at him with the dead-eyed gaze which asked for serious trouble. Gears shifted inside me and my discomfort with the formality of the ring became the contented anticipation of violence with a personal edge.

Dragon honed his glare, whittling his anger into a sharp, pointy stick.

Round two was a serious effort from both of us to dish out some pain. I split his eyebrow and swelled that eye shut and he laid two more knees to my right side. One I blocked, the other was a solid smack that flung me a metre and made sure I didn't inhale again for a good thirty seconds, also known as forever. My master did it to me regularly though, for practice, so that was just an endurance test. Try as I might, after that I was slow and he got me pinned back to the ring edge a few times, laying into me with his fists in the hope of battering up through my guard. I could only defend while he trod on my feet and tried to clash knees – a hopeless move but effective in its message. It probably looked worse than it was but looks counted for a lot – most of the crowd didn't know a fight from a hole in the ground. I survived it ingloriously, nothing else to say about that.

Round three and he showed no sign of exhaustion. I knew I wasn't going to make four with my cracked ribs. He had a good chance of puncturing a lung too. I stared at him and gave his ugly mug the blank face. They stopped the blood pouring into his eye, which was a pity. I got tape on my side. I knew by now that he was nowhere near as ambidextrous as he liked to feint out. He had good legs but his arms weren't up to much even if they looked pumped. Most of his knockouts were from kicks and until now I'd only taken one of those.

One more was all he'd need. I struggled to think of some master plan but unless he lowered his hands significantly I was out of ideas. Body shots wouldn't save my score. So far I hadn't really tried to kick him. Kicking a kicker is hard – they know what all the setups look like. If there had been no rules...

The bell went and I had nothing. All this defending was annoying. I danced around him, pretending to be much fitter and easier than I felt; it nearly killed me. He was slower now, though; not much, but some. We traded a few flashy attacks that didn't go far but looked good. I realised he wanted humili- ation, not just a win: a defeat, maybe a rout. I moved slower by degrees, tilted left a bit, thinking he'd be glad for any chance to end it fast. He went for a jab to the head, I slid forwards inside his arm and put everything into an uppercut. He did hit me, but glancing. I hit him square, driving off the floor hard, and he went down like he'd been pole-axed.

A glass jaw, who knew?

That was my lucky fight.

The two after weren't like that.

The second fight was a top billing against a seasoned pro who was less kicky and showy and was out for a slaughter. He had a dagger and rose tattoo where the rose was stabbed through the middle; charming. Betting was heavily against me. After the previous fight my boss had won big so she pumped up the prettiness angle. No surprise that he went immediately for my face and nothing else, ignoring legs, torso and any effort to grapple or lock. He'd been told to make me ugly, I guessed, so I didn't take it personally.

Regardless of his aims he didn't get to plaster my nose over my face or ruin my teeth but I didn't get enough on him to do much other than stand up for the statutory rounds. There was blood, there were moments of head-rattling, body-shocking savagery; and I lost.

When I got home Two looked pissed off. She fixed food, chucking things around, stressed.

'You wanted me to lose,' I said, surprised, as I watched her over the dinner table. I realised she must have watched the fight. My face went hot. I stared at my food, hating the sudden sensation of deep humiliation that ran over me. All our lives I had won in front of her. I didn't let her down. I'd been a champion. Now I was – what? I don't know. Human. A college reject. A thug.

'Yeah,' she said, and added in faultless logic that made me go cold, 'You have to lose or you'll just carry on.'

I took my plate out into the common room and sat with

Jayda. She was high, took a selfie with me and my untouched face, 'So later, when you're a big famous fighter, I can prove I knew you!'

It was hard to smile.

Between fights two and three I got a summons from the boss. I went dressed in an upmarket bodyguard's charcoal grey *hitatare*, cut to show off fancy ceremonial swords worn on the back, but concealing the usual blaster weapons in shoulder holsters. My hair was back to blond now and down to my waist. Jayda braided it.

'I look like an arrogant prick,' I said, eyeing the result with quite some wonder. The extended training had stripped my face and left me looking angular. The cold, ice-chip eyes that stared at me seemed too hard and calculating to be mine.

'You look badass, Pretty,' she said. She hesitated. 'Kasha Dann ain't got no boyfriend.'

I checked the safety was on with both guns and put them in place. 'You think a refusal often offends?'

'She got no interest in keeping a man, from what I hear,' Jayda said, packing up her beauty case. 'Picks what she likes, puts it down again. Pays good. No questions, no heartache.'

'I'll see you later,' I assured her and looked beyond her into Two's room. She was there, slung in cyberspace, doing gods knew what. I may as well not have existed. 'You can use my bedroom if you want to sleep.'

'Always do,' she said, hi-fiving me; and then she caught me at the door, hanging on my wide sleeve. 'Say, Pretty, don't you ever want to ... you know?'

I smiled at her and slipped out and closed the door. Refusals always offend.

A car waited for me. It took me to a whole new district of the city, where skyscrapers reached up to the blue vaults, their feet dressed in fountains and green parks.

Here in a corporate high-rise that sheltered much of the city's gross white-collar crime Kasha Dann's offices perched close to heaven. The elevator-car ride took nearly a minute. I stared out through its plexiglass into the lives of legitimate people, wondering how many of them were like me and how they coped when you could hardly walk ten metres without coming across a shrine, a balancing point, a call to prayer. The higher I got the better I felt. I noticed, briefly, that Dann's building stood cheekily jowl by jowl with Harmony's most successful bank; no accident I was sure. A silvery night operation beside the solid block sun of money. There was no better Alchemical set-up than that.

Dann's ordinary guard let me in, so pro they were able to check me out, open the doors and wait for me to pass without giving any sign they were aware of my existence; they might as well have been rehearsing for a future event. The cartel was big on letting those who were favoured pass unnoticed, as if they weren't being screened and followed and watched with several missiles trained on them at all times. Nothing grotesquely obvious, no droids shadowing me. It was a sign of some odd rise in prestige. Usually I was the one doing the official ignoring. I had to check myself from trying to make eye contact with them as I handed them my guns.

They let the swords go through. I wouldn't have.

Kasha Dann had everything I'd come to expect of wealth and power: lots of space with nothing much in it, big art on the walls, a shrine the size of a shop with a personal priest in attendance and a view over the city that was genuinely breathtaking. I couldn't help staring at it over her shoulder as she stood to receive me. For once there was no galaxy-sized desk for the person who does nothing much all day. She had her room arranged into three 'receiving' areas, opulent but tasteful. Dann herself wore black, her golden hair in a high twist. The severe tailoring made her full figure even more impressively hourglass shaped. She must have been about forty-five but she could have passed for twenty less.

'Ah, hello Pritz,' she said, shortening my ring name to a pet version. Behind and to her flanks, subtly shrouded by huge planters filled with green fronds, I saw my compadres from the cartel guard pool, calmly staring into the middle of nowhere although their ears must've been stretching to the limit. 'Come right in.'

I obediently descended four steps into the sunken well of exotic couches she indicated and she did too, as if we were dancers about to do a routine. An occasional table covered in fruit displayed at knee height prevented us from meeting. She surveyed me from a five-inch height disadvantage and, close to, I realised how petite she was. Even in heels.

'Miz Dann,' I said to her, bowing my head as I'd seen other inferiors do. We'd never met in person before.

'Take a seat.'

It wasn't a suggestion. The swords had already proved annoying enough in the car on the ride over but drawing them even to get rid of them was out of the question. I didn't fancy stabbing the soft furnishings so I moved to a bare patch of carpet by the coffee table and knelt down in *seiza*, hands on my knees. It looked better than it felt.

Dann cocked a slender brow at me, partly amusement and partly something else. 'You're Twostar's personal guard, are you not?'

Ah, questions to which the answers are already known. Never good news. 'Yes.'

'Her childhood friend, I understand?'

'Yes.' Interesting turn.

'You know, of course, how valuable Twostar is to us?'

'She has three guards and that's only two less than you do.'

Dann smiled. 'She told me that you were smarter than you looked. I think she's right. She also asked me if I would consider

62

withdrawing you from the fight circle and instead send you to university to study.'

I looked at her, feeling angry with Two suddenly, but also hopeful.

Dann's expression became the resigned smile of someone who isn't happy with what she's going to do but knows it's for the best. 'So pick your course and you will be on it.'

My surprise must have shown. She laughed. Probably thought it was for this act of generosity. It was because I couldn't believe that Two had them over a barrel. But clearly she did. Still, it didn't feel right. I didn't trust gifts from these people.

'Your next fight is already advertised so you will be fulfilling that appearance,' she continued. 'I want you to go out on a high note. Win it. That's my first condition.'

Ah, conditions. Here we were. This was not about favours or education. 'And you publicly withdraw me to send me to school?'

She smiled. 'I always fancied extending my repertoire to philanthropy. And how better to encourage the best young fighters to my stable than by offering genuinely worthwhile rewards?'

She was right, even if a qualification wasn't a reward most people in Chaontium had much ambition for. It wasn't education but the prospect of getting whatever you wanted, and Two must have told her I wanted college. I assumed my attendance on said course was of no importance, only the PR spin for her plan, which was good as I'd no intention of attending. I wouldn't mind leaving the Arena though. Since I'd started the gap between Two and me had grown to gulf-like proportions. I was spending way too much time away and I'd have given up that whole prove-myself schtick in a split second if that would've healed the rift. Maybe this was a way out.

'Me and you, the ghetto heroes?'

'I bask in your reflected glory,' she said, making it sound like that was remotely plausible.

I was thinking about my master's shrine. Tea on her floor. Twostar in that cradle, always so far away. 'Was there another condition?'

She hesitated and I saw her considering a lot of things as she looked at me. 'I've been offered a lot of money for you from a rival who would like to consider himself my equal. I have refused, several times, but I feel it only fair to warn you he will not be pleased about it. My priest consistently casts twin suns for him.'

And there it was, the sunny elephant in the room. In addition, I could read easily into the *not pleased* line. It was the way of these people to ask first, offer to pay second and then take whatever it was they wanted. A chill went through me. This was not about fighting alone. The fact she labelled him twin suns was also a normal way of saying that the interest went beyond that. No Chaontium citizen talked openly about their orientations whether they gave a damn or not but they'd pretend to spit on it whilst dishing the information.

Dann looked directly at me and I knew she knew.

'Of course, if you stayed on as my fighter, you would retain the protection of your vow to the art.'

'And if I take the college ticket?' The more this went on the more sure I became that staying on at the Arena meant losing Two. I could feel it, like an outgoing tide inside my veins. Maybe she knew about this other guy too and was trying to spare me. Maybe. In the old days I'd have known for sure. Suddenly all this was too much for me. I wanted out of the complication, the manipulation. I wanted old Two-and-Nico back.

Dann shrugged, 'You are part of our establishment with all the rights that affords. And you can take good care of yourself.'

So, fight and get protection or stop and you're on your own with a shark hunting for you. I felt that either way I was screwed now. Stay and fight, lose Two. Don't fight and something worse might happen. She was honouring Two's request at the same time as she was suggesting I go the other way. Typical. 'Thanks for the advice,' I said in my best asslicking tone, not too cute, in case its deep underlying hatred burned through.

She beckoned and I stood, unfolding as I'd been taught. It made her smile again, and there was a hint of genuine feeling in it, even if I was hard pressed to say which feeling. 'Be a credit to me, Pretty, not a liability. Not even Twostar is irreplaceable.'

I wondered how many dead people she'd looked at just like this shortly before they were dispatched. We disposed of bodies at a city incineration plant: easy part. Their official records were a little harder to reconcile. That was done downstairs just a few floors away. It would take about ten hours to make Two and myself vanish as if we'd never been but they could take as long as they wanted, nobody would come looking, would they?

A credit. Me. Worth saving. 'Count on it.'

'Give me your answer about the college tomorrow,' she said, indicating with a mild move of her gloved hand that this was where I got off.

On the street outside as I got into the huge whale of a car, I saw another vehicle fly close to us, blacked out, slick, like a gun. One of its cameras whirred and followed me as I closed the winged doors. We flew an avoidance route, one of many designed to pick up or lose tails, and they didn't let me back out until they were certain we were clean.

Four Mistakes

I relayed my news to Two late that night as we sat watching a movie together and drinking beer. The Girls were out and the guards were stationed outside and on the balcony. We had the sound loud so there was no danger I'd be heard.

'Go to college,' she said, flatly, staring at the screen. 'You'll end up in the Pit otherwise.'

It was hard to disagree with her assessment. I got that she was trying to save me.

'And you'll have to spend the rest of your life dressing up like a twat.' She glanced at me sideways, tipped up her beer for a swig.

'It's not the college, is it?'

'Go to the top of the class,' she nodded, swirling the last third of her drink around in the bottle and belching.

'Two, why didn't you tell me about Tashin?' I thought I'd sling that javelin out there and see where it went since I might not get another chance.

She jumped as if I'd literally struck her. Then she tucked her feet under her and grasped the bottle tightly. 'I dunno. I couldn't. The thing is . . .' She started biting fiercely on the edge of her fingernail and said the rest around her savaging. '. . . I wasn't sure about it, you know, what it meant and was it serious. So I didn't and then it had gone on so long and you were always at

66

that fucking dojo or talking about your stupid fights and trying to be nice to me and I couldn't.'

I'd thought about this a lot already so it wasn't difficult to say, 'But it's OK. Nobody said you can't have relationships and fall in love and all that stuff. I never said that. It's OK.'

'It's not OK!' She pulled her finger out of her mouth with a wet snapping sound and leaned over to hug me, her beer bottle whacking me on the back and splashing my neck. 'Where's your love affair?'

'You know me, I'm one with the force,' I said, hugging her back.

'Idiot,' she said and thumped me with the bottle again. 'But seriously,' she drew back, 'there's been so much going on. Tashin's... she's really into the resistance and she kept pressing me to join them but if I do it puts you in danger so how can I?'

The resistance wasn't something I'd given any time to. I should have been right there for it because of our common hatred of the establishment and our will to overthrow it but nothing about them as a group or a set of ideas lit any fires in me. They were like all politicians, all talking and statements and very little action. There weren't enough of them, they had too little backing, no significant firepower and no hope of success without some radical change in the status quo or unless they persuaded one of the cartel mavens to adopt the cause. Since there was no profit in that without a guarantee of a win they'd be waiting until the sun froze over. They were on the losing team and that was that. There was no point pitching in with them, you'd be wasting your energy.

'Not much more danger. I don't think they've done anything but foam on forums for the last ten years. What's a little Purging between friends anyway?'

'Stop joking, Nico. I'm serious.'

'You seriously want to join the resistance?'

'No. Yes. I don't know. The thing is we're doing nothing here, are we? It's been years.'

'But if we're going to survive long enough to go anywhere we shouldn't be pasting a target on our asses. That's what *you* said.'

She made a groaning, unhappy *nuuuh* but it looked like frustration or something akin to it was eating her up inside. 'Something's got to give,' she said, looking into her bottle.

'If you want to go with her...'

'No! It's not like that.'

'OK.' Maybe not, but it was like something. There was no more forthcoming though. She put her head against my shoulder and we watched the rest of the movie in silence.

The next day I told Dann I'd take her college ticket. Over the next month Two spent more and more time immured with her honey, getting deeper into politics, and I spun my wheels, wondering what I was going to do after I quit the Arena. Two asked me to hang out with them but although we had a few cordial dinners she let it go. I didn't like the way Two looked, trying to split herself between us, feeling that she had to do that equal shares thing all the time. It made me tired. Tashin was so passionate about rights and unfairness and the way the Alchemy was actually an offence to the wider solar system's vision of rights. Out there you couldn't indoctrinate children with any form of religious or ideological ideas until they reached age of majority and could choose it for themselves. She banged on about it endlessly, as if we didn't already know Tecmaten was filth, but that was so much pointless chatter to me. I couldn't think of a thing to say and *yeah, so what?* seemed like it might drive a wedge between us. Changing the world was a dead end. I wanted Two to be happy, but she wasn't.

My last fight came up. It went four rounds and I took a hammering but I was faster and fitter after another month of training and when Viper Bite went for his signature move with all its split-second telltales I was quicker. Dodge, slide in, hammer up to the jaw, end of story, the crowd go wild – all right, mostly they went wild because of the odds against me and the fact that a good percentage of them were in the money, but I still got showered in beer and rice and could see well enough out of my left eye to take the belt. It felt like nothing to me. The second of victory was sweet, sure, but after that I felt like an emptied shell-casing – no fire inside. We were already at the end of the road, but we didn't want to admit it. We had no other plans. We were coasting to a halt.

I guarded Two in her few engagements around the city over the next few weeks including a minor bank job where we were stuck in a van with a ton of tech for about ten hours – not as exciting as movies would have you believe. Everything flowed along in its normal gangstaland way.

I trained at the gym, in silence and alone. Notionally I went to college but I paid someone else to attend for me while I hid out in the campus gym for my regular date with the element Iron. The Girls came and went. Two and Tashin remained an item, although Two made a big effort to be around more than before. I didn't join the revolution. I swept the dojo and made tea and pretended that I didn't know Two was working on systems to skim money off the cartel casinos. That way I didn't have to tell her it was a suicidally stupid idea. I figured she was the smartie, she already knew that, but my vigilance over her increased. This went on for nearly a month – just enough time to forget there was any other problem lurking.

Then one day as I was walking off campus I saw the strange black car again, the one which had followed me the day Dann told me I could stay or go. It was gliding very slowly along the road towards the lift-off zone, the rear window half down and figures visible inside, in particular a face cut across by a long dark fringe or veil. It carried on and I'd begun to get over it when I heard running feet behind me, soft and near silent but fast approaching.

After that things turn blurred and out of order. I know there was a fight, at least four others involved, and that I lost it fast. They took my pack, cable-tied me, bagged my head and carried me a short distance. There was a dead guy. I felt his body slide over my feet, heavy like a strange, soft sort of lead, unmistakable. They stripped my comms and my hidden gun with such ease I knew they were pro.

I managed to kick off one of my shoes, just so there was some trace of me, because this was bad. I was put into a car, laid on the floor, and driven a long way. The doors banged shut one after another. They left me in it when they all got out. I heard the hum of various engines at close quarters, like a garage or a bay. My car was silent. A few hours passed in which I got cold and stiff and desperate to pee. The hood smelled strongly of synthetic waterproofing. I recognised it. I'd seen other guys use it on people to scare the crap out of them although it was loose enough around my neck that I wasn't going to die soon. It wasn't very breathable, so after a while my face and hair were wet with condensation.

The door opened some time later, I think it must have been night. Someone heavy got in, a man, I guessed. They moved clumsily around me though I was trussed up so hard I couldn't move. The plastic ties were almost cutting off the blood everywhere they touched. My hands were numb.

Fingers fumbled at the control strap on the hood, figured out the release of the catch and pulled it off. I held my eyes nearly shut but I needn't have bothered, only a single weak cabin light was on.

A man was crouched over me in the tiny space left by the two rows of plush seating that ran either side of the windowless interior. His hands were resting on his knees, hanging down relaxed, one empty, the other holding the hood. He jogged the hood a little as he spoke, the heavy cut of his fringe swinging over his face. He was reasonable looking in a corporate sort of way, middle aged, trim, groomed as only a man who spends a lot on grooming and clothes can be. A fine white scar ran across both lips and over his chin. It had the characteristic precision and colour of an electroknife's work – vanity or bitterness must have made him keep it, there was no other reason to.

He looked at me for quite a time. I looked right back at him. There was an interest in his eyes I hadn't seen before and slowly it percolated through my flashfrozen mind that this must be Dashain VanSant, Dann's two-sun rival. A surprising and unwelcome flicker of heat ran through my body and his face moved just a fraction towards amusement, so I knew he'd picked it up.

'The vids don't do you justice,' he said eventually, sitting back on his heels and tossing the hood onto the seats. The movement opened the folds of his heavy long coat and revealed blunt, dark shapes near his armpits: high-end blasters, one a Gul Sazer by the line of lights on its grip. Customised to his gene profile. It would be no more than a fancy club in my hand, and I couldn't escape anyway.

I didn't speak. Safer that way. Beneath the small of my back my hands ached and I flexed my legs to lift some of my weight off them. He looked me over then, a long up and down check that took in my old training shoe – just the one, that made him linger – then my street-kid's combat pants, cheap long-sleeved skinshirts and sweat-top.

'You dress like a vagrant.' He had the careful accents of another self-made man, trained to disguise any origins. 'That must change.' With an impersonality that made it no less invasive he put his cool hands around my neck and into my hair, behind my ears, under my collar, searching for hidden tech or implants. He pulled back my eyelid and stared into the depths of my eye, a piercing light arrowing from inside his own pupil and beaming into my unprotected retina. I guessed it was some wetware of his, though I hadn't seen anyone use any before, only heard about the illegal trade from Two. She searched constantly for any leads on the kind of stuff that we could have found useful, always supposing there was any way to get our hands on it. What we'd do if we did was a point we never discussed. There were very few doctors in Chaontium capable of splicing it in properly and too many failures buried in the desert to count.

His eyes glazed for a second as the machine worked, spilling information into his mind, and he grinned. I stared, sight bisected by the black line his scan had cut into it. 'Really careless of Dann to let you out alone and uncut. Not even a tracker. But don't worry, you won't have to endure her stupidity any more.'

He reached into his pocket and took out a multipurpose disposable blade, held it in his hand loosely, resting that wrist on his knee, so I could get a good look at it. I'd always told myself in this situation I wouldn't flinch but I was ready to do it. His gaze was stone cold. He clicked out a finger length of razored edge and with his free hand reached out and took hold of the cloth over my right leg. The blade hummed as he cut easily through it and peeled back a flap. He looked at the tattoo underneath for a minute as if it meant a lot to him.

'So,' he said conversationally as he placed his left hand and the blade with it up under the angle of my jaw. Expertly, he pressed so that I was pinned to the floor unless I wanted to cut my own throat. 'Here's how it's going to be.' He put his right hand down between my legs, found my treacherously half-hard cock with his fingers through the light fabric and adjusted me so that I rested against the length of his hand with about the same ease and comfort I'd expect him to use on himself. He began to press and stroke me gently as he talked, his face showing no emotion other than workaday intent.

'You're going to get out of the car and take this bag –' he indicated a holdall that was lying on the floor beside him '– with you. You'll go into your apartment and exchange it for a bag that will be given to you by my operative inside. You will not speak to that person nor give any warnings to anyone inside. Once you have made the exchange you will bring your friend Twostar back here to me and we will leave without further complications. At no time will either of you do anything to obstruct events as I have explained them.'

I was hard now under his hand. He looked at me with focus and then began to pull open the tabs on my trousers. His voice was mild, reasonable. 'I'm sure you're wondering why you would do this, loyal as you are to your generous employer and your dear friend, so I'll show you.' There was a small click and then the in-car screen came on and some shaky video blurred into shape on it. I was able to see it, even though the angle was bad from the floor and part of the image was blocked by the seats.

As the pictures soundlessly unfolded in front of me he slid his hand into my undershorts and moved back, bending over me though his knife hand never faltered in its position.

At first I didn't understand what I was seeing, but then it became more clear. I saw black-gloved hands pressing lines of what looked like modelling clay but which was all too familiar and grey, into long, careful strips under some flooring. They laid the explosive neatly along the joists, periodically inserting the small, square pins of remotely controlled micro-detonators into their handiwork, the sort used in multiples as failsafes, connected to many potential controllers on varied signals. It was standard cartel operations for a no-shit visible hit, usually triggered only after a 'sports news' message was broadcast to whoever the victim's protectors were, as in, 'You're so shit we can take you out with our eyes closed. Have a fun minute trying to stop us.' Then *blam*.

No sooner had it clicked what I was watching than he went down on me.

On the screen the gloved hands finished laying the explosive

73

and began to wriggle back out of the service gap, jolting the image around. Pipes and cables slewed back and forth. His tongue and lips were warm, slippery, in constant motion – the sensation mind-blowing in its intensity and newness, so long desired and denied. Fear, hate and arousal combined effortlessly into one all-consuming cocktail that wiped my ability to think.

The bomber withdrew from the hatch entry in a jog of bad transmission. As they emerged from the dark confine of the floor-space the camera blazed white, slow to react to the sudden lighting of the room above. As if he knew very well the timing of the video Dashain's mouth surged forward, his tongue demanding and hard, flicking and writhing. He pushed the blunt bulk of his blade hand into my throat in a commanding choke that hurt fiercely, razor edge pulsing against my skin with every violent thud of my heart.

I saw my own apartment on the screen, the black gloves refitting the access panel and laying the rugs down in place again beneath Two's sling. Two was there, she didn't seem to mind. I saw the logo of a major electronics company on a jacket as Black Gloves picked it up, put it on. Gloves took Two's commset from her, did something to it. Two smiled, thanks. She put the commset back on. The video feed switched off.

I was sure he'd intended me to come at this point. That I didn't was only down to the fact that years of denying pain access to any significant awareness had also left me numbed to everything else nerves had to offer by way of feedback – I didn't react that hard to pleasure either, even when it was delivered so professionally. He wasn't about to be denied his moment of dominion though. He wrenched my clothing down, yanked up my knees, rolling me onto my side, and forced his fingers inside me, pressing hard internally until he found my prostate. I came then: release, no great euphoric delights, no thrilling pleasure. It satisfied him however. When he sat up he looked oddly immaculate. He drew a pack of sterilising wipes out of his pocket and used five of them to clean his hands, a sixth for his lips, flinging the used ones into the corner. The whole fucking time he never moved the choke point, the blade never quite cut my skin open.

He looked me over as I got my breath back and then leaned across me to cut my hands free, then my ankles and my knees. If the numbness was bad the recovery was agonising. He gazed at me with lust and calculation, a half-grin on his face. 'Remember you have no idea who holds the detonators.'

So he'd made sure I was going in and getting out the door with Two; what about the rest? As if in answer to my thought he said, 'Once you leave the apartment you'll call the elevator to this parking bay. My guard will meet you on it.'

If they blew the charges I reckoned about two floors would go out. Anyway, what did I care really? He was wrong about my loyalty. I had no illusions about who was least important in the schemes of things. Me. And one boss was much like another. I owed nothing to the cartel, not even to Dann, and there was no point trying to trade with her now. Even if she'd take me back, supposing she even could, I knew the rules. I'd be dead within a week or sold out to the authorities. Most likely the latter if she felt truly offended. I nodded at him to show I understood. Only Two would care.

'You don't talk much,' he said. 'Keep it that way. Now get your pants up and get moving.'

I did as I was told, the only thing in my mind the thought that I knew one useful piece of information at least. There were no bugging devices or recording gear in that car cabin. If there had been he would never have dared do what he did in case it would appear one day as blackmail material. I got out of the car and found a gun at my temple. His personal guards were there, two at the car and a line of four between me and the exit, all focused, all calm, all armed.

Dashain got out with me, the clicking of the blade audible as he stowed it back in its grip. I felt him stand close behind me, then the slide of his hand into my trouser pocket, caressing me as he left the folded knife there for me. He patted my shoulder as he moved aside, like a friend.

'Just in case your brothers in arms aren't all that willing.'

I turned around and picked up the holdall from the car: it was quite light, no telling what it held. The gaping flap in my trouser leg was cold and irritating as I walked. I thumbed the elevator call and the doors opened. The ride up was the only minute I had to myself. By the end of it I still had no idea what I was going to say. My body burned in a sullen glow at the places he'd touched it.

I opened the door, let myself in. Inside the hall Jayda was waiting. She held out her hand for the bag.

A refusal always offends.

'I'm sorry,' she whispered as I got near enough to hear. I looked at her, giving nothing to her even as I put the handles of the holdall into her waiting palm. She went into my bedroom, came out with a different bag – a large grey canvas tote stuffed to bursting and tabbed close.

'Your stuff,' she said.

I opened my mouth, looking into her half-defiant, half-shamed face, and a relaxed, tough guy spoke out of my mouth, slightly impatient and demanding as he talked loudly to someone in another room. 'C'mon Two, let's go get take-out at the Park.'

One thing we had, as kids, was a series of inane lines used as code between us – essential for escaping the long arm of the law and other kids on occasions. This was a bastardised one of those. *Take-out* and *Park* combined meant we were out of there, no questions, no hesitations. Tone of voice didn't enter into it.

I didn't know if she'd go for it but it was the only thing I could think of that wouldn't start a long, drawn-out yap of trouble. It was also not unheard of for us to take trips together into the city, now and again, and we existed purely on take-out food. The other guards on duty looked up in the kitchenette. I was ready this time.

'You want something?'

'What's in your bag?' Temas asked, frowning as he looked up from his comms.

'Laundry.' The laundry was in the basement. Dropping it off was another regular trip. Jayda usually did it. Jayda wouldn't be doing it any more.

Twostar appeared in her doorway, dishevelled, hand in her pocket, commset still on her head. 'Huh?'

Commset. 'You wearing that out?' I asked her.

'Huh? No...' She took it off, leaving her choppy hair in a startled-rabbit look. 'Sure you want to...'

'Yeah,' I said, giving the nod.

She was ashen faced but she went with me, muttering her usual goodbyes to the Guys and Jayda. She looked at my pants leg but didn't say anything. We went out the door, into the hall. I keyed the elevator car on cue and then locked gazes with her to share a look that went right back twenty years into the freezing cold and hunger.

The doors slid open and there were four armed men inside. I got in between them, Twostar following meekly, and we stood in a wretched silence all the way down to the garage. It made me sick to know how much she trusted me. Not that harm would come to her. I was sure it wouldn't. That wasn't the point though. She'd have followed me into a point-blank showdown just as readily. But I was supposed to look out for her.

I shoved the useless guilt aside and opened the limo door, getting in first so she'd know she wasn't being spirited away alone. We sat on one side, Dashain and his bodyguards on the other. One a man, the other a woman: karma combo. Both of them wore black armouring and held their guns on their knees. I felt Two's leg trembling next to me and pushed my foot against hers in solidarity.

VanSant saw it and a faint smirk, not pleasant, crossed his face. 'I'm—'

'I know who you are,' Two blurted in that sudden, aggressive way she had when cornered. She was weak, yes, and out of condition, a thin, angular creature that lay around with its mind elsewhere most of the time, but cornered she was ratty and grim. 'Don't worry. I know what this is too.' She glanced at me then, tears brimming in her eyes, and then down at her hands, fumbled together in her lap like two big, clumsy spiders. 'I'll work for you.'

'Well, it would be such a shame to separate you,' Dashain said. 'I'm glad you're being so co-operative. Very professional.'

The car got underway, all its movements so hard to follow because of the air suspension cushioning, the compensatory fields. I lost track of where we went in less than thirty seconds. I wished it mattered more to me, but where was there to go? The road led here. It was always leading here. Who thinks otherwise?

There was a mansion in a private zone of expensive estates where Two and I were put. It was high up in the most prestigious code, at the sky level where every glass room had its own vista of poor schmucks to look down on. VanSant's operations outdid Kasha Dann's by a small margin, but in terms of fortress-building he was way ahead of her. Whatever our theft meant to her was something she could consider at her leisure. We'd moved up in the world. The old districts were decks below and her base on the other side of the Enclave altogether so any view of that was blocked by the massive pyramid of the high city.

Two had her own building, not that it mattered, all those gyms and swimming pools and entertainments were wasted on her. She was in the same position as before. As far as our personal lives went, however, they were both ruined. Tashin was Dann's personal offworld agent and remained in the unit Two had left behind. They didn't see each other any more, obviously, though Two found a way to establish infrequent contact using some of the revolution's parlay channels; there were sympathisers in VanSant's slicer squad who readily lent her their help once identities had been securely established. I guess joining wasn't that bad an idea after all, though it wouldn't have protected me.

As for me the sudden confinement to the estate meant I was cut off from the dojo. It emphasised all the more starkly that I had nothing without Two, was nothing if I wasn't her guard dog. That duty was gone too. I could see her, but I found that I didn't go. In spite of the fact there'd been no choice I felt responsible for her being here and for my position as the plaything of a rich and unpleasant man. One thing I'd always been was free in my own estimation; I grafted by choice. That illusion was shattered. I chose to be here, sure, because the alternatives were extinction, but it was still a demerit. I didn't want to see Two because I didn't want her or me to feel my shame. Without anyone I knew left then I was on my own, shut into myself and finding that after you stripped off the attitude and the belligerent hate there wasn't anything else in there.

VanSant had my gear incinerated, far as I know – I never saw any of it again. Anything that could have connected me to the past vanished. I was escorted to his personal apartments in the penthouse where I was shown to a walk-in closet which contained a strictly reserved array of clothing to fit me and nothing resembling a weapon of any kind. I couldn't even connect to the datmosphere without using his – protected – terminals. Given the nature of our meeting the meaning of this seemed pretty clear but in case it wasn't he gave me the guided tour of my new, tiny universe which ended on the open balcony where his infinity pool shimmered in a huge hemisphere of blue light over the night-lit vastness of the city – the Harmony Enclave out to the right as if its massif of gold was only a tacky add-on to the spectacular shine and blink of the city stretching into a darkness without stars.

Kidnapping, enslavement, I could say with confidence I hadn't expected this. It felt like my body contained an invisible wall beneath the skin suddenly, a piece of dragonhide to keep inside in and outside out. I felt it grow distinctly thicker as we looked out over that spectacular view and I searched, following roads I knew, trying to find a glimpse of the old world, but the little stucco building with its fairy porch lights I was looking for was blotted out by the insentient blue of the pool.

'I had you booked in for some upgrades,' VanSant said. He held out a glass of wine to me, his head tilted to one side, amused, waiting to see how this was going to go. 'But do you know, I was surprised. The lab said that you didn't need any. You were already sequenced optimally and there was nothing they could do. Millions of credits they couldn't charge. You should have seen their faces.'

The wineglass was the deal we were about to make. I looked at it. 'I guess I was born lucky.'

'Born...' His face creased with a sudden, immediately like-able smile and he laughed, all his perfect white teeth on show. I could see why he was so successful. He was likeable. He nearly spilled the drink. 'I understand there are people who still believe in chance instead of the fate of the Alchemy and the destiny of money.'

'I didn't say that.'

'Here.' He re-offered the drink and there was a steely glint in his gaze that said the longer I waited to take it the more of his displeasure I would earn. The smile lingered. 'And just to speed things along, let me make the terms of our engagement clear. Your friend's life, in all its particulars, lies in my hands. I know what that means to you. It was very foolish of you, to become so attached to only one, vulnerable, fragile, ephemeral thing.'

I met his gaze with my own. My master's oldest nostrum was that the essence of a warrior lay not in their ability to dish out the pain, but in their ability to restrain themselves from action.

80

To have the power to make irreversible change in the world and not to use it – I felt it now; the impulse in every fibre of my being had already calibrated every movement it would take to destroy him, had already done it sevenfold by the time my hand reached the glass and took it with the lightest of gestures, the most neutral of faces. In every gesture I made lay a deep ambivalence, a power of extreme intensity paralysed by opposing impulses: to kill and to claim. I know that what he did was meant to master me but the extremity of his commands revealed the truth that he was fearful of losing and this infused me with a peculiar desire. It wasn't for him, though he wasn't unattractive, but to reach out and take the position that was rightfully mine because I was the master here, the one without fear. I did look as if I submitted but I wasn't the one enslaved to his impulsive lusts; instead those drives had enslaved Dashein to me, tangled him fatally with me and now I could choose to tangle myself or simply to take him and use him as I wanted, a toy for myself. These two paths vibrated in my every nerve, each with its own terror, its own joy. I should have hated what he did, but was I going to? The decision was suspended like a sword over my head. Suffer and fall or revel and rise.

I was amazed at how hard it was to take that choice. Suffering had defined everything until now, had been the cause and the reason, the motive and the driving force, but I realised the lie hidden in its macho promise of superiority. Suffering was a state of being that only poisoned – it had nothing to give but more of itself. I could consider myself beaten, or I could take a path that I had never noticed existed before. It was so unfamiliar I didn't have a name for it but it felt like pure energy rising in me, fierce and unstoppable, like it had the force to turn over the world and consume gods. I could have power. I took it.

I knew that this sudden joy had hidden my predatory nature perfectly, making me an instant master of deception. It took everything I'd got not to crow with delight – both in what I had found and in the change it made to the world. I saw that from now on this was how it was going to be at every moment. My life had been easy until now, decisionless in its meander along the paths of the possible, Two's survival its only goal. But there had been freedom in that limited world and as my fingers closed on the glass I felt that it was this Dashein wanted most from me – my choices given up to him so that he would never be in danger from me and never be in danger from himself and the things he would do to win me. I would never let him or anyone take that. I'd lie and give him what he wanted so he became mine. I'd laugh and wait and stalk until the moment came when he was finished and I stood on his wreckage.

As he let go of the wine I felt his fate already sealed inside me with the finality of vault doors slamming shut.

He saw it and mistook it. 'I wonder how long you'll last,' he said, eyes fierce because this kind of game was what he lived for and it was going so well for him, he thought. I saw instantly how he wanted it to go: we were hunter and quarry who would run and run. Since that was the truth of it I let it go there – he moved the few steps across to me, gaze on mine, daring me to do anything about it, and kissed me, a tender, loving touch of lips to lips. My lips agreed, soft and promising while my gaze said that with one mistake he was dead meat. He almost swooned and pleasure filled me to the core.

He caught himself, stepped back, pretending to fan his face with one hand. 'Well, aren't you the surprising one?'

No. The only thing that surprised me was how much I enjoyed it. Until this minute I hadn't realised that the minotaur had other modes than battle or that war could be conducted this way.

My career at the Arena was over. VanSant's taste for bloodsports had long since sunk into the Pit by the time he acquired me and it was there that we went the first night, not to compete but to watch. He made sure that Two came with us. He was showing us off to the other bosses, to display what he could openly do to Dann when he knew she wouldn't be there. Word would get back, though, he'd make sure of that. He had other motives too – he wanted to show Two what I'd be doing. He knew everything about us from Jayda's tattling. He enjoyed Two knowing I was going to be exactly where she didn't want me. He wasn't about to bow to any demands about my safety from her. He was demonstrating that neither of us could use the other's value as a bargaining chip. He'd do all the proposing and disposing.

We had front-row seats, a mere half metre from the cage wall with its wide-set bars that most adults could have squeezed themselves through if they had really wanted to, if they had a minute or so to work on it. The floor and the seats were stained with blood.

We were late. The first fight on the card was finished, the second underway by several minutes. The air stank of sweat and every kind of human filth that sawdust and sand couldn't muffle. He sat between us and ordered everyone in his retinue popcorn and drinks except me, then he nudged Two.

'So who do you fancy to win?' he said, conversationally, one leg hooked over the knee of the other, his foot jumping and jogging with glee.

'Whoever you do,' she said, not looking at the struggle in front of her but trying to stare down instead.

'Oh come on.' His words were punctuated with thuds and cracks as an arm was dislocated, an elbow broke. It was hard to hear him for a moment over the gasping whine of the victim. 'I insist you make an educated guess... rather easy now, wouldn't you say?' He put his hand out and turned her head with his fingers in a claw grip over her small skull, made her watch. 'Or do you prefer to root for the underdog? Or with the underdog?' Then he looked at me with his scintillating grin.

'And you, Flower. Why the straight face? I thought you liked the thrill of mortal combat.'

'There's no thrill if you're not in it,' I said. The guy with the broken, dislocated arm was trying to go into shock but whatever his blood was full of wouldn't let him. The limb dangled in a grotesque fashion as he staggered and slammed himself back into his assailant's next assault.

VanSant pulled a face. 'I do hope you're not going to be a terrible disappointment. That could turn out to be very painful.' He let go of Two's head but caught her hair in passing and pulled some out with a yank that almost lifted her out of the chair.

I pushed my foot against his, as if it was a kind gesture to distract him 'I wish that you could feel what I feel when I'm there.'

He laughed and dropped the hair strands with a delicate little rubbing motion, as if he was sprinkling salt on his dinner. 'I bet you do. Popcorn?'

I took it. The pair of fighters were so high on stims they dragged it out another fifteen bloody minutes. Neither of them had enough energy or skills to end it faster. They were hardly adepts. The one with the ruined arm lost, strangled within inches of Dashain's shoes, his rolling eyes wildly trying to connect with anyone else's, until they didn't.

'Spirited,' Dash said, first to clap though the sound was lost in the general uproar of the packed crowd. Bodies went out, fresh meat came in. 'Now give me your professional assessment of the next bout. I want commentary, rolling analysis, make me care.'

Within a second my hatred escalated to a burning need to eat his liver. I glanced at Two and saw how green she was, her dark hands holding the chair so hard they were knuckled in white. I relaxed, waved my popcorn hand airily. 'Well the problem here is that this guy is letting that guy hit him.'

VanSant looked at me with a stare like a knife being slowly drawn. When it was nearly free I added, 'If you're looking for some kind of style guide you asked the wrong guy. Fighting is simple. Don't be where the other guy's hitting. Destroy him. That's all there is to it.'

Our gazes locked. I should have looked away, but that wasn't possible. I could feel time trickling away for all of us and I had no idea when the sand would run out on his demons. I think if I'd wavered he would have broken into a rage fit but my calm grounded him, so that he couldn't. He felt this happening too, I could see the confusion and the resentment in his face as his energy wandered away from where he'd expected it to ground out. Physically, he could make me do whatever he wanted and I'd agree freely in order to save Two and myself. I was OK with that. It was my decision, pragmatic and nothing else. But the rest of me which he so wanted to make crawl and break was out of his reach.

I wondered if I could playact broken, if I had to. It'd be difficult to convince someone as versed in degradation as he was.

There was a sickening noise of breaking bone from the ring and Two started in her seat. I glanced at her.

VanSant laughed his studied, devil-may-care laugh. 'I never met anyone so willing to gamble their life. You really must feel invincible.'

I didn't reply. I was too busy wondering how I could get Two to a safe place for long enough to dispose of him. But it was too early to say – it would take time to figure out how many and who among his retainers would be loyal enough to take revenge, execute orders or inherit the throne. I could act at any time, but I needed an escape route that would save Two.

The last three fights came to their depressing conclusions, witnessed by the same rows of wet-lipped men flanking VanSant's cool pose, my indifference, Two's sobbing repulsion. Those faces I filed away into the long lists of negligible prey. I didn't see anyone in the ring who would have given me too much trouble, but maybe all those fighters were already dead because only death would have been enough to make them quit.

'You must struggle to find enough fighters,' I said at the end, as we watched another body being dragged away by the ankles. I'd got the conversational-asshat tone down pat by then. I was used to playing too cool to care, it was my oldest and most comfortable overcoat.

VanSant tossed his half-finished popcorn down on the floor. 'They don't seem to last.' He smiled at Two. 'Are you ready for dinner?'

As we came out of the venue VanSant's black cruiser drew up to collect us but before he could get in there was a sudden blur of motion and a crash as something heavy landed on the car hood. We all watched in a stunned silence as the body of a young woman slid off the paintwork and onto the hardtop. She rolled onto her back, revealing a neat bullet hole in the centre of her forehead. It was Jayda.

A courier bike sped past and its rider screamed, 'Compliments of Kasha Dann!' and gave a jaunty salute.

The guards around us grappled for their weapons and aimed a few shots but they got nothing.

Jayda was wearing her hairdressing overalls. On the white material someone had used her lipstick to scrawl the words, 'More to come.'

We got into the car. VanSant's face was cold, thunderous. Two and I shared a glance. Jayda might have betrayed us, but what choice would she have had? I could see Two thought we were in serious danger and I knew she was right. Whatever value either of us had, our new boss was prepared to spend it.

Dinner was served on a floating barge as high above Chaontium as the Pit was below it. The glass room was full of his cronies and confidants and the early hours of the morning passed with them in full exploitation of the facilities. I managed to get away from him for a while and stood at the wall, looking out towards the desert, watching the excess behind me in the reflections. I tried to see the minotaur, but he wasn't visible. Spectator sport wasn't his thing.

I watched something that seemed to be moving in the high air corridors for a while without thinking much about what it could be. People did sneak about for assignations at all hours of the night in unlit vehicles, so there was no reason to be interested until what turned out to be two assault drones put their lights on and it was clear they were coming right at us: high speed, a signature yellow glow in their gun ports. Dann had hacked a couple of cops.

I was already running, shouting, straight for Two at the centre table as the first shots punched through the glass. VanSant's personal guard had corralled him and were taking him to what I assumed had to be the nearest, best and better-armoured escape vehicle. The furore would've made great cover for an escape but I had no idea where anything was on this vessel and the constant *ackack* of the drone guns was already tearing the place to shreds. Two and I crocodile-crawled under tables and rolled down into the sunken stairwell I'd seen VanSant take. Bullets the size of fingers slammed into the structure all around us. The air shattered and burned.

We got to our feet, sliding in blood, stumbled over the bodies of dying guards and then I picked Two off her feet and ran for the exit – not hard to see, the figure of VanSant being pushed inside, doors of the huge craft closing as the engine came online. The last guard looked back and saw us, held the door for a second – long enough that I got Two over the threshold and into the interior with me as the car declamped from the mooring and dropped like a stone. The door slammed at my back and the driver suddenly engaged a harsh angle of acceleration, flinging everyone around in a heaving mess.

When everyone was back in their places, belted in, the sudden smoothness of the transit let us know we'd escaped. Two was bruised but not really hurt. I didn't realise I was staring at her until VanSant said drily, 'I'm touched by the speed of your devotional return.'

He was shaken, pale, his voice the only part of him still able to manage laconic.

'She must really dislike you for some reason,' I said.

'Nobody likes being outsmarted by a better player,' he replied, a bitter grin on his face because he was still alive so whatever Dann was doing now counted as a fail in his eyes.

I saw in Two's face the same doubts I had about how long we'd survive here. Then she glanced up at me as VanSant was giving instructions to his driver and I saw her give me a shaky smile, more bravado than confidence, and whisper the words, 'Game on.'

It meant she had a plan, but our chances to discuss it were rendered impossible as she and I were taken to different locations – she to an estate in the country, me back to the penthouse. She was the brains of the company and in a much better position to gather intelligence. Whatever I'd thought to do was now on hold. She had a plan so I had to wait it out. She had a plan. We were back in the game. A rush of air burst into my lungs and I sat back and coughed to cover up the return of hope.

It was now that my master's oft said but little considered (by me) teachings came into my mind. She told me that being a warrior is not about fighting in the physical world – though you do that if you must. She said the task of a warrior is to end war. All war is internal... At this point a lot of the disciples nodded as she was talking, but you could see their eyes glaze. They'd grown up on the streets and war there was anything but internal. Then at this point in the teaching there would be a long silence as the master waited for us to understand.

'War is a dream of war,' she said. 'All illusion. End war inside, then war outside ends.'

'But that leaves you doing nothing while everyone gets killed,' someone said.

'I didn't say do nothing. I say end war inside, then war is over and only what must be done remains.'

'Aren't you redefining war as what must be done, then? If I have to defend myself and fight – how is it different?'

'All difference in world,' she said, with a tinge of sadness as she saw that we were not getting it. 'Saving self not war. Save others not war. Defend weak not war. Act is not fight. Fight is fight.'

They used to mock her for speaking as if she were a foreigner – there are no foreigners in Harmony and no reason to drop half the words, but she always did it. When prompted she only said, 'Less is more.' I think that her guru, whoever they were, had adopted the same way of speaking. It was memorable at least.

Once a guy asked her how he could become an undefeated champion, never lose. She thought a minute and then said, 'Sparrow never lands where tiger walks.'

Outside the dojo students liked to joke about her sayings, made up stupid ones of their own. 'Prawn not rise like sun,' that kind of thing.

If I could have gone to her now I'd have asked how to retain control of all my decisions and so keep myself true beneath the skin of whatever had to be done on the surface, because there was no escaping the surface now. I did as VanSant wanted or we were finished and although it would've been authentic to challenge him, me and Two'd've been authentically dead at the end. I even went as far as sneaking off to go to the dojo in the old district. I stood outside in my hooded sweats, hands in pockets, head down in the rain. I could smell the incense and resin coming through the door but I couldn't bring myself to go inside. Since the Pit I didn't want my master to see what I'd become and what I was doing now. She came to the door at goodbye time, waving off the students, letting the children come in off the porch, and looked at me. I'm sure she knew it was me. She waited for me. I walked on. I was soaked to the skin.

So, hunt war. Hunt fucking war.

I had as much of that as I could handle and some days accepting reality and flowing with it was so hard I couldn't think of a physical comparison. I died a thousand times a day as the old me tried to assert himself and came up against the strange energy that had yanked me in the other direction with that hopeful intake of breath. My thoughts dashed themselves against its immovable mountain but at some point my struggle with what was going on began to stop and I started to see what she was on about. I stopped thinking all this should never have happened, that I should have foreseen it, avoided it, done something about it. I stopped thinking that anything was meant to be different. Even VanSant stopped annoying me. I started to see what the end of war was and it wasn't what I thought. Nothing changed in my circumstances but I no longer felt upset by it. I even thought that all this happened purely to teach me this.

School! Who'd have thought it?

Even Two noticed.

'How can you be so sunny?' she asked once when we met for ice cream in our allotted weekly hour. Her little droid sat on the table between us, hidden by its soft fur costume of a brown bunny rabbit, shielding all our conversation with a bubble of frequency blockers.

I shrugged. 'I know you've got a plan.'

'You liar, that's not it. But anyway I'm glad you're not suffering too much.' She waited, hoping I'd fill her in and tell her it wasn't that bad, but I couldn't talk about the great sex and the stalking hunt, the joy of the long death of VanSant, without shattering all her illusions about me. I waited her out and she went on, in a much lower voice, excited and unable to hide it. 'Tashin's got hold of a pilot Switch.'

A pilot Switch was a fever dream, as real as a flying unicorn and as attainable. We talked of them in the winters at the heap when it was too cold to sleep – tech from the far distant world of the Diaspora, which interfaced human and machine, allowing both to expand and take advantage of each other's abilities. Of all the Switches, a pilot Switch was the grail because it synced with a starship and starships were the only way out of Harmony other than death. Tashin had a pilot Switch.

'No shit?' I said, wondering suddenly when, where and how she'd managed to meet Tashin and how Tashin could have met anyone ever who was in possession of such an article. At the same time my heart was thudding with excitement.

'Dashein keeps pestering me to get you wetware upgrades so he can be sure you won't die in the ring,' Two said, ignoring all the questions in my gaze and replacing them with a bunch more about VanSant and his anxieties, his weakness. 'I told him I had contacts but they're non-cartel, infiltrators. One whiff of trouble and they're gone, never hear from them again. He bought it. I met Tashin. She got the Switch. But as far as you know it's transcendent wetware, right? Machine upgrades. Nothing else.' She hesitated, briefly grinding her lower lip against her top teeth, her own uncertainties in how this all worked too strong to be kept inside. Looking her in the eye I could see we both felt the same ridiculous sense of possibilities, chances and the same urge to grind those possibilities into the dust before we got our hearts and everything else broken.

It was remarkable how you could dangle something so valuable in front of someone and their fixation on it would blind them to all the warning signs. Dash had gone for upgrades and the offworld glamour. He didn't trust me and he was going to make me fight in his death ring, but he was jealous and he wanted to keep me too. He wanted to win and he'd gladly cheat.

Me? I wasn't sold quite so fast. So Tashin got the Switch. Then she wasn't just Dann's tech fixer, was she? No way she was using those offworld links without Dann figuring it out. So Dann was in and that was trouble for VanSant for sure. This double-cross sale, posing one thing as another, had to be a Trojan horse that was going to race for Dann even if it raced for others too. My mind churned, jumped to an obvious starting conclusion.

'He doesn't know Tashin is the contact.'

'No. She was disguised. We took every precaution. Bunny's been upgraded too.' She patted the toy rabbit.

I glanced at its oversized, plaintive eyes. 'I wouldn't bank on that lasting a long time.'

'I'm assuming we have ten more minutes before someone objects,' Two said. 'So listen because I have more to tell you. I have the Switch and there is a ship. I'm going to present it as your wetware upgrades to VanSant, telling him that I have altered them to sync with your genetics, which obvs I have, and to make you better. But I'm really giving him the full package. Which means it will sync you up with the ship, depending on how the surgery goes. Actually, that's minor. It's made to install itself. There's not even any intrusion other than a few injections.'

I'd been imagining saws cutting my head in half and nodded, too relieved to say anything. Then a fresh wave of anxiety hit. 'How can you be sure it's legit?'

Her excitement level was too high for it not to be. She was jigging her feet at the ankles, talking fast, eyes lit like party candles. 'I've been all over it, Nic. It's the real thing.'

'And Tashin?'

'She's giving it over so that Dann can screw VanSant, of course. Because when you get the ship up and running we're off with it back to Dann's cartel. That's what Dann believes. She's getting the whole deal.'

'How?'

'The ship has dropships for in-atmosphere work and exits.'

We were locked into each other's gaze now like we used to be locked in each other's arms in the dump. 'We're not giving it to Dann.'

'Fuck, no, Nic. We're off. Up, up and away. But nobody knows that but us.'

I wondered if Tashin was now included in Us, but I didn't ask. 'Are you sure you're not being played?'

'I'm sure. Or ... if I am then I don't see how it's going to go down. The Switch is real. And we've got it.'

It was too good to be true. But then again, how often do you even get part of too good? I didn't like it at all, it felt all over sticky with sweetness, but I couldn't have said no and then lived with the consequences.

I nodded. 'But wait. Will it help me fight?'

Two sucked her lips into her mouth through a fine gap in her teeth, dragged them out again. 'I really don't know. I'm going to do my best but there's a lot I won't touch in there, 'case I screw it up. Maybe.'

'Hope I live long enough to enjoy it then,' I said.

'You'd better.' She grinned, but it was fleeting. Her minder came in through the door, waved at her. Time to go.

She picked up Bunny. 'It'll be soon, Nic. Stay cool.'

I pushed away my uneaten sundae. Cool. Sure. Yep.

I don't remember a lot about what happened on the day Dashain was killed. There was a fight the night before.

The gladiatorial combats were always held at different locations throughout Chaontium. Although the desert would have seemed a natural location a large number of expensive craft heading out of the range of patrols would have caused suspicion so most of the meetings took place within cartel buildings far beyond the reach of police actions or Crusade intervention. That didn't mean they went unobserved by the authorities.

Among the hooded and veiled patrons in the stands many from Harmony came to spectate, some in disguise but some in their ceremonial robes. There was always a guest priest present, one of the high-ups, to lend to the air of corruption by their willing participation. They were Nostrums, palliatives for the Alchemy which would otherwise have been offended by such a gathering of negative energies. They came to channel higher vibrations and convert the heavy downforce of violence and death into something more transcendent. At the time of this meeting I considered them no more than vultures of an ordinary kind; it was only much later that the real purpose of their presence there came to me: they came, like everyone else, to trade. The event was the cover, the real deal was going on in whispers outside the ring.

This particular day the announcement for the venue came late – a cancellation and restructure that made Dash hiss and curse as he was forced to change all his security details. We arrived late, the cars battling with those of five other cartels to get to the best parking spots on one of the highest and most prestigious decks of the SkyLane – a building controlled by a rival of Dash's and Dann's, Cor De Leon. There were some standoffs between guards as we disembarked onto a ramp Dash deemed too far from the entrance, but we got inside without any shots going off. I was slightly high, as usual for this stage on a fight day, striding after the master in my fight gear under the huge drape of cloak and hood. It was always these moments I expected to get shot by a sniper and hated the feeling of trusting myself to the vigilance of a bunch of other bozos. I breathed a sigh of relief once the doors were behind us. Given what was to come it amused me that this was the worst part over as far as I was concerned.

The light and darkness of the fight theatre was so familiar to me now that it was a kind of homecoming to walk in to its stark, anonymous vault. The cheap stinks of the amateur ring were long gone, replaced by the scents of much more refined delicacies, but the sense of ravaging hunger in the air was the same. It was nameless to me at first, but I knew it now. The crowd had a limitless appetite for more experiences and felt by raw instinct that witnessing this violence, extreme as it was, was going to enhance them, give them a larger reservoir to hold more of life. They wanted more and somehow they felt it was here, to be taken by the Alchemy's subtle process. Even the priest said so as he burbled on effusively about the energy of vitality in the presence of death, reverent and sincere as he trembled with anticipation. A vamp is a vamp; I was used to them too and their drooling desire meant nothing. Only Dash's focus interested me. He was my life and death, as I was his, and this dance was growing stale.

Sometimes I felt there *was* a curse of too much sun, two essential factors meeting, yet always ending up unfulfilled after the hormones, the athletics and the pleasure were finished. Whatever the attempt at union meant, at whatever level and even through whatever avenue of emotion, it was hopeless. What was about to happen in this room was the same. It would and could never fulfil the dream. It could never be enough. The entire universe could slip into that maw and not be enough.

I watched him walk in front of me as we made our way to the ring and fancied myself intuitive for knowing we were soon to be done with each other, seeing only a minute later that it was because I had already done with him. The Switch and its promise had replaced him as the focus of my interest and my survival now lay with it and not with him. He had to go.

My opponent, Wormwood, tattooed with the image of his own skull all over his body in a repeated motif that made him a living ossuary, was tricky and determined to live. I forgot even the Switch as we began our circling. In the black-ringed sockets of his gaze I felt he'd seen a part of me that had been willing to die here once and that he would conjure it up again.

There was nothing left of the original fighter I'd been with my swagger and pose, my arrogance and my sham humility back in the amateur ring. This was not my first no holds barred fight to the death either, but it was the first where I felt my own mortality present with me, as close as my opponent. It wasn't him, but through him it could come for me, I only had to decide if it would. There is no opponent but yourself after all, whatever form he takes on the outside. I hadn't known that a part of me had died until now. If it hadn't that seductive lethargy of the grave wouldn't be looking at me through the ink and loathing.

I felt how easy it would be to give up and the weight of all that the Switch promised as liberation and as trap would be lifted, not mine to bear. I'd never have to face my fear of it, which wasn't only what it would do to me physically but what it could do to destroy me when it was revealed that Two and I were the patsies once again in a greater, better-paid game. I'd bet my life on getting out. To be thwarted with the very thing that was the only real hope of escape seemed worse than losing now. It would make everything a joke on me. I did want the Switch and I didn't.

Wormwood landed a punch that knocked all the nonsense out of me in one instant. I got off the mat in agony, spat my broken teeth on the floor, and lispingly thanked him for saving me – from thinking. He looked confused and I returned the favour. I went after him, horned and tailed, ready to eat his liver and that of everyone in the room.

He went down in nine minutes. He was taken to hospital in a coma. They never told me what happened to him. I never asked.

The apparent brevity was something VanSant hated. He wanted things drawn out to the point where unrecognisable creatures crawled to each other across the floor, so desperate to live that there was nothing they wouldn't do. And lately his inability to needle me was needling him like a new, too-tight suit.

After the fight I was back at the house, wearing the sweat and bloody evidence of my business in the way Dashain preferred, and nothing else. He was fully dressed in one of those designer outfits that cost more than my life, watching the fight again on video.

He sat up on the end of his bed and I lay on it while his personal medic – a shy, tiny woman who never spoke unless she had to – used the latest healing technologies on my injuries: cracked nose, cracked jaw, broken ribs, bust knuckles, missing teeth, minor internal bleeding and a bunch of the usual superficial cuts and swellings. She'd doped me with some shot so I really didn't feel much. Dash was impatient, replaying seconds, his foot twitching with dissatisfaction, freeze-framing whenever I got hit. When the medic was done we were left alone and Dash indulged his fetish which was to keep me naked in his lap while he sipped whisky and watched more matches from the past. He watched me on the screen getting the stagey bullshit display kicking I'd been told to suck up before taking my opponent out with a sudden return to brutality as normal. It was his inclination to use me and the more demeaning it was the better he liked it. He wasn't sadistic in the traditional sense. Pain didn't interest him, only power.

At first my hate for him had morphed into an exquisite creature of near physical presence but I kept it under control by calming myself with thoughts of killing him with the ease I knew I could. It would take about three seconds. Five if I was feeling mean.

I did it again in my mind, purely for entertainment, as he made his soft appreciative sounds at my softening, accepting body. I broke his neck; I rammed my finger through his eye and into his brain; I tore out his throat in a bloody chunk of red wet flesh and shuddering white pipes. I itched to do it. The movements ran in my nervous system like a constant illness sometimes, making me shake with the inherent joy of their unexpressed power.

He mistook it for arousal and pleasure and that vain error

pleased me with a deep thrill. My perversity ran rampant. It had nothing else to solace itself with. Real fights were nothing on this game between us. Even the fact I knew and named its shame didn't dampen its thrall. What I did in the ring was tame in comparison. I didn't hate those men, they were simply in my way. It was here, on the bed, that my battle was won. And I must think of a way to end it that satisfied me. I didn't want to be swept up in Dann's schemes again, robbed of my prize. I wanted blood.

The last fight video finished. He drank and poured the remainder of his forty-year-old offworld alcohol over my ass before licking it off.

He cued up some orchestral music, the kind he listened to when he couldn't sleep. I was nearly comatose when he said, 'Aren't you worried about tomorrow?'

It took me a minute to process what he was talking about: the wetware installation. It was something I hadn't thought about because it was inevitable and so what was the point? What happened was beyond my control. 'No,' I said, doped on painkillers and too woolly to lie.

'You know why I trusted your friend to do it? Because she would never let you die if she could help it and I need a return on this investment, Nico. I need you to become a legend – and also there are other rumours of technology smuggling routes and I need you to be a good pioneer for the future. Once you're proven I can expand. You'll be the first in a long line of connections offworld into very lucrative markets.'

It took me as long again to consider what he said as it took him to say it. The music had a sentimental, sad tone. Listening to it was his way of getting to that state of contemplative melancholy he fancied was the necessary weather of great minds when they were set on putting the world to rights. It made me want to smash the sound system. But I was too busy trying to flip his words inside out, see if there was a hidden threat there, some implication that I should always be his pet or we were dead. It was hardly like him to be reassuring. But then I figured he was nervous – not for losing me but for the money and the chance at kicking the other cartels in the face. Sure. That was worth a sad song or two.

'Are you looking forward to becoming a god?'

A god. I'll be the worst god in the world. 'I'm just waiting to see,' I said, which was true. Wait and see if this tips the scales in my favour at all, so I can kill you and be done. Yeah, out of here, that was first on the list but surely there'll be time for the fond farewells? 'What will happen to Two if I don't make it?'

'Unfortunately I have no insurance policies put aside to cover the expenses of your failure as a host.' And there it was. He let the last drop of drink from his glass fall on my spine. There are some people whose hearts you'd eat to claim their power and some you'd spit out and rinse to avoid. There'd be no ancient rites for him. But also, nothing simple like a shot to put the rabid animal down. I fancied something much more human and personal. Time for a few well-chosen words.

'No protest to make, Nico?' he asked in a pitying tone, but laughing as well, since he knew the answer. 'What is it like to be completely without a choice in the world?'

I considered it but I was exhausted and my mind was still boggled by the vaunting scale of his ambitions. They were ludicrous. He was insane. He thought he was going to become an offworld broker. The state would have him for an example and string him up.

But I had no choice, I told the truth. 'It's easy,' I said.

'But inside.' He was really in pursuit today, searching for every little trace of the good stuff. 'What is it like to feel the anger, the rage of rebellion against cruelty and unfairness and not even be able to let it show? How much of it must you eat before you break?' He sighed and I heard his irritation as he signalled for another drink. 'Your lack of resistance is itself the most infuriating resistance. I fear your patience for a fight is going to long outstrip mine. I couldn't decide yet whether or not to have you made more obedient. It's a difficult choice. I have no interest in a flesh robot that does everything without a care, but then, I can't risk a viable fighter getting out of his place if he has some kind of super power. I can't risk you turning on me. I don't know what to do...'

Perhaps I should have been touched that he'd lie to spare my feelings. I knew what he'd do. He'd vote for me to get axed in the wetware installation so that he could protect his investment. He'd ask Two to tame me. That was only business and a personal fetish was something he'd find another, cheaper way to fulfil. I was sure he'd already signed off on it, but also sure Two would not do it. There was nobody to prove it either way until I woke up. If I woke up. But then again, when your mind is altered it's altered and what once mattered won't concern you any more. This was death itself come calling.

I tried to work up some mortal terror but the drugs were too strong and my inner fire was weakened by the time I'd spent here, on this bed, in this way. I'd taken pleasure out of what was on offer simply because it was there too many times. Purity was diluted by ambivalence. Hate was love gone bad, clinging, gripping love that wanted to suck the life out of its object. My focus had scattered. I was just like Dash: a sad vampire searching for one more hit, one more taste of something that was a perverted echo of bliss, but good enough as it's all there was to get. Surviving a kicking was one thing, surviving a transformation – that never happens. That's the meaning of transform. Out of one shape and into another. If I lived I knew only one thing, there would be no more waiting to escape.

You tell yourself these lies. I'd waited much too long already.

We slept: me very badly due to the pain in my hands. I saw the minotaur as I fell asleep. His back was turned to me. It was

100

raining on him, steam rising off the mountains of his shoulders, water dripping from the points of his horns, boiling as it ran only to evaporate into thin air.

The morning after was spent in prep for my operation to receive Two's black-market upgrade. We went out to the country estate all together.

One of his rooms had been turned into a surgical theatre, although there wasn't a lot of surgery involved – a tiny keyhole was sufficient, nothing you wouldn't recover from in a few hours. I had to be anaesthetised with special drugs, attached to monitors – it took a long time. Two was there to oversee her end of the works, synchronising and activating the Switch itself, checking and setting up the wetware so that it merged with my natural systems seamlessly. She held my hand. The last thing I saw was her face, her smile a confident white semicircle pasted on for my benefit in an effort to counter the terror in her eyes.

'You'll be fine, Nic,' she whispered. I think her hand stayed on mine but I felt the touch of it fade away as sedation pushed me under, the anaesthetist muttering about how much she had to use, enough to drop a fucking horse.

Five – if you're bothered about sectioning up your information into a tidy order

I opened my eyes.

I was in a brightly lit hospital room. The lights were oscillating too slowly to be efficient. I could see into spaces I shouldn't. I opened my eyes into the spaces of the building. And instead of being just me I existed in a series of parallel parentheticals, a kernel of me encased in endless onionskin slipcovers of me, all doing different things. I could *even say* phrases like 'parallel parentheticals', which included words I didn't know until the second they popped into my inside-out head like invisible rabbits from equally invisible hats. Balance is everything.

At the same time that I was groggily trying to lift my head I found myself poking about in police networks with relatively little trouble like I was some kind of automatic signals ferret. Other agents of me were swimming through the Upper Datmosphere, tentacles in every orifice of the Harmony working day, watching traffic and sneering at the security protocols. Plus, the lights were inefficient all over the place...

I closed my eyes and willed the horrible zoo to go away. Be a bad dream. Bad zoo.

I became human again.

Meanwhile my thought-hacking should have triggered every alarm from the hospital to outer space, but it didn't. Instead of screaming sirens all I heard was my own hand rustling against the sheet, heard it with an unbearable precision of detail which let me count the threads – a hundred per centimetre but half of them synthetic so they'd last a lot longer than any patient looking for a final second of luxury. They'd been washed but soap was still left in the weft – my skin could taste it.

I had to turn that shit down a notch too, but as soon as I had *that* thought Something did turn it down. It restored my skin to skin, my ears to ears, eyes to eyes. I stopped hearing the conversation in the next room and the shallow breathing of the unwaking at the end of the hall.

The bed sat me up with a whirr of a quiet motor and I found myself in a private room, the really expensive kind, with a window and everything.

It was a wet day, grey, drizzling, with light winds pushing more cloud banks over the city. I could feel the rain if I wanted to. It was on the sensitised glass of the building and I could be that building or any number of other buildings and machines. Their surfaces could be my skin. Everything I was connected to could be me. For an instant I was so enchanted by this that I let me be everything and that was the last thing I did for some time. I drowned in a storm of information, not even time for a last wave.

When I came to, the intolerable reality of that mass-consciousness had gone, but gone like it was hiding behind the curtains waiting to pounce, not gone-forever gone.

A silhouetted person stood at the bedside, me in their shadow.

'Nico Perseid?' That kind of voice which knows very well who you are and is merely completing a formality for someone else's sake. The kind of voice which is really saying, 'You are so screwed.' It was a real person, not a curtain-lurker.

'Yes,' I said. 'Who the hell are you?'

'Lucian Shan, Inquisitor General of this Purge cycle. I am here to arrest you.'

I had to laugh, only I couldn't because I was still drugged to the eyeballs. I managed to muster a fucking civil sentence to my surprise. 'On what charge?'

'For the murder of Dashain VanSant. And a number of other charges ranging from grand theft to gross moral indecency. Do you wish me to read the list?' He was doing a good job of sounding thoroughly bored and a bad job of hiding how much he was enjoying it.

Wait, what? VanSant dead? Two minutes ago he'd been staring at me through a high-res panel with the expression of the goose that laid the golden egg as anaesthetic faded me to black. I groped around my memory for the past and felt it come in bits and pieces like it was some loose change lost down the back of a seat.

I recalled our arrival at the makeshift medical centre set up behind Dash's country house. I'd felt sick with apprehension. I remembered Two being with me, holding my hand as they sedated me though it was her touch that kept my heart in pace. We were both excited to pieces because our secret hopes were coming that bit closer to reality. With this wetware we could be connecting me to a ship that I could captain without the interference of others. I'd be capable of getting us off this dump, details TBC and screw anybody else's plans.

I'd had to have extra sedatives. Then a few more. The consultant complained that I was using excessive drugs – 'dope a horse' – and made them run extra bloods to see if I was high. They scanned my gene pattern and I recalled hearing the surgeon make a joke about new mutants. He'd not come across this kind of constitution before. It was virtually eating thin air and if they kept me under for long I might grow a second liver.

VanSant had been there in the background, behind the safety glass so he didn't have to bother scrubbing up or changing his suit. The lights blazed. After that, nothing. Murder? When could I have done that exactly? It was impossible. But here was the

Inquisitor asking *do I wish to know the full fucking list of my crimes*. No, I couldn't give a shit at this point. I have way worse things to deal with. And apparently no ship I can detect.

'Just send it to my lawyer,' I told him straight from my cop-show vocabulary, trying and failing to muster some dignity. The metal restraints on my waist, neck and wrists and the tubes coming out of me somewhat got in the way of that.

His return look was priceless: condescension, pity and contempt. I remembered it to play back later whenever I needed a rage-surge of adrenaline.

'The stars smile on mercy.' His voice was an old, dry snake, slithering in the well of his throat. Must have taken hours to perfect. 'But they cannot smile on those who choose to commit the deepest of sins in return for that mercy.'

Well, nothing looks worse for a fundamentalist cult of gengineers than the ones who turn out wrong in spite of their tinkery mixology. They always love it when you screw up. Makes their predictions of your failure look so good.

'Thanks for clearing that up,' I rasped.

My breath must have been special. His patriarchal lean over my bedside turned into a recoil of disgust. 'Do you even have a lawyer?'

I didn't, but a name appeared in my mouth of its own accord, as though it had been waiting behind my molars for that very purpose, 'Juliette Noughten.'

He almost stepped back. 'Of Dice and Dice?' That bad-liar's voice said I had to be kidding.

'That's her.' Apparently. I tried to swallow, not through dry mouth but a sudden fear of what was happening to me. Summoning lawyers was not my thing. It wasn't anybody's thing without a phone. I didn't like it.

He left, furious, with a sweep of his black cape. I may have made up the cape. I blacked out again.

*

105

This time waking up was not so fun. The puking started as the tech misunderstood my sudden urgent need to escape and tuned me into sixteen different fire escapes inside the hospital walls.

A doctor ran in along with the nurse. As my guts hotly disputed the nature of reality I heard the doctor say the vomiting was normal – my brain had to adjust to a new sensorium. I guess it was good bedside manners that he didn't say it might never adjust and then I'd sick myself to death shortly before they scrapped me and hacked all their expensive work right back out of my still-warm corpse. I just took that as a given.

After the doctor had gone and I was more or less myself again I took a moment to will my ordinary senses back and shut down everything else.

– Listen, machine. Shut down and shut up. Totally. Maybe make me a bit smarter because I need to figure out what's going on here.

I went back over what the Inquisitor had said. VanSant was dead.

And then Pandora's Box was open and where I'd had nothing but denial and silence and resignation before a billion paranoid options reared their ugly heads and I got to look at each one in turn.

All along the trading chain anyone could have been taken for a ride. None of us were expert technologists, the reverse in fact on all counts except for Two. There was no way to know that the gear was what it was claimed to be. I trusted that it did look good enough to fool Two, but Harmony is a long way out on the edge of nothing and our pitiful mechanoids are as dust compared to the fantastic creations of the greater Diaspora, not to mention the Forged community. We literally would not know shit from a shovel. We could be taken for as long a ride as you liked on that score.

So that was one. Quite a wide-area kind of infinite 'one' that didn't bear thinking about.

Then there were the agendas, open and hidden. We all had those. At least two of us wanted VanSant dead. Given what happened to me just now it's possible the tech took over on one of my delirious whims and did the business without me – I wouldn't put that past its genie nature. But Dann would have used me in a heartbeat if she'd had the means to do it. I should've asked how he died, that would have given me a clue as to whether it was on my ticket or someone else's.

That was two.

Then there were the amazing upgrades, all as promised, apparently. But at the same time, as I was spacing out into the world I wasn't finding a massive interstellar craft poised like a metal angel to grant my wishes. How I'd find that I don't know but if I could find the nurse's hairpin stuck in the air-conditioning unit causing that annoying buzzing sound two floors down I could surely have found something the size of a city that was supposed to be connected up with me and there was nothing, nada, squat like that. Maybe it was only upgrades and no ship.

So that was three.

Then, for some reason it had never occurred to me previously that all the apparently criminal trading was tacitly allowed by the state. Now it was obvious. Those secret shame parties in Chaontium at the fight club, the Purge to cover the lifts of goods from one area to another. The entire black world of mine with its precise rules and carefully managed badness was a state-sponsored venture in being just naughty enough to make it seem like there was a legitimate resistance and a genuine underworld. It allowed officials to obtain by seizure under Inquisition what they could never obtain openly without breaking all their own laws. If there was such a thing as a *legitimate resistance* to the orthodoxy it wasn't in the cartels I'd gotten used to. They were merely glamorous furniture in the state's dining room; cheap furniture you smash to make a point and impress. Hence the

Purity Crusade's eternal advance and retreat, the trials, the executions and the stubbornly continued existence of Chaontium with its crowds of poor misfits, failed experiments, queers and weirdy-beardies. Every hero needs its nemesis, that's balance in action exactly like the Alchemy says. So maybe I wasn't a rich bastard's toy goon so much as a way of getting something for Harmony by the dirty route. After my arrest I was state property. Deal done.

That was four.

I started to wonder what else I'd been missing under my own nose and my wish to know was immediately granted.

It hit me like a truck. Yet again, it'd never occurred to me to wonder that someone like VanSant thought he had a shot getting involved in seriously big-time crime like offworld piracy. But he must have had someone pulling his strings from behind. He wasn't stupid, he would have had assurances from greater powers that he would be looked after as he went about this little venture. I tried to remember meetings he'd had, places he'd been that were unusual and there were several opportunities for clandestine operations. But even if there were more players than I thought, that didn't help me out at all, it only explained the how of things. The fact he was dead meant he was the weakest link and the fact I was arrested meant I was no sooner in the game than out. So I was the prize or the instrument.

Only Dann had instrument as a motive. That would effectively waste me, and that seemed like something she wouldn't do, unless my arrest was a misstep.

There was another alternative. Two's revolutionaries might really be trying to pull off a master stroke and infiltrate Harmony. VanSant was not a target then as much as a means to getting a very altered me into the Inquisition. And that meant the revolution had people outside. VanSant and Twostar and I, we were all stuck in the great singularity that is Harmony's complete isolation from the outside world. Someone from the outside had to have fenced the item. It was more than possible we'd all been the victims of a switch.

I decided I hated being smart and wanted no more of it and the magic upgrade granted my wish with what I was learning to see as a degree of excess. I blacked out.

Two hours later and this time the drugs were having a go at me since the escape stairs seemed to be obeying orders, cowering in their usual places inside the walls. I was puking nothing into a cardboard bowl, shaking from the weight of the kilogram manacles which had replaced the bed restraints, while a complete stranger stood over me brandishing roses and waiting for me to spit: Juliette Noughten, of Dice and Dice, specialists in criminal law cases and known across Chaontium's elite for getting the most unlikely people off the hook.

'I didn't do it,' were the first words out of my mouth.

She dropped the roses into the trashcan and pulled a wipe off the stand, passed it to me silently.

'Thanks,' I said, holding it close after I'd used it, as if it was a teddy bear. Finally I was able to lie back.

Juliette Noughten was about twenty-five, tall, lanky and brown all over from the top of her hair to the sole of her shoe. She carried an antique palmtop computer with her which may as well have been a huge placard saying 'I Am Disconnected'. She'd chosen a chocolate-and-cream spotted suit. I was trying to decide what that meant while she opened a tiny case from her pocket and let out her Privacy Droid. She waited until it had whirred and checked for surveillance and set up its interference fields. When it bleeped the all clear we were legally, professionally *Alone*. Then she said, 'Good to know, though not important.'

'It isn't?' I stared at her.

'No,' she said, smoothing the lie of her perfect tailoring.

If I could have changed bodies with her I would have, in a heartbeat. She looked so well. I felt so unbelievably ill.

109

'Nor is your defensibility an issue.'

'Why not?'

'Because this is going to go down another route,' she said. 'Do you know where you are?'

'Uh ... The VanSant Cashimir Estate,' but even as I said it I knew it wasn't true. How could it be? That had been a temporary room built to order. This was a full-sized hospital. The view from the windows was city not country. I stopped, gaze locked on to her as the only still point in the universe.

'You are in Atiso Maximum Security Holding One-D.' She waited to see if it rang any bells. Then continued. 'It's a facility for the criminally insane in Harmony Enclave. In the shadow of the Citadel.'

I puked again. Nothing came. Anything inside me was long gone, there was only my stomach, trying so hard to dispose of everything that was poisoning me, not understanding that its valiant efforts were in vain. The poison was everywhere but in my body.

Juliette handed me another wipe. I obediently passed it over my mouth. She gave me a few sips of water although I felt I'd be seeing them again shortly. Her kindness extended to not waiting for me to ask for an explanation.

'Your operation was a success,' she told me as I closed my eyes. It helped a little. 'But not without complications. You've been under heavy sedation for four days. When the police discovered VanSant's body and then your whereabouts they had you taken from the estate and brought here to be arrested – which is when I was called, I believe.'

I managed to organise my mouth. 'Dash is really dead?'

'Yes. Four shots. The weapon, weapon residue and genetic material all tag you as the killer. Plus a witness and video footage records the crime and, well, you had plenty of motive unless those indecency charges are real, wouldn't you say?'

Four shots? Ridiculous. A professional like myself wouldn't

110

waste three extra bullets on him. Personally I wouldn't have used any to do the job. Fists were what he needed. I felt offended but also interested; I was sure it wasn't me that had done it and that was worth knowing.

But motive. Yeah, I had plenty of that and the fact she seemed to know about it meant that she'd been briefed by someone who knew. Not too many of those around. Twostar. Perhaps her lover, yes, that fit – the revolutionary.

'Yes. No. Yes,' I said, breathing carefully, easing my aching stomach muscles.

'Any idea who set this all up if it wasn't you?' Juliette tried to give me water again but I pushed it away. She bore it patiently.

The great big nothing out of which previous inspiration had come was empty. 'No,' I said, not daring to shake my head. It wasn't entirely a lie. I had no proof, only a lot of suspicion.

She made a note of it on her palmtop. 'I need you to be examined by an independent doctor and a slice expert. Also by an Inquisitor working for me. It would be better if we used the Court Inquisitors, it will look more like co-operation. But you can call for a different one if you think of someone who might be sympathetic.'

I opened my eyes and looked at her to see if she could possibly be serious. There wouldn't be a sympathetic Inquisitor in existence. The idea filled me with dread. Now it would all come out. I only just grabbed the bowl in time as the thimbleful of acid-tainted water came back out of my mouth in lieu of an answer. I wondered if Juliette knew.

'Why am I in Harmony?'

'Because someone wants you here.'

'The Inquisition.'

'No.'

I gagged. 'Then who?' Another tissue. I took it, used it, added it to the two in my hands. 'What's going on?' I asked when I was able to, my voice sounding as raspy as a dying man's. I felt like I might be dying. I wanted to call a doctor but I wanted to know what this lawyer knew even more. 'You sound like you've got privileged information.'

'I think it's better that some information remains confidential at this time,' she said, looking sympathetic though her gaze said she wouldn't be moved. 'You should also know that the wetware in your body is abnormal in some way that has yet to be determined. I understand from our employer that you knew the slicer?'

Our employer?

'Who's your employer?'

'I can't say.'

So, my random selection of lawyer was nothing like a random selection. She was already waiting to come and see me, because whoever had framed me was footing the bill and that person also had access to the wetware in my head. The notion made my blood into ice.

I wanted to use any pitiful lever I had against Juliette's professional silence so I played it as miserable as possible. Not difficult in the circumstances. The constant shaking that crept over my limbs, part exhaustion, part fear, was irresistible.

It didn't work. She continued, 'We can discuss this later when you are stronger. In the meantime better the doctor sees you in as poor a condition as possible. May I send her today?' She was automatically reaching for another tissue from the box as I convulsed with another agonising spasm. I ended up lying on my side, staring dully at the roses in the trashcan. Belatedly I realised she hadn't thrown them away, there was just nowhere else to put them.

'Yeah, sure,' I said when I could, feeling her push the wetted paper into my hand. I looked down her long legs in their fine synthmesh covers, feet in their amazing stacked shoes. Something about the shoes made me trust her. No strait-laced servant of the state would wear such rebellious shoes with their outer primness, their classic laced lines and so much fuck-you elevation.

'Is there anything else I can get for you before I go? I'll return this evening when I've done some preliminary research and checked in with the investigating officer. They want to interview you but I'm sure I can have that vetoed for at least a day or two by the doctor. Is there anything else you'd like to tell me?'

'Yeah,' I said, mustering enough saliva to say anything. 'Thanks for the flowers.'

She paused and then I felt her hand on my shoulder. 'This will get a lot worse before it gets better. Just try to recover as fast as you can. When I come back I'll need everything you know.'

Juliette returned on time accurate to the minute. I was in better shape, or so I thought, but by the time I'd finished telling her my life story with all the pauses and backtracks to answer her exacting questions I was wiped out again. Then, since I'd shown her mine, she returned the favour and showed me a recording of the shooting taken by Dash's security cameras.

There I was, time-logged two hours after the op, verified by the good old DNA, walking up to the garage in my scrubs, barefoot, opening the door, shooting the guards in the face with a precision I rather admired, my expression bland as white bread. Dash took cover inside his car but for some reason as soon as the doors had enclosed him in their protective cocoon they sprang back open like he'd trod on the wrong emergency button. See that and you know your systems have been hijacked, but I looked like I expected it and, bored as bored, I stepped over the bodies, got an angle and made four clockwork shots. Then I dropped the gun on the ground, turned and walked out. The door closed at my back, cutting off the light and closing the scene.

In every bit of footage the pathetic medical pyjamas make it clear I've got an erection.

113

I point this out to Juliette. 'That's because I'm asleep.'

She closed the display down and composed herself. She might as well have been watching lettuce grow. 'That is the moral indecency charge basis. You don't remember any of that?'

'Nothing,' I said, thinking back carefully, but even as I said it I could feel the memory of the pistol in my hand, the closing of my finger on the trigger. 'I'd never have done it that way.' It could never have lasted long enough. I felt robbed.

'Still, I think we know where we stand,' Juliette said and patted my hand. 'Get some sleep.'

She left.

If I'd paid more attention to Two, I thought, and who she was hanging with, I might have realised that she was in her own bubble of change: falling in love with ideas and the person who handed them to her and getting in over her head. What defence could she have against things as heady as that? Whatever Tashin had sourced and handed me was no upgrade and no ordinary Switch. I really should have done some background work on her a long time ago instead of assuming that anyone Two loved could only be a harbinger of good.

But I was still alive and that was something. For now.

I thought of Jayda's body falling out of the dark onto the car bonnet.

Dann could still have ordered it as a hit. Tashin could have done it for the money, although the more I remembered her the more I bought her as a straight idealist, someone devoted to the cause enough to do anything to further it. Would that include murder? If it didn't cause too much inconvenience, probably. She was passionate, if dry, in her arguments. Criticism of Tecmaten and the Alchemy flowed out of her in furious torrents given half a chance. She was genuinely angry, connected to her beliefs. But she was one of us so how the hell had she got away from Harmony and into the Diaspora and then made a return with hot gear without being picked up? I really couldn't figure that one.

I thought about Two's happy clinging to her, the agreement without too much critique. Throwing your brains away for love, that was a classic mistake a lot of people could fall for, right? Did Two program me to shoot him? If she were going to kill him she'd have chosen that method, I think. She was always much too merciful for her own good. But I didn't think she'd use me. Unless... it all became too complicated at that moment. Excellent as this wetware might be it didn't do telepathy. I had no idea what anyone else was really thinking or feeling. I could feel myself super keenly though, as if I'd never been more alive.

Yeah, I was lucky. But where was Two anyway?

The answer shot into my head with the subtle nuance of a brick arriving at high speed. One second I didn't know and the next I was sure of all the details. She was alive and well. She was working for the same people Juliette had cited – the 'resistance' were our bosses now – she was updated on all my developments and glad I was going to be OK. She was glad Dash was dead and that I'd done it even if I hadn't really done it.

Her pleasure felt like gritty chocolate, a feeling and a taste, a sensation like slipping on an unexpected patch of oil, but this bizarre sensory insight broke up in signal. There was a flicker of the world and I suddenly heard her voice in my mind, more clear and real than if she'd been sitting next to me. Seems I was a bit off on the telepathy, but then I realised it was some kind of internal phone.

'Can't use this channel for long. I don't want them to notice the extra band.'

We went through a half-giggling bunch of 'Can you hear me? And now? What about this?' for a minute or two as I figured out the linkup could stay just with 'voice' or go as wide as I wanted and include real input from my body or imaginary things or access to my memory. That explained the gritty oil-slick feature. That made us laugh. She was ahead of me on the curve as usual, I didn't have to explain anything, in fact

I launched all my questions at her in a barrage of lightspeed bursts; anxiety's minigun.

'I still have take-out from yesterday,' she said.

I struggled to sit up, as if being vertical was going to help. She was using our code again: our plans are still underway but we're under observation.

'It's still good,' she said, on cue. 'I think it will last a long time.'

So, the truth was that it wasn't anywhere near done. But knowing it was in play – hell, just knowing I wasn't alone was good enough for me.

'I can't use this channel often but someone will be in touch using the Switch. You can trust them. They're your connection to the organisation.'

'The lawyer said it's the resistance,' I said. 'Is it?'

'The name's not important,' she said. 'Follow the plans and we'll get out of this.'

I didn't want to tell her how hard following other people's plans and waiting was getting as more hidden players showed up without any warning; but she knew, because I felt her answering jolt of fear and anxiety like an electric shock in my gut. Our memories and bodies exchanged information rapidly at a super-conscious level. I was sure that she was playing straight and sure that she suspected Tashin wasn't doing the same, but she was in denial, she'd never admit it. She got that it hadn't been a one-way street with Dash. We were more up to date in a second than we had been in years. And unwittingly honest. I forgave her. She forgave me.

My stomach complained – wasn't handling my worries bad enough without all this extra? We both snickered half-heartedly at that and our dual embarrassment and then she said she had to go. She was leaving everything I needed in my memory. I just had to review it when I was ready. It would be like having read a book. Easy for a college dropout like me. I was not to be alarmed if the Switch relayed voices to me, or visuals.

Her goodwill tasted like honey and the aftermath of a hot shower. It was so startling in its own right that I lay still, eyes closed, fishing around in my senses like a drunk at happy hour searching for his dropped credit chip. Wishes used not to taste of anything.

The word you're looking for is synaesthesia.

I opened my eyes. Everything was normal. Hospital room, wilting white flowers, drips, drugs, camera drones watching, nurses moving about in the corridors, the smell of antiseptic not quite covering the smells of urine and fear hardboiled into every surface. I was still in this little pocket of hell. An observation drone was perched on the ceiling in mosquito form.

The synaesthesia is an optional response built into the systems. It is intended to give you physical feedback to very complex incoming data of all kinds, up to and including astrogation information, ship diagnostics and engine protocols. Would you like to keep this function operational or close it for now?

In the past if I ever found parts of my inner talk spoken in voices that weren't mine I've always figured them as crap to ignore. Obviously it's some part of me that's lost the plot. Except this time it wasn't.

I talked to it as if I was talking to myself.

– I want to sleep without pain, without dreams, and wake up in eight hours. Then I want to know what I'm meant to do to escape.

As you wish.

– Wait. Are you there?

Mmn.

– Are you the wetware?

Not exactly.

– So you're a person using it, you aren't actually – it?

I am using it from a distance. You can close the connection between us, but you can't close it all the time. I will help you with all the things you need to know, when you need to know them.

117

– Pardon me if I puke with gratitude. No.

You don't want my help?

– I don't want you at all.

It's not as bad as you think. And you are under-informed.

– Really? It sounds like I'm your puppet.

That's much too harsh.

– Who are you working for?

For you, you are my host. Of course.

– You had to add that.

Add what?

– 'Of course.' You lying shit.

You need my help or you will not survive.

– Thanks for pointing out the bleeding obvious.

I am here to help you. I need you as much as you need me.

– I highly fucking doubt that, but I'll play along. Why?

I have no other way into Harmony Enclave.

– All right. What do you want to do there?

I only want to see, to hear, to investigate. That's all.

– For now? Or until you get to be a real boy?

For now.

– Right. And if I say *No*, what will happen?

You won't say no. You want to get away from Harmony, to be independent and free. Without me you're only going to die. A few fist fights we can put down to you, but from now on your enemies will all have big guns and bigger motives. You have no chance without me.

– You're a total mindfucking shit of a shit.

You're smiling.

– Not like I don't know you, even if we've never met. Player is a player. Now, what supermental bullshit is this revolution trying to pull off by fiddling with the Enclave?

It must be determined whether or not the claims of supernormal powers are true and, if they are, by what means they are achieved within the Alchemy.

– Not that garbage again.

Ah, but I thought you'd be a believer.

– Me? I'm the last person who'd be into that.

But weren't you resurrected? Didn't you 'see the light'?

I took a mental step back and put two and two together and got Two. How else would the sneaky bastard know about that? My heart sank, faltered, got up, considered – would she really have sold me out?

Two was a believer. She was the type.

– Hey, Snowflake. If you used me to kill Dash without my knowing it, why bother letting me live now? Why not take charge, cut out the middleman?

There was no need to make you a murderer.

– What? Oh, so it was a moral kindness? Taking me over.

I'm not a murderer. Allow me to correct myself. I'm not YOUR murderer.

– You are the most fucked-up machine I've ever met.

You were simply in the right place at the right time. Consider yourself a substitute. One from the bench. I will be paying for your services.

– Colour me fucking overjoyed. Now get lost. My head's not for rent.

I imagined door upon vault upon locker slamming shut – *bangbangbang*. Seemed to work. There was no more irritating chitchat from then until the moment I was sitting in the car on the way to Khor's Gyrus and my imminent demise, scrabbling about the back of my brains for any connection to anything that could save me.

In the hours when I rested and waited for Juliette's return I considered whether or not this could all be a vendetta against the house of VanSant. It didn't really add up though. Dash was useless to everyone but himself. Surely he was an embarrassment, yes, but even Dash's father didn't off his embarrassing children;

119

he paid them a huge yearly allowance and left them to get on with it as long as they didn't get caught. Dash would never do anything to drop off the sacred gravy train and his only rivals were people like Kasha Dann; vendetta was their sport and it was no fun if it was played too quickly.

Barring that I didn't see another obvious horse in the race.

When I woke up a second time and found Juliette quietly sitting at my bedside reading the lit screen of her palmtop I knew Dash wasn't the point at all. He was collateral damage. His death wasn't personal, he was only a bit-part player in someone else's drama and that was why he was dead. I braced for the puking to start up again, but it didn't. I dared to move my head and immediately Juliette sat up and gave me her full attention.

'Water,' I said and she gave me some. I managed to drink it by myself.

'Listen, Nico,' she began, keying off her little machine and leaning forward, her voice soft. 'You will have to stand trial in this cycle of the Inquisition, be condemned and go down for the murder. It'll be in a closed court but that's the only thing we managed to pull. You'll get the death sentence. You will not be receiving this sentence, however, though I don't know the details of how that will be circumvented. You're needed elsewhere.'

It never occurred to me to protest. It felt like something inevitable that people like them did to people like me.

The doctor from the morning's reverie returned and injected some more drugs into the tubes leading into my arms. She checked and removed my catheter bag and took a blip of her machines' readings, all in silence. She nodded to Juliette once and they smiled at each other politely as if they were meeting in a store. When she'd gone I turned to look at Juliette's eyes again: brown, steady, unsurprised, a little sad.

'Did your employer kill Dash?' I asked, for confirmation.

She nodded. 'Yes, although technically you did it. As far as the state is concerned you'll be executed and autoclaved so that the tech can be recovered. They're very interested in getting their hands on it. As far as we're concerned, you'll work for us.'

'Work how?' Although it wasn't so hard to guess an answer I wanted to hear it from her. It would feel better from her, as if she was telling me something for my own good. Her wholesome authority would make it seem welcome. I needed to hear something good.

'You're a gun,' she said, in the same kind of voice I imagined she used to tell her parents what time she'd be home, don't wait up, no dinner please. She'd already washed her hands of that end of things. All that concerned her was how to get this job done. 'I expect you'll be assassinating someone, or kidnapping them. After you've finished you'll be let go.'

Let go. That's cartel talk for 'dumped in a shallow grave out in the desert'.

Just because I didn't see a way out didn't mean there wasn't one.

I noticed the flowers were in a red glass vase now, on the nightstand. Juliette saw me looking and looked at them too.

'I brought it from home,' she said and I forgave her on the spot for everything. I felt a pathetic twinge of sadness at how cheaply I could be bought now, but it only lingered a moment.

'What's in my head?' I asked her.

'You'll have to ask your friend Twostar about that. She's loyal to the organisation.' She paused and sighed, deliberately deflating herself to my level. 'She talked to me about you. About your life on the streets together.'

Except...

The quietly dropped mistake, because Juliette assumed that such close friends could not have omitted to tell each other a vitally important fact. Twostar was *loyal to the organisation*, that batshit feelgood name for the revolution. The Organisation. She was part of an organisation that didn't include me so it had had to steal me. I didn't even get that in the speed bulletin. How long had she been in it? I guess she couldn't have told me while I was still in the Arena, but then I knew exactly when, of course, it was when she started talking about college and parroting universal justice secondhand from Tashin. Like Tashin knew something we hadn't known for ever, like it was new, like it was something different that was better than us. She'd already got out of 'us' and she wanted me out too. Guilt accuses others of what the guilty party has already done. You only have to listen and pay attention. Which I rarely did. Gotta break that habit at some point after I'm done breaking my heart over being left in the cold.

I mean, I'm not. My heart breaks when I tell it and not before. Not like I didn't really know anyway, is it? I knew, I was pretending I didn't know because it might not be true and as long as that's happening I'm OK.

I felt sick and blown open, like I'd swallowed a live grenade and it's just gone off.

Shit.

'You'll recuperate here until you're well by which time the trial will start. However long it takes it takes.'

My lack of reaction must have worried her.

'Nico?'

'Sure,' I said. 'I'm tired. I need to sleep now.'

'Of course.' She gathered her items and hurried out.

I swore silently at the wetware, forbidding it to act under any circumstances and to leave me the hell alone. I didn't care what happened any more. If Two had abandoned our plans long ago because she had a new love and was doing shit without me, with a separate organisation that had a hold on her such that she could only co-opt me by stealth instead of honesty, then our whole lives together and all it meant was over. I may as well be dead.

Six – in which we are back in the car again

– Now would be a really good moment for some help. If there is any.

I flexed my arms against the grip of the manacles. They were solid, a bar of plastek that gripped my wrists snugly and showed no signs of breaking under any strength I was able to use. The whole thing flashed white to show I was resisting and Jobsworth turned his own wrist to check his mail.

'You won't get out of them,' Number One Fan said. 'Everybody tries.'

'Do this a lot, do you?' I looked around the cabin and shifted, testing the state of my back after all the sitting.

'Not a lot. I do what's on the roster.' He sounded defensive.

I felt the car tilt into the characteristic sweep curve of a landing approach. 'Didn't make the torturing schedule today, then?'

'Only Inquisitors handle investigations,' N1 said.

I started to hear music in the middle of my skull. There was some messing with the volume and bass. Some girl started singing a cute pop piece of fluff. I recognised it then as one of Two's favourites. She had only two musical tastes: pink girly cat pop and techno metal – if they combined so much the better.

'...call me, baby...'

I looked down at the manacle keypad. I knew its number – it

had just arrived along with the music. What a pity you needed hands for that kind of thing.

'Nico, don't move!' she said in her DJ voice. Its tension made me obey. 'Really, really don't move. I can feel that you're gonna do something stupid. Don't. Just wait. We're on it.'

I felt the touch of her small, bare hand, a girl's hand, on my arm – the same touch she'd used to keep me on the ground after that priest woke me up and the car'd hit me, the same hand that guided me into the operation; the same, a stitch out of time. The same. I realised she was playing my memory, like a track. It wasn't only my memory. She was *hacking* me.

My vision expanded. I could still see the car cabin all around me, but it was transparent suddenly, a ghost sliding swift and casting a shadow over the rocky ground a hundred metres down. The guards had become red silhouettes. I could see their comms operating in digital lightning.

Steel guitar slid and rang. The range on my awareness was snatched out of my head into orbit. In the deep darkness of the planet's shadow a leviathan twitched a fin and a black dart lanced forward into the faint light reflected from the atmosphere. Something strange caught my attention, a ribbon of blackness flowing out in a huge arc... but the shape was snatched away as I was pushed away from the space visuals and back to the essentials.

There were no defensive vehicles orbiting around Harmony, only a ring of satellites. None of these reacted as the dart shot out of the shadow and into the gravity well. It slipped between them and emerged from the night's edge into a strange blindspot between surveillance sweeps – a spot that was created at its bowfront and which vanished in its wake leaving no trace. It mimicked the curve of the descending car as it tore into the higher layers of the envelope.

'We're here.' Jobsworth closed his mail down reluctantly and shifted.

'I'll take care of the formalities,' Number One Fan said, cueing a protocol off his glove that tripped the car's automated landing routines and security clearances.

High in the atmosphere the dart began to burn with a searing heat, an unmistakable light. Weather drones reported an incoming meteor. There was no upset, it was predicted to burn up before it got anywhere.

I felt the heat begin to melt the triggers of release systems.

'...Mister Bojangles...' sang a pink kitten in my mind's eye and the car door jammed.

Jobsworth tapped the control key with his gloved finger. *Pitty pat.* No answer.

We touched down to ground with a clank from a loose piece of bodywork.

'What the— ?' Number One Fan's door opened for him after all. A wall of intense light replaced him as he got out into the glare of the noon sun.

The 'meteor' accelerated to many times the speed of sound. It splintered the air. Shock waves began to break windows in far distant towns long after it had passed over their horizon. It broke up into three pieces, each incandescent. Two were no more than piloted shrapnel of a material that seamlessly converted heat into energy for their basic engines. Burning made them shrink en route as they broke through the cloud layer several hundred klicks from the car, decelerating hard.

The third was slower by some seconds, stately by comparison. It tasted the atmosphere in a leisurely way and connected itself to the datmosphere with world-weary finesse, the machine equivalent of a hand in a silk glove softly turning the tumblers of a combination lock. As it dropped, its pregnant cargo belly expanded and began to give birth.

Back in the car the other door catch gave way at last under the onslaught of a stabbing finger. Jobsworth pushed it open, waiting for it to prop itself on the strut so he could get out.

'Nico,' Two whispered. I heard her fear as if she was there with me, under the plas-sacks of yesterday, clinging on for dear life with the roving scrutiny of the security drones passing over us in weightless beams. She had not expected the meteors. We didn't know what they were, but we knew they came for me. I was relieved I wasn't the only one who was last to know.

'Ah yeah,' I thought, hoping she could hear me. 'Don't sweat it. I was already starting to think there was more to this than they'd let you in on anyway.' I was talking about Tashin, but also her bosses or handlers, whoever was in the chain of smugglers that gave her the Switch. I felt terrible exhaustion at her sad surprise that there was more going on than she could detect.

She held Tashin responsible. Her voice broke, hoping that things would turn good. 'But I love her.'

Through the infinitely refined nuances of the connection I felt her despair and the shutters falling closed on her hopes – you can't trust anyone.

It didn't matter what was going down now because it was out of both our hands. I folded her into my heart as Jobsworth finally heaved his ass off the seat and moved out.

'C'mon,' he said as he went, to me.

His head cleared the doorway and a dart of dark shadow hit his face with a soft pop like he'd been hit with a kid's puffball gun. At the same time I caught a glimpse from outside the car: Number One Fan looking a bit quizzical, sweat running in an oily drip to the end of his nose as a silver fish became a lilac cloud of dust in his eyes.

They hit the ground in two ladylike crumples of armoured cloth: two grey geishas. It was quiet after.

The sun beat relentlessly onto my right side so I shuffled over to the left and swung my legs out, put my boots to the ground and stopped. I looked down at Jobsworth's shocked expression where it was frozen. The lilac powder on it – the remains of one of the missiles – melted into a liquid. It blended with his sweat and then sank into his pores. It looked like a toiletries commercial, aside from the fact he was dead.

I'd never seen tech like this, only heard about it. Was this Forged? Was this for me?

A shadow of buzzard wings swept the ground beside him. It crossed the shadow of my head and the car's bulk, then split free and angled away. I squinted after it.

It wasn't really a bird. It was the child of the third meteorite. I could see from its viewpoint – the car is parked on the stand inside a security perimeter. Doors are opening in the walls some metres away on a corridor that leads into the side of the huge concrete sarcophagus that houses the city autoclave. Droids are visible, on duty, but no living people. It's a sacrilege to involve the living in the reprocessing of living things from flesh to ash; the undoing of a mystery and a miracle.

I heard the scrape of movement and was instantly back in my own body.

Behind the car Number One Fan slowly got to his feet. Under my stare Jobsworth's eyes opened.

'Nico,' Two whispered.

'It's OK,' I reassured her, empty of conviction. Until this was done neither she nor I trusted a damn thing. It was weird but I noticed that this state of things was actually pleasant. No fucking clue and no fucking hope. Who'd have thought?

This may get a little weird, but not to worry.

I felt Two scrabbling around to identify the voice. There was an anxiety in her I recognised as the urge not to know even as you sought to know and my little theory of calm vanished. I watched it slide away from me like shit off a shovel. The only reason I didn't crap myself was that my system was empty. I hadn't eaten in days. I hadn't wanted to. Shootouts and hijacks I understood, but this was way beyond anything I had imagined.

Jobsworth and Number One Fan looked like they were back on par. Jobsworth took hold of the shackle and used it to help haul me out of the car seat and I was suddenly standing. One thing I had right, worrying was out of the question. Worry is for people who assume they have a future. Jobsworth and Number One Fan used to have worries. Now they had none.

Jobsworth waited for his partner to come round the car. They took up their positions and nudged me forwards. We crossed the few incredibly hot strides to the door. I looked up. Blue skies, massive cliffside of the building. Fuck that for a last view of the world. As we continued indoors I was blind, between the zombies, wondering why the hell we were still going on here when this was supposed to be a rescue. I didn't get executed here. That wasn't the plan, right? Right?

I tried to stop but the gun from Jobsworth shoved me in the back. His voice was flat and toneless. 'Keep going. We have to make the five-minute window.'

'Who said that?' My own voice was raspy. The dry air. The shackle weighed on my biceps. Was it the same person who'd been talking in my skull now using them?

'Nico.' In my head Two was whispering; she had something bad to tell me.

'Well this is shit,' I said to her, like the last ten years hadn't happened, like we just got into the first car, the one we never got into, the one that hit me.

'Nico,' she whispered. 'I didn't know she'd do this.'

'Cut to the fucking chase. There's not a lot of time here.' We had reached a pair of sealed blast doors.

'I didn't know she was a pirate.' The last word was agonised, betrayed, miserable.

Privateer.

Tashin. 'Your girlfriend is a lot more than some bleeding heart revolutionary.' The doors had opened, revealing a dingy concrete bunker. Huge scrapes on the floor and charred, scoured walls. Cracking. Some patches crazed like glass. I should be

128

kinder, forgive her, of course she couldn't know and anyway, love's blind, right? So I should be blind too.

'I had to make the deal,' Two said. 'It was a one-time offer. I don't know who she is or where she really came from. I thought I did. Everything checked out.' She sounded utterly miserable.

'I guess our luck had to run out sometime,' I said as we entered the crucible. From there a glance up revealed a tall black chimney with a circle of sky at the top. The walls were part of the machinery which cleared whatever was left from the burn, shoved it left to right and out to some other part of the factory.

'The last thing I wanted was for you to end up like this.'

I believed her. 'Don't worry about it. There's no point.'

I looked at Number One Fan who was turning his head slowly, gazing at everything.

'This is it,' he said, and turned to me. This is where they left me alone for the focused rays of the sun to burn me back to hell. He had three minutes or so to clear out of the way or it would get him too. From my bird's eye view I saw the huge mirrors and lenses tilt into position, one, then another, another, in an automated sequence. Come in Nico, your time is up. Now your atoms will be liberated to make something more acceptable.

I could count my life out in seconds now. If this was a rescue it was cutting it way too close for my liking. I got ready to run although I'd inexplicably started shaking so hard I could barely stand. A few more ticks and this place was going to be glass.

Blue flashed at the side of N1's eye showing that he was talking to someone silently on an official line. At the same time Jobsworth came around and removed the shackle with a press of his hand. As it let go I felt a sharp stab into my wrist and I felt instantly weakened, tired and listless.

'They've pumped me full of Slow,' I said, thinking surely this was not good. I started to bend at the knees.

'Oh god.' Two – crying.

'I don't get it.' It was hard to slur the words out. 'I thought this was … a … rescue.'

Shit, I forgot about that. Nico, concentrate. Get undressed.

I started to laugh.

I can fake the camera feed for a minute, but we have to have enough mass to get the clearance on the burn. Undress.

Number One Fan smacked the side of his helm and the voice that was talking to him came into speaker mode. 'You have two minutes to clear the area. Please take all belongings and leave the crucible.' He began to take off his clothes with a speed and precision that was incredibly unlike any movement he'd made so far. Pieces of ceremonial armour hit the ground at my feet.

Get into the uniform, you idiot.

'It's the old switcheroo!' I said to Two, fumbling at the grips on my shirt. The drug made it seem incredibly funny. My fingers felt like they belonged to someone six sizes bigger than me made of clouds. I was light, floaty and everything had a strangely glowing quality of pleasant exhaustion which made escape seem much too much like hard work. I vaguely grasped what I was meant to be doing, but doing it was drifting out of my reach. I thought it was rather nice that they gave the condemned a bit of dope, yes, it was all right.

The world tilted and spun around and I ended up looking at a black field with a blue circle in it. I could hear people arguing in the distance; Two and Tashin. They sounded like honking ducks.

'Nico, I need your permission,' Two was saying or something like that. I thought I might have been jolted a bit this way and that. I thought I probably had fallen over some time ago in the past but the Slow meant that I was only becoming aware of it much later. I wondered what 'permission' meant.

He's dead in thirty seconds. Here, let me do it.

I drifted, a little angry about what was being said. It seemed a bit ominous in a way I couldn't quite place. I felt two women

130

arguing fiercely and I wanted to say, *No. No, don't fight, girls* but before I could do that I forgot whatever it was.

Then there was a lot of movement and I was like lightning in the clouds. I stood up and I thought, clever and smug, that I was going to feel some pain by and by, but that would be later. A man was lying on the ground far away, my clothes on his head covering his face. A boot lay on his torso.

We were in the corridor. The doors were silent, like iron breezes.

We were in the yard. The sun was so hot all on its own, staring at us.

We were in the car. The world is broken in bits.

I've got a gun. Came with the uniform.

I had a dream in which the car was flying low over the desert but I could see it from the outside. A buzzard the size of a horse came right at the windscreen. It was carrying a big rock in its talons. It let go at the last moment. Light glinted off its metal feathers. The rock went into the engine bay like a knife into butter.

We crashed into the ground at a shallow enough angle we only spun and tumbled. I was stuck in the back seat. The buzzard landed on the car's upturned belly and plucked off the drive units and the battery before stripping out the plates between the internal cage bars. It was quite a pro bird.

It pulled me out and then opened its beak and sicked up a body into the space I left behind. The body was mangled in a slick caul of red slime. If I'd thought it was real I might've found that disturbing. The buzzard picked me up in its right foot. As we gained height it rocketed the car. It must have been a solar frag missile because the whole thing broke into bits and all the bits turned into white fire and light. So pretty.

I woke up with the world's worst hangover, lying on some wet muddy grass, and wished I was dead. Whoever said pain is only information needed to be eviscerated.

131

I looked down on my own body from very high in the sky for a moment.

Sorry about this. I need to restart the in-system.

– Fuck you, Tashin. I'm gonna get you for—

I woke up again.

Two was so happy I was alive. I noted that and held my tongue about the motherfucking pirate asshole living in my skull who was also her hottie, but I did give Tashin a look – I don't know how you give a look to something that's only riding in some wetware you're carrying around in your head but go with it, that's how it was.

I was sitting on a hill in a huge piece of countryside marked with trees, grass and some handsome buildings in an old-world style, the kind you could see on shows about the distant past. Between me and the buildings a few people were edging closer, carrying a stretcher. I tried to get up but that didn't work out too well in that nothing happened. I was awake, kind of, but I couldn't move at all by myself.

They put me on the stretcher and carted me indoors.

I don't know why you're so angry. I saved you and I saved her.

– Hijack, possession, interference. That's why we're not on speaking terms any more, shitbird.

You're being very unreasonable.

– Get on with it. The sooner this is all over the sooner I never have to listen to you again.

Seven: sins

I woke up braced for pain. There was none. I felt back to normal except that I couldn't remember much since we landed at the autoclave. There was some dumb stuff about a bird but that couldn't be right. It persisted as the pieces of other memories slowly returned. I could perceive a highway heading out from just over the top of my head up into the vastness of the sky somewhere around the back of my left cerebral hemisphere. As I followed it my sense of it began to disintegrate so that again that glimpse of a vast being beyond the sun's light, finned and tentacled, floating in the darkness, was felt and then dissolved before I could make out what it was. Origin of horrors. Was it my ship? My supersenses vanished or perhaps they were my imagination. Whatever, they were gone again leaving me frustrated and disturbed

I looked around me at the calm beauty of the room I was in. It reminded me of some spa that Dashain had visited once, taking the place over for his cronies, everyone in a private room with treatments and drugs on tap. I'd stood in the corridors mostly. The smell here was the same: cedar and grass and a faint tang of the sea.

Don't worry, your memories were difficult to piece back together because of the overrides – I had to rewrite a few links and I may have made the odd mistake. From now on things will be much more normal. What doesn't kill you makes you stronger.

– There are no words for the level of *fuck you* that I am telling you. And the word you're looking for is 'bitter'.

I can feel it well enough, words are not required. You're such a sore loser, Nic.

– I'd punch myself in the face if I thought it would hurt you.

How like the bite of a serpent's tooth is your ingratitude. But carry on. I think that time will justify my actions.

– We'll see who comes out what of it. And don't even say that didn't make sense or I will find a way to fry your circuits so help me g—

– Did you delete something?

Something wrong?

– My curse doesn't feel cursey any more. It's like all the force drained out of the word.

Should I reinstate your former attachments to the notion of a possible omnipotent being? I would have thought you would have—

– Just put it the fuck back.

There, is that better?

She restored god.

– Shit, no. I don't know. I hate you.

That is the axis of certainty around which I am beginning to revolve all other concepts.

Clearly I was going to need more practice at the banter.

One wall of the room was a window that looked out across a huge vista of grassland, bordered by tall stands of trees. There was some faint calming music in the background. It was warm. I was incredibly uncomfortable thanks to the guard's uniform buckled all around me and the fact that both my hands had locked in a death-grip around a gun two hours previously and not given up since. I had to work hard to persuade them to open and put the thing down. Bereft of death-metal my fingers remained stubbornly insistent they wanted nothing else. I started doing some exercise with my arms to get the blood moving.

– Where am I?

The wall opposite the bed I was lying on flared with light and began to answer my questions with images and the groomed machine voices that I associated with offworld video. No sooner did I wonder something than information faded in onto its blank surface.

I think you prefer this way of finding things out, yes?

– It's fine. Isn't there an elsewhere you could be?

Certainly.

– I mean really, I want you to go away, not lurk about eavesdropping.

You only have to ask.

I played along.

It was a safe house, fifty k from my last known position, the home of a wealthy widow who had six of the things and had never visited this one. She was getting to the age where buying hope of eternity through membership of temple organisations seemed like a good bet and was planning to sell up to fund the works. The property management company taking care of it was owned by people in Twostar's revolutionary movement. I called them to complain about the tenants while I went looking for something to eat.

The kitchen was immaculate and bigger than our entire previous apartment. It had an air that I'd soon come to find in every room, as if someone had left just before I arrived – a person whose mission was to make everything just as I would have made it, but who had been instructed to leave me absolutely alone. I opened the cooler and stuck my nose in.

The cold air and the lamplight on the packaging suckerpunched me as I saw shelves of products that Two and I had liked since we'd started spending the cartel's dirty money. We

135

felt we were owed these luxuries in return for the theft of our freedom; they made things feel more like a trade. By the time I stood up with the food in my hands I was ready to cry.

I ate in an empty lounge, counting bites and calculating energy until I reckoned I'd had enough. I threw the wrappers on the floor to break up the alignments of the furniture and the walls which were seriously starting to fuck with my head. I felt like I was ruining an otherwise perfect world, and I couldn't ruin it fast enough. There was nowhere to be that wasn't the conjunx of a pacifying pattern of colour, texture and shape. Presumably this sold like hot health snacks in the housing markets of the overly wealthy. I went back to the bedroom and looked for evidence of how I'd got there. I smirked a bit over knowing what 'conjunx' meant in Alchemical terms, although I suspected I might have made it up as shorthand for whatever the feng-fucking-shui was doing.

After a couple of hours I'd pieced together the incontrovert-ible facts: that I'd been let out of some kind of trackless vehicle in the yard – a decked area surrounded by sculpted land and planting that hid it from view except by air – and then been carted to the bedroom and laid down alone in a frozen foetal posture, cuddling my new best friend Mr Gun.

I picked him up, stripped him down to his empty chambers and examined his rounds. Kyro-shells. They don't so much kill as vaporise to a degree you don't even need stain remover. Mr Gun really had no intention of letting anyone get away, though nobody ever had got away from a capital sentence that I knew of. For a second I wondered about the guards but whatever zombie trail was left behind wasn't my problem. That was a problem for magic bird dust to solve and me not to think about too hard because there's a specific number of mindweasels you should let in your head to remain functional and survive in a dangerous situation and that number is zero.

But in case the zombie trail was *a* problem I put Mr Gun

back together and set him in a harness so that he lay snugly ready for a fast draw. It didn't seem like much in the face of giant birds that came out of ballistic missiles but since that had been on my side I wasn't too worried. I made a full tour of the house and estate, checking everywhere for spies, droids, wildlife, anything. Blank. I was alone. Then I had to check the place I was dreading – around the spooky corners in my mind where the tendrils had been drifting upwards, upwards to the foreign objects far away in space. I went back to the bedroom for that with a lead heart.

I closed my eyes briefly and reached for the leviathan I'd seen whose scales had tipped fate in my favour.

It was there, far back left in my head, tiny, the size of a single cell, two billion klicks out from Harmony's sun and as big as a reasonably sized suburb. Its violet tentacles idled against the stars, feathered through the range of the visible and the invisible, holding it to anchor within the oceans of dark matter no human eye could fathom.

I suddenly felt like I was being watched. Icy drench, stomach cramp. Shit. Not literally.

I opened my eyes and it was gone like it never existed.

I closed my eyes and it was there, so near and so far, but mostly far, like we'd mutually zoomed out on each other. I was pretty sure it had sent those missiles. How the fuck would the revolution on Harmony have something like that in the arsenal? What the fuck even *was* it? Were there outworlders who had an eye to ruining Harmony and if so why weren't they shooting from where they were already?

I sent Two a code note, cursing Tashin with every word I could think of and hoping she was eavesdropping: *Dis is some bad fish.*

While I waited on her reply I took off the guard's uniform and searched for something else to wear. It was all women's stuff in the wardrobes, still in the bags from the store. There were some kind of lounging meditation pyjama things in milled organic hemp flavour. I put those on. The belt went round me twice.

I was studying the controls of the heated bubblejet pool when Two pinged me back.

Your execution was on the news. I'm coming to see you. Don't do anything dumb.

I figured she'd be a while so I put the jets on medium rare and got in the tub. Mr Gun didn't fancy the water but he was happy to rest on the side with the safety off. For a few minutes being dead really wasn't all that bad.

They arrived an hour later: two cartel guards and Two herself. I didn't recognise the guards. They wore Dann's uniform of grey and blue functional armour and carried the usual arsenal. Two ducked and ran through the sifting rain on her way from the car as they scowled and made an obligatory security tour of the outside. I'd never paid any attention to the relationship between the cartels and the revolution, but here it was again. Maybe Tashin had bought Two's safety from Dann with VanSant's death. I'd've offered that deal. I might even be forgiving if it was true but Dann's return to the fore made me uneasy. I couldn't think what she wanted with a revolution.

Seeing Two was a huge relief, though nothing dissipated the gnawing sense of unease I'd been trying to ignore that insisted someone else was with me, unseen and inaudible, but distinct. It may have been some effect of the wetware. Maybe Tashin was surfing me. There was an unknown quantity to it, however, that prevented me feeling any confidence in my judgement.

We met in the entryway which I'd searched a minute before to convince myself we weren't accompanied. She looked startled as she glanced up from her wrist phone, face beaded with water, braids scattering drops as she straightened up.

'Nico!'

We were in a vice clinch for about ten seconds of blissful relief from the whole world. I knew every bone in that little ribcage and every heartbeat. It really was her. I felt like I'd made it over the finish line of something.

About three seconds later when we parted the situation washed back in like sewage on the spring tide, but it didn't dull my buzz much. I adjusted Mr Gun where he'd been pressed into my ribs.

We looked at one another in a way that said a lot, wordlessly; water moving under a bridge, murky and shadowed where it had once been clear, seething into the past. Talking is for people who don't know each other and who don't listen.

Two threw her dripping raincoat onto one of the priceless damask occasional chairs that nobody would ever sit in. 'I've so much to tell you. You must have a million questions.'

'You could say that.' I folded my arms in my outsize pyjamas, shivered a bit though it wasn't cold.

Two smiled awkwardly, suddenly shy. 'I love her and she loves me. Doesn't seem such an explanation now, though.'

'You didn't know it wasn't legit.' Legit meaning what she'd been sold, told, what she'd bought at first, the original deal about the 'ware.

Two hugged herself as I led her into the house proper, 'No. I've never seen this kind of thing before. Offworld weaving. There was much more to it than I could have learned in a lifetime. I trusted that the extreme difficulty of getting it and Tashin's promises would, you know, guarantee it would be the bare minimum. It is a Switch. It does work like they're reported to. I do know that.'

We reached a lounge where neither of us sat down. I didn't want to be dishonest but I felt entitled to some testing. I wanted to know how much she had known when she held my hand and let me slip into this. 'Yeah, well it was way more than that. Nobody mentioned AI enhancements. Or puppeteering.'

Two nodded slowly. 'No. They didn't.'

My fingers bit into my arms. I bit my lip. 'I believe you. But do you think Tashin really didn't know what she had?'

Tears rolled down her cheeks, dripped off her chin which she suddenly scrubbed with her shirt cuff. 'I did, at first. But once I started to analyse the tek – I couldn't even understand half of it, Nic. But I couldn't say so because then VanSant wouldn't have trusted us. Tashin promised there was nothing harmful – I'm such a fool. She tricked me and I still love her. How is that worth believing?'

I wanted to comfort her but I wasn't done. 'You said pirate.'

'I did.' She folded her arms and nodded at the door behind me. 'But I'm not sure that's right either.'

I glanced out the windows. It was still raining. The guards weren't visible though I could *see* them mooching around, nursing hot drinks in the security room, with that vision that wasn't anything to do with my eyes. I pointed at the wall to our right and showed an edited highlights version of my trial and the subsequent trip to the autoclave, missiles, space, birds and all. My virtuosity with my new AI add-ons was fucking impressive as I used the house's inbuilt systems to their max limits. The sound reproduction was spot on and I watched Two closely, listening. I wanted to know if she was fully aware of what was going on, if she knew Tashin was still hitching a ride. The actual voice in my mind wasn't like Tashin's real voice here, however, so I didn't expect identification of her personally. I didn't care if it was actually the woman herself or some mechanoid lackey – the principle of it was the thing.

Two watched in silence, chewing on her thumb. 'That voice,' she said.

'Only I hear it,' I said.

'Where did the shots come from?'

'I don't know.' From the leviathan-monster in space that she definitely should not see. It cringed from the idea of being seen and I found myself absurdly convinced that I must protect it. I decided not to talk about it either – see if Tashin had kept that a secret too.

'But offworld and out-atmosphere tek.' She nodded. 'A ship? I suppose it's hers. Or ... maybe she's not alone. That's the fucking problem, Nico. I don't know if I can believe a word she says any more. She waits until after the fact with everything.'

'Where bits were missing here,' I pointed at the wall again, 'that's where the AI, or whoever, ran me.'

Two sucked in air sharply through her gritted teeth, lips spread in a grimace of hatred. 'Shit. I'd never have agreed if I'd known it could do that.' Her face, pinched with fear, was so gaunt. She worried her knuckles. Two would never crack them, but she pulled and bent them in a tortured silence. 'I think,' she began with the special emphasis that meant this was something she had been studying a long time, 'I think that VanSant was killed and you were set up to prove to Kasha Dann that Tashin was a bona fide cartel operative and not a revolutionary agent. So that her cover was good.'

'What?' I hadn't thought of that.

'VanSant just wanted to make you a better fighter, and maybe eventually into a pilot he could use to smuggle stuff from outworld. That was the sell. Fight now, pilot upgrade later. He'd been fed a lead on a ship a while ago but he'd had to sit on it because there was no chance of getting the wetware.' She paused, to see if I was registering the new information. It was the first I'd heard that the shipware was something anyone but the two of us had ever mentioned.

'And you didn't tell me.'

'I couldn't mention it. If anyone overheard they would know you were in on something.'

I nodded. Nothing's easy when everyone's paranoid.

She drew breath through her teeth and went on. 'All the traffic on that deal was coming from outworld cartel ops; they're all offworlders, no natives, and they don't use ecomms so there was no way for me to trace it but I think VanSant never knew there was anything more than a chance to score a ship. If he suspected Dann was behind it he was too slow to put anything into action about it.'

'So who came up with the idea first?'

'Tashin. She put the idea to Dann.'

'Yeah, but she must have talked it over with you. Why else would she use me?'

'Of course we talked it over. I had to convince her you were trustworthy...'

That got a snort from me and Two blushed, picked at a knuckle, but then made herself continue though she looked out of the window. 'She got someone else to convince VanSant's contacts that this was legit and she was going to get him the Switch if he'd guarantee my safe return to her personal custody. She said she was doing it to get me back.'

She must have seen my face in the reflection, because she stopped and sighed. She turned and sat down, leg tucked under her, cushion suddenly on her lap, being twisted. 'I wanted to believe her. But everything fitted together a bit too well. I felt, you know, to be honest I felt like maybe she'd stalked me, both of us. Maybe she was looking around a long time for a chance to do something like this and when I told her about our plans she kind of bit my hand off. I was so thrilled to think I knew someone who was so cool they could get their hands on that kind of stuff. I felt like... I don't know! Like finally our luck had changed and I'd made it, you know?'

I nodded again. It was hard to see her so torn up. I wasn't able to keep my poker face. I went and sat with her in the oversized armchair. 'Too good to be true.'

Two groaned in assent. 'I'm not sure, I can't prove it. I mean, I'm sure there's more to it than just preserving her cover and getting me out of gaol... sorry... you know what I mean. I was worried about it so while she was off getting the goods I looked into her history and it looked fine. Except that I couldn't track down a single human being who knew her before two years ago. So even though she checks out completely as Harmony native, she isn't. Which left me wondering what an agent from outside could want here. I don't know what it is but whatever it is she needs you to get it.'

After a few sad sniffs she turned to study me, moved her head back in surprise. 'You don't care, do you?'

She was right. I had no interest in what anyone else wanted. Thwarting them or helping them didn't help me achieve my goal of leaving, never to return. 'No. Wheels within wheels, one boss, another boss, it's all the same to me – does any of this speculation help us?'

'No, I don't think so. Whatever she's got you into now is much bigger than I can touch. Shit.' She put her forehead down on her folded hands, set on the arm of the chair, and her voice was muffled from there. 'I screwed up. I screwed up so bad.'

'It's OK,' I said. I butted my knee against hers, *thump thump*, and laid my head back on the headrest as if that could cushion the weight of what went on inside. 'You were distracted.'

'I don't know who she is,' Two wailed softly. 'I do. But I don't. I don't know what she wants with you. Does she even like me or was I only convenient? How do I get answers? I don't know how we get out of this.'

I was reasonably sure there was no getting out of this. 'We don't.'

She lifted her head, then put the cushion to her face and wiped it.

I shrugged. 'Trying to be free here, as if you can walk out of the cartel, as if I can pull this out of my head and walk – that's no use. We got to play the cards we're dealt.'

'This was so not the plan.' She was defiant, as ever, but her tone suggested she knew it was futile.

'Yeah, well. Gotta have a plan though. So – you're in love

with a thieving liar. Who the hell else were you expecting to meet in Chaontium, anyway?'

'Nico!' She leaned over and punched my shoulder, smiling in spite of herself. 'Don't you care?'

'If caring means I have to lie around wailing about it, then no. Shit happens. Deal and move on, same as always. One god-moded sock puppet at your service.' I touched my forehead and pretended a fancy bow.

'How can you be so calm?' She pawed at my arm gently, plucking, like she wanted to take something off me as well as reassure.

'I'm lazy,' I said because if I was serious now she'd get so intense she'd melt down and that took too long to recover from. Two had confidence but only about certain things and rolling like a boss through the world of the cartels wasn't one of them. I wasn't exactly lying. If panicking had been a way forward I'd have given it a shot. But since I suspected even my own thoughts were capable of being monitored it didn't seem like much of a plan to try thinking a way out of anything. I fully intended to get the hell out, but it was going to have to be done by some super-badass mode of *wu wei* where even I didn't know how I was going to do it until I did.

'You look so grown up suddenly,' she said, gently moving a strand of my drying hair out of my face with her finger.

'You mean old.'

'No. Maybe. Did they tell you about your assignment?'

'No.'

'I may not be able to contact you.'

'I'd assumed that.'

'I'm still not sure how you got through to me just now, before I came here. I got your message but all the ID tags were scrambled. Cartel security isn't the greatest but I would have thought calling out from here would have tripped some Harmony oversystems.' She looked at me, a slight frown puckering between her dark brows. Strong arches, messy edges, never one for plucking and colouring-in, our Two.

I shrugged.

'What did you *do*?' she laughed nervously.

'I uh ... thought about seeing you. I sent a note. But I didn't actually make a call and then here you are.' I sounded like I was a kid caught lying, making up stuff to explain doing something dumb. What should have been entirely in my control wasn't, at least not in control of the parts of me that usually made the decisions. I didn't want her to know it freaked me out. Too late for that.

Two looked at me with misgiving and some annoyance. Her voice trembled, giving away her fear. 'Whatever it is, if you ever find out how it works tell me. I could use some of that.'

I decided to change the subject. 'How's the bridge club?' The Bridge Club was what we called our savings that we'd defrauded various casinos and bosses of over the course of our lives. I had no idea where it was kept or, well, if it even existed as more than a fantasy. I didn't mind if it was a fantasy and Two had made it up for me. What would we do offworld with a load of worthless Harmony dollars anyway?

'Some of the members dropped out so there are no meetings right now.'

For the best. Who needed more people digging?

I sensed movement. 'The guards are coming. Your time's up. There's an inbound car with my ex-lawyer in it headed this way. Maybe other people. Were you expecting them?'

Two frowned a little and chewed on her finger. 'You really are turning into droid of the month, Nic. I—' She paused and we shared misgiving looks of fear and grim determination. In over our heads. Back in the garbage tip, running for it. Then she lifted her chin. 'You need to get a handle on all you're able to do with that stuff. It might be the key to getting through this. Whatever you can do I'm pretty sure nobody here has a clue about it and they should stay that way. And I'm not exactly top of the food chain. I was surprised they even let me come here.'

Now that I had a chance to consider it, so was I. Neither of us needed another prompt to get moving. Two hurried to the door but I knew she wasn't going to make it off the property so I caught her arm. Better with me than without me.

She looked up and we shared a moment of listening, reading cleanly the danger that one of us had spotted, even if the other hadn't, waiting for a cue.

'I should show you the rest of the house,' I said and without a sound or protest she followed me swiftly. I went to the room I considered mine for the duration and we pretended we were hanging out chewing the fat.

I sat with my back against the headboard in a lounging position. Two sat cross-legged on the end, hugging a cushion. I put a vid on the wall and pushed it forward twenty minutes. We fast-talked our way through what bothered us – my adaptation. Two was sure that it was only a way of augmenting my interface with the world, that there was no separate AI doing its own thing.

'I'm only a backwater engineer but I'd know if something that big was in there,' she said and I believed her. Which just left Tashin and automated systems, so nothing to worry about.

There were good and bad aspects to being in a tek-silent zone. The house didn't even have an alarm, just old-fashioned locks to stall anyone with malice in mind.

If it was so silent, how come I could see so well?

It bothered me because if I could there had to be something going on that could be sliced into by someone else...

No, you merely collected information from ordinary sources: city traffic, observations on autocams and the car's GPS.

– I knew you hadn't gone.

You didn't actually ask me to so I'm here on a technicality.

'Tashin talks to me as well as taking the driving seat sometimes,' I said to Two's raised brow. I hadn't meant to say it, but her expression was so vulnerable and hopeful with trying to read anything positive into things that it was out of my mouth before I knew it. I managed my usual don't-give-a-fuck tone until the last word when my voice suddenly lunged upwards into a plea.

Two pulled on her knuckles and took a look at the monster movie where sea creatures from the depths of a lost lagoon were making a stealthy approach to an unsuspecting passenger cruiser. 'Nico, there's something I need to tell you.' Her joint popped and startled her. She shook her hand but I saw the rest of her shaking too.

Outside, the new car had arrived on the forecourt. The occupants disembarked. Juliette was there in blue. Three henchpeople in a uniform of drab greys and body armour clambered out of gullwing doors at the front, gold-sheened masks covering their faces so they could have been androids though they moved with the sluggish fumbling of bored humans. They didn't look armed but I wouldn't have bet on it for any money. The last was a tall, attractive woman with dark hair, of a type I always thought of as Catalogue B, the most common gene pool with good but affordable assets, the family-saloon of the human female Harmonite world. She wore sunshades over her eyes, edged in gold that shot the sunlight off itself in starbursts. Her shoes didn't go with her trousers. She straightened her spine with a distinctive move, as if steeling herself for an onslaught.

– Tashin. How good to see you at last. Long-distance wiring not enough for you any more?

No need for silliness. I'll be there in a moment.

Tashin waited for Juliette to meet her before they walked to the door together. In the kitchen the men who'd come with Two looked up briefly and then turned back to the snacks they were eating.

GPS and local traffic my ass.

– Got a better explanation up yer diodes?

Not at the present time.

Aloud and in person, in the bedroom, I was still only one beat from Two's revelation, 'Tell me what?'

We could both hear approaching movements in the anteroom now, the two sets of feet.

Two glanced at the door, then at me. 'She's come to meet you.'

Which she said with such depleted tones that I knew her statement was the pitiful last cousin of whatever she was hoping the next five minutes were somehow going to explain. Whatever, though. She wasn't an actor. She didn't know Tashin was talking to me already.

Two cringed from my look that said *that is some weak fucking tea from you.* I was immediately ashamed of myself. The door opened but I didn't drop my gaze from Two. I had to suck all the information out of this for my own sanity. She'd lied a few minutes earlier. Surprised they let her come. How many lies were there and what for?

'Did you think I'd run?' I asked her.

She couldn't keep my gaze. Hers flicked out to the first person through the door with guilt and entreaty, glanced at the second – no reaction. Right, then. The first one was Tashin, wasn't it? The second obviously Juliette. I'd have known those stack platforms anywhere. I waited long enough to watch Two's face take on a sickly gratitude for the arrival of backup against me and then I'd had enough of that and the jealousy burning up my stomach. I turned my head.

Tashin carefully raised a hand and lifted the glasses from her face. Against Juliette's darkness in the background she was a rich tan with natural emphatic colouring, no make-up. She'd had a haircut since I last saw her but not much else had changed. There was a strange excitement in her, nerves maybe. She greeted me and then looked at Two. A flash of lightning heat shot up from the burning point in my stomach. So, it was requited love all round and I was included in the memo.

I gave Tashin the nod of one bloke to another. 'You don't look like you buckle much swash these days.' Over Tashin's shoulder I saw Juliette bite her lips together to prevent a grin.

Tashin ignored me to go and hug Two, though the brevity suggested they'd been together very recently. Then she gave me her attention. 'Nico, you're looking so well.'

'Pleasure's all yours,' I said.

'Nic,' Two said. It amused me she was still keen on us liking each other but I felt bad about giving her such a hard time.

'Ninety per cent yours,' I said, still watching Tashin.

'Such a charmer,' she said to Two.

I patted the smug form of Mr Gun in his holster. 'Charming isn't paying out these days. Wanna tell me what's really in my head, agent Tashin? Or whoever else?' I glanced pointedly at Two because I was pretty sure the extent of the buggering interference hadn't been revealed.

'It's a Forged Interface. A Chimeric Avatar Switch. You shouldn't blame Two. I didn't tell her what it was.'

I was so wrongfooted by this that I lost the plot of what I'd been doing before. Two's complicity faded into a background made grey with a creeping sensation that I'd been infected. Machine interfaces were one thing, they were only connections. The Forged made these things to help monkey-base humans take a step towards their infinitely technological worlds. That's what a Switch was, the ordinary kind. But Forged Chimeric interfaces made you into something else. They were Transhuman converters. To use them was the most abhorred activity there could be on Harmony. It was the antithesis of everything I had ever known or valued and it was strange to find how repelled I was now by it. You'd think I'd be happy to stand against that fucktard Tecmaten and his ideology any way but it wasn't so. I

149

was polluted. I was corrupt. The thoughts went like that and I had no defences against them.

I stepped forward and punched Tashin with all the power of my right hand or – I would have done that but as the impulse moved into my legs and arm it was circumvented. I lost control, tripped over myself, fell heavily off the bed instead of leaping forwards and ended face down at Tashin's feet.

Two gawped at me. 'Nic?' She was terrified something had gone wrong with me. It had.

I waited for sensation to return and then bounced up to face Tashin's pale face – it had cost her something to manage that. I looked at Two. 'See? I can't even touch her.'

'Oh, gods, Nic...' Two started crying. Tashin went to put a hand on her shoulder and she shook it off violently, then turned and slapped Tashin hard across the face. Two was small but her viciousness was real. Tashin staggered backwards, hand to her cheek, gasping. Tears stood in her eyes. I glanced at Two and gave her a nod. Now the extent of her guilt made sense to me. She'd suspected things like this. 'But...' I tried to gather a thought, pushed away my rage. I wanted to be sure. 'What is a Chimeric Avatar Switch?'

Tashin regained herself, rubbed the tears off, took her hand down. Emotion made her hoarse. I was glad to see her upset. 'Anyone with a linked Switch can interface with anyone else, if they're allowed to or if they have access. Unlike a normal ship interface this Switch allows a Tek or Forged ship entity to pilot human or other biological avatars in environments they couldn't otherwise reach.'

Suddenly I got what bugged me about Tashin and always had – everything she said to me had this 'need to know' feature on it. 'So now I'm Forged?'

'Technically. But look, don't blame Two. It was my doing.'

Wow, again the defence. I should have been grateful that such feeling meant someone this powerful and manipulative was on

Two's side but all I wanted to do was crush Tashin to a pulp. I was a hairsbreadth from trying it again when Two interrupted me.

'Tash, don't lie for me. I'm sick of it already.' She glanced at me like a dog looking up to see if the owner's still mad. I couldn't make my expression alter from murderous hate and she looked away, up at the roof, trying to prevent herself crying.

So she did know. She had known. Even when she held my hand.

Tashin moved towards her but Two's hand snapped up, stalling the action. She shook her head, both lips bitten to white between her teeth.

I took Mr Gun out of his place, checked the magazine, the load, the power cell. I could feel them watching me; in my peripheral vision their movements had become abrupt with fear. I cued the shell into the chamber, set it to single fire, calibrated the trigger pressure to a double pull so there wouldn't be any mistakes. I took a deep breath, let it out and felt a fraction of control come back.

'So, tell me, if I do this – are all your plans fucked for ever?' I put the barrel of the gun into my mouth and bit on it, angled so there'd be no danger of missing the critical parts. I waited. I wanted to see if that bitch was still there, was going to have her way with me whatever happened. Could she stop me if I wasn't assaulting her? Was there some rule to it?

'Nico!' Two shrieked, jolting with an attempt to leap for my arm, jolted in turn as Tashin grabbed her and restrained her, making her be still.

I looked questioningly at Tashin and started to squeeze the trigger.

'Don't be an idiot,' Tashin said, her voice staccato and squeaky with weakness.

'Nico, please...' Two breathed, her hands stretching towards me. Her fingers were shaking. She didn't have the strength to break Tashin's embracing grasp.

I kept Tashin's gaze as I felt my finger reach the end of the primary pull. Firing required one more definitive, forceful movement. I thought that her chatter about permissions was bullshit. I just wanted to prove it for sure. The price for being wrong was stupidly high.

'All right!' Tashin blurted. 'It's not up to you – the Switch can override you. It can do anything. *I* can do anything.'

'What?' It was Two's turn for the shaken surprise, the crippling dismay.

'She thinks I'm her bitch,' I said. 'And she's right. Still loving her?' I sat down on the bed, gun at my side.

Tashin drew breath but it was Two that spoke first in her low determined voice as she shook Tashin's hands off her and took a step back, 'You said that anyone with a linked Switch can communicate with you in any way the Switch permits. You said there had to be permission. There was no override. He'd always be able to choose. *You said that.*'

Tashin held herself back. 'I had to say it, otherwise you would have changed it, you'd have made us wait, and there couldn't be any waiting. I'm sorry. Truly. But what if the next fight killed him? What if VanSant lost his patience and killed him? We could all see that coming, couldn't we? Even Nico knows he hasn't got the self-control to last for ever under a psychotic shit like Dash – he'd have cracked and then it would all be over! But now we're free of him.'

Two's face was warped with revulsion as she shook her head slowly and silently, looking at Tashin. Her mouth worked but no words came out.

'Your apologies and reasons and well-wishing doesn't mean shit to me,' I said to Tashin. 'But after all the insults and the abuse you owe me an explanation.'

'And to me!' Two hissed, backing to sit down beside me. She

took hold of my foot in her hand to steady herself. 'I thought you trusted us. I trusted you!'

'Fine,' Tashin said, twitching a little at the use of the term *us* for me and Two. She was having a hard time keeping her own anger in check but she managed after a couple of breaths and straightened up. 'I need Nico to get into Harmony Enclave. I'm investigating Tecmaten's claims about evolving superhumans capable of apparently magical acts, using only *original* DNA manipulations. I can't go myself because they will be able to trace me through this body's gene sequence and kick me out, but I need to be there to witness what goes on. Hence the Switch.'

'Why?' Two asked. She rubbed her feet together. Seated as she was they didn't quite reach the floor.

'I've already been logged in the datmosphere...'

'No,' Two said firmly. 'I don't mean that. I mean why didn't you tell me the truth in the beginning? I thought this would be the end, that once you'd killed VanSant and cleared Nic's identity we'd be out of it. I thought... but all you wanted all along was another avatar for some, I don't know... police work. Is that it? Just for some business?' She looked at Tashin, tears streaming down her cheeks and dripping off her chin.

'I know it's not... I know it's a lot to expect you... Yes. But. I'm going to give you both what you wanted in return. That was no lie. It's a promise. Please, believe me. I may have dealt with this wrongly, I... all right... but the stakes are so high you don't even know—'

'We don't know because you didn't tell us!' Two screamed suddenly, bent nearly double with the force of her rage as she spat this at Tashin. 'I told you everything about us and you didn't even give us a chance! All this time I thought you believed in the revolution and that we'd end up running an escape route for people to get out of fucking Harmony. But *you* had other plans and *you* let me believe. You let me...' She ran out of air and out of anger at the same moment, ending on a huge gasp that gave way to sobbing.

'Two, please,' Tashin began to beg, approaching with her hands out, pleading, 'Everything will be all right.'

'Yeah, it will be,' I said and the authority in my voice made Tashin look up. 'You're going to make it so.'

'I think I'll go make some tea,' Juliette said. She'd been so quiet we'd all forgotten she was present. Now she slipped out of the door but her sudden reminder brought us back a bit. I started asking questions again, mostly to bring things back to a less emotional level. 'So, it's not an AI in its own right, not like a droid or a synthetic agent?'

Tashin took a breath, sighed. She turned and sat down opposite us, elbows on her knees, head hanging, 'No, it's not a machine or a softbiont. It's an entirely biological interface that connects you to the other Switch holders.'

'Doesn't sound like pilot software to me.'

'It is, for Forged ships.'

'I thought they were all people.'

'Not all of them. Some didn't work out as planned so they don't get to be people but they're still functional, still useful.'

'And now I'm one of their slaves.'

'No, you—'

'It wasn't a fucking question.' I looked Tashin over again. The Catalogue B stuff wouldn't stop running through my mind. And she'd said she was logged as going offworld. 'How many of these things can one person have?'

'Switches?' Two was confused now.

'No, avatars.'

'I, uh ...' Two looked at Tashin, who was watching me closely.

Juliette returned with the drinks at that moment, in time to hear the question. She handed out cups with an expression of detached if acute interest.

'More than one but not more than one at a time. It's illegal

154

tek, even within Earthsystem. Only the Forged out in the Diaspora use it and then only for these – as you say – botchling Forged who couldn't be saved.'

My anger at last had frozen over, powdered into an inner snow that was starting to settle.

Tashin took a swallow of nuclear-hot liquid and composed herself. 'I told Two that it was a standard mechanoid pilot Switch for a freighter that had been stripped of its IDs.' She paused and looked at Two with such a yearning sadness I wanted to punch her so hard she'd bite her own heart out. 'But of course as soon as she started to slice the code element she knew it wasn't. So I did explain that it was a way of direct-interfacing one person to another. With permission. Which ... I have given you ...' She turned to me as Two refused to meet her eye. She had some front, I'd give her that. 'We want the same things, Nico. You want your freedom, off Harmony. I want to ruin Harmony's overcaste. These goals will be achieved with the Switch.'

'I wouldn't make too many assumptions about us being on the same case,' I said to her. 'But let's pretend. If I stick to the original deal and do whatever shit I have to do here, are you going to keep your end of the bargain and give me and Two a ship?'

'That was the deal I made with her.' She looked at Two again but I wasn't hearing *Yes*.

Something did not fucking add up here. There were things still missing from the equation – Tashin's reasons for being here in the first place. If she wasn't native she could be anything, but Forged was my bet.

I watched Tashin go and tenderly entreat Two's attention, taking her hands and holding them on bended knee, murmuring some crap or other. But she still hadn't apologised in any way that rang true to me. She was sorry that things had got to this, sure, but she wasn't sorry in any way that would have stopped her.

She reminded me of a guy from the dojo I'd met near the beginning of my time there. A too-sincere, dedicated nice-guy, he was a reasonable student who was constantly preoccupied in a way that meant he never gave anyone else the time of day – but nicely, like he was too thoughtful, too spiritual to really be of the world. He was the one who one day in satsang asked the Master what he should do to become invincible. Master told him that saying, *The sparrow does not land where the tiger walks*. I don't know what he made of it but to me the meaning was pretty clear: if there's a good chance you'll get eaten alive, don't fucking go there.

I bet he thought he was the tiger.

Now watching Tashin I didn't think she was insincere, I even believed she loved Two – shit, I could feel that – but I stuck with the vain and selfish interpretation. She thought she was the tiger. What did I know? Maybe she was. So I left the question of her motives aside for now. I'd got more practical things on my mind.

'This Switch,' I said, seeing Two's head turn at my voice which made a spike of victorious spite run sweet in my heart – suck it up, Tashin – 'who's got connections? Where's the ship?'

'Just me. And the ship, but it's quarantined off. I've kept it out of the loop for now. You won't be bothered by it,' Tashin said, but she hesitated and I *knew* she was hiding something.

– I'm going to cook you for this, motherfucker.

We can settle our differences after this is all over, of course.

– Bet your Catalogue-B avatar's cheap ass on it.

Aloud I said, 'Does your *boss* have the ship waiting too?'

'It's safe. In-system but out of reach of Harmony's Security.'

The leviathan. That figured.

Two cleared her throat. 'How did you get it? And why? Is it one of those Forged that didn't pass the Human Test?'

'Not exactly,' Tashin said. 'It rejected every personacraft that was created for it, so it was fitted with Switches so that it could

156

have a human or a Forged companion, a pilot, interpreter, carer, what you will.'

'Whaddya mean, rejected?'

'I mean rejected.' Tashin looked at me directly. 'I can't explain persona creation very well. Something about the ship's structure meant it couldn't become what it was meant to be. It didn't mature into what we could consider human. But it was too human to be treated as something else. It was assigned to permanent deactivation so it wasn't difficult to persuade the owners to part with it.'

Two looked at me, 'Is it real, Nic?'

I nodded, 'Something's real. Whether it's a ship or not I really couldn't say, not being sufficiently informed.' I gave Tashin the evil eye.

'We should go,' Tashin said to Two, straightening up. 'We must get back to Dann's before we're missed. She's expecting us. Juliette will stay to brief you, Nico.'

'Wait outside,' I said. 'Me and Two have things to say before she goes.'

Two stood and rubbed her palms down the sides of her jacket. She was chewing her lips as she scrubbed her face with her sleeves and then tilted her head. 'We OK?'

I couldn't answer. We were, but saying it was too much for me at that moment – what had happened was too big. Though I needed us to be OK because otherwise I couldn't go on. 'You know, I'd say I'll write but I'll probably be too busy.'

She laughed, once, coughed it off. 'I'm gonna make sure she keeps her word.' Her face was racked with doubt.

I asked the question on my mind. 'If she doesn't want to go, in the end, when we're leaving here, will you still go?' I didn't want to think of a life without Two but I'd seen her come around to Tashin so fast I couldn't kid myself there wasn't a real risk that we were over.

'If she . . .' and I saw she hadn't even considered that her lying, two-faced lover might have other plans.

The slow sinking in me was only my heart feeling the crush in advance, for her. I cleared my throat and patted Mr Gun. 'Ah don't worry, the shit'll've hit the fan so hard by then she'll have to leave,' I said in my best breezy voice, smiled the white teeth smile I used to give the cameras at the Pit. 'Won't even be an issue.'

Broken people, broken ships, broken promises sat between us in a huge pile of shit.

She was trying not to cry but the snotty tears were starting to leak out of her nostrils, made them glisten. 'Nico.' She worked her mouth as if she'd speak some more but she couldn't and only shook her head. She made like she'd hug me but in the end she didn't do that either because she felt like she couldn't now. I had to leap up and sidestep, stand in her way as she moved for the door so that she hit me full on instead. I hugged her and her arms closed on me like a vice. A few moments later we parted and she walked out of the door.

You like to play dangerous games, Nico.
– What was your first clue, Big Ears?

Bold words, but there was really no hiding the fact that I was up monster creek without a paddle. Tashin was lying when she said the leviathan had been salvaged. When she spoke about it her own anxiety level was so high she lost control of her thinking and I'd seen the truth of it. She'd done a deal with it to get it here, this inhuman thing she'd spliced me to, and it was getting impatient. Her credit was running out.

Eight – is a sacred number, two fours, double the stability of the already stable, the points on a cube, six faces, three dimensions, you do the math

After they left Juliette returned, lace cuffs and collar perfect, her expression curious and composed. 'For your information, no, I am merely employed by the revolutionary Tashin and her associates. I am not part of their number. And to my knowledge the cartels only supply funding and guns when they need to take the heat off themselves and offer the Inquisition something else to chase.'

I leaned back on the bed's headboard, as exhausted as if I'd done ten rounds in the ring. Another reason to kick emotions into touch whenever the chance arose. Who needs that shit? 'This must be an interesting case for you, but why bother being here now? Surely your job ended when I died?'

'In public, yes, but my contract defines the case to be you and the sum total of your operations for the revolutionary.'

'Inquisition know you're a dirty outfit?'

Juliette shook her head, smiling. She sipped her tea and pulled a face with a wrinkled nose at the taste. 'That's quite an accusation, though given your condition I'll allow it. Dice and Dice offer perfectly legal services within verified terms and conditions which are acceptable to a surprisingly large client base, including the District Prosecutor's Office.'

'Conflict of interest?'

'Is triggered less often than you might imagine. In Harmony Enclave our branch has an immaculate record. But in Chaontium the rules are a little more... elastic.' There was real weight in her brown gaze, every word carried the significance of eight. Seven nuances to say that there was plenty dirty in every direction, though it stuck only in one. It was interesting to have her confirm what everyone knew in their bones but no one could prove. Even the evil in Harmony is secretly legit.

'It makes Harmony look good.'

'In every possible way.' She nodded, then her gaze fell on Mr Gun. 'I will have a cleanup team come for that. I'm afraid I can't let you keep it. Meanwhile I am to provide you with physical and uploadable copies of your briefing. If we can deal with that as soon as possible I'd be glad to be out of here and on my way.'

'Do your worst.'

'Excellent,' she smiled, and brought out her anti-spy droid, set it up, and then meticulously assembled her materials. 'Let's get you a new life.'

At least my past was easy to fix in the datmosphere. Two had given me a model background: school yearbooks, childhood photographs, a tragic family bulldozed by the infamous cargo aircrash at our hometown of Sabadre fifteen years prior. The trauma had set me on a serious, studious career in the priesthood, devoted to the study of the Alchemy. My search for spiritual cures and the power of mind over flesh had led me, exam by test by paper, to a scholarship at the Ito Seminary right in the beating white heart of Harmony: Tecmaten's personal academy. I was reserved, quiet, shy, polite and took out any violent impulses I had in the formalities of the boxing ring.

All the files of video that had me smashing noses and kicking blokes flying into midair, or alternatively of me being pasted across various bloodied arena floors, crossed my mind. There was no way to erase all of those, surely? The cartels were well known for selling any profitable files off-planet. I guessed the revolution brains didn't think any offworld investigators would be sent to check on me and that homeboy agents would be banned from offworld travel. It always surprised me that people higher up than street life so rarely relied on word of mouth. They just looked at files and verified signs and took that as gospel. Personally, I gave my cover a few months to run at best before I slipped up. Given that, I was forced to assume that this job wouldn't take long.

I looked up from the presentation Juliette had given me as she took a pause. 'That looks great but I'm no priest. I can't stand these people.' I spun Mr Gun around on my index finger to reinforce the point.

Juliette gave me a patient but pained look. 'Do you mind?'

'Safety's on. Or, well, it is now.' I put him down, but kept my hand on him. He was really kind of comforting.

'Thank you. Actually Tashin assured me that you can be quite the actor.'

'*She* should be doing this but hey, we went through none of that already.'

'I'm afraid I can't reveal privileged information about the reasons for your selection.'

I sighed. 'I need beer.'

'No drinking. You're ordained.'

'What the fuck?'

Juliette pointed to my long list of qualifications. I was seriously boring, but worse than that, I was deeply orthodox.

I rolled my eyes and slammed my head back against the padded board.

Juliette smiled, 'Shall we go on?'

'Yeah, sure. And all this is automatically committed to memory? Because I can't even read some of that.'

'Not to worry. As I proceed and you – ingest – the details they will all remain box fresh for you whenever you need them. In fact there is a checksystem running which will only release me from this job once your memory add-ons are sufficiently well configured. Rather nicely put together actually. No danger of either of us suing for malpractice.'

'Oh good. I was so worried about that,' I pouted.

She laughed. 'Come on, Nico. There's still a long way to go.'

I nodded. 'I'm not the one delaying with chat about lawsuits.'

'You're impossible.'

'That's been observed many times before.'

After I'd ingested my own fake past and committed it to my newly minted memory I flipped open the dossier on my target.

I picked out only names at first. Mariwyn, the mother. Ashtier the sister. The father – Branforn, meaning *proud citizen* in the old tongue. The son, Isylon. Isylon Selamaa. Selamaa being *peaceful dawn*, a family name even I recognised. *That* dynastic family.

I checked again. Could there be two. Cousins? Distant relations? A misspelling?

No.

In her seat opposite me Juliette smiled vaguely and pretended to polish her manicure as she took a break from talking.

'Selamaa?' I ventured, tapping the display. 'Are you serious?'

Juliette smiled and nodded with the satisfaction of someone whose problem it isn't.

I began to sense a clusterfuckage of epic proportions headed my way.

In the rarefied universe of true Collegiate and Canonical power there was no greater name. Three Sanctified Masters had come from that family. Isylon's daddy was being obsequiously modest in sending his son to the Ito seminary. He could probably have self-declared him the next Grand Master in waiting, given it a couple of years for politeness, kicked the incumbent off the pedestal, installed his pride and joy and nobody would have said boo.

But the matter nagging at me wasn't the sudden new glamour of being attached to this well-known group of power-mongers, or even the terror of being inside a snake-pit like the Alchemy's central power base: it was the magic, the nagging scratch of grit at the core of the universe that turned to pearls for believers and cancer for the sceptics. In Harmony you don't talk about magic, you make some wa-wa tones about spirituality and faith healing and the power of mind over matter and the grace of god surpassing all understanding or, if you're at a safe distance, you lift a cynical eyebrow and claim it's all propaganda. Selamaa was virtually a synonym for wa-wa.

Isylon Selamaa was, if blood ran true, going to have the kinds of unexplained-by-public-science abilities that could strip the disguise off an intergalactic bounty hunter from two planets away. A bounty hunter cyborg. In a lead coffin. Inside a warp-ship. Riding out a gas giant atmospheric storm with his fingers in his ears singing 'Don't Look Down'.

Not that I believed in that kind of thing.

My Switch might be some fancy bioshit but it would still fry under that kind of scrutiny. Wouldn't it? Or maybe the legendary qualities had amplified in the telling and he was only up to levitating a pineapple and curing gout. I had no idea.

I started hunting down some kind of hard evidence on the situation re spooky powers of wa-wa. Tashin had kindly provided a full breakdown of her extensive research and world-busting passion on the matter. It consisted of one word: unknown. *This claim of the priesthood to have engineered paranormal capacities in their most advanced evolutions is the primary reason that I'm here.*

– Ah, so your schtick isn't merely a popular uprising of the people against the Alchemy's tyranny, it's thieving-bastard business. Are you looking to steal or buy?

Oddly, I respected that angle. Though that wasn't saying much.

Actually this only came up late in the mission. It is not known about offworld. Harmony supplies the finest gengineered products but none of them claim anything remotely related to the so-called evolutionary projects of Tecmaten's priesthood.

– So you originally came here on a spying exercise?

Oh, no. We had successfully managed several double agents for decades who gave us all the information that we required. We had no interest in Harmony. They were a minor supplier of the Solar Diaspora; one of thousands, generally superior in product but otherwise unremarkable. We're under a strong official directive from the core worlds to tolerate spin-off states existing in voluntary isolation for ideological reasons – like this one – so long as they make no efforts to evangelise outside their borders. I took a personal interest in the Alchemical Manufactory because quasi-science is my hobby.

Quasi-science? What the hell was that?

– How do you get from there to backing revolutions and murder?

I heard about the miracles from one of the double agents. They said there was living proof. That Exalted forms were more than a theory.

– You don't believe in them.

I, no. But she had been sent out into the Diaspora to look for certain things which made me wonder if there was a technological aspect involved in creating these effects. The grail of the Alchemy is—

– A cup of ever-regenerating youth.

The Sol System medical protocols have never included resurrection as a technological goal – it was merely considered a part of ordinary healing and longevity assistance and there has always been a large gap between the swift regeneration of the body from massive trauma and the return to life. The return to life part happens far less often than it seems it should, given the restoration of the body to a theorised operational fitness. Even if it regained system function there remains the annoying lack of response – the subject remains apparently comatose with little

164

or no brain activity beyond autonomia – and also, there is the anomalous weight loss. A few grams less per cadaver. We see it even in the Forged.

– You're weighing souls out there now? Ah, come on. I was hoping you'd be way past that bullshit. It's my dream community. I don't want it full of superstitious crud. Stop spoiling it for me.

You hold on to a great ideal of the world beyond Harmony.

– It's much better than here. It has to be.

I thought about Number One Fan's peculiar reanimation. If that was resurrection then I was a horse princess. Then something occurred to me.

– You occupied the bodies.

Yes, temporarily.

– What technology is that?

It's rather crude. It can mimic life even in the worst of corpses. But it doesn't last very long. The decomposition process…

– Zombie tech.

If you like.

– You could have just made me a zombie. Why not?

I am not an immoral agent, here to execute my will at any price, Nico.

– But you did kill them. You need me alive and you need me to believe I matter enough that I still have some choices. But we both know that's crap, so if it's all the same to you I'll hang on to my own motivation in this.

You want to leave a free man.

– With Two. In a ship of my own.

And that is what you'll get. As I've said.

– After you get what you want, which is the secrets of the Alchemists within Harmony Enclave's Holiest of Holies, right?

Right.

– I smell a rat's *ass*.

Meaning?

– You're telling me about the profit and loss angle because I believe in that kind of thing. But before that you were passionate about Two's convictions. I felt it when she was talking to you. So, what's with the revolution?

That is personal. You wouldn't understand.

– Try me.

Let's just say that coming here for the sake of my personal conviction that it is correct to attempt the overthrow of states which steal choices from citizens is a private matter that has cost me everything. How would you put it? I have bet the farm.

– Rogue agent?

You do like a glamorous label.

– Without it we're just hustlers, baby. Does your boss know you're here?

Not yet. But soon.

I turned to some pictures so I'd at least know whose face I'd see just before I got carted off to the dungeons.

Dominion robes suit a lot of people. They have black and white panelling, big hoods, the kind of tailoring that makes even a gluttonously ruined dog's ass of a man look like he's some big-shot with the wisdom of the ages oozing out of his every orifice.

Isylon Selamaa actually managed to hide in his, at least in this photograph, even with the hood back. The bulk of the robe fell off his shoulders and chest in a straight drop, disguising everything except that he was relatively tall and hadn't porked out as a result of years of meditation and catechism. His hands were hidden in massive sleeving. Forget cards, you could've put a blackjack table in those sleeves, croupier included. Everywhere I was used to checking for signs of trouble on a person was concealed. That usually meant a lot of trouble. Quiet, skinny ones hidden in bulky clothes? Bad, bad news.

The bad news was looking down and to the side of the camera, half his face curtained off by a straight fall of camel-coloured hair. So far so emo. That probably went with the job. The visible eye looked like it had seen enough of the world and wasn't going to share anything without a warrant in triplicate.

Juliette moved over to see what I was looking at. 'Oh, dear.' She glanced at me.

Selamaa had the brooding, sulky look of a teenager forced to obedience with severe threats – that was in the mouth. But as a whole there was a cool, refined aloofness to him that spoke more of an older adult, an adult with plans. Contradictions. My speciality.

I was going to die over there, in the onstage meaning at least. Maybe it was Fate's idea of a joke to dump me in the last place in existence I'd choose to go.

'He's two suns, isn't he?' I wasn't sure what prompted me to that guess. I think it was Juliette's words, her tone of sympathy, now.

'Think so,' she said.

'That's why Tashin didn't go. Zero extra leverage.'

'I couldn't say.'

'He's Exalted, isn't he?'

'Oh, Nico, two for two,' Juliette patted me on the back.

Tashin tried to talk again, obviously thinking we were mates after our last bout, but I told her to fuck off and asked Juliette to continue, intent on making it through my remaining time here without having to dwell on the revelation of my true role – as bait.

A week later I was still on site in the gym, sweating on the treadmill. I enjoyed it: the old run-to-nowhere, music in my headspace, nothing in my mind.

I saw Juliette come up behind me in the mirror. Her cream and brown suit, her ballet boots were perfectly judged. I slammed my hand on the Slow button and jumped off. I was bending down to pick up my water bottle as she handed me a towel.

'You look much better,' she said, smiling warmly.

I thanked her and scrubbed off my face. My legs ached and my lungs hurt.

'You ship out in two days,' she said. 'I came to tell you and get your measurements for the clothing and gear.'

So that was what the small scanner in her hand was for. I tossed the towel and held my arms out obligingly. My vest and shorts stuck to me with sweat. I was pretty rank but like I said, 'I won't get much more naked unless I'm naked.'

Juliette frowned and smiled at the same time and walked around me with her scanner, taking readings. She studied them and then looked up. 'You have eighty per cent active take-up of the systems. That's very good.'

Ah, not just a clothing reading then.

'Don't get anything too fitted,' I said. 'I still don't have my body back.'

'I'm sure your allowance will be sufficient to buy new,' she said. 'But you have to pass muster first. Think you can make it?'

I knew this wasn't so much a question as a warning.

'I'm used to faking it,' I reassured her.

A wan little smile turned up the corners of her mouth, almost without her noticing.

I felt no response inside. I could have been made of concrete for all the reaction inspired by the idea of the priesthood raking me over the verbal coals.

'Will I have to kill him?' There, it was out.

She shook her head. 'That's only a fallback option. If Selamaa were to be killed by some crew of nutjobs it would only give the Alchemy a bigger resource in his martyrdom. The revolution wants him safe and in his place. Tashin wants to investigate the possibilities. You listen and learn. That's all for now.'

'Until?' I prompted.

'Until we tell you otherwise.' She sighed and seemed reluctant to leave. I decided she wasn't as deeply into Tashin's loop as she thought she was. She believed that the revolution was the priority. They wanted Selamaa for something else, maybe something they hadn't even thought of yet. They could hold him hostage for something big. But Tashin had plans beyond that.

I drank and watched her watching me. 'Something else on your mind?'

She looked around at the machinery. 'This is all you do: run, lift weights?'

'No, I punch bags and ... what do you mean?'

She sighed and looked at me. 'Let's take a walk. Have a shower and meet me outside in ten minutes,' she said.

I obeyed her like a good zombie. Tashin had informed me that she had pressing business elsewhere so she would be offline for a few hours. I felt her connection to me drop, as if my bones were a hollow stone chamber and a coin had fallen to the floor. It was the first time I believed she wasn't eavesdropping.

We walked the cycle path, me in layers of training sweats, hooded, she in her overcoat and heels, an umbrella over her head to protect her from the faint drizzle. A security drone whirred through the wet grass, rubber wheels squeaking as it surveyed for other people's surveillance. I had no idea where I was. The place was nameless. In every direction countryside stretched in a warp of green and brown.

We strolled out of reach of everything except the drone.

Juliette turned to me when I stopped, 'Quiet enough here, is it?'

I nodded. The biophony was rich but the technophony nearly silent. Far overhead satellites and shipping signalled amid the two hundred channels of radio. Yep, quiet.

She smiled thinly. 'I'm glad you've adapted to your wetware. Now listen, about Isylon. As far as I understand it he isn't a mind-reader, a Confessor. So in theory you'll be able to keep your secrets so long as you keep your mouth shut.'

So far as she understood it I was relieved. Put me in the viper pit and say they'll only bite if you make 'em angry. I hoped she was right. 'You got an exit plan for me?'

She looked at me steadily, 'If all goes well you'll have a life much like your last one, maybe better.'

Yeah, right. 'How can you be sure if things go wrong that they won't connect me all the way back to you? Not hard to figure out who I am if they want to check the DNA.'

She looked at me through the falling rain and then stepped closer, the gap between us down to inches. Her gaze moved back and forth between my eyes as though she were trying to see me.

A stream of rainwater fell from her lowering umbrella and soaked me in a long line from chest to hip, 'Perhaps the opponents are not so clearly defined as one might assume. Don't let anything go wrong.'

I wished her away but she stood there, dripping. To my surprise a look of hurt came over her face, quickly turning to humiliation, then shame.

'I'm sorry,' she said, finding her professional voice easily so I knew there had been a lot of times she'd had to fish for it as a shield. I wasn't sure what she was apologising for but I filed it under *there's shit ahead*.

She sighed. 'I'll brief you for the interview. We can practise a few things. And your 'ware will help. Your guest. I think we can make a good go of it.'

Guest. Yeah that was exactly how it was. Nice try. 'Bribery not the noble pastime it used to be?'

She smiled warmly at me. 'I wish it were. Then we could all sleep easier. But even if there are Cardinals open to cash buyouts I don't know who they are. Now, let's go through your briefing material, at least the major points.'

What followed was such a marathon of question and response in practice for my Ito assessment that I wished I was back in hospital. One upside of it however: I remembered everything verbatim and pitch-perfect.

170

I'm lying. There was a part of the Alchemy that grabbed me which I didn't want to grab me. I wanted to hate it, to rip it to pieces as unconscionable shit and to reject it in a global apocalypse of disdain, only I couldn't, and as I found myself getting drawn into its labyrinth an old, dull, dusty creature forgotten from my boyhood stirred into wakefulness.

Juliette was parsing me through the Rote. Any priest with the mind for it studied the Alchemy. Some stuck with theory, piling image on symbol on element, bickering over dogma; some researched and developed it. I was going to be one of the latter.

For the purposes of my rapid, cheated education we went straight into my speciality. I thought it had to be a bad-taste joke on Tashin's part. Cisnormativity. That isn't even a word and if it is a word it shouldn't be a word. It shouldn't even be an idea, it's so ruinously ugly in every way. It should be destroyed in hellfire.

It was right then that I got a stab of pain in my stomach, a goring from the minotaur. I remembered him suddenly. My stomach remembered him too, with a twist, trying to close around him, to protect his pure and undiluted nature from what I'd been made to swallow.

He was a cisnormative bull-man: buff body, oiled tan, head of a black longhorn monster, size of an ox, what else? He snorted steams of pure hate. His eyes were surrounded with the white and bloodshot of primal outrage. He was all my love and there was no way I was letting this Alchemy dreck poison him with its preaching about the ebb and flow of human behaviours. I hadn't thought of him in ages and I was surprised to find him now, guilty for my neglect, until I looked around me – oh yeah, we were back in the orphanage. No wonder he showed up and no wonder I was looking around for the antacids.

Cisnormativity was an ancient term, stolen like everything else Tecmaten had ever thought of to throw into his little podule of hate for actual nature. In that he was an arch transhumanist, ironically.

171

In the Alchemy it was essential that one's gender matched one's physical form but, as with my particular variant, this was something that even the most refined Alchemist had yet to assure. The biology was understood at the level of the gene. Why the biology developed as it did was understood. Mostly. Preventing 'mistakes' was not understood; whatever measures were taken they didn't always work. Vast efforts scrutinising every micro-reaction were now being undertaken to solve the problem of variation that came apparently from nowhere.

This tiny coalface of OCD joy was where I would be spending my days from now on.

'Are you all right? You look ill.'

'I need water, some indigestion tabs,' I said and got up to go find them.

I'd once believed in the cold hells too, once, felt safe within Harmony's caring arms, even if they didn't care so much about me. The minotaur had appeared then, to stamp around mad and wild inside my guts. *No, we're not having that crap, we're not accepting it even though we must look as if we do. We're not swallowing.*

I suppose that had set me up now as someone who knew very well how to put on one face and do something completely different inside.

I found and chewed some bland tablets and followed them with a glass of water, picking the bits out of my teeth as I went back to the briefing. The minotaur grumbled, mildly annoyed by the chalky pills but soothed by the fact that whoever had prepared my education had dismissed Harmony, dissected it, had already been through the Alchemy with a fine tooth comb and found it was all nits. But he remained resentful, snorting, because he saw with his rheumy eye that this outsider culture viewed the Alchemy as the curious lifework of a madman: aesthetically it could be appreciated as a creative gesture, as a piece of art, and all of us were a part of it in its living entirety.

Our lives. Appreciated. As art.

The minotaur belched horribly in dismay. We crapped on that idea. If you could see the Alchemy as a bizarre spiritual aesthetic worked into genetic engineering for entertainment purposes, for philosophical whimsy – then you were someone we were happy to sacrifice. So we may not be at home anywhere. There might be no escape. What if the Diaspora found abortions like Tecmaten merely amusing, part of the grand play of life against the infinite backdrop of the cosmos or some garbage like that? Who wanted to spend ten minutes with that kind of people? I could leave Harmony with dreams of the stars and find only more assholes.

Still, it was something to know that the Alchemy's claim to have exhumed the patterns of greater mystical energies sewn into the deepest biological bonds was the only feature that set it apart from a thousand other Übermenschen cults devoted to the pursuit of various everyday grails: eternal life, everlasting youth, the transmutation of elements. Harmony was a Utopia with a twist. Enough for an essay. Maybe not enough for a doctorate. It's quite something to see your whole life as some dipshit's master's thesis footnote.

I belched with considerable force so that I sounded like a growling bear. Maybe a few tablets weren't going to do it.

'So, cisnormativity.' Even Juliette struggled to pronounce it.

'Yeah, yeah,' I said, sitting down on the couch, rolling my eyes. 'I make sure everyone's born into the right body without a trace of disappointment or confusion. The right mind for the right job.'

'Creating all people in the image of god,' Juliette quoted from Alchemy 101 with a wry smile.

'Tecmaten's Tecnormative vision of Normativegod. I wonder what Tashin really looks like. Do you think she has tentacles?'

'I cannot speculate on the matter.' Juliette at least looked surprised. She smiled and hid a chuckle.

173

'Of course you can't.' Anyway, I had a feeling that the tentacles in outer space didn't belong to her. They belonged to whatever it was that made the bird. My botched, gagged little friend. 'Do you believe in magic, Juliette?'

'Something's going on. Confessors, for instance. They can tell what you're thinking. Don't you?'

I thought about the car. I did not believe and I'd seen tech that made me even more convinced. It might look like it, but really? 'I don't think what's happening here is because people are suggestible. Something happens that makes it look good. I don't think Tashin's looking for it because she thinks it's real. Just a fake that's worth having.'

'You may be right. Shall we continue? There's a lot to do.'

We continued examining the mystery of the Alchemy, the symbols of archetypal creation hidden in the physical world. What makes you think you are male or female, both or neither, is a mystery both of neurostructure and biodynamic grace. Sometimes it is weak, sometimes strong. It depends how the sun was, how the moon swung, whether or not there was enough iron and fire, earth and water where you were as you grew, your mother's tread and breath the mandala of your spirit.

If you can't blame god (and in the Alchemy you really can't) then you can always blame Mom. Artificial gestation was not permitted. Nature must be entirely natural. Obviously as the last card in the deck it was all down to what she did.

The minotaur frothed at the mouth a little. I popped another pill from the end of the roll.

'Do you think that if Tecmaten had had more success with the ladies we wouldn't be here now?'

'Nico.'

'I know, I know. Focus.'

'No. I wanted to say I'm glad it's not me going in there. I don't have many dealings with Enclave people but I have friends in our offices there. I know what they're like. Nobody feels safe, even at the top. Especially not at the top.'

'Tecmaten paranoid about his successors?'

'Wouldn't you be, if you were three hundred years old and showing it? Even with technology he's not going to survive that much longer and surely the vultures have started to gather.'

'Is there even a state without him?'

Juliette shrugged. 'Think of it as a cartel. Does anyone care who runs it once it's rich enough to fend for itself?'

By the time we were sitting, exhausted, with boxfuls of food, I was ready to be one of the dullest and most reliable pieces of pulpit fodder it had never been my pleasure to meet. The minotaur had galloped into the labyrinth of my intestines under a gassy cloud of misery.

Juliette left after dinner. Tashin returned, my bones told me, but I didn't want to talk to her. She could stay in my skeleton and enjoy the extra calcium from all those antacids.

I went to bed and found a card on my pillow. One of the droids must have put it in place. There was also a chocolate in a purple wrapper which I sniffed suspiciously and found to be violet-scented. I read the note on the back of the card, written in Juliette's impeccable handwriting.

'Was told to pass this on. Trash it when you're done.'

I read the front of the card again with a sense of deja-punked.

Fine. This went bone deep so let's summon her up.

– Was this your idea?

Hardly.

– So I take it you're not the only one jerking the strings around here?

I've had to do many stupid things in the name of achieving a greater aim.

– This smells of Kasha Dann to me.

Revolutionaries appear in unexpected places. One takes what one finds and makes use of it. I need her for now so it must seem I am a true servant. As far as she is concerned this is a cartel operation.

You can never know how many groups someone belongs to, nor which of them commands the highest loyalty. I took the card as a typical cartel gesture: a reward on the face of it, but also an insult of the deepest and most personal kind, a barb of poison aimed at the soul in order to set up a time bomb. It gives with one hand and strangles with the other.

I studied the credentials and video intro on the card for 'Tabu'. All I had to do was call.

He looked like the men I used to work for, only he wore his sharp tailoring with a friendly smile and easy grace. His body said he was commanding and his face said he was anybody's. But you can't sweeten the unsweetenable.

A whore gift for a whore. My body ached everywhere it remembered a blow. I screwed up the card and flicked it into the corner.

Then I lay awake in the dark and studied Isylon Selamaa's picture, trying to read anything sympathetic or likeable into it. But he was no Tabu with his open grin, his knowing eyes. Isylon's look was bathroom-familiar because I saw it every day: Out Of Contact.

He just didn't want to know.

Ditto that, bro.

The journey into Harmony Enclave was long and boring. I slept most of it away and arrived yawning, startled by the sight of a black-robed priest with a glower like holy vengeance under his cowl. After a second I realised it was my own reflection in the car window. As I looked through into the street the first thing I noticed was the absence of litter. You could have licked the pavements and it would have cleaned your tongue.

The architecture of the city spoke of a considered elegance

and design far from anything seen on Chaontium's boulevards. The buildings wore uniforms, habits and mantles. The street paving was laid for pilgrimage; the beliefs of the faithful were made manifest in stone, glass, steel, concrete and tile, and the people themselves moved like sleek, secure angels as if every step was a dance into grace. I guessed they must learn it at school. I'd have to work to fake it and imagine myself in some eternal dojo.

The stores were almost indistinguishable from the temples. Seeing the undeniable beauty of it did something painful to my overworked guts. I wasn't supposed to be here. I could never touch it without defiling it.

But then the cold power of that thought pleased me.

The car purred up to the kerb by the cathedral in a line with more than twenty others. Once we had been relayed into position the door opened and I took my first step out into the Enclave proper and my first breath of its purified air. The car door closed and it moved away behind me. I pretended to admire the cathedral's front face although I looked past it to the slight haze in the air – the shimmer of the distortion dome that shielded the Enclave from common and unwanted things in Lesser Harmony and her ugly sister, Chaontium.

That first breath was an intense pleasure, the same exact reaction as I used to get stepping into the arena for the first bout of a night. I took a moment to soak it up: nobody knew who or what I was – the black cuckoo right in the middle of the nest.

You may have to dial that back a notch.

I ignored Captain Killjoy and went for a thoroughly plausible tourist goggle at the temple of doom, practising my entitled waltz technique. One, two, three...

The lack of heavy firearms at my side was disconcerting. As I leaned back to decipher the montage of statuary ranging up the temple pyramid's ascent, I found myself reminded of the vast and strange inner ocean I was avoiding, because I could see echoes of it in the intricate carving of this massive structure.

For a flash that almost had me off balance I understood that the universe was 'in there', as well as 'out there'. All I had to do to find anything was look – inside. It was such a horrible sensation of being on the brink that I rammed it firmly away from me and put all my effort into studying the architecture.

Look at all the work and effort people had put into this shit. I didn't give a toss about what it was for, but it clearly involved some major convincing of the thousands. I found that I knew line and verse of the theology. Every line, every verse…

– Have you been filling up my memory?

Knowledge is fuel and, in this case, armour. I put you slightly left of centre in most theological and Alchemically debated hot topics, since you're from the provinces and economically at a disadvantage. Nothing to stir any interest. Remember, you're here on an Alchemic scholarship as an engineer of excellence and orthodoxy but with a hint of creative radical. A HINT. For flavour. Nothing to arouse suspicion.

– And there I was thinking you had no fudging sense of humour. Oh my— Wait. Why aren't I swearing any more? You deleted my ***** swear words?

Profanity is the…

– …way of the infidel, for those of weak mind. FYI: when I get to godhood you're toast.

If you get to godhood there is no god.

– I'm well on the way. Or didn't you read that part on Personalised Transmutation? After experiencing the nine circles of ascent I achieve actualisation and parity. I've already done four of them, according to the story on this pyramid. You, on the other hand, aren't even initiated. Go back to the start, do not collect any goods and chattels.

The gongs and bells sounded, shattering apart unwanted negative energies, apparently including Tashin, and announcing that prayers were about to begin. I tore my eyes from the frieze of angels and labourers and stalked through the doors, hoping I could make a decent fist of getting lost among six hundred identically dressed others.

Men sat to the right, women to the left. I found my spot in the golden glow of artificial sunlight and stood on the solar disc set into the floor. Runes glowed. Kind of a cheap effect, especially when you know it's reading you and authorising your credentials – who needs god when you've got AI?

Above our heads the four planes of the pyramid rose, their faces displaying the stars overhead as a permanent night, our side featuring the beaming face of a golden sun, the female side a moon in its current phase, a thin crescent of white pregnant with darkness. Harmony does have a moon. They had it made specially, and placed it where it could be suitably shaded. Someone said they painted it white with blasted marble dust from Earth, but people will write and believe any old rubbish.

– 'Rubbish'? Who talks like this? Come on! Can't live without the swearing, it's already driving me insane.

– I love how you go deaf when it suits you, you urine-soaked weasel.

But I was talking to myself, jabbering away at the edge of the dark for one more moment whilst the thousand people around me stood in unison, in silence, witnessing the devotion of their minds to the great cause of achieving divinity through the rigorous application of science and spiritual principle. I'd always mocked it but now, among them as one, I felt a twinge of sentimental grandeur.

My heart twisted in on itself with the old revulsion, the old hatred – it knew the sublime sweetness of this sense of innocent purity and righteousness among the chosen, and that we were forever outcast from it for no fault of our own, but for their fault. It hurt with a fierce stab like a narrow pin thrust between the ribs. Gored by the minotaur again. Furious at this mortal strike against myself my anger rallied me as it had when I was a child, but then as now the monster was not so easily defeated. My master said you only ever fight yourself. Only a fool was not on his own side.

She was the one I thought of as we intoned the prayers that renewed our commitment to the Alchemy: reality and its symbols are magically entwined so one becomes the other in the endless round. What is created as thought, seamlessly becomes real in the Alembic of the mind.

How right this was.

My heart thudded dumbly along in donkey-punched staggers as it felt itself ripped out anew. The first time it had happened was at some early age, when I realised nobody wanted me. I did my best to cauterise it at the age of seven: in throwing out all of Harmony's ideology I threw out its ability to harm me, so I'd thought. Good riddance to bad rubbish. But I hadn't the skills to perform the necessary total extraction. I left a huge, bleeding hole behind into which loathing and resentment seeped steadily, changing belonging into not belonging and love into rejection.

Now in this glorious music, chant and space there was a curling and fawning part of me that wanted that lost love and approval. It was there for the taking because nobody knew I wasn't supposed to have it. I wanted that love from these people, everywhere around me, cheek by jowl by shoulder to shoulder.

There's your poison, Nico. That's what ails you. Soak it all up.

And with that thought all wanting ceased. I remembered myself.

If they gave me love I'd bite off their hands.

Nico.

Tashin's emotion, a flicker from elsewhere, myself seen from outside by pitying eyes: that was all it took to snap me right out of it. From open season to ice block in one instant.

– Thanks. That was out of hand. But if you ever communicate sympathy towards me again, I will kill you.

I'll kill you! It's what little kids say when they're so furious and know they have no chance. Only I wasn't little or a kid, and I had plenty of chances coming. And I meant it.

The ceremony moved towards a conclusion. I watched the back of the guy in front and wondered if I could put him out with one hit. I thought it was pretty likely. I could probably lay waste to a good portion of this bit of the room before someone got a grip on what was happening. By the time my fantasy had run its course reality was back on its razor precipice between imagined and actual: I was shriven, as they said, lighting their incense, sprinkling their salt and water.

We filed back outside on a walk to a nearby assembly hall where dinner was being served prior to the individual inductions. Meals were collected from a servery, eaten at long trestle tables illuminated by huge salt-crystal lights.

I'd decided that Fake Nico was a very shy, insular guy whose idea of being social was sitting within six metres of another human. That would save me from having to indulge any social impulses from other people. This turned out badly for Fake Nico, as I'd no sooner found a place on the end of a bench at the most remote table when someone stepped in beside me and put his bowl of noodle broth down next to mine.

I watched an elegant hand make a considered motion of placing the spoon and sticks precisely on the placemat before the figure turned to face me.

'Hello. You're Nico of Sabadre. I'm Isylon of Delatan. We'll be sharing rooms and labs. I understand you specialise in gender engineering.'

Slam, knockdown, facepunch. I really hadn't seen it coming.

I finished pulling the disposable chopsticks apart and set them down, then with a sense of foreboding drew back the heavy cowl I'd been hoping to hide inside for the rest of the day, or for ever, whichever proved more achievable.

'Your hair is white!' He looked surprised. I couldn't help smiling at the way it made his serious face comical. Now others were looking our way. It was rapidly turning into a spectacle.

'Not quite,' I said quickly.

Coloured hair was a sign of insecurity or maladaption to some – like criticising the High Alchemy – so in addition to antisocial disorder Fake Nico was obviously an avid sunbather or outdoor nut. I felt Tashin cringe silently but gave her an internal order to shut up and stay out of it on the promise that I would absolutely abandon her and the project at the first sign of meddling.

You need to relax. Be yourself. No, wait. Be someone nice. Don't blow it.

Isylon and I clasped hands and he blinked in surprise at my grip. I dropped his hand as if it had bitten me.

His interest went back to my hair. 'It's nearly silver. Platinum Blonde #28 if I'm not mistaken,' he corrected, peering closer.

I returned the favour as a professional kind of competitive courtesy.

Caramel everything, hair, skin, even his facial hair was only one tone darker, like his parents had been all out for toffee, then had second thoughts and gave him blue-grey eyes in case someone thought they were batshit. 'You're synchronised, but you've got the Takata #30 Nordic Eye Variation. Family pattern or another reason?'

I impressed myself with that, hoping this would defuse any stupidities I came out with later. The eyes weren't a vanity option, I thought. Takaa Eyes were linked to the expression of key sequences of genes that had only lately been evolved to viable states. They were new, expensive, experimental. They were also incredibly pretty, pale at the centres and fanning out in starry rays to dark outer rings.

I caught myself staring into them and nodded, like I'd been looking for iris flaws and telltales instead of gawping. He was more handsome close to. He even smelled good and this distracted me. I turned back to my dish trying to hold on to my breath and keep that scent as he leaned away, inspection concluded.

'You're very dark for such bright colours.'

'California Tan was the perfect fashion for my mother,' I said, suddenly stabbed by another unexpected pain in the heart. 'I don't even think any of my family knew what California was.'

'Is,' Isylon said cheerfully as we were joined by two more initiates opposite us. 'It's still there. At least I hope it is.'

'I didn't take much interest in Earth.' Anything to do with the origins of Harmony was a no-fly zone for me. Had been.

'Earth History is my passion,' Isylon said, like passion was a word anyone could use at lunchtime and not something only an idiot would say if they wanted to get punched.

All my social warning flashes for the cartels heated my nerves. I looked at the faces of our new companions to test the waters. They seemed pleased, in fact used the statement as a way into the conversation and soon they were deep into some historical chatter about Earth's old states while I studied the rest of the room for exits, weapons and threats with a kind of sad nostalgia. When that sorry moment was exhausted I went back to studying the enemy.

'Unusual to find someone with your look in here,' the dark-haired man opposite said to me and this time I knew I was being tested. 'Facial structure is all out of the intellectual and into the strength and power spectrum. Not saying they can't combine of course but it's a very unusual, almost blasphemic alternative.' He looked at me directly, obviously used to issuing bigass challenges. I got the message – we weren't going to be friends.

But a fight's a fight; I'd take it. '"If thought can't stand friendly criticism, it can't stand." My dad used to say that. Our family was whimsical. Creative. The fiery phoenix to your more plodding workhorse person,' I said, quoting one of Two's favourite sayings and only then wondering where they came from.

There was a startled pause and they all looked at me, noodles adrip on the end of chopsticks. I examined the speaker's face intently. The insult had landed; he was glowering like a wet weekend in the slums. His companion, sensitive and erudite but no less intense, said:

'My mother always told me you can't trust someone who deviates from the eight archetypal modes.' He had the weak chin and collapsed cheeks of the contemplative – where the mind gets pushed inwards on itself by preference and for some reason the skull goes with it. His forehead saved him but he had a mean mouth. He was, like his friend, deeply attuned to the obeying of authority; it was like catnip to them. I read it in their eyes and knew that these were dangerous people, very smart and very alert loyal fans. A brief vision of smashing their heads together gave me pause.

'Creativity requires some experimentation,' Isylon said before I could reply and then went on to talk with them about all he had heard of the latest refinements in spiritual attunement through the latest neural designs; compared to those *in vitro* today everyone present was already so very yesterday, don't you know? He was delightful.

I had to concentrate on eating with the best of manners to cover up the way I was watching them. He was very funny, but not as funny as the pair opposite us made out. I realised that they must know of his status and then I realised what we were doing here – we were sorting out who was going to be trading up.

Well, that made life familiar. Cartels are all about connections.

I thought how Two would have loved this, for the science anyway. She'd have been as keen as me to rip them a new one for other reasons. But while I was wondering what she'd have said Isylon turned his attention back to me. 'So, Nico. Sabadre. Have you been to the Enclave before?'

'Uh, no. First time,' I said, looking at my empty dish. I put my sticks down and gave a hopeful grin. 'Maybe you can show me around if there's time later, once we've moved into the rooms.' Eat that, suckers. We're room-mates.

'Of course,' Isylon said. If he was aware of what was going on he didn't show it. I guessed he was used to being used as a ladder.

I turned to the pair opposite, graciously. 'What about you two?'

They stared at me. 'We live here,' Esan said, the first and darker of the two. He made it sound like everyone who was anyone lived in the Enclave and that was true.

Kyest, the thinkier one, rolled his eyes but part of that was at Esan's childishness. 'If you can't manage it I'm sure we have time to give a tour.' He smiled at me with a cool assessment that promised a lot of trouble if I didn't take up my allotted position at the bottom of the heap real fast.

I glanced at Isylon, eating his food serenely, showing every sign of the grace that priests were famous for. He smiled with his eyes only, which said *No*, but not a No you could do anything about.

Kyest cleared his throat, pushing his bowl away from him untouched. 'There was a rumour about you,' he said to Isylon, conversationally.

I felt the local temperature drop a little.

'Oh?' Isylon said, looking up with every sign of curiosity.

'But of course these things are always coming up,' Esan said quickly as if he was dismissing it, though the opposite was true. His gaze slid over to me, slid back without blinking.

Coming up, hm? 'Huh?' I said, blank of face. 'What do you mean?'

Kyest actually looked uncomfortable, which I thought was

big of him since we were talking about the revelation of a potentially capital crime – unless I was mistaken and Isylon was a closet kleptomaniac or something. Kyest was going for the two sun knockout combo.

Kyest cleared his throat. 'One should never repeat gossip. But once on the lips, always in the memory.' He gave Isylon a glance of apology, who shrugged lightly.

'You're right,' he said.

There was a pause. I noticed people several seats down listening. Even I looked at him.

'That does come up a lot.'

I liked his timing. I found myself grinning and made myself stop.

'Yes, well, only because of what they said about the other Exalted,' Esan said with a dismissive gesture. 'All those test runs but no active responses except in one subject with a double moon. It's bound to be a question for any true scientist, and if it were factual then the conditions of the doubling would suddenly be of great consequence, not to mention something that eludes exacting control. Still.'

Isylon gave a formal smile, composed his hands. 'Quite so. My own status is not Exalted, however. That has yet to be proved. I am merely a channeller and there are plenty of us around.'

I felt a sensation that was entirely new to me. The people in Chaontium were bastards and rejects – scum to a man – and most of us weren't much more than slaves, that was true – but here everyone talked proudly about themselves in terms of being a product and that struck me as way worse. I might be a bit dodgy but at least I wasn't a *thing*.

'Do you have special powers?' Kyest was looking at me, impassive, objective, that cold stare I knew from VanSant, a look which was calculating the value of everything to him personally.

'No.'

'You look as though you should be on the regeneration spectrum to me. Very unusual maxillary proportions. Are you sure?'

'Kyest is a Seer,' Esan said with a veiled pride in their association. Not that veiled.

'I've never been ill, really.' I hadn't thought about it ever, but it was true.

'Maybe you were never badly hurt enough to test it,' Esan suggested with one brow raised in speculation.

Ouch. 'Yeah, that must be it,' I said. 'But I'm not throwing myself off a bridge to answer your question.'

'Don't you have faith in the Overseer?'

I had a lot of feelings about the Overseer, Tecmaten, but faith wasn't one of them. I really know how to walk into these things. 'I have faith that all is as it should be, I don't need demonstrations.'

Isylon glanced at me with approval and I felt a sudden zing of excitement. I wished we could go before Kyest decided he was going to *see* a lot more interesting features about me.

'I'll have to look you up in the Registry,' he said, voicing my worst fear. The Registry would lay out all that I should have been. I'd have to pray it had no lingering connections to what I'd become. Who knew what VanSant had put on record? Everything, most likely. I wondered what Kyest's face would look like when he saw some of that.

I gave him a confident nod, 'You do that.'

I was spared more by the sounding of the bells. We cleared away the meal and were sorted into small groups. Each one was led to a different interview centre where we awaited our inductions. Most people involved themselves with some kind of study on their palmtops. I checked mine and pretended to use it to see if it worked. It brought up the apparent latest on my personal research. Reading the first few excerpts was one of the most surreal experiences of my life. I suddenly realised why appearances were so intensely scrutinised and why my field was worthwhile for the Alchemy.

Your genetic inheritance is all revealed in your face. Kyest could see it intuitively – that's what a Seer was. Faces revealed how 'normative' a person was – Seers vetted on sight. That's why he'd said my upper jaw structure was unexpected for a priest. But it wasn't odd enough to be impossible.

I wondered why Tashin hadn't changed my face at all.

A woman in grey robes walked towards me. 'Nico Sabadre?'

I rose and put the palmtop away, followed the robed woman down some halls to a meeting chamber lit with lamps that mimicked the constellations of the most favoured hour. It was decorated half as a candlelit retreat, half as intimidation chamber. My interviewers sat in a triad on a raised platform, an altar before them holding the sacred signs and sigils of the High Alchemy. I entered and walked to the obvious centre point in a circle of tiling before them, but not so close we'd be anywhere near personal spaces.

I put back my hood correctly. They did not remove theirs and I couldn't see their faces. Their hands were on view, folded on the altar top, right over left to signify mind over nature and possibly to convince me they were alive, because they didn't move a muscle. From the moment the door closed behind the usher an unpredictable, elastic silence began to stretch out.

VanSant had been a jabbery idiot, incapable of waiting a microsecond, but every other cartel don enjoyed a good line of dramatic tension and routinely wrote extra hours into the diary for scaring the crap out of people, maliciously or for laughs. I'd been on the receiving end a few times and here I knew that I couldn't speak first, or at all, without losing. This left us in my other expert ballpark: standing around doing nothing much while you wait for someone else to do something.

I checked out the room, looking for hidden exits, trapdoors, viewing points and handy weapon-like objects, a feat made more interesting by the fact that I couldn't move my gaze from the altar's focal point.

'It is noted that this is your first visit to Harmony Enclave,' the one on the left said eventually, without apparently moving. Her voice sounded like she suspected me of killing children and hiding the bodies under her floorboards. Since it wasn't a question I didn't answer. A frosty minute went by and then the one on the right spoke.

'We have never been out to Sabadre. What is the appeal of such a place, so close to the wall?'

I experienced a blistering second of images, repeating some of what I'd learned at Juliette's behest about my 'home'. None of that had dealt with the wall. I'd never been close to it either, but now I could see a human angle on it – Harmony's border with the neighbouring region – a massive, grey cliff, a klick high, of billions of panels that cut straight up from the sandy ground in a perfectly straight line that ran for thousands of miles in both directions. High on its summit a field blurred the edges of the sky. Drones patrolled in groups of three, no cluster ever out of sight of its comrades. Nothing had ever passed through or over this structure. Anyone in Sabadre could see this wall to their west at any time. They couldn't not see it every day of their lives. I'd never once thought of it until then.

'I have nothing to compare it to,' I said, but I did. In the orphanage we never went beyond the garden wall, high as a cliff to a child, concrete and topped with razor wires. We thought of nothing but what was beyond it. 'But it is habit there to turn one's back to it.'

One of them chuckled, 'Ah, the dislike of so much cold iron, it's only to be expected. We anticipated that such things would happen. Those outlier places are useful in their way though. Speculate?'

It wasn't the iron, though I wouldn't correct him. It was the endless reminder of the unknown. It called so that you feared and longed for it with unbearable intensity. At night when there was nothing to block it out any more the pull of it dragged on your bones, whispering its seductive, thrilling invitation. I just needed to translate that into crapola they would approve of.

'Far from the centre the centrifugal outweighs the centripetal. Unusual mutations and development are more likely. Mental disturbance is more common and rebellion and radicalism encouraged by proximity to the edge.'

I waited, on tenterhooks. Were they going to buy it? There was a level at which that made sense – energy – but the one on which it was pitched – science – transformed it into complete bullshit. Saying it made my mouth taste bad.

'Yes, yes,' the central figure said. His fingers tapped on each other. 'Of course. Some study here will manage to grind off that predictability of yours. Do you have anything new to offer, given that you will be studying alongside one of our better students?'

It occurred to me that this was why I had been able to get into that spot – Isylon was completely from the centre and I was from the rim – it was a simple balancing compensation necessary to produce the tension required for creative work. 'I…' No. My mind was blank. Nothing came because it would have to have been new and I hadn't done my own work.

The priest on the left interrupted anyway, 'There are some cases from this year's Purge that remain to be judged. Please, your considered views. The first – the leader of a child gang that roamed the lower Chaontium levels. The usual crimes: petty theft, trading in illegal paradigms, vandalism, but also the destruction and dismemberment of government property, to wit, two drone police droids and selling of parts of the same.'

There was no way they could know. There was no way.

I was frozen; only years of having to have a good poker face saved me.

'Or the second one,' she said, as if there was all the time in the world and my hesitation had meant nothing. 'A prostitute with a double moon who also acts as a smuggler sourcing medical supplies from Enclave shipments for buyers in the cartels.'

Maybe they didn't know. I wheeled out the safest responses. 'Age of the child precludes capital judgement. Reform school until the age of majority.'

'And the other?'

'The law requires a capital sentence.'

'Do you disagree with the law?' the centre figure asked, quiet but intent.

'I comply with the law.'

'That is your second avoidance. Do you have some criticism to make?'

It was always impossible to know in this kind of situation whether you were about to kill yourself or not. The questions were direct and gave no clue about what kind of answer they expected. I knew the tactic of asking someone to dig their own grave and I felt it loom now at my feet, a beckoning space.

I felt around for my inner Juliette, thought about her shoes. 'Premature termination of any experiment provides less than optimal information and on those grounds I disagree with capital punishment for offences that are not themselves capital crimes.'

'So you don't deem criminal tendencies and double moon to be sufficient information in that particular case?' A note of sarcasm or some related condemnation had leaked into her tone. The central figure leaned forwards a little.

The doubled power was a capital crime, in the book. But it was one of those things that was more hate than Alchemy. Tecmaten was just a bozo who couldn't overcome his personal reactions when he created his edifice of statutes. 'Unless the doubled power is active it makes no difference in the greater Alchemy and it can always be balanced out by the presence of double suns.'

191

I felt warning signs all over. I was meant to be Orthodox. I should have gone for execution and shut up, been dumb, like I looked. I could feel this very clearly now but it was too late, my anger too intense. I began to sweat with the idea that I might have ruined any chance I had now, not only mine but Two's and Tashin's as well and that made me even more angry. I was surprised my clothing didn't catch fire. Into their absence of response I decided I might as well go down burning.

'In addition re your cases: the first, the child, is beyond the scope of germline engineering at this point but within the grasp of social engineering. Their actions are entirely driven by the circumstances of existence in Chaontium. The second is a fault of the state's incubation and development practices and the persistence of natural variation, not the individual concerned.'

There was an instant of wintry silence. Then the left priest spoke. 'So you believe that individual crimes are to be laid at the Alchemy's door?'

'No. Aside from the twin moon. I'm saying that circumstances are outside the reach of the Alchemy.'

I was pretty sure that was heresy. It was certainly more than enough to warrant a trip to the Inquisition. My body was weak at the surface, nothing, a skin of feathers to hide the molten iron that wanted to burst out everywhere, spray all of them, everything. I was fire. I wanted to burn. Their condemnation was the only spark required to set me off.

I was so the wrong person for this job. I had barely even got to the door.

The right priest moved their head slightly, shrugged one shoulder in a movement so slight it must have been involuntary. 'At least you have the conviction to speak frankly. I suppose we must be grateful for small mercies. What is it that you intend to achieve here in your time at Ito?'

Boom. Poof. Extinguished. Smoke rising. Wind blows it away. What? What did I want?

World domination and your extinction, but that might take more than a few months of lab work, to be honest.

I accessed the phrases Tashin had prepared, a robot repeating its code. 'I want to understand the degrees of expression of key personality features within the physical body to complete the Seer's Vision path.'

The left priest sighed audibly. 'You have no aptitude for Seer's Vision, but perhaps... hm, these things can occasionally be learned. Your own germline is part of the Resilience pattern. Have you ever been seriously ill, suffered major or substantial injuries?'

You could say that. 'No.'

'That is rather unsatisfying in terms of experimental data, is it not?'

I thought about it and the implication of it. Satisfying data would be my return to health from near death, I guessed. 'Not to me.'

I felt someone smile, the centre one, I think. The parallel of their implied threat and the one I had received from Esan could not be a coincidence.

'You can go.'

The sudden dismissal took me by surprise but the door was opened and my usher present almost in the same moment. As I followed her into the halls, burned out and clammy, she turned and half-bowed. 'Welcome to Ito, brother. Please, come this way. I shall show you to your room.'

The interview repeated itself a few times in my mind on the way but I couldn't figure out what it meant. I decided to assume the worst and that I was being let go only so that I could be watched. The only question was whether they'd wait to see what I did, or spring their trap early for 'research purposes'.

My usher, a grey shadow of a woman, gave me the full tour of the facility. Halls and galleries, filled with art, rooms on the scale of football fields, laboratories with every instrument built of light in scented mists, Alembics in fractal racks, attended by priests like giant jackdaws hopping from one beckoning cauldron to another... the scale and devotion silenced me. I didn't listen to her words, I trailed after the breadcrumbs of her furry voice like a kid, deeper and deeper into the stranger forests of the Alchemy where all of us were born, where all of us were thought of first and set in motion. It reminded me of clockwork. Everything was calculated. The more I saw this, the more chilled I became. How could anything here be deemed natural or accidental?

In the midst of it all Tashin returned – I felt the coin picked off the glass floor inside me, all my strings gathered in a moment.

Goodness. What happened to you?

I didn't answer. I couldn't. The radical alteration of my perceptions had fundamentally shifted everything about the way I understood the world. Everything was too big and somehow painful. I could avoid the worst of it by drifting after the woman, a ghost of myself, horned and cloven-footed. I saw beyond physical sight. I let Tashin soak up the information of the last few hours in a moment.

Don't panic. You're still good.

If she meant I was still at large, then she was right. Good, no. My usher let me out of the laboratories and gave me my library key. I exchanged pleasantries with her as I spoke with Tashin.

– Where have you been?

The Inquisition has launched a Purge. A war broke out among the cartels as people tried to leap into VanSant's power vacuum. They're preparing for a lockdown. But the rumour about the ship, that it might be here already in-system, waiting ready, and your death – things are very unstable. I can't divide my attention between you and what's going on here. It's not safe.

– Is Two all right?

194

'Here are the cards that let you into your room and your individual Alembic suite,' the usher said, handing them to me as we reached an unmarked door on one curve of a snaking corridor that was featureless. Underfoot the carpet was thick and grey, swallowing all sound.

For now. But my vigilance is required here. Nico, I need you to focus on looking for strange or illegal technicalities in the Alembic records. Especially around the Exaltation.

The door opened silently at the card's touch.

'Is there anything I can help you with before I go?'

'No, thank you,' I said, meaning 'Yes, get me another life and another task. One I can do. Let me out of here.'

To Tashin I said,

– I don't know how long I can last in here. It's not my game.

The usher bowed to me and I bowed to her. She left and the door closed behind her.

Just focus on the job at hand.

I looked around. My room was austere but pleasant. My belongings were set in the middle of the floor ready to be unpacked. A second door opened into the Alembic – a miniature version of the vast laboratories I'd seen before. On its other side the second room, Isylon's room, was dark and vacant. I wondered what induction he was having. Maybe it was tea and cakes, a little light banter about social matters.

– So, you're not reliable. You won't be around to save me with a quick quip.

You didn't want me around anyway.

– I suddenly missed you while I was facing discovery and torture. Funny that. And I thought you were interested in this priest.

The Exalted. Yes. Learn everything about him.

– Sugar on a shovel, Tash, you must be in it up to the eyeballs to give away your candy like this.

As you so crudely put it, we're all up to the eyeballs here.

Dann seeded a rumour that the ship Switch was still in VanSant's possession and now they're busy ripping up every warehouse, dock and apartment he ever came within a breath of. That's why the Inquisition are here, too. They want to make sure they get it.

– What if they figure this out? Why didn't you change my look?

I don't know if you noticed but there's nobody in Chaontium with the surgical skills to give you a new face, and certainly not one that would fit your gene profile. The only reason I could give Two the Switch is because it virtually installs itself. The chances of anyone recognising you are almost nonexistent. Please think before you open your lunking great mouth again.

I'd never thought about the mismatch of a face and a germ-line being the reason not to change it, which was pretty funny when it wasn't busy being tragic. I hadn't understood that a new face meant a whole new me, when I'd be surrounded by people who can read your being in your features and had the science to back it up. Duh. Tashin was laughing at me, but in the way you laugh at someone crazy who's holding a loaded gun: because things can't get any more dangerously stupid. I felt sorry for an instant.

– I'm just sayin' I don't like any of this.

Your feelings are noted in the book of tragically lost causes. I'll be back as soon as I can. Her anxiety was like a crackling cloud of static, prickling in tiny volts around my skull.

– Yeah, sure. Whatever. Keep Two safe for me.

And there I was, alone in comfort and security with nothing to do but shuffle fancy clothing around into the right wardrobes while my place was occupied by – well, I'd never even seen Tashin in a fight. I'd no idea if she was up to the job.

I sighed and wondered if searching for surveillance cameras was too obvious. Of course it was. I willed myself to the magic way of the Switch as I went to sort my things out. Thinking of it as magic made me smile, well, it nearly moved my face. Look at me, the sceptic cynic getting all whiffy-whoffy about his tech.

It was quite the stoner to realise, two minutes later, that there was no surveillance of the rooms at all, only a copy feed of the Alembic data to see whatever was being done in there. Unheard of. Did they *trust* each other or what? I demanded a recount but no matter how many times I demanded a different answer the result remained – my bones said no, there was no observation in here, no secret door, nothing but the temple's huge stonework and its hive of virtuous labourers, serfs and overseers. No technological observation anyway.

I glanced up suddenly, sure I'd seen a shadow move at the edge of Isylon's room door, but when I looked there was nothing. The steady floor lighting of the lab glowed softly, uninterrupted. My skin felt strange, though, so I went across and stuck my head around the door. Nothing but a mirror image of my room with a box trunk on the floor and a canvas tote at its side. He travelled pretty light.

As I came back through the lab I saw a flash at the corner of my vision. I thought maybe a light had blown, but a couple of blinks later everything looked normal and there was no sign of anything being damaged.

Before paranoia could really grip me I set about the complex task of changing clothes. Off came the formal robes of sanctity and in came a much more practical set of grey overalls, that particular shade that represented elision – smudged out of existence as an individual one is ready to work unencumbered by ego. It was warm and functional. It might have been made for me. Only my great unease with the place I was in made me shiver. I didn't want to feel so at home that I slipped up.

I'd nearly found a place for everything when I heard the outer door on the opposite side open and close, the usher's voice repeating her query. I busied myself fiddling with the lighting as I listened to the noises of departure, unsure as to whether I should be friendly or respectfully distant. I hadn't seen anyone here who looked like they barged around, disarming people with a grin as they nosed where they weren't supposed to be. In addition, my mind kept straying to Chaontium with longing thoughts of easy violence. So I was surprised when Isylon appeared in my doorway and knocked a quick three-rap announcing himself.

'Did I make you jump?'

'Yeah.' I straightened up and turned, everything in my brain going quiet at the sight of him in the glowing uplight – the contrast of the robes of doom and his casual posture, head to one side, a grin on his face, a bit of a quizzical expression around his eyes as if I might be funny but I was certainly interesting. It all hit me like a punch in the gut with a dandelion clock fist. Hit me hard and I like it. Hit me softly and apparently I buckle like cheap wet paper.

'Are you all right?' Concern added more charm to him.

No. I'm staring like a drunk at an unopened vodka bottle. I had to cut this out before the depth of my attraction became unmistakable. My body was smiling in every cell like it recognised its forever home. This is it. This is the one. Catch it. Keep it.

'I'm fine.' Fine and dandy, cat with the cream. 'How did your induction go?'

'Ah, it was a formality,' he said, glancing around my room and then back at me. He blinked a couple of times with a curious little nod to himself. 'Mostly they ask about my father and his work. Then they ask if I've performed any miracles lately. I say no. Then we're done.' A twinge of something sour turned the left side of his mouth down. 'And you?'

'The same,' I said. 'Minus the miracle part.' I hesitated, seeing that for some reason I had his attention. I wanted to keep it. 'Oh, and they asked me to sentence some criminals.'

He blinked.

'You know us people from the edges,' I found myself saying,

198

wishing I hadn't as soon as it was out because I sounded like a blithering idiot. 'Always too radical. They must think I'm here to poison you with my ideas.'

He shrugged, tipped his head the other way. 'Maybe I'm here to poison you.' Then he smiled, faintly. 'Reclaim you to the fold, I should have said.'

'But there is something like that going on? We are here on purpose, to cause some change that they want to study?'

He made an equivocal face that became harder as he spoke. 'Always. Action, reaction; salt, metal, water, fire.' Talk of the Alchemy made him heavy again, crushed his shoulders a bit lower, his head drooped down. I noticed a fine line of sweat at his hairline.

'You're tired of it?'

His eyes turned, head stayed still, calculating, much like I'd seen him in the first photo – out of contact – but then he relented. 'I know they placed you here deliberately, either as a reagent or a catalyst. I'm tired of knowing those things, tired of everything being an experiment.'

'So you thought you'd befriend the catalyst?'

His grin returned. I felt an inner click, then a slight fall as if two interlocking pieces of a puzzle key had matched; we got each other. Catch it, keep it.

'I like to adjust the parameters,' he said, waggling his eyebrows until he felt foolish and shook it off. He cleared his throat and looked aside, searching for a way out. 'Did you leave a lot behind? I mean family. People.'

'Sister,' I said, deviating from the background story without thinking about it, thinking of Two. I realised my mistake but it was too late. 'But other than that, no. They were killed in an accident. It's just us.'

'Oh, I'm sorry.' He made the sign of peace for the past with his hand and retreated a step.

'It was a long time ago,' I said. 'So, at dinner, those two

fools...' asking his opinion of the two who'd spoken to us – though I wasn't asking about that; I was asking for us to bond over them, either way. Whatever he said I'd agree with.

'Don't worry about what they said.' He leaned on the door frame, willing to stick around a bit longer. 'They're kind of... the undead.'

I nodded, feeling comfort as if it was natural for him to state this kind of dangerous opinion and I was free to agree or disagree without causing trouble. As if we lived in a safe place. He peered at me, gauging my reaction. Talking to strangers can be too easy, but he'd given me the connection as I asked for it. In words I'd have used, though he didn't even know me.

I smiled at him because I agreed. Flirting with strangers can be too easy, too. I felt that sensation of being one step from the precipice.

He absorbed my reply and stayed put; glanced away though I thought his eyes had darkened.

'Those two are just afraid,' he said, because we were all afraid.

'What of? They've got it made. Here they are.' Here *we* are.

'Do *you* have it made?'

He was good at the feint and switch. I turned and lifted my chin so he could see my face properly, feeling a death's head grin on me. I was on fire again, in a completely different way; but it doesn't matter why you're burning, at the end you're still toast. The reaction between us was simple combustion. 'Oh yeah. I've totally got it made.'

He kept my gaze for a long moment and then smiled before a sudden shyness cut it off. He went back to his room, ducking away with a speed that ceded me the bout and left me wishing it would never end.

I wondered what I was going to do with this horrifying sense of lightness and air that had filled me up from top to toe.

Three Threes – the charm

Although the Ito Retreat was in the midst of the Enclave and at an elevation of more than twenty decks above ground, it maintained a stone theme which extended to odd granite towers on the exterior platforms. A huge arboretum was housed in an atrium at its heart, open to the sky. The entrances by the temple where we'd come in were all modern but inside, and on its private decks, Ito was one big garden crisscrossed with both ground-level and aerial paths in the form of an ancient Earth mandala that meant a big deal. We were high up, in a building festooned with flowering vines. Our personal rooms had no exterior openings, but our laboratory did. It had doors which gave onto a deck where you could enjoy the canopy of the mock woodland. Birds fussed and rustled in the twisted old growth of ivy beside the frame. Insects hummed, giving the air a syrupy quality. Tiling and wooden block seats denoted it an area for contemplation.

I sat on the floor at the centre of the sun's symbol, crossed my legs, rested my hands and thought that here, in the bird garden of the damned, I could at least manage sitting meditation for the first time. But after a minute of quiet I found myself turning to that strange ur-space at the left back of my head. It was that or think about Isylon so the ur-space was winning hands down.

As soon as my attention landed on it I saw the way it

expanded out of my mind's limit – I was a fractal mote on the edge of a far vaster space and time. This vastness shared my awareness but not my form. I thought this was the ship mind. It seemed inactive. I *asked* for a total scan of the immediate environment, to know where everything was and what it was doing. There was a pause as long as one of my heartbeats after which I knew what I wanted to know: the information from that greater entity replicated immediately in the small mote.

The ship insisted that there was an astonishing lack of spyware everywhere in the Enclave and not simply in my part of it. I sat with this uncomfortably. It didn't ring true.

During my childhood everything was spied upon with cameras, peepholes, secret mirror glass – there was no privacy of any kind and if you thought there was you soon learned otherwise. I'd assumed that everything in Ito was like this, just as everything in Chaontium rested on ratting other people out. Only the cartel bosses could get their hands on technology and that was used exclusively for the security of their personal castles. But after a minute or two of contemplation I started to understand that Ito had tattlers of its own kind. It had Confessors and preferment for weasels. I hadn't noticed the resemblance because I was so unused to thinking of other humans having abnormal powers of observation but Confessors were walking truth extractors, or viewers; I wasn't sure how they worked but there were plenty of them about. I was wrong about the spying. They were everywhere, in fact.

Once I realised this I immediately felt at home. I couldn't say at ease, there was nothing *easy* about anywhere I'd ever lived – but it was familiar, I knew how it worked. We were all the police and we were all the suspects. *Do not engage* had become my mantra from the first minute I could think my way through it. I figured that people were all crazy and they'd never get out alive. If I was going to get out then I couldn't engage with their bullshit. I'd use it, abuse it and move on but never believe a single word. It was a deadly game where nothing was real but the consequences.

Only I was real. My head was sacrosanct. Nobody got in. And I had my minotaur in my gut.

My head *used* to be sacrosanct. I looked at my co-host again and it was so vast, it made me nothing. Then, without warning, the sense of scale switched around. I was huge. It was infinitesimal. I liked that for a moment. The scale then began to oscillate back and forth. I was an eye winking at itself. I felt sick.

I opened my eyes with an involuntary yell and the feeling that I'd been pulled apart and all my insides were on the outside. Really, *really* needed my swearing back. 'Aaagh' did not cut it as an expletive for existential destruction.

Isylon came out of the laboratory – I heard his shoes whisper across from the wood to the tile. 'Nico?'

'I'm all right,' I said. 'Fell asleep. Had a bad dream.'

There was a pause as there always is when someone is deciding whether or not to go with your implausible excuse.

'OK. I'll be in here.' Excuse accepted. Obvious stated.

He padded off and I heard the soft chimes of his Alembic restarting its program.

His kindness in view of my role here made me feel like crap. I hated lying to him. It felt like lying to my old master about the Pit. Their being lies of omission didn't lessen their power. In a world of liars she had always been straightforward and honest. I felt that I couldn't give her anything other than my honesty in return so I tried not to give her anything, but the nothing spoke volumes anyway. I felt a pang of longing, but what was the point? What's gone is gone.

A shimmer caught my attention and I looked out at the arboretum. The leaves and branches shifted in the breeze. For a moment I thought I'd seen a shadow winding between them but when I looked straight at it there was no sign. Every leaf was sharp-edged, every shadow dancing with its caster. This had been more like smoke. It had possessed an aliveness in its movement that was nothing to do with the weather.

I looked at the sky, testing my eyes, but nothing floated against the cloudy grey. I'd have dismissed it except for the uneasy but very distinctive feeling of being watched. The skin between my shoulder blades prickled as all my external senses, even my Switched ones, insisted there was nothing extra, nothing out of place while my intuition screamed at me that we were under the microscope.

I couldn't understand this paranoia. I had enough real stuff to be concerned about and I'd checked a million times but this conviction that I was observed directly would not shift.

In desperation I tried to ping Tashin for information but she didn't reply. My mind supplied a montage of arrests, beatings, tortures to fill the gap; the Inquisition spared no efforts when they wanted something found. Any loose tongues could easily put Two and Tashin within their grasp.

The itch to do something violent and decisive ran through me, making my hands shake.

I had to act.

I got up and turned my back on the silently screaming trees to go into the laboratory and try doing what Two was so good at – research. If I couldn't help them directly I could get on with fulfilling the conditions of my parole as fast as humanly possible. If someone noticed my deviation from the timetable, then so what? I'd say inspiration had struck.

Some revolutionary's research-fu had been good because I found myself easily able to activate my Alembic's virtual machinery. Vague intimations of thought brought possibilities streaming out into glowing holographic visuals that expressed what I'd never be able to say aloud. I started to understand why Two liked sitting in her sling all day; it was exhilarating to think this way, like thinking with godly power. She'd never had an Alembic. I don't know what her vision was like, or her mind.

I'd taken everything she said as gospel because she was smart and plugged in and I – wasn't. Now I'd got this to play with it was like having a moment's insight into how it felt to be Two.

I missed her. She would have loved this. It would have been her element. I could hear her in my mind's ear, talking a mile a minute with impassioned force about Tecmaten's acquisition of older thought systems and folk wisdoms: '...and yet, his real evil is his sheer unimaginative banality. Creating this pathetic *bolster* to shore up a childish insistence that the way of Harmony and eugenic perfectionism was the ultimate good for all. Like Utopia wasn't a dirty word. No sacrifice left unbled to prove what his ego has to have true. Toss in some half-assed desert religion morality and a desperate desire never to die and voilà! – the Alchemy, a concept album cover for a fascist totalitarian state!'

Then she'd start singing, 'Dess-tin-*eee*,' in a mockery of a popular song and I'd be telling her to stick it in her kitbag and shove a sock in it whilst being pleased that she was my friend and glad she could hate things that clearly and out loud. Having it said was a kind of relief. All I felt up until then was the steady, skull-burst pressure build of a lifelong loathing with nowhere to go. Listening to her was a safety vent that kept me calm.

'You like that song?'

I looked around, startled, to find Isylon standing at the edge of my Alembic's outer rim, eyebrows raised.

'What?'

'You were humming "Destiny of the Ancients".' He looked amused though his smile faded fast. Beneath his eyes were heavy dark rings. I got the feeling that he was doing the same as I was – searching for a distraction from something that bothered him.

'I uh... didn't realise I was doing it.'

'It's a bit of an earworm,' he said and I nodded quickly.

'I can't stand it,' I admitted.

'I'm not sure anyone can. What're you working on? Is that your germline code?'

Was it? I'd been thinking, not reading. 'It's a bit easier to work with something you have a direct insight into,' I said.

He nodded, studying the display with me. He was so at ease that his question caught me off guard. Again. I was going to have to up my game.

'Did my father send you here?'

I turned to look at him but he didn't look up from the Alembic display.

I never liked being on the back foot. 'Why do you ask that?'

'You don't feel like a priest to me,' he said, still polite, still studying the workings of comparison between the outright raw germ data and the actual present-day expression – the DNA and the me it had become after years of iteration.

I thought about the lead-lined starship in the mantle of the gas giant and a few bars of 'Don't Look Down' went through my head. In all that had happened I'd forgotten Isylon could pick up vibes and read them like signed affidavits. I couldn't answer because he was right, I didn't feel like a priest.

'It doesn't matter,' he added. 'I guess you have your reasons for being here. Though I am fascinated to know how you survived this long.'

I looked across at him and found that I suddenly didn't like the idea of being shopped to the authorities and executed. He could easily do it. He'd seen through my cover.

'You're thinking of someone else, someone left behind,' he said, glancing up past that curtain of hair, his gaze suddenly acute. I recognised a hunter on the scent.

'I don't wanna be rude or anything but, what's it to you?' Aaand stonewall. Let's see how you like that.

He straightened up a bit to face me, hair out of the way. 'I want to get to know you better.'

Wow, full frontal assault. He was confident.

'And if I don't want to? I came here to study.' Let's see if he reacts to irritation.

'I'm studying right now, Nico. I'm studying you.'

And again the straight jab. He used my name. Such a power play. I grinned at him and his smile answered slowly. A dance it is, a fight it is, then.

I was charmed. 'What's your dad got to do with it?'

'He's kept very close track of me in the past,' Isylon said, turning a bit so he could read something in the Alembic which was set at an angle to him. 'It wouldn't have surprised me if he'd paid someone to report back.'

'In case you stray?'

'I think in case I'm endangered, but for the sake of appearances, yes, it does look like in case I stray.'

'And why would you be endangered?' Why would you stray, more to the point? Tell me, so I can help you do it.

He slid his hands into the pockets of his linen trousers and shrugged languidly. 'There have been threats from some revolutionary group targeting me for kidnap and extortion. And if not that then we always have people at dinner using the soup spoons to pry into my private life. A great many people would derive great satisfaction from holding a death sentence over my head while they suck up to me in public.'

Now his smile was knowing – he looked sweet as a pie saying 'how'd you like them apples, bro?'

He knew. And I knew he knew. And he knew that I knew that he knew.

'You're not telling me, in a very coded way, that you are what they think you are.'

He smiled, watching me with a curious fascination, his lips slightly parted, so I guess I was giving the goods away so effectively that I might as well be parading them before him on a conveyor belt. All I could think of was the last thing I wanted to: hot, sweaty, full-on sex.

I turned to Isylon – might as well finish it since I was out for the count. 'That goes double for me.' My voice was throaty and a bit giddy, lurching upwards at the end as self-consciousness kicked in full volume because such an admission really put me in the shit now I thought of it, and then it struck me – I understood the gravity of what I was doing. It was very unlikely either of us, any of us, were going to get out of this alive. I'd admitted the inadmissible and my prize was to let go of it and find out that it had been conveniently hiding the true peril I was in. I felt dizzy and had to put my hand out onto the Alembic's frame.

Isylon stopped partway through a shaky inhale and whatever he was going to say became, 'Nico?'

'Post-traumatic stress,' I said, anger replacing disappointment fast as light.

I felt suddenly gutless. My dreams of escape were dead and trying to drag me to the grave but sod that, gutless and apparently shirtless and clueless I was going to forge the heck on. And I wanted my swearing back so badly it hurt. I had to have a recovery moment. Where was old horns'n'tail when I needed him?

'If you're twin sun and your family knew, why did they let you live?' I said.

'Why did yours let you?'

'I'm an orphan. A pre-parent orphan,' I said to clear it up after he looked nonplussed. Under Harmony law a defect found after it was considered too late to abort had to be allowed to grow to adulthood to give it a fair chance of being somehow nurtured into the shape nature didn't want to make. After the age of majority a life on the poorest rung of society awaited the breathless survivors, and a lifetime of pious gratitude to the state for permitting them a second chance, but nobody was going to waste actual parenthood on that.

He nodded. 'I wasn't spotted until much later and I was part of an Alchemical project that was too important to stop at the time.'

I felt that gutless sensation alter to its opposite. We were actually having this conversation! It damned us, but it was on the way to clearing my exit at the same time. Excitement and the sense of intimacy it created made me able to say only one word in reply. 'Exaltation.'

He smiled with a bitter twist of his mouth. 'Part of the legendary grail within which we forge a new humanity free from illness and death.'

'Yeah, I read the brochure, it's very impressive.' He was hurt, I could feel it, but still feisty. I approved of that. What doesn't kill you makes you bitter.

'That's heresy. But I'll allow it.' His smile became amused. His expression sparkled with life.

Time to poke harder. 'You're your father's science experiment?'

'Warm and delightful story, isn't it? Not that he doesn't care, don't think it's as cold as that. If he didn't I wouldn't be here.'

'Everyone's an experiment in something.'

'*Now* you sound like a priest.' He flicked his fingers and my Alembic displayed the particulars of my make-up in a different format. He peered at it closely. 'But why are you here really? What do you want?'

I looked at the same place he was poking around in: the fusion of the elements. Metal, metal, earth, earth. I was ore made to heat and bend. I was tough. I wasn't the luminiferous aether of air and fire of which most great minds were made. I was some kind of large blunt basic implement, or a rock.

I gave up the game. I'd lost it anyway. 'I came to kill you, or to save myself.'

He watched me for a minute's worth of calculations and I tried hard not to flinch from his stare. 'I vote for the second.'

I nodded. 'That might not exclude the first.'

He seemed to sink on himself. 'I don't get it. You're telling the truth, but why would you do that here, now?' Bafflement creased his forehead.

'Because I don't want to kill you. It'd be like killing me. And I've had enough of that.'

His eyes widened enough to show the whites all the way around briefly. At last he said, 'Well, this was very unexpected. A disillusioned assassin. But my original impression remains the strongest.'

'And what was that?'

He was nervous. 'Sulphur and quicksilver.'

He was talking about the Alchemical Wedding, where mysticism, symbolism and reality met to give rise to a new kind of being. I didn't miss the wedding part. He was quicksilver.

I felt seen and vulnerable, excited and ready to go, go, go. Have to put a stop to that. Let's talk some more about stuff I don't care about. 'Not male and female?'

He grinned and shook his head. I bet he'd got my *Yes. You caught me, now keep me,* way before I came up with my delaying tactic. 'Ahh, the sticking point of so much theology, experiment, theory, formulae and agony.'

'Strike you as odd that so many Alchemically powerful people don't fit the prescription?'

'They fit it perfectly. The mistake is in translating a spiritual equation about balance into a material universe as if they are interchangeable.' He paused and bitterness filled his tone. I felt the tide of the moment turn in him, surging inward. From then on he seemed to talk against his will, biting words out and regretting them on the spot but they wouldn't be stopped.

'I was convinced before I came here that revealing this flaw in the translation of spirit to matter was my destiny. In rewriting the theory, fixing the Alchemy's mistakes, I would bring about a re-evaluation of Harmony. I am the revolutionary. I was. But ...' he stopped there, mid-sentence, staring at me.

We were on the cliff's edge and I felt the jump call. The slightest touch would put him over the brink. He wanted to tell me more than he wanted to hide. 'But?'

His face became masklike. 'But that was naive. Do you know what they asked of me in my interview?'

I shook my head – obviously I didn't – but I could feel an oncoming rush of energy as clearly as if it had pressed a wave of air over me and I knew that here was what was eating Isylon.

'They brought in a body. A child. Lately dead. An Inquisition execution. Electrocution, I believe. They wanted me to resurrect it, if I could.' His hands had become pale fists at his sides. 'I wasn't sure whether or not they had killed him only for this moment – I asked what the crime was. They said that he was the leader of a gang: theft, fencing, the usual things. Petty things. He didn't have any shoes.'

My skin had become cold, icy.

'I put my hands on him,' Isylon said, holding them out in a copy of the gesture, looking at the space between them. His voice faltered, the cool calm recollection of a scientist lost in a bewildered, childlike shock. 'He was warm. I could feel the spirit around him, broken in bits, some of it trying to leave. It didn't know what had happened. It asked me why he couldn't get up and open his eyes. I could feel that there was a way. I could push the spirit back and its presence would let the heart start again. He could live. But if I did that – they might kill him again. I don't know how many times they could do that and ask me to... do this.' His hands moved slightly, pressing, pressing the invisible.

'I didn't want to hurt him but I couldn't think of a way to get him out of it. So I cut him free. He clung to me as hard as he could. He was desperate not to let go. He was terrified because he had no idea what was happening. But I made him go. Every last bit of him. In pieces. Into the darkness. Alone. And I said No. No, I can't bring him back. He's dead.' He lifted his hands up, air-light, and slowly let them sink back to his sides. He exhaled, slowly.

I believed him, but every word he'd said had undone my

211

world. There were no souls. Were there? I didn't want anything to exist that could make the Alchemy more plausible for a microsecond. But he had told the truth.

Seconds passed. I knew that whatever I said next would make or break whatever lay between us but I didn't know what he was asking for. I wasn't sure what I was giving. I might've approached it differently to him, but only because I'd have killed everyone in the room first.

'You did the right thing.'

'I know I did!' he yelled and spun around on his heel. He threw his hands out, shaking them as if he got rid of some filth on them. 'But everything I thought up until then, every hope I had for reform for—' He made a spitting noise of contempt. 'It was stupid. For nothing. A waste of time. If people will do this there is nothing that can move them. Not a damn thing. What would my great rewriting be? Buried, burned. I'm here only to fulfil Tecmaten's great work and if I don't do that I'm nothing. And if I do do that then this continues for ever or until—' He broke off. I could hear sobbing in his tone though he didn't show another sign of it.

I didn't want to insult him with sympathy. Your world breaks, you give it space to fall.

I gave him a minute, then – 'You know, it goes both ways.'

'What does?' He was so confused and guilt-ridden and focused on being a good guy I knew he'd never think of it on his own.

'Resurrection. If you can put it back you can take it out. I'm just saying, you're not looking at the whole picture.' *You could send them to eternity in a heartbeat*, is what I didn't say, but it hung there between us like a huge, open maw.

He took in a breath with a sharp rasp. His head moved as if it wished it would move him back in time, around some corner. He looked at me. 'I'm – not ready for this. I need to be alone for a while to collect my thoughts. I'll see you at evening prayer,

212

assuming you don't finish me off before that. I wouldn't blame you if you did.'

'Killing you wasn't my first order,' I said and put out my hand to forestall him leaving.

He half turned back, reluctantly, listening. 'Oh?'

'Don't you want to know whose ticket this is all on? You're not the teensiest bit curious?'

'Ticket. You mean who might want me dead? The details don't matter. If anyone in Harmony proper had wanted it they could do so by far easier means than finding you and creating a ridiculous scene.' Even though he was still talking sense his face was grey. He sounded like he didn't care what happened to him. 'Knowing wouldn't help me to stop them.'

I babbled, false cheer coming out of me in its inappropriate, gleeful way as I attempted to fix the hopelessly unfixable: 'Yeah, my boss doesn't want you dead, that would only be if things went wrong and it had to be covered up. They want me to find proof of wrongdoings in the Alchemy that violate Harmony's status as a specially exempt state so that a ton of galactic justice can fall on Tecmaten's head from on high. They're some offworld cowboy gunning for him for personal reasons which somehow tie into some kind of Diaspora police system. So they said. I can't pretend I'm being told the truth, but that's what I'm here for. If I can find it then according to my plan we're good to go.' I stopped.

He nodded, humouring the psycho so I'd shut up. 'That's very interesting. I need time to think. Excuse me.' He gently unhooked his arm from my grasp.

I let him go and his door closed at his back.

I stood with the lit patterns of my germline code shining all over me like cheap giftwrap. I wondered what that kid's name had been and what had happened to his shoes, if he'd ever had any. Would I be afraid when the Inquisition came? Would I beg for my life when begging was all there was left? Was Two somewhere out there in the same night wondering the same thing? If all that's left is one more minute and you can get one more by sacrificing up others, would you?

I'd forgive her. The silence from her was killing me.

As soon as I recognised it weakening me I crushed that line of thought and went back to work, searching for the material that Tashin insisted must be somewhere in the massive archives of the Alembics. It had to be there, because even if the secret of life was written out right in front of me my ambitions had changed. I didn't just want to escape and forget. I wanted the proofs of the crimes and then I wanted them all dead. In the absence of proof I'd settle for dead.

Many long hours later, Isylon ghosted out of his room and back into the laboratory. He walked straight up to me and waited for my attention.

I was weary from standing so long, reading and thinking. A lot had passed under my radar and I'd run into problems, the worst of which was that I could not access germline data from the Exaltation program. It was out of my area of expertise so the system did not allow it. I'd been thinking I could ask Isylon about it, supposing I wasn't on a torture rack somewhere after he changed his mind about handing me over. For him that was the most sensible course of action. I wouldn't have blamed him. I was obviously incompetent at subterfuge and a blabber of secrets. Nothing to inspire confidence there plus my crazy story. But here he was.

I closed down the systems and looked up at him. A strange vibrancy about him made me wonder if he was high. I'd felt it off VanSant several times, when he was on drugs, raving about his ambitions. Come to think of it he'd sounded that way when he told me about the Switch and now the same quality set my nerves on edge. He was here to dish out my fate. The next few minutes could not move fast enough.

214

'I've been part of this for far too long,' Isylon said, with measure, rehearsed and still rehearsing like he'd struggled to find the words. 'I thought you'd come to help me. I mean: that you'd be some kind of key to my work in proving the mistaken basis of the energy doubles.'

He stopped and started again. 'You did help me. Not in the way I planned, but it's better it went this way. I bet everything on my research working out but since the interviews I see that's just fiddling with the details of a much greater insanity. There's no possibility of changing this from within. There is no foundation for the Alchemy as the system of the world in science, only as a sociological system.' He smiled wanly, as you would before you apologetically threw up a friend's terrible cooking. He looked embarrassed and deeply sad, continuing, 'But, even that's nothing. Once I looked at it all from that angle I realised that the real trouble is the people who all benefit from things as they are. They'll never give it up. And I'm one of them. How can I criticise it when I'm part of it? I have been here, holding this up fervently, thinking that it was the Alchemy that required adjustment. You must think I'm a real idiot, that I knew what was going on all along...'

I started to say No but he held his hand up and I shut up.

'Now that I've done what I've done to that boy I can't stand by while these cruelties go on.' He looked me in the eye and a certain steel came over him, straightening his spine and lifting him a good two inches in height. 'I don't know if you have justice on your mind at all. I don't know if what will happen will bring only greater evils that I can't see yet, but I can't not act. I can't live with myself if I do nothing, because I've spent so long asleep and we are already here.' He stopped, looking frustrated, impatient, hand moving before his face as if he was trying to extract a better vision from himself, or something he couldn't articulate but wanted me to know.

I waited, not sure if I'd heard him right. He was going to

help me? I'd never seen anyone turn around this fast before. I wondered if he was stable, mentally, but then who was I to judge? It had taken only hours for me to unhinge in here and start shooting off the secrets like firecrackers at the end of Purge night.

He rubbed his hand compulsively across his forehead with a scrubbing action that looked painful and restless. A few deep breaths later and he was composed again although he'd aged about twenty years in the last ten seconds. 'Look, Nico, I'm going to help you get what you want and get out of here, whatever it leads to. But there isn't much time. A day at best before one of us will undergo Confession. Then it's over. So tell me what you need to know.'

He had changed completely from the cool confidence of the afternoon. All I felt from him was exhaustion and the kind of insistent doggedness which comes from trying to suppress despair. A frisson of relief that my time hadn't arrived yet was washed away by a grim sadness for him. I stepped out of the Alembic towards him but he backed off. Comfort can be worse than pain when it threatens to take away your suffering and suffering's all you've left to cling to. I got that. I stayed where I was and tried to make my voice calm and gentle.

'I'm not sure exactly what I'm looking for. Something which proves beyond doubt that the Alchemy is using outworld technology when it makes people. I don't think it matters who, but we suspected the Exalted line because you're so weird. Unlikely. I mean, supernatural has to be super technology doesn't it?' It came out more insulting than I intended but it was too late to take it back.

'Reality is very much a matter of interpretation,' he said stiffly and I knew we were both thinking about the dead kid but I shook my head at him anyway.

'No, it really isn't.'

'You don't believe me. That there is such a thing as spirit, aether, call it whatever you want.'

'It doesn't matter what anyone believes right now,' I said, weaselling and hating myself for it but getting bogged into philosophy wasn't going to happen on my watch. 'Reality is: I need evidence and you can help me find it and that's it. Here. Now.'

He struggled not to snap at me. It was obvious that a host of burning issues were eating him up and twisting his features with disgust but after a few moments of internal wrestling he bit out, 'Very well. You won't find the data you're looking for in any of the Alembic mandalas available to us. I've been through it enough times to know.' He was ashen but as he kept on speaking and thinking his voice came back on an even keel. 'Consider: if you want to prove that I am part of a procedure involving alien tech; wouldn't it be in me right now?'

'It might, but if it's purely biological or its work was done *in vitro* then it won't show up in any scan we can perform for that. I was more hoping that you may not have been given the real data to work with.'

He opened and shut his mouth. He really had been a believer. It hadn't occurred to him that anything he worked with could be censored. I saw this fresh disappointment crash over him in a wave but he was getting used to the ebb and flow now and within a minute he was back.

'You don't think that in all these years of testing it would have been found out somewhere?'

Nice try. 'Do you believe that everything in Harmony works as it says it does? If you're a special snowflake that has to pass muster until the day you graduate because you're being farmed, don't you think you would work as you do and find what you find? What if there's a layer of priests higher than you know, fixing everything, telling nobody? Even Tecmaten could be a voicebox.'

217

He made an ugly face of dislike and suspicion. 'I cannot prove otherwise so let's assume that is possible, even though it makes our situation more hopeless. I still think the first thing we should do is test my germline from a sample taken now. I'm sure doing so will draw suspicion but I don't see another way forward. It could be that evidence is there but was never looked for previously, so was never found. Perhaps we can say it was for your research, because I am a convenient subject.' As he started to plan, even though it was weak, he began to look better.

I wanted numbers. 'By *draw suspicion* what action are we talking about and how long before it starts?'

He ran both hands through his hair, tugging it backwards. It made the whites of his eyes flare for a moment, he did it so hard. 'They check the Alembic data every half a day or so as standard but I can't say when. So hours rather than minutes. Action is most likely to be an investigation, so – Inquisitors or a Confessor. If they have no suspicion so far they'll assume scientific interest first but if they have an eye on you or me then they'll be a lot faster. Is that vague enough? Besides, as I speak I realise that if you're right about things being hidden there's no reason to think this Alembic will deliver the truth to us.'

He was right. Trying it was more trouble than it was likely going to be worth. 'Is there anywhere we can go, or anything we can do to get more data out of the system? Some access point that wouldn't be compromised by secrecy?'

He thought it over, eyes closing in concentration. 'No. Perhaps Tecmaten's personal Alembic, supposing he is the one orchestrating and not merely a front. Or the Exaltation Alembic itself, but that is in use and guarded at all times.' He sighed heavily, arms folded. 'There's a second option. We can fabricate your evidence, but since we don't have access to genuine alien tech that could backfire badly when it fails inspection by some greater expert.' He sighed. 'Maybe we should keep with tradition – would a confession suffice? Suppose someone who was part of the Exaltation project were to admit contagion with foreign technology?'

A speed check returned a positive response in my onboard, silent AI. 'If it was by someone in authority.'

'Then I can call my father and ask him. You could eavesdrop on the conversation.'

'He'd know about this kind of thing?'

'He's Inner Council. And he did make me, albeit under Tecmaten's supervision. If the idea of using alien gear is all new to him I'll know, he won't be able to hide it from me. If he does know then he might admit it and try to stop me from making trouble. But if it is new to him then he'll start an investigation and we're back in the Inquisition. Even in the best case you're going to be first to come under suspicion and you won't survive it.'

I nodded and noted his harrowed look as I took up the offer. Calling his father implicated him in whatever followed. The whole family might be pulled into it. He would have betrayed them all and I knew he must be thinking of this. I saw no other choice. I filed away my feelings carefully for later use against those responsible for it all. 'Call him.'

'He'll be at evening services,' Isylon said, tersely. 'I'll do it when he's at home. Besides, as soon as I do that then there will be no time for you and me to talk. As it is, the evening is young and prayers are not until midnight.' He stuffed his hands into his sleeves and walked out past me onto the viewing deck.

I followed him a moment later.

He thought for a while and we watched the stars turn over the black silhouettes of the trees. 'Let's say we find your information. What then?'

'Then I get out of here.'

'And what will I do, when you vanish without trace and they ask me for an explanation?'

'You can come with me.'

'Nico, you don't know what you're saying!' He laughed without any humour. 'I can't leave. Even with outside help I doubt you'll make it very far. And where would I go?'

'To Earth,' I said, though I'd no idea what was there. 'You could look up all those old empires.'

A brief, boyish enthusiasm lit his face but he shook his head. 'What would I do? My entire existence is all about... this! Do you have any evidence the Diaspora exists or that your master is what she claims? I have your word. Your ill-informed word. And you're a liar, and a spy and a pawn.'

I let him have it. It had been a long day. 'Don't worry, you can hand me in right now and all this will just be a bad dream by tomorrow.'

'And you'd let me?'

'I'll probably wait until you go out and then make a break for it over the balcony, to be honest,' I said.

We looked at each other and both of us cracked a grin at the same moment.

'Why have you been so confident that I *wouldn't* hand you over?' He spoke with genuine puzzlement.

It was a good question, though I knew he was clawing me for reassurance, not really asking a question about why my decisions were so batshit. Wait, was my swearing back? Was that a good sign, or a bad fucking omen of an ill destiny as Tashin's grip faded for reasons too bad to think about? *Shit.*

Isylon still had his head tilted towards me waiting for an answer.

'I had a feeling about it.' For a more comforting measure I added, 'You hate the regime as much as I do, but you've looked the other way until now.'

'You couldn't have known that.' He was smiling, teasing a little with his tone. 'I thought you had no belief in spirits, let alone kindred ones?'

'I've always been intuitive.'

'Attuned?'

'There are people here who are attuned more than I am and they never outed you...' I stopped, realising the stupidity of my words even as I was saying them. 'I guess because they're waiting for you to reveal it.'

'Or,' he said, his voice soft enough not to carry, 'they don't know and they're merely guessing but the risk of being wrong is too great.'

He really could think of a way out of anything. 'Not even you believe that.'

'Meaning I'm able to believe anything?' Self pity and bitterness.

I hated those things so much I wanted to punch them out of him. 'Yes.'

'What was your previous occupation? Drive-by killings?'

I made my right hand into a gun shape and pointed it at his head. 'Nailed it.'

That jolted him. 'What? You're kidding.'

I shook my head. 'Did I ever tell you where I came from?'

'Strangely enough in all our long acquaintance you never mentioned it.'

And there it was, the arrow to my heart. Sarcasm, cynicism, barbed wit, fighting by stealth and – essentially – no quitting and the crying had stopped. If he started making direct insults and taking personal liberties I was done for. 'It might take some telling.'

I found his index finger pressed against my lips. 'Another time. It doesn't matter.'

Personal space violation? I bit his finger, not too hard.

'Ow!' His eyes flashed with rage as he snatched his hand away, finger straight in his own mouth in reaction. He watched my response like a hawk. I was so turned on that I nearly missed a movement out wide to my left.

I saw the silhouette of a figure at a balcony, the light behind

221

making it impossible to tell who it was although I felt a familiarity in its awkwardly hasty movement. My heart sank as I watched it hurrying away.

Isylon followed my gaze, finger in his mouth. 'That hurt.'

'I don't think so,' I said, meeting his look with a disgusted one of my own. 'Whose room is that?'

'I don't know, I'm not a directory,' he snapped. He rolled his eyes and turned back into the interior, finger still in his mouth. 'Of all the chances and situations. I can't believe it. And *you're* my opportunity?' He was clearly appalled by my careless stupidity one more time. I was a bit baffled by the sudden surge of playfulness over reason myself. Must be the end-times feeling that did it. Still, punch counterpunch.

'I'm *the* opportunity,' I said, sauntering after him. 'Were you expecting another one?'

We shared a glance. Looks really are worth thousands of words. We got married somewhere in the middle of it, had our first fight, broke up, made up, got into the second.

He folded his arms. 'You know why you don't feel like a priest?'

'Enlighten me.'

'You have no sense of self-preservation: socially, or any other way. Or you have a death wish. No, some other thing. You dare death like a little boy, sticking his tongue out. You're not serious, about anything. You think it's not going to happen to you.'

I understood his envy and grinned at him. I gave him a gang sign for badassery. 'I've died *twice*.'

He frowned, not sure whether he wanted to believe me or not. 'You're proving my point.'

I stood up on my spot and gestured at myself with my hands. 'Do I seem dead to you?'

He smiled and turned away. 'I'd have to get closer before I'd be willing to say.'

I caught up with him at the Alembic's shining curve, spun him around by his upper arm and kissed him.

A flicker of movement in the darkness of his bedroom door made me break it off before it was properly begun. Right. That did it. 'What the— ?'

I left him protesting and ran across to the spot, determined to catch whoever it was who'd been spying on me all day. The shape had seemed too short for a person, and too quick, but it had been solid and real. No way was I going to miss it this time.

I got to the doorway and went straight inside, senses on high alert. Light from the laboratory gave all the objects definite grey shapes. There was nothing. I checked behind the bed, under the side table. Nothing. I opened the closet. Robes and shoes in neat alignment looked back at me. A slight smell of sandalwood was all I could detect in the air.

A cold, greasy feeling slid down my spine. I wasn't used to being wrong about this kind of thing. No way I'd been wrong. Something had been there.

'Nico, have you lost your mind?' Isylon stood in the doorway, hand on the frame. He sounded hoarse, all cultured cadence gone, undone in a romantic way I should have been exploiting but instead I was standing like a dumbass looking at furniture.

'I saw something right where you are,' I said, reluctantly giving up on the search and closing the door.

'Some*thing*?' He emphasised the last syllable with a drawn out scepticism.

'It was too small to be a person. It was more like an animal. It stood in the door and then it shot off to the left inside the room.' I checked the outside door but it was closed and anyway I would have heard it open and there would have been a change of light from the corridor.

'I hadn't noticed anything like that.' He pushed off the frame and came into the room proper with a cautious step. 'I don't sense a presence.'

'It was here.' I had started to doubt that, but I had definitely seen it.

'There have been reports of hauntings in the Seminary for years,' he said, exploring the small spaces with fingers outstretched like he was dowsing. His suspicion remained but he was making a show of effort. I wished he would stop.

'This wasn't like that. It had weight and it moved like a solid object.' I kept trying to re-create it in my mind but it had been so fast that my initial impression of a creature was all I had.

'There was a theory that the spirit fragments of those the Inquisition dispatched are attracted here and try to materialise when they encounter enough energy. Does it seem colder?'

'No,' I said truthfully, and not just because I didn't want the vengeful dead added to the mix. 'Maybe it was my wetware malfunctioning.' I was much more worried about that than spectres.

'Your what?'

I explained as concisely as possible about the nature of the Switch and how I'd come by it. As I did so he listened with rapt fixation.

'You came here with it, undetected.'

'I think it's connected to a – system . . .' I stumbled, the whole of my lacking knowledge revealed, embarrassed. 'A system that has reasonable infiltration and control of Harmony's datmosphere.'

He nodded slowly, his eyes wide. 'Something that can god-mode even the security here, at the Citadel?'

'Maybe. I wouldn't count on it.'

'Nico . . .' He shook his head, pale and serious so that I wanted to hug him to put colour back in his caramel face. 'You trust this AI which is so powerful? If it is an AI.'

'Thing is I don't have a choice. I have no way to . . .' I groped around in the air, pushing, resisting an invisible force. 'And I know all the time that it could take control of me because it did before. I want to get this done, not have to live with this hanging over me all the time. I'm dangerous to you and me, whether I want to be or not.'

'What a terrible thing to live with.' He was the one who reached out although we were too far apart to touch. His hand raised in a gesture of kindness, his face lit by sympathy and pity which made my sense of powerlessness intensify to a pitch that I'd sooner kill myself than live with it. Then it shifted, a rock altered in the riverbed, and the water of his sweetness touched me instead as if he had said aloud that there is a limit to all power and not being able to use it is not the same as being without it. I went from feeling despair to feeling limitless and it calmed me. I clung to his gaze, to what he effortlessly did to me, as though he were the only straw on the surface of the sea. But he wasn't done: 'Then what you are seeing and feeling may be this entity that your handler refers to as the ship. It could be looking for you. Its spirit tries to reach you when its voice cannot. Even machines are a part of the universe and may be the transmitters of the aetheric, as well as the electric.'

Time to shut this down, too. 'I don't believe in that shit.' And I couldn't, even though everything he'd said was true. True for him, I rationalised. Maybe it was real to him and not to me. I'd never seen or felt anything like it myself. But I felt a sudden shame in denouncing him and in my fear that he was right. I was so much more lost here than I had imagined I could be.

He sighed, gave up his own exploration and straightened. If he took offence at my assaults he didn't show it. 'So, my hand-some cyborg anathema, defiled creature, slayer, spy – before you rushed off on the ghost hunt...' Every name was an acceptance, an invitation, as if they were the codewords to the secret vaults of my being and he used them that way. I hadn't got a defence.

I turned to him, 'Oh, you think I'm using this as an excuse to avoid intimacy?' Because that is exactly what I would have done, if only I hadn't seen some shit that apparently wasn't there.

He shook his head. 'No. I got the impression that you were really startled. I just want to know what you think you were doing back there. What that was.' He regarded me with quiet patience, his lips turning to press themselves very slightly as he did so.

I made a few final futile efforts to scan the room. 'Nobody ever slap you to bring you to your senses before?'

'Not with a kiss.'

'Well, now they have.' And there we were in the half dark, standing awkwardly without a single distraction and the momentum all gone.

He stepped forwards, head lowered, a kind of prowl about him as if he'd scented weakness. 'You want to run away now. You, with your powerful ghost machine. You're scared.'

'Always,' I said. 'I hate feelings.'

'Perhaps that's why you act on them without thinking?'

'I act on the ones that are doing something useful.'

'So, what feeling was that when you were kissing me?' His eyes glittered gold.

'I don't know, do you expect me to name them all? They're snowflakes in a blizzard.' I was now going to have to step back if I didn't want him to walk into me. I held my ground and he stepped in, nose to nose, and looked into my eyes. We shared breath.

This is why I never did this kind of thing. My body was an overclocked nuclear reactor melting down on all fronts. It had only two settings to deal with anything: icy disdain or Defcon One and nothing in the middle. Icy disdain had served me very well. The other one existed only in dreams where it blew up the universe. Neither of them was any good for this. But as he faced me I couldn't back off. I could see touchyfeely was his ballpark. He was right at home in the filthy, miring horror of it, happy as a pig in mud. He probably had more emotions than a harp had strings. Defcon One was trying its hardest to burst the straitjacket. The minotaur stabbed me in the guts for good measure. I couldn't even blink.

'A blizzard, hm? I'll name some then,' he said. His breath was sweet, the breath of a well cared for specimen. 'Curiosity, fear, anger, lust.'

'Yeah,' I replied, unable to see anything but the vague features of his face, the darkness where his irises were. 'And I was, you know, sorry. For uh … everything.'

'Sorry?' All the self pity was gone, replaced by a serpentine questing. If all priests could sniff out a lie that fast then I wasn't ever going to try it with them.

'Do not engage,' I muttered to myself between my clenched teeth, aware of my face scowling by the heavy sensation in my brows. My lips buzzed with a tickling fury where his finger had pressed. Maybe I didn't like drama after all. Maybe I hated it.

'Life and death hang in the balance and you say—'

I say stupid things to prevent myself thinking. But now I have to say something and I need it to sound convincing to me, if not to him, though I'd like to impress him so much it hurts. I'm keenly aware he's kicking my ass in the hardball game. Here we are at the gates of hell and half a day ago we were carefree lads about to step into the best graces and brightest futures in all of Harmony. Then a few words here and there, bloody words, and we're here. I feel that his good opinion, his attention, is more important to me than life itself and at the same time I'm aware that this is dumb and probably created by all the circumstances that led me here, a bull by the nose ring. I hate that. I hate being me. I have no idea what I'm going to say or do even as my mouth starts to shape the sentence, operating on automatic in my absence. 'No fucking talking,' I said. 'That's what I say.' I kissed him again and this time there was a brief altercation in establishing lockholds about who was stronger that lasted all of two seconds because it was me but I wanted to give him the illusion he'd had a shot at it.

At least I hadn't punched him.

A moment later I realised I was no good at kissing. To me kissing was war.

I let him go.

His eyebrows were up in a question, hands and arms held up and out to hold the space I'd been in. I held up my hand to ask for a time-out. His mouth was swollen now. I touched his lips with my thumb, trying to feel through the calluses. I couldn't get close to him in the way I wanted, not with bodies but with feeling. Even in a deathgrip it wasn't close enough. So this might be a way. I barely registered the softness of his skin but I did feel the change over the lipline, the curve of the bow, the dampness where my lips had tried to break the ice.

He made to move but I kept my free hand up in the *stop* position. He peered at me and I saw comprehension alter the stress lines in his face, smoothing them out, creating new shapes as his expression changed in the golden salt light. I watched those microshifts closely, my fingertips flowing over the contours, skin velvet and gilded. I watched the brute shape of my thumb trying to find the touch that would undo my armour on the fine lines of his mouth.

The still, hard container that I had made of myself didn't open. However, the texture of him altered in reaction to my touch. He became firmer and stronger. I tried for less, for lighter, until there was almost no contact and then no contact at all and I thought I was imagining the shapes under my skin, feeling the heat across the space between us that I couldn't cross. Frustration became despair. My sense of isolation was agonising. This was the only crossing that mattered. I wanted to touch him. I wanted to *meet* him. And I couldn't.

I had been much too good at disengaging. With Dash I had been a cold prince, playing games. The only hot moments of real passion there had all been within me. I was in love with my fantasy of being the tough guy, the survivor, the one in charge.

Dash was only a thing that fulfilled a role in that fantasy. I saw, through the awkwardness I was in now, that I had been alone there too.

And Two – that was born of some other form of desperation. It was real but again, the memory of hugging her close to me told me that she had helped create my story that I was strong and capable, not alone and vulnerable. I did care for her. I did love. But I'd never met her either. I met something I thought was her, I met what she meant to me and it was so precious; but I felt now that I had never touched *her*.

The minotaur existed only to personify my anger and make it into something noble so that I could use it and not die of it in helplessness. But in this situation I was stupid, vulnerable, helpless, doomed and now unable to make contact with this person upon whom it seemed every remaining second of my life depended. If I could not touch him, if I could not meet him then I would never have been alive.

The dramatic self regard of this struck me as comical. What a crock. Who believes this crap anyway? We're alone and I'm a master of self pity. Boo fucking hoo. And there we were back in cynicism, my shield, which let nothing come near. I wanted it gone but it could not go. I had made myself so that I could never be touched by anything that might disrupt my inner world. I had made my fortress very well, but I had not put in a single door.

As this realisation came over me I felt my eyes heat up and fill with tears. My chest hurt. The need for contact intensified to a pitch that was so hot I felt that I was being incinerated but nothing within me would let go. Another piece of me was looking on in disgust: give me five minutes and I'll get over it, stuff all this useless shit back in the box where it belongs and become functional again. For the first time in my life, though, a different part of me turned and said, 'Yeah, but should you?' Should I get over it? I'd watched Two mire herself in all kinds of this crap from a safe distance and thought I was so superior for my detached command. But should I have? Wasn't it callous to step aside and become so inhuman there is nothing included in the world at all but yourself? Had I hung her out and left her to dry alone?

Yeah, I had watched her burn. My hands fell useless to my sides.

I saw Isylon moving. He was still in command of himself. He seemed sure. I didn't know what he was going to do but I was going to stand and take it.

He opened his hand and gently stretched it towards me, slowly. He moved his fingers and I felt them on my face from inches away. His lips were parted in wonder. Nobody had looked at me like that before.

I wondered what he saw. And I knew what he saw. He saw what I was seeing or trying to see – to really see someone for the first time, without a lens, without a war, but there was something in the way. I couldn't feel him.

I thought this was about sex but it wasn't. I'd thought it might help but I knew it wouldn't. My body was desensitised to invasion. I should tell him not to bother.

Isylon blinked and caught my attention. His eyes were dilated, the light casting a faint star in each of them at the side of the iris. He lifted his hand and the warm sense of touch crossed my cheek. I felt it so clearly, so tenderly as it ran down over my forehead, across my bones, light as air, as a ghost's touch.

The icy skull beneath my skin melted. I felt it start to go with a sudden leap of fear in my heart that made my flight reaction kick. I almost smashed his hands out of the way but by superhuman effort I held still and I understood the truth that the body holds all the feelings that the person doesn't want to acknowledge. My face held all my self-hatred and he was undoing it so that suddenly there were hot tears on my cheeks, running down my nose and over my mouth. The sensation of the emotion was almost unbearable. I was burning from the inside, with shame. I was eight again, seven, six, five... I was terrified and horrified and in despair. For every time I was strong, for every blow and every thought and word and minute I'd played it cool in my whole life – I felt *everything*. And all the while his clever fingers kept burning loose the nuts and bolts that held me together.

I wanted to run. I did not run. No more running. Today I die in a fire. I looked at him with abject gratitude, hopeless surrender. Tears ran down my face and tickled my jaw.

He smiled at me and his gossamer touch flowed on. Over time the melting of my old self started to slow down and the crisis ebbed. I began to feel the stroking guidance of his hands more physically and less acutely. The heat of the Alchemy faded to a firefly glow and at last I stood before him completely empty.

He held out his hand to me, palm up. I placed mine on it. I closed the small gap between us until the length of our bodies touched. Beside our thighs our hands entangled on both sides. I tilted my head down very slightly so that I could look into his eyes.

'Extraordinary,' he said and I wasn't sure what he meant until his mouth twitched up at one side and he added, 'I never met anyone as receptive as you. And I thought you'd be the worst of the lot.'

'Worst of what lot?'

His eyebrow quirked up and he rolled his eyes around to look everywhere. 'All of them. You're like...' He paused and I resisted the urge to fill in the gap for him with the tears still wet on my face. 'Clay.'

'Charming,' I said, but I was pleased in a perverse way. 'And I thought you were going to say blotting paper.'

'Ah, no,' he grinned. 'Not quite so much absorption. Malleability. Sculptability?' He kept trying words out to see if they would shift my pretend-insulted expression.

'I'm putty in your hands,' I said, cringing from the cliché

but knowing it was exactly right in a profound and unexpected way. Through dumb buffoonery I had hit a home truth. I was my own opposite. I was open to anything. I was joyful and he had allowed this or made it. It didn't matter. Everything about me was screaming 'Yes!'

'Can't be an accident,' he said and as the implications, good and bad, of that ominous statement sank into the mush of my brain we kissed properly for the first time: the softest touch of lips to lips without a fight or a game anywhere. I felt myself vanish in sensation. His expertise in living honestly within his skin became mine instantaneously, transferred like a print.

He was much more skilled at undoing tapes and the fasteners on the ceremonial clothes than I was but his speed faltered once the outer layers dropped and he started to find scars. He traced them first with his fingers, then with his tongue. A faint burning deep in the flesh followed his touch but it wasn't painful, it was good. Cool air from the air conditioner drew our skins tighter. He stopped as my shorts came off and he found the tattoo.

I glanced at it, braced for the reaction it had always given me though until now I didn't know that I braced when I looked at it. The reaction of defiance and rage didn't come. It was a flower on a green leaf field, with two stars.

'Pretty,' Isylon said, without voicing or even whispering, his lips forming the word. He leaned forward and kissed the stars.

A long time later the night was well advanced. I was in bed, arms behind my head, staring at the ceiling. My body glowed so warmly I felt surprised it didn't illuminate the room but only the glowlights in the wall sconces cast a faint yellow gleam over me.

I couldn't find a trace of Tashin in all the silence. Every other minute Two's face popped into my mind and my stomach plunged like it was in a failed elevator.

Isylon came back from the bathroom, towelling his hair, composed. 'I don't think we can achieve any more from here,' he said after a moment. He sat on the edge of the bed and brushed my still-wet hair back from my face.

'We need to squeeze someone who has access to the whole mess.' I flipped the covers back with one arm. He got in and lay with his head on my shoulder, adjusting until we fitted right. We watched the ceiling together, listening to the sounds of other students waft across the leaf-heavy night through our now opened doors. Their voices were too quiet to be deciphered, animal song. My eyelids would not stay open. I stroked Isy's shoulder, lingering in the simple peace that brought.

A sudden howl from somewhere in the arboretum made every hair on my body stand on end.

'Did you hear that?' I sat up, dislodging Isylon who propped himself on his elbows, frowning.

'Hear what?' He was alarmed but also annoyed at being jolted wide awake. I apologised with a touch of my hand.

It sounded again, a wolf's plaintive call, lonely and distant – too distant for anywhere in the enclosed garden. There was a pause. I listened and Isylon watched me. I could see he didn't hear a thing.

'What is it?' he asked.

'A wolf, howling,' I said as it came again, closer now, definitely somewhere close beneath our eyrie. This time there was no lonely moon calling and the wolf had mutated into a dire form – the howl was a furious declaration of bloodthirst, the edges of the sound raw with slobber. I could feel the vibrations of it running in my bones. It was glorious, and it called to me with the sweet, addictive promise of savage slaughter and brotherhood.

'Nico?'

I glanced down at Isy's face in the soft glow. I listened but there was no more. A vague sense of urgency, anxiety and questing remained in a low resonance in my body. It knew for certain what my mind denied: something had come. In the night it hunted me and it called me to the hunt.

No explanations. I was sure it was something to do with the Switch. Personal, like Isy had said, only not a ghost but something definitely alive and connected.

Isy was about to speak when his comm burred. He sat up and reached for the small palmtop, moved carefully before he answered it.

I listened for the few minutes until he closed the line and gathered before he announced, 'My father can't come today. I couldn't tell him what for, of course, so he couldn't know the urgency.' He sat, hunched over, and slowly replaced the palmtop onto the nightstand.

'Probably for the best,' I said, super rational to save my own feelings of despair. 'Don't want him dragged into it.'

He sighed. 'We missed evening prayer. That's acceptable a couple of times but not ideal for those wishing to keep themselves above suspicion. You have a backup plan?'

Sure. Turn into a werewolf, kill everyone, squeeze Tecmaten for information and get the hell out of here. 'Should get some sleep for a couple of hours. Maybe one. People are at their worst at four a.m. That's when we go.'

'Go where?'

'The Exalted Alembic.'

He tried to argue me out of the idea, first of us going and then of him going but I ignored his assurances we could last another twenty-four hours on the chance of his father's interview. Maybe we could and maybe we couldn't but it didn't matter. This place was my death if I wasn't out of here at that point. My bones told it to me, as they continued vibrating to the ringing tones of the howling. Tashin might not even be alive to care any more for all I knew and I didn't feel like I owed her anything. Two's silence hurt like a strip of missing skin. No way I was waiting for the enemy to close in.

We settled down again. I listened, watched the shadows. Eventually I fell asleep.

Immediately I was snatched into a vivid dream that I was in a jungle. It was very dark under the mass of growth which had covered all of the planet overnight. There was no way out of it, I knew this. It wrapped everything and was everywhere. The only light was a red haze in the tiny chinks of visible sky.

I was running for my life along with everyone else: priests, gangsters, drones. We were running away but something was coming. You could feel its presence on your back and in your bones; fear had turned them to water, limbs wouldn't work. The running was like swimming through mud. Shockwaves from the monster's dread approach shivered us into pieces that we had to gather and carry before we ran on.

The closer it got the more we panicked. Eventually everyone stopped running and tried to hide. I threw myself into a hollow near a tree and covered myself in leaves but there weren't enough of them. I froze there, too scared to even breathe, hoping that the increasingly rapid beat of my heart wasn't enough to move my skin and give away my hiding place. The presence grew stronger, a heatwave of searing invisible radiance, a breath of hot, fetid rot. I was going to breathe in a moment, I had to, I had to, but it was too late and didn't matter because there was nowhere to go, it was everywhere, reeking and burning. If it didn't get me I would die of fear.

My mouth and nose filled with blood and the visceral stench of emptied guts. A foul musk seeped into my skin, marking me. The sheer oppressive weight of inevitable, agonising death hung a hairsbreadth off my face. It was in all places, at all times, a consummate hunter, a ruthless killer: the Beast. It had found me.

Nico, what the hell are you doing? Stop it!

Tashin's screech shattered the dream. I filled my lungs with cool air and found myself sitting bolt upright in sweat-drenched bedclothes. Isylon was gripping my arm with a pretty impressive vice-hold-of-death. Relief flooded me so intensely that I almost cried.

The room was dark. It was the hour before dawn.

Tashin's panic barely made an impression on me.

'Nico, you wouldn't wake up,' Isylon said, letting go with slow caution. 'You were growling and...' He held his face with his free hand – I must have elbowed him or something.

'Bad dream,' I said taking a slow breath.

'I'll get you some tea,' he said, getting up and releasing his hold with a care that told me his muscles had nearly cramped in that position. As he left I saw him ease his shoulders and back, shivering.

– What's the problem?

By the time he returned Tashin had me understand that whatever had gone down over in Chaontium was almost over. Two was in hiding, Tashin with her, but they were somehow separated for now, taking different routes to a rendezvous. Guns had been in abundance, blood spilled over into the streets in a brief but furious cartel war that ripped through in the wake of the Purge which had towed away several kingpins. Gangs had been swept up in it, no chattel left unused in the efforts to seize the chance to wipe out opponents and take their resources. Kasha Dann had lost a lot and Tashin was using the maelstrom of rebuilding and bloody vengeance as a cover to take herself and Two out of the game altogether.

– Where?

I wanted to know immediately. The one reason Two and I had never done the same thing was the simple fact we'd already worked out there was nowhere to go. Beyond Chaontium's reach were the wilds – uninhabitable geography without a single sustaining feature. Harmony's terraforming had been successful but basic; people had gone out into the wilds but they never came back and anyway, we didn't want to become free skeletal savages, we wanted civilisation.

Kalunkat.

Not good. The Demi-Sauvage fringes where the agricultural

basin petered out into scorched canyonlands. It would be the first place anyone with half a brain would go looking once they'd licked their wounds and got reorganised.

I can get us out from there. At the wall edge we could climb to the Dereft Plateau and get airlifted.

If you had atmospheric aircraft on standby I guess you could. Supposing you lived long enough to get up there.

– I keep hearing things. Is the Switch faulty?

There was a pause. A long pause. I sensed misgivings, regrets, steely determination. *No. Since I've been on the run I haven't been able to keep as tight a grip on things as I should. You may be experiencing overbleed from the ship.*

I know a lie when I hear one. I was about to pursue it when I realised Isylon was standing beside me, holding out a cup.

'Nico?'

'Hn? Oh, just thinking about the dream,' I said. I took the tea and drank it for something to do to cover my outer silence while I inwardly railed at Tashin's poor judgement. Trusting the revolution, running to Kalunkat.

The Diasporan revolution took a long time in the making. They have people there, a base.

– Oh so it was you all along, was it? Been here a while?

Years. On and off. Mostly off but it hasn't been easy to get down to the surface. Most of the work was done through offworld comms.

– Who are you working for? Really?

I told you. Myself.

– There must be some big profit I'm not seeing. You know a revolution has no chance here.

Then that can't be my goal, can it?

– What's wrong with the Switch? Tashin?

And she was gone, just like that. I fished around but I couldn't bring her back. So she didn't want to talk. I felt the distinct impression that she had been hurrying off to do

237

something urgent and dangerous; the vision in my mind's eye was of someone rushing to plug a hole in a dam with a rag. Ship-bleed. Right. Birds and the beasts. What kind of fucking ship was that?

'Nico!' Isylon was shaking me.

I put the cup down. 'Sorry.'

'Who were you talking to? Is it that thing?' Isylon asked, moving his hand next to his head.

I nodded. He looked like he wanted not to believe any of it. His face was ashen grey and I saw how tired he was. He needed sleep, though neither of us wanted to waste a minute when our time was counting down in hours.

I finished the tea and thanked him, put the cup down and got out of the bed. He was warm and pliant when I embraced him and kissed him. I would have given much to stay there with him for ever and I tried to tell him so through my passion. At last we parted and I made myself let go.

'You're not really going?' He was afraid now that we were up against it and so was I but damned if I was going to let that get in the way of the exit plans.

I started to get dressed. 'No time like the present.'

'But what are you going to do?' He watched me with disbelief.

In the wakeful minutes I'd had time to fillet the AI for inspiration and it had supplied me with some. 'I'm going to Confession.'

'Don't kid around. What are you really doing?' Anxiety filled his voice but he hastily put down his own cup and started grabbing clothes and putting them on.

'My only chance of getting to the information I want lies with people I can't fool who want me dead, but I can delay them if I cut a deal.'

'What kind of deal? You can't trust them!' He was desperate.

'They can't trust me either but they'll believe they've got the upper hand long enough for me to get something.'

'And once you're under arrest how will you get out?'

'Don't know,' I said. I was thinking of the plateau, the bird, the shadows. I felt a confidence that was entirely misplaced but it occurred to me that a diversion of enough interest here would buy some time for Two as well. If she got out it would be like both of us getting out. I didn't have to make it. One would be enough for me. But then I looked at Isylon and I knew one was not enough.

'You don't have to be involved. I can explain it all as my doing...'

'The hell I don't,' he said. Then he paused, stock still. 'Nico, are you leaving me?'

'No,' I said. 'I can't leave you.' I looked at him with my true face. I meant that it wasn't possible for me to leave him even if I wanted to. I might never see him again but that wasn't the same thing. 'I'm leaving the room.'

Resolve replaced the uncertainty in his face as he understood me. 'Wait, there's something I have to show you.'

'I don't have time...'

'It'll only take a minute.' He reached out and took my hand. I let him lead me into the Alembic. Its light swept up from standby into the fierce golden symbols of my germline code. He expertly flipped the display out of that mode and then showed me a cartouche filled with coloured forms. 'I guess you might not have looked at this. It's the record of who made your germline.'

I hadn't looked. I didn't want to look now. I pulled my hand out of his grasp, ready to leave. 'What does it matter?' I had never liked the idea of being abandoned and I liked the idea of being designed and then screwed up and thrown in the trash even less.

'Read the name.' He had hold of my wrist now, insisting.

I humoured him, made myself read the dedication and the signature. 'Bitna Valkyrian.'

'Bitna Valkyrian,' he repeated softly, 'is the missing Exalted. She vanished without trace three days after your inception date.'

I stood there, in limbo, not sure what this meant, decided it was too late to mean anything and that knowing it probably wouldn't help me. I hugged Isylon to thank him and reassure him. I couldn't handle any more revelations. I had to rebuild cold-hearted bastard Nico and get the job done. 'I can't figure that out now, I have to go.'

'I'm coming with you.'

'Bad idea,' I said, 'I'll come back for you if I get—'

But my heroic speech was broken by an incredibly loud bang from the arbor. It made the glassware in the lab chime, and was followed by a muffled crashing, snapping sound and a final muted thud.

We both rushed out onto the balcony to look. The lights in the arboretum had all come on and the birds and bats that lived there were spiralling around, shrieking and panicking. Up in the broad arch of the dome a large pane of glass showed a huge round hole with jagged edges, silvered lines streaking across the entire roof. Directly beneath, a dark shadow on the trees showed where whatever had come through had broken its fall. Voices and torches were already hurrying beneath the canopy. At other balconies figures stood and leaned out as far as possible. Through the smashed gap in the planting we could both make out the cleared patch on the ground where the infiltrator had landed.

'It's a bird,' Isylon said, puzzled. 'A giant bird. I never saw anything like it.'

The bird was twisted and broken. Not a feather moved or eye opened. It was as big as a car and stone dead.

'What does it mean?' He looked at me but I couldn't tear my gaze away.

'That's my diversion,' I said.

He looked at me, aghast. I nodded at him. Yes. We looked back down again as one.

A faint shadow like a kind of smoke seemed to plume from the bird's wings before the breeze dissipated it into the air. Pretty sure I didn't imagine it. I wasn't about to waste this chance however.

'Best time to go is now,' I said. 'You should expect to get caught anyway but it will take them more time to figure things out if you stick around and play the fool here. I'll get you out. But I have to get the information first.'

He blinked. 'Is this . . . is this bird something to do with your machines?'

I nodded.

He looked down again at the creature, now being poked and prodded by a large party of guards and priests, and repressed a shudder. 'I was right, you see. It came for you. But I don't know how long I'll last. I'm not so good – under pressure. But at least this proves we're not alone.' He looked at me, eyes tear-filled, his hand on the rail shaking. 'What are you still doing here? Go get your information.'

Light the Blue Touchpaper and Count to – Ten

I put up my hood and left as though I was simply going out to collect something from somewhere innocent. As I went I thought about my other options in the way you'd look over a box of biscuits you knew you weren't going to eat. Probably, if I went now, I could leave and go back to Chaontium and find Two. Tashin might be persuaded to save her own skin without the evidence she wanted, though I had the feeling that it wasn't her only exit possibility. If she loved Two enough, she might agree. Or I could go to the Inquisition and hand Isylon over, pretending that I had fooled him into admitting his loathing of the Alchemy. That was a bit weaker and I didn't think that I'd last long if they used a Confessor on me. It wouldn't get me anything worth having unless I lucked out and got a chatty interrogator who was willing to trade secrets to someone they felt sure was a doomed prisoner.

The walks and colonnades were busy with figures in all colours of robes striding this way and that, agitated by the sudden assault on the arbor or else about business that had been rerouted because of it. There were only a few students around, but enough that I didn't stand out on the paths I chose. I followed my inner map of the buildings, fabricating fresh destinations and excuses for my journey as I passed them in order of plausibility: the kitchens, various stores, the postal drop, the porters' cubby, the overseer's office, the Ordained Laboratories, the Supervising Magisters' apartments.

Once I'd reached the silver towers I had no possible reason for my presence. Here doors stood open, light radiating from them across the wooden floors of the hall in clear rivers that I'd have to risk crossing if I was to carry on with my idea. At first I'd thought I would simply go to the Office of the Chief Confessor and see where we got. I'd bet the farm on my story being so bizarre that they'd talk, but now that I was so close and saw the open doors and lack of patrols I decided I'd delay that in favour of some spying.

As I approached the first door I listened as hard as I could for evidence of its occupation. Voices in conversation. I couldn't go in. I'd look for an empty room instead and see what I could eavesdrop. I slowed down. My shoes were nearly silent, which was double-edged. I'd sneak by but they'd sneak up on me too if I wasn't careful. The talk was of the bird, unsurprisingly.

'…a terrible creature. Never seen the like. Not a native creature, surely. Where could it have come from? Are there unobserved breeding grounds in the wilds before the wall? It's a ridiculous notion. And to come right here…'

'Paphotis says it must be from beyond the wall.'

A snort of derision. 'Man never had more sense than a table-top. Beyond the wall. Does he know how high it is? There's no atmosphere up there. I suppose some migratory error could be responsible.'

Neither was convinced but they were thoroughly excited. I'd passed them before I heard any more. Then to the left an apparently empty room yawned and I walked directly into it as if I was meant to go there, searching quickly for signs of life before I even registered what else was present. An Alembic was spiralling gently, illuminating one corner. Comfortable chairs and rugs furnished the place with an air of sleepy comfort. Personal items were scattered here and there in a way that suggested whoever had left intended to return soon. I looked around, not knowing what to look for, angling to see what the Alembic was showing.

It took me a while to understand what I was reading. The scope of the machine's displays was incredible – every cartouche part of a huge set of nested ideas and concepts, names, germlines and connections. Besides that a personal mail system was in operation, the last caller flashing their ID which was the only thing that made me look twice at it. When I did I couldn't quite believe what I was seeing. The tag was Dash's personal ID.

A sickly cold crept over my skin from the top of my head and shoulders downwards, like a mantle of congealing grease. A keen sense of personal danger and the knowledge of passing seconds burned in me, urging me to leave, but I opened the conversational record.

'...the continued supply of specific germline requests to the locations you identify will continue as long as your credit remains good...' My eyes scanned lines, so freaked I didn't understand them the first time, had to try again and again to comprehend their meaning. After a second some assistance from the Switch must have kicked in. The sentences cleared up and their implications shone out in gleaming clarity.

It was quickly apparent that the owner of this room was the author of a reassuring contract which they had agreed with Dash – to send kids to orphanages. They were aware that Dashein was dead now but had decided to carry on business as usual with whoever had taken over. The guys on the Chaontium end hadn't even bothered to alter the account information because it wasn't the people that mattered, only the deal. The user here didn't care either. Dash was a middle guy, shielding people further up, but a fast trace back in the history revealed he'd been instrumental in trafficking children out of the orphanages and into the cartels. Their names meant little to me, but they could have been changed. The news stalled me out, dry-mouthed as my hands operated on automatic, pulling up data files for my AI-enhanced brain to scan.

I didn't need to be consciously aware for that, which was good because rage and denial were fighting to a standstill for control over my brain. I thought I heard a noise in the hall and twisted, the action freeing my combat instinct to shut down the irrelevant drama. There were no shadows, no further footfalls. I could feel the presence of others like a flicker of static in the air, but they weren't close enough yet. I paged on while there was still the opportunity. I would have searched for myself and Two but that would compromise me later, if not set alarm bells ringing all through the system.

Then within me the AI took aim with the sniper rifle of its own, much faster, machine attention. It saved me the trouble of using the Alembic and showed me the numbers, the dates, the names, the prices that I was looking for and hoping not to see. There were other things too, videos: me in the isolation room. The face of Two watching her favourite teacher being executed on state television. The smooth arc of a car as it swerved in pursuit of a running teenager and knocked him flying.

So there were fewer accidents than you might suppose. So I might have been sent as some weird shipment to bozos for reasons. So there were schemes afoot. Well, so fucking what? Like I wasn't in it over my eyeballs already? News about history wasn't going to get me out of here. Rage was a luxury that had to wait in line behind necessity as I stood here indulging my personal hate and blew my chances of finding the right information.

I watched Two, huddled in a doorway, gutting a service droid, shivering and hungry as a block away two police officers leaned on their car watching her and doing nothing and I slammed my hand onto the Alembic's delicate touchpad and shut it down. Softly. I opened other logs and threads as fast as I could, randomly, trusting the Switch AI to save and search.

They went back years, decades even. Say what you like about the Alchemy, they have admin to die for.

I tried searches for *technology, offworld, special* – nothing, until I entered *import*.

'...the imported supplies will be sent with the usual couriers...' but it only meant that Dash had been selling something into Harmony more than fifteen years ago, it didn't say what. I tried a cross-link on the same word but it had been used only twice. In. Not out. Into Harmony, from the outside world, something fishy. If there was going to be something it had to be here.

There was no concrete reference to anything. They used generic terms that were virtually meaningless: shipment, order, material, product, transaction. I persisted, feeling like I was onto something big and wasting time at the same moment, sure to miss whatever was useful. After a minute's frustration I began to pick up the faint murmur of voices in a louder conversation from the hall. A door opened and closed. Feet in slippers hurried past in a rapid pitapat that wasn't interested in my room though they would have seen me if they'd only turned to look. Capture was certain.

I switched tactic and tried to search on the germline codes that were mentioned now and again, not knowing who or what they were. I was scattershot. Page after page went by but the resolution of the AI helped me to understand that among all the things I was seeing were shipping manifests, invoices, contracts all attached by ID to the line codes of individuals. I'd done it. I'd got a connection. Now all there had to be was something illegal and we were done. I mass-searched the ID codes and the Alembic made a soft chiming sound of three tones that made me lurch around, listening, looking. At the same time the displays dissolved and a beautiful colour image replaced them.

'Welcome,' said a warm, feminine voice, 'to the Harmony Catalogue.'

I shut it down as it was still speaking. I listened. The hall was quiet except for the continuous burble of voices at their halfway station. They weren't reacting to it. Maybe they heard it all the time. Catalogue. The prices were marked in Solar Credit. Offworld money. There was an entry on the order form for multiple renders of individual items.

Bought, paid for, traded, with purpose. Suddenly Two and I weren't accidental freaks. We were product, commerce, nothing so natural as mistakes of concoction and human error. Deliberately crafted, but to what end? Was this going to be be my proof, and not something more flashy? But no, no sign of technology in us or in any of the other products on offer. If it was in use there was no trace of it in the sales literature. Why would there be? That's the last place you'd put something that would ruin the claim around which you'd built your entire business. Your world. Purity. I'd gone the wrong way. I needed manufacturing information, not sales.

Instead of getting it I was standing, staring numbly at the blankness, Dash's ID flashing like a crafty little imp winking at me – got you, got you, got you.

In the hall the talk turned into the tones of people bringing things to an end. Soon they'd go their separate ways.

Tecmaten was selling people. Well, not news really. I'd heard about the trade to Chaontium as a rumour and I was cynical enough to believe it some days though most of the time I'd figured it was apocryphal. Selling offworld, that was new even to me.

Then I stopped, frozen. What I'd said to Isylon before had popped back into my mind – *what if the information Isylon had always been given to work with wasn't the real thing?* If I was a devious sod trying to pass technologically engineered genetic code for naturally developed code (and fuck knew what the difference was but give a psycho a rope and he'll knit you a knot) I'd strip any markers off it. I'd have my minions work with stuff without telling them the origins. If they asked I'd find a way to stop them. A bit of Confession, a bit of redirection. I'd hypnotise him into thinking everything was legit, so that his own honesty fooled him as it looked trustingly out of those big, grey eyes.

The eyes had it. The eyes. I tried a search on the Takata eye variants, linked with his name and, on an impulse, the name of Bitna Valkyrian.

Sweat was running freely down my temples and body under the heavy robe. My mouth was ash dry as the Alembic whirled like a universe around my head, spiralling to a slow standstill as it showed me what I was looking for, together with helpful prompts for all the other places this particular combination of genes and their expression controls were seeded.

Now all I had to do was find a connection between this Takata code and an offworld supply.

– I hope my memory is set in stone, I said to Tashin, even though she wasn't there, as I looked through every reference, faster than I could reliably read it, moving at AI speed. If I could even show that there was a trace to put the method, if not the material, offworld it might be enough. Tecmaten hadn't been bringing in objects at all, maybe. He'd been importing ideas, information, techniques. So he was a hypocrite. It didn't make him criminal. Though being a slaver might, as long as he was doing that offworld too.

But couriers. *Think*, Nico. They had to bring something more than talk because talk was all here in this overconfident stack of OCD correspondence and all the connections out of Harmony were buried in codenames and other shit I didn't have time for. I had the Takata list but it wasn't informative other than to highlight how rare it was.

My mind quit on the undoable. Forget genes. What if they were enhanced like I was, with machines? I'd already proved the systems could be fooled into not noticing that stuff.

I searched on all the bland codewords and generics, looking

for something that crossmatched with Takata, and meanwhile, as if of their own accord my fingers tapped in a second search sequence before I was even aware of what I was doing.

Tashin.

The Alembic glowed, the system spun down into a lower fractal.

Tashin DeKalfu. A name on an invoice paid for a catalogue model.

Hot rage, like the minotaur, is a big dumb brute. It can take you only so far. But when the brute's forge is quiet and the steam has hissed away and that comforting animal has gone to sleep what's left is cold steel, all edge, all razor-sharp point. It wasn't something I was used to but I already sensed that with that I could do my best work, even better than with the empty sweet obliteration of the pit and the ring. Everything personal that had been holding me back and getting in the way vanished. Time itself slowed as I entered a state of focus and purity.

Tashin's germline was, ironically, the same standard female that I'd mocked her for being. It was marked as *Sans* – the one word I didn't understand. Sans. (An ancient term for *without* said the AI.) It had been delivered five years ago. The model's incept date was given as twenty-one years prior. There was a reference code which linked back neatly to a huge database of detailed 3-D renders of every part and parcel of a human being. She was from the catalogue of bodies you could buy. Bodies and parts. Bodies and infinitesimal parts of them. Sequence codes for particular enzymes. Everything stamped with the sparkling moon, sun and star sigil of Harmony's flag. Its trademark. The scale of the truth blew me away. I wasn't sure how long I stood there with my jaw hanging, shot through every cell at point blank range into total silence.

I was so fucking stupid. Like everyone else on this dumb, cursed dump I'd thought the Directory was what it said, the directory of knowledge protected by the priesthood, the bible of how we were all lovingly crafted for the good of human development, our birthday book and our valuable history. But it wasn't. It was a sales tool. Not so much a holy document as ten thousand pages of profit opportunities. Then again, to a cartel, that *was* holy.

My complex search on Takata plus returned its results, all the possible combinations and then a caveat saying that this was still under research and would not be shipping until further notice. There was no mention of special properties. There was a repeated reference to something called 'Inceptor'. As soon as I saw it my body flooded with relief. The AI grabbed it and ran. That was it, apparently. I still didn't know what it meant. I'd found the grail. I needed to go, I was off the hook, contract fulfilled, I was free! That was all I knew, but it made no impact on me as I stood there, looking at that one word.

Sans.

Shipping. People. Sans. What the hell was that 'sans'? Tashin had to know so this could not be the information she wanted because she had already had it, whatever it was. This was going nowhere, other than fuelling my rage when I couldn't afford to have it overpower me with another hot surge. I already felt grievously in the way of doing harm. I wanted to run, to destroy, to go down in a blaze of fury, taking it all with me, but then I'd never find out the truth. If I ran and went full destruction I wouldn't keep my word to Isy and that I had to do.

I typed in 'Inceptor'. I got a query message asking for a passcode.

The squeak of a shoe sole from the corridor startled me. They were here. As I looked up a shadow crossed the doorway and the brief intoxication of having found one guilty bastard's lair was replaced by the liquefying-gut sensation of being caught. It had always been my plan anyway but it was one thing to think about it and another to have the last seconds of my life cut down to the stark visual of three figures arriving in the dimly

250

framed door, the light casting each of their unhooded faces into comic expressions of surprise and disbelief.

I must have looked pretty stupid too although most of my face was hidden by the cowl. Maybe they only saw my slack, unpriestly jaw as I registered them: a Confessor, a Cardinal – Saffan, I thought – nobodies to me. But then, at the front, a face that I'd never forget although it was so far out of place here that it took my conscious mind seconds longer to find it than it took my body to set me up for running with nowhere to run.

I was fifteen again. I was about to bargain one more time with people who never kept a deal. It was the woman from the car, the one who had leaned impatiently forwards, trying to entice Two inside. She was older, of course. Weren't we all?

I didn't bother trying to hide what I'd been doing. Far too late for that. Without a pause I started to wonder how I could trick the information out of them before they finished any business they might want to conduct with me.

The moment of silence accompanying our startled surprise ended as the woman tilted her head. 'Might I ask what you are doing here?' She made a gesture that would summon the guard and moved forwards cautiously, one step at a time. The others flanked her, blocking the door.

'I'm here to audit your accounts,' I said, the old, glib patter coming to me as naturally as breathing. 'In particular the ones where you buy in outworld engineering to create superhuman whatever it is that you're making here. Sorry. *Tecmaten*'s making here. I always lump you guys together as if you're the mindless servants of an insane dictator. Bad habit.' Hopefully that would have pulled enough triggers that they'd be interrogating me for weeks. It must have pulled a few because they didn't get it together very quickly. There was glacial time passing as the looks on their faces slowly changed from shock to contempt, to disturbed wondering and then to outright loathing.

The woman was the first to recover her wits. She took a

breath and indicated one of the chairs that were arranged in a comfortable semicircle around her fireplace. 'Sit down. I can see we have much to discuss.'

The polite ones who were in control were always far worse than the raging pricks who leapt for your throat, but I hadn't been able to goad them enough for that. Probably I couldn't. It was their turf and I was in a minority of one.

I reached into my robe front as if I was about to pull out a gun and they all flinched. I kept my hand inside as though I was holding on to it, waiting for them to decide what to do. I didn't have to wait long. A second later I felt the strangest sensation of pressure around me, as if I were dough being compressed into a neat, tight ball. I saw the Inquisitor's expression of concentration and knew him for the crusher, then the Confessor put her hand up to her forehead as if she had a headache, but it was my head that felt a soft blow, stabbed through with a down-feather scalpel.

My hand closed into an empty fist.

Their relief was palpable, even I felt it as my arm withdrew, partly under my control but the movement entirely suggested by them. A dull hate filled me, and a resentment.

'You are used to being used,' the Confessor said softly. She had a voice like falling thistledown. Used to comfort someone it must be effective. Used as a weapon its sweet gentility was the repellent antithesis of her action. 'You are not here for yourself, but – there is a friend, somewhere.'

'Sit down,' the woman from the car said again and I walked over to the seat and did so entirely without my own will. She and the other two, clearly an experienced tag team, took the other chairs at their leisure. 'Who sent you?'

'I don't know,' I said.

She made a finger rise and fall on her hand. The Inquisitor made a move with his hand as if signalling across a crowded room and my own hand lifted up and pulled back the cowl of my robes.

'Nice puppetry.' I looked at him directly, trying to meet his eye and not show fear though I was showing plenty of the repellence I felt at his smothering clutch on me. It was curiously intimate, as if it had a physical component to it, his overplush body the actual weight shutting me in and yanking my strings. 'You get a lot of holiday work? Children's parties?'

Meanwhile the floss scalpel of the Confessor continued to work. The sensation of her presence filled me with a violent disgust even though there was nothing I could physically feel. Only my body was capable of recoiling and it was held in place by the Inquisitor's psychic vice.

'Wait, there's something...' her candyfloss voice murmured. Her eyes were half shut and her fingers made little spread-out, fishing movements as if groping around looking for lost lenses in a field of broken glass.

The woman from the car frowned. At that moment the guard arrived, breathless and hot, clearly having run.

'The High Alchemist has declared a closed investigation,' the first said, reporting in with a salute. 'You are to go immediately to the autopsy of the... of the...' He faltered.

'Of the bird,' the woman finished. 'Very well. Escort this priest to the interrogation cells. Under no circumstances is he to communicate with anyone.'

The Confessor glanced around at the door, looking irritated. The interruption had foiled whatever clues she was sponging up and her annoyance was peevish and childlike. The guard nearest to her cowered and leapt into position, weapon drawn.

'Yes, your Holiness.'

They waited until the other guard found his tape and bound me. Then, even though the three of them left together the Inquisitor's choke-hold remained. I could feel his presence long after he was gone and it remained alert even as I was taken out of the high apartments and down, past the entrance to the arboretum floor and into the warrens of cells and labs that lay underground. We dropped three floors to a level that was carved out of stone and I was left in a cell that was large enough for me to sit or stand, with a stone bench and nothing else. When the door closed its seam with the walls was so narrow it was barely visible, like a fine pencil line on the soft, chalky whiteness. A glow from an overhead panel provided a dim, unwavering light.

The Inquisitor's grip vanished once the door had closed. The mercury salt in the rock prevented it. But he wasn't needed. There wasn't even a window, merely a slatted vent carved into the ceiling. They had left my wrists bound up. In the sudden quiet, which was absolute, I felt a crushing sense of defeat. I'd always imagined myself and my warrior training to be more than the equal of any souped-up magician priest but the truth was I'd had no counter for either of their advances and even now I couldn't think of anything useful that might stop their command of me again. Perhaps it wasn't effortless, but they'd hardly sweated over it. I was going to get picked apart. The humiliation of it cut much deeper than I thought it had a right to. The worst part was that even until now I'd held out against believing a word of it. Against anything Isylon'd said. Fine. He was a dreamer and full of imagination, let him believe. Belief would have you imagine all kinds of powers you didn't have. But I was the one without the powers now. My mind still insisted Two was right. We lived in a materially ordained universe. But alone here, waiting, that was a tough story to swallow. I might be better off thinking she was mistaken and buying into the woo-woo. I wasn't going to be able to manage what I didn't believe in, was I?

I lay down on the bench after a while, thinking at least I could rest and store up some energy for whatever came next. I wondered if they were interrogating Isylon and what they'd

254

make of the dead bird. I kept thinking of that dark smoke that had left its body, a departing spirit coiling in the air.

I put my head on the bench, eventually found a way to rest it on my arms and hands and lie so that the robe was a small comfort. I thought about Two and Tashin, that two-faced bitch, lost somewhere in the marshy nightmare that was Kalunkat, hunted by the relentlessly well-provisioned forces of the Inquisition and by the vengeful cartels too. Maybe they'd all die in the swamp shooting each other. Fat chance.

I couldn't stop thinking about Tashin, particularly Tashin's body. You don't grow an adult in a vat. They have to be someone. I guessed that somehow 'sans' meant without a person inside. Tashin as I'd met her was an avatar. She had bought a body from the catalogue to use here on Harmony. Was there a good market of sales for these things where she came from, then? What happened to the person? I couldn't understand how it could possibly work, not that I understood most of how the world actually worked. But if you sell *sans*, where is that someone now Tashin is in there? What happened to her? What was Tashin's great, humanitarian excuse for that going to be? Because Tash riding me was one thing but in all the times I'd seen her I'd never glimpsed a hint of anyone else in there. Though I knew from experience that it was possible they were.

My disappointment and repulsion were so crushing they were worse than the Inquisitor's grip. It felt as if the bottom had fallen out of whatever vessel my heart had been in and the contents were now lost and splattered behind me. I realised that I'd held a faith in Tashin, a childish trust the same as the one I'd had in Two and myself until this moment, and suddenly I understood that belief was built on nothing but hope, because I needed to believe that someone was coming to the rescue, somehow, somewhere, even if I was going to do it. There would be a rescue, we would get out.

It was a decision to believe so, based on nothing. Tashin,

whatever she was, was a thieving liar who cared only about her own goals. I'd believed that her demands for evidence were all heading to a justified policing action against the people I hated, but had she proved that, had she told me so? No. I'd wanted to believe it, to make sense of what was happening to me, so I could choose to take part in it. So I could pretend I wasn't a stupid mule, pushed this way and that from the first. But why was the woman in the car a Cardinal from the Harmony High Echelon? What was she doing there at the very moment we ran to Chaontium? Was she the one who drove the car which hit me? Was Bitna Valkyrian within a hundred metres of that by accident? How could a person read another person's mind? How could they force a spirit into or out of a living body? How could there be such a thing as living fire and the energy of life? Surely it was Alchemy-talk for spooky bullshit nobody can prove or touch except the 'chosen' who are going to call all the shots? Even Isylon had to have a language to explain what he did so it made sense to him. He said 'spirit' but that didn't mean that's what it was.

And then there was the death and resurrection. One out, one in? Couldn't be possible, even as a nightmare. The body is a storehouse of memory infinitely more vast than the mind. A mind can't be an interchangeable entity and what is a life but a body in action? What is death but the body's inaction? The secret of the transition between one and another can't be an occupying presence of energy that exists above and beyond all that. Can it? And would that ghost have information? Could it think and suffer and love and diffuse without any connection to the physical? Was Isylon literally telling me that souls existed for brief moments of time or was he explaining an insight that had no other way of expressing itself within a human framework? Was Tashin a murderer in such cold blood as to take a body from someone not done with it? Without an Exalted like Isy, how did you even do such a thing? But maybe they had one. Valkyrian.

I wasn't dead though, that time. I was knocked out. I couldn't have been dead – look, surely I'd have *known* something like that?

Sleep threatened and I resisted it, but the queasy moment of confusions where images became words became drama whirled with an unexpected force. My body fell asleep, untouchable and unknowable suddenly, while my mind cleared.

Sst, Nico, can you hear me?

After a moment I realised that it was Two's voice, coming from the Switch. Relief tried to grab me but I waited. I didn't trust the way things were going enough to allow the full wash of joy.

Nico, it's me, Two. Tash is asleep. I'm using her Switch thing to talk to you. I've hacked its frequencies with some comms tech. Don't talk, just listen, I haven't got long. Every transmission to you runs the risk of discovery…

All right, maybe a smidgen of joy.

– Are you all right? Are you really in Kalunkat? What—

Shut up, Nico. Yes, yes. But the cartel fights have triggered an Inquisition of epic levels. They're arresting everyone. There's no going back. Someone gave us away. They know there's a spy, but for now they think it's someone still in Chaontium. We'll be on the move again soon. Earlier you were talking to someone else. Not Tash. Who was it?

– I wasn't.

My mind flashed back to Tashin's first hysteria.

That was an Offworld transmission. Something was talking and it wasn't her. If you keep doing that they'll find you. That stuff can be seen by the Aegis satellites. You have to stop it.

– Seriously, I have no idea what you're talking about. Unless it's the ship?

Shit. Of course it's the ship, you doof. But you didn't know? That's weird. She said ... ah, shit!

She cursed! A bit of a first for her. I felt a glow of paternal pride.

– Lover girl not the all-star revolutionary you were hoping for? Been doing a bit more cheating and lying, has she?

I could feel her annoyance with my bitterness but it was the hurt that was like a lance in my side. I hoped my apology would be transmitted with equal effectiveness, perhaps less lethal in quality. Sorry sorry, I sent, trying to say I was unable to do better.

I love her but I don't trust her. She was very upset before and she wouldn't talk about it. I've looked at the time logs on this stuff, I know it's going on a lot. But if it isn't talking to you then what's it doing?

– Well there's been an interesting incident here.

I filled her in on the dead bird missile, thoughts fast as light, including all those about Isy and me because it all tied together. It didn't go across as words, it just went.

Oh, Nic, she said and she was sorry and terrified in equal amounts. And happy for me. And sad.

I started to receive brief sense impressions of where she was: a fetid, murky place, ripe with the burr of frogs and the methanic wallop of rotting plants. Then there was a sudden uproar so intense I thought the monster from the black lagoon had come but in a moment it resolved to Tashin, awake and fulminating with rage at both of us.

You hacked me!

Two kept her presence in the Switch. *Well, you're keeping secrets and it's a bit late for outrages of that kind, don't you think?* She was sour with disappointment, wretched with all she didn't know and couldn't touch that seemed to lie so close to her fingertips.

Nic, I told you to stop talking to the ship. Her dismissal of

Two's remark was all but invisible, it happened so fast. She was all pragmatics and no care but under that I felt a terror of things coming apart, sliding out of her grasp, rushing headlong. *What have you* done?

– Doing all I can to get your information, Master, I said in my best asslicking tones. – I haven't called the ship even once but I think your grip is getting leaky. Interesting that it doesn't seem to want to obey you either. But don't worry about me. I'm good and safe in the Inquisition dungeons. I would guess you've got about an hour tops before I'll be decommissioned.

There was a pause as that sank in. I could see glimpses of a miserable shelter, wooden planks and a bodged door locked with a splintered piece of wood. It was as if my vision was clearing over time, or maybe their two inputs were strong enough to give me a better picture. I realised they were in the ground floor of an abandoned structure and outside there was a distant, intermittent sound of gunfire and the howls of dogs.

Out in the swamps something inhuman that was soaked into the ground told me that the Inquisition was coming, by twos and threes in their pale, fungal squadrons. They knew very well who they were looking for. They had the scent.

As soon as I knew it the others knew it too. Two moaned in terror, clutching Tashin's upper arm in her hands as the bigger woman got to her feet and started ransacking a holdall that had been under her head. She cursed at what she wasn't finding. Something was missing, or hadn't been packed, or had fallen out somewhere in the mire behind them. I felt her slump, her defeat and rage and resentment a familiar carcrash cocktail in my body as every part of my awareness was suddenly sucked down the invisible tunnels of the Switch into Tashin's avatar.

Eleven – are they guideposts
or spears in the ground?

In despair she knew she had to ask me. I could be shunted around like a railroad car but that was only location. If she wanted more there was only one thing she could do.

Nico, I need your help.

Rage warred with amazement and mostly lost.

– Shit, Tashin, am I in *you*?

I am giving you equality of control and perception. So: yes.

We were peering around some kind of barricade made out of rubbish. A head-turn to the left revealed the crouching figure of Two beside us. Her grip on our arm was vicious and hurt. I was so pleased to see her I reached out, only my hand didn't quite want to do it enough and struggled to stay put.

Shut up and stay still. They've found us. I need you to help me get out of here. Help us.

– Fine, but you have to stop getting in my way.

I tried to see, hear and feel for a better idea but dream-muddiness clung to everything, leaving it all blurred and indistinct. Tashin's refusal to let me grab control, I guessed.

Don't fight me, this is already hard enough. You'll get your minute. We're at the edge of Kalunkat by the gasworks, in an old furnace shed.

Despite the poor quality of the senses I could clearly hear gunfire and the characteristic puffy explosions that betrayed beam weapon assault. They were outside and not too far away. My guardian-fu had a very bad feeling about this.

– Sounds like a dead end. Tell me it's not.

There's a chance that if we can get out of this we can cross a ridge on the spoil heap to the north and then cross the coolant lake and get out into the country on the far side.

Vague impressions of this, a kind of notional map, came to me. It was possible, but a stupid position to be in.

– Why aren't you already going? What did you wait for?

I tried to make her show me Two so I could get a good look at her and see how she was doing. She'd let go of us. I saw her hands hard at work on some control pad, with those stabby, sudden moves she always had when she was anxious, but not the super-calm steady ones when she was frightened out of her mind.

The Inquisition have sent two guards here to mind the door until they could come back with reinforcements. They've got handguns, shock weapons and neural bolts. I could maybe get one but not before the other one gets me. But you can do both. You get rid of them and I'll take it from there.

– I want to talk to Two.

No way, there isn't time, Nico.

– Give me control.

I knew by her hesitation that once she handed over it would be up to me to hand it back and she didn't trust me. I didn't want to hand it back and she could feel it. But there was no choice.

With a sliding rush of sensation I felt suddenly, furiously awake.

Don't fuck it up, Nico.

– I hate it when you use my name.

Tashin's body was a lot less to work with than I was used to but I didn't let a little thing like that stop me. I grabbed Two's arm, as I'd always grabbed it in such situations – clamp on the wrist that looks hard but isn't – and she glanced up in surprise, whatever she was working on forgotten. She looked like she'd seen a ghost.

I signed to her that I was going to clear the way and she was to follow at my signal.

I had to grip harder then because she nearly fainted. 'Nico?' she mouthed, eyes wide.

I nodded and then pointed twice at the ground for *stay here* and made my move for the exit. It occurred to me as I slid past the old vent panels and saw the shadows of the guards outside that even if I did fuck this up it wasn't going to kill me. Only Two.

As it turned out the panels were too neatly piled in place to be handy cover for a secret approach. All that turned in my favour was the fact the two guards weren't expecting a breakout. I waited to see if any helpful gunfire or dog mayhem would come in our direction but it had moved off. Behind my eyes I could feel Tashin's apprehension and terror. It gave me quite some pleasure.

Surprise is always worth a good second or two.

I was honestly surprised that even with me on board Tashin's avatar didn't move faster and strike harder but it wasn't made for killing, more for lying around talking and drinking cocktails. Given its astonishing lack of power and fine motor control the cocktails might have been inbuilt. I watched my initial attack land and achieve nearly nothing – instead of breaking a neck and giving me a meatshield to deal with the second body I managed only to grab the guy around his collar and give him a mild choking.

The guards worked well as a pair so his first instinct was to spin to put me in the way of his partner. I botched that by pushing as hard as possible off the remaining foot of mine in contact with the floor. Something in my ankle hurt but I ignored it. Together we staggered and lurched against the second target and the only thing I could do at that point was let go and face two well alerted and seriously pissed off fighters.

– Why don't you have a fucking gun? This is all much easier with a gun.

Ran out of ammo yesterday.

First guy went left, other stepped right, both drawing weapons.

262

I went left and hard forwards, keeping him between me and the partner, going for his arm. The kind of blackout that focus brings fell on me. I was aware only of being alive, the moving and doing stuff was all being taken care of by some bit of me that didn't require a mind. I'd learned to stay out of things and watch at this point, prepared for nothing, expecting nothing. I heard and felt things breaking, the vibe of a weapon, the scorching heat of something, weakness, failing, impacts, my finger pulling a trigger clumsily over someone else's finger, then a strange exhaustion and then quiet.

The guards were down but something had gone badly wrong with Tashin's body – the right side didn't want to work, it slid around and had lost all sensation. I was lying over one of the guards. He wasn't moving. I tried to roll over. Nothing. We were down for the count.

Oh shit, what have you done?

– You said put them down. It's not my fault you're made of fucking paper.

Really, handing back the control wasn't such an issue, though I felt a bit bad about it, giving back a broken toy. Guiltier when I thought it was stolen too, as if it wasn't Tashin I'd let down but the original inhabitant who might be somewhere waiting for the day it would be returned.

Nico... I can't move. I can't leave now! How am I going to lead Two out of here? What's she going to do on her own?

I watched Tashin try to recover but it was clear to me this wasn't going to get anywhere. She had nerve damage and internal bleeding.

'Two!' she called hoarsely, her voice unrecognisable with weakness and a panicked gasping for air.

Two was out of hiding in a second, her own gun – why oh why show me it now?? – slung across her back, her kitbag hanging off her shoulder. Terror and panic blanked her expression as she bent over us.

263

'Fucksake, Tash, Nico – what's...?' She was looking around, putting the scene together, there was no need to ask or to say, it was all too obvious.

I could feel the damage – it was impossible to go anywhere – but yet not bad enough to kill quickly. It would take Tashin days to die.

From their distance the guns and shrieks of the battle they'd tried to escape came clearly around the derelict buildings and abandoned heavy gear. On the dead men some comms crackled and piped with voices demanding answers.

– Who is it?

Inquisition and the cartels. Both after us but got stuck fighting each other...

'Come on.' Two was getting out her first aid kit, looking for a splint.

Both of us knew that was never going to work.

Tashin grabbed weakly at Two with her right hand, almost able to touch her sleeve. 'Listen. It's just you now.'

'No!' Two shook her head, flicking at a syringe although there were tears in her eyes and she had to slash them against her sleeve to see what she was doing. She put a shot in but I didn't feel a change. 'I'm not leaving you here. Not for *them*.' It was the first time I'd felt and heard such pure hate in her voice.

Something banged and crashed – a gate going over, some rumbling vehicle pushing at a resisting panel. I heard drills and the scream of more beam weapons. That was Inquisition work. Now they'd lost the contact with their two idiots here they were heading back with a vengeance. Two wasn't going to be alone much longer.

Two knew that as well. She made a decision, dropped her kit and tried to pick Tashin up. For a moment she nearly made it but we were dead weight and she was thirty pounds lighter than Tashin on a good day. This was not that day.

'Two. You can still get out along the ridge like I showed you. Leave everything. I'll find a way to reach you again.'

Two wasn't listening but the lift had defeated her. She held Tashin in her arms, clinging. I could hear her murmuring 'No no no,' in a dead mantra.

Nico, you have to sell it to her. Make it fast.

I saw the sense of it and agreed. My heart hurt for Two.

'Two,' I said. 'It's me, Nico. Tashin's going to make it, just not gonna make it here. But she's not gone. I promise. She has other bodies, at least one.' The last was a guess but I felt its rightness as soon as I said it. And I was out of my depth again. How could you have multiple bodies? But that wasn't my problem right now because I was about to head back to my own.

'Nico,' Two whispered. I could feel her hands on our face, shaking in shock.

'If she stays here the Inquisition will find her and get their hands on the Switch. Then they'll have me too. You have to shoot her and take out the Switch, Two. Get it and take it with you. Understand? Because you have to do it *now.*'

The vehicle was winning its fight with the gates. Voices yelled. There was the whine and pop of a signals droid coming out of plus-mach high air travel.

Two made a horrible moaning sound. It was quiet, but continuous. I saw her take off her jacket and then nothing – she'd thrown it over our face. There was the hard press of the gun over our heart, then the sudden fierce fire of a beam-knife and a shocking explosion of pain which ended as Tashin broke the connection to me.

I lay alone and alive in the Inquisition cell, my bones sore from the stone bench, silence everywhere. I moved slowly, the echoes of destruction inside my limbs. I shook off the phantom deaths, made myself move to get myself fully anchored where I was supposed to be.

She was tough, Two. She'd make it.

I didn't believe in god but I had a deal with him that if anything happened to her then all bets were off with me. He had to take care of her or I'd unleash everything I'd got left into his world with the sole aim of ruin. Kind of a bullshit thing to do, but I fucking dared him to let her fall.

That is a kind of bullshit only you could come up with.
   – Ah and I knew you had another fucking card up your sleeve.
   This is the last one, so you'd better not screw it up or we're all finished.
   – Where are you?
   She didn't bother to answer. *I need you to tell the ship to stop.* There was a weary impatience to her tone, as if she were a parent faced with an endlessly disobedient child who has no idea of the reasons it's forbidden to do things and can't care. Dying had clearly rattled her.
   – I don't talk to it. I already told you.
   Yes, that's why it launched an infiltration protocol. I don't know how you're getting around my collar but the important thing is that you stop, or Harmony will alert the Sol System Security forces and they will find us before we find you.
   I felt extras in her concerns, intangible, uncertain, connected with the ship's provenance. Not only the sensation that she was losing control, but a feeling of being tracked in her own right.
   – You stole it.
   I took it without permission. I was ... there are reasons which needn't bother you now.
   – You are one psycho bitch, Tash, I'll give you that.
   I knew you'd admire me in the end.
   – You killed someone to use their body like a toy. Admiration is not what I'm feeling.
   Without it I would never have passed in Harmony. I used a Switch. She wasn't dead. We had a deal. It's unfortunate that your carelessness killed her.
   My anger became white hot. The clay of me became glass,

clear and crystalline with the purity of my intent that some-where, somewhen there was going to be a reckoning for this.

– It's all on your head. You never told me. And I hope you have a great time explaining it to Two. I'm sure she'll love you after that.

Was it my imagination or was that a sweep of crushing shame? Someone was very hurt. Someone was smothering their pain, boxing it up and shipping it out to a place it could explode later. It was both of us. Even as I'd been talking I knew I never wanted her to explain it to Two. I never wanted Two to know that there was a good chance that the person she loved was dead or had never been what she thought they were.

I don't have to tell her, and neither do you.

She was a spineless bitch, but that was true.

– I'm sure you'll find a good reason to split up with her before I have to do it for you.

Let's stick to business. I need all my resources to restrain this ship. Believe me, you don't want its full attention.

I considered the implications of her threats. Really, at this stage, what possible leverage could she have on me? But I found she had some effect, namely hardening my resolve to never, ever connect with someone else's bullshit. The feeling of rage, hubristic, crazy, ready to burn anything in order to burn what it hated, was a fire in my nerves. I enjoyed the curious pain of not moving as it lived in every cell I possessed, invisible as it strove to incinerate me. I thanked eternity for my master, who had taught me that you could feel anything and not act on it, that you could love even hate for the sheer gloriousness of being a thing capable of such magnificent hatred. I felt the minotaur fully restored, his bones my bones, his horns and tail mine. He had wings now too, ready to fly. Old skin and bone, tattered from war, they thrummed in the rising winds.

– What drives you, Tash? What is all this really about,

because I'm sure as fucking hell that it isn't about getting some dipshit like Tecmaten on a technicality charge.

I need the proof. That's all you need to know.

– And if you don't get it?

Then you can kiss your ass and Two's goodbye. We're rather closer to that than I'd like as it is.

– And yours?

That won't be your concern, will it?

She was right again. She had the cards and I had to suck it, for now.

It cost me almost my entire being to acknowledge that. I felt like I was going to explode. But if I was ever going to get my hands around her throat I had to survive this first.

And she was gone.

I lay there, considering. Pirate. I guess that means someone out only for themselves, to whom nothing and nobody is an expense too far. She and Tecmaten seemed more like bedmates than opponents, as I'd first imagined. I was the prisoner of pirates, pretty much out of the game unless I did something unexpected and possibly unimaginable. The only thing on my horizon was the ship.

My pride hurt me as it died another death.

What kind of idiot believed there was *only one Switch*?

A sudden change in environment startled me out of my self-hate and all my senses turned instantly to the outside, forgetting. I saw a jaguar sitting in the pattern of the grey shadows on the white stone wall in front of me cast by irregularities of the stone. It was watching me. A breath moved the pattern on its coat. The tip of its tail made an impatient, irritated gesture. Instinct told me this was the shadow I'd glimpsed before.

I stretched my hand out towards it. What did you say to an unhinged, inhuman creature prowling your subconscious?

I said, 'Come on, bro. Come and get me, if you're coming.'

It was gone. There was no discernible pattern of any kind on the rough surface and the light of the distant sun was also gone, leaving only the dim glow of the salt light.

The locks sounded their whirr and clack, far more bolts than necessary.

I sat down on the bench as the door opened, and slumped, trying to look defeated and stupid and miserable – not that much of a stretch, but I'd take any advantage I could get.

The man who entered was small, hunched over with age, using a stick to support himself. His hands on it were knobbed with arthritis and the skin was so thin and papery that the veins stood out, even the smallest of them, in strange blue and red traceries like a map scribbled by a child. His robe was made of lighter cloth but it was supremely fine and only this gave away the answer as he asked, 'Do you know who I am?'

'Tecmaten,' I said. If he'd come in person then things were pretty bad.

Everything about him was struggling to carry on living. I could feel it as clearly as if his body was shouting it. He was exhausted, animated by a thin breeze of will blowing through an entirely worn out husk. When he tugged his cowl away with several motions, impatient with his failures but at the same time accepting them so that his stoicism transmuted his anger into a kind of strength, his face was the drawn skull of a man who has burned up every bit of his energy and is existing on fumes. The bone visible through his fragile skin was shockingly yellow, his eyes a colour I couldn't really see well, because they were so sunken and blinking, red and glistening with ointment.

'Yes,' he said. 'And you are a creation of my greatest creation, Valkyrian.'

When I didn't answer he looked annoyed. I watched the corners of his mouth with their brown lines of uncleared saliva left there unknowing, stickily tacking against one another up and down as the words kept on coming. I supposed I wouldn't get to be that old.

'You ended up with the catalysed mistake, of course, just like the others.'

I wondered why we weren't cutting to the chase and having me mentally vivisected like before. Unless the whole point was to annoy me? Now I considered it that had to be his major MO anyway, given the nature of the state he'd created. My choice to take the silent high road started to veer. What would the harm in talking be anyway? Hadn't I decided on this master plan with exactly that idea?

'It's not a mistake, it's a feature,' I said. Ugh, I'd have to cut to the chase myself. The words came easy, like jabs. Sliding into a fight was always good. 'I was sent here to prove you're tricking the outcomes and the Alchemy is bollocks. Not the idea about creating gods part. Everyone thinks that's bollocks. I mean the actual science part. The Exalted. Spirits. Life after death. It's not real.'

An Inquisitor and a Confessor eased into the cell behind him, more or less filling it.

'They're not necessary,' I said. 'I'm glad to tell you whatever you want to know.'

'They're necessary,' he said. 'I don't want to hear it from you.'

The vice of the Inquisitor descended. I lay down in his grasp by my own movements, a puppet again. I wondered if I would survive this. I could accept it either way. Some part of me had run to the end of its rope here. To be beaten like this, without a whisper, without a breath, to be helpless, it was a defeat that was equal to death because I had no power against it and it took me with effortless ease. There was no shame in it other than missing a fight. I could exert my will but there was no apparatus or contact point through which I could convert my opponent. I didn't have whatever it took and there was no story I could tell myself, no joke that lessened it. Whatever happened now I was only a witness.

With the knowledge a strange relief came over me, a lightness like that feeling I'd had when I met Isylon and crossed over from one life in which he didn't exist, to another.

'Interesting you think this to be unreal,' Tecmaten said, though there wasn't much relish in his tone. He was beyond relishing anything. 'And you don't accuse me of making them with help from the unholy technologies.'

A fox moved, winter white coat white against the snowy wall. Its feet left no trail but snow swirled up around it in the finest frost flakes. They glittered, dust motes, and settled onto the shoulders of the Confessor and the Inquisitor, melting suddenly into nothing.

My thoughts became foggy, distant. The Confessor said, 'He is with the Sol System spy. There is a technology inside him that connects them.'

'But what does she want?' He was puzzled. 'Why is she here? To steal the Exalted?'

'He doesn't know,' she replied. 'He's only a hand she uses.'

Tecmaten thought for a moment, then turned with an effort and shuffled out between the two. 'Well, ensure that you cut off that hand, Inquisitor. But leave him alive.' He paused at the threshold and half turned back towards me. 'No doubt you're here full of righteous justice at the inequitable society I have made, particularly for someone of your ten percenter-ness. Perhaps you wonder why it is that the Exalted and so many others of the talents that arise from the Alchemy are miraculously part of a vilified underclass, doomed to spend their lives in miserable hiding and with feelings of great inadequacy and shame heaped upon them, the spectre of their death always close at hand, hmm? Those are indeed factors well worth some thought. Do you suppose it's really true that for all our abilities with the elements we still manage to output this level of error? That will be something for you to consider from the situation you have got yourself into.'

271

He left and the door closed behind him with the soft crump of a single footstep in a deep drift.

The Inquisitor scratched his neck. He glanced at the Confessor. 'How am I supposed to do that?'

'I don't know,' she said. 'But it's not my problem.' She gave him a pitying look and shrugged. 'I wouldn't do too much. He's got a temper when he's disappointed, but it's up to you of course.'

'This can't be what he intends to use as...'

'I wouldn't second guess it. Just disconnect him. That will be enough.'

Suddenly I couldn't feel my body at all. I could think, see and hear, but there was nothing beyond those two senses.

'I'm not sure that will cut the contact with whatever tech is in there,' the Inquisitor said unhappily, 'but I can't do any more without killing him. I don't feel the technology. Check it.'

She came back to me, my eyes still turned to the door so I could see her very well. She was scratching her ear and frowning. 'I... oh, all right.' She stood there. I felt nothing. 'It's fine,' she said. 'You've done it. Let's go.'

The door closed behind them. Step two.

The fox came out of the wall and stood in the middle of the floor. The fact it was a fox and not a cat didn't alter my conviction that it was the same being. It could manifest as any form it liked. I guessed jaguar was stealthy but fox was crafty and here we needed some craftiness. It shook its luxurious coat and a scatter of tiny diamonds fell out of it. Then it leapt lightly onto my chest, sat down and with its nose turned my head so that my skull was aligned with the rest of me. I was still staring at it as whiteness closed in around its dark eyes until the eyes were the only thing left to see, ever larger and darker until the eclipse was total.

12 – three fours or four threes: yes, it's important which one

I woke into what I knew was definite dream territory by its familiarity – a place I visited frequently when asleep that was made up of a mishmash of places I'd been as a runaway. It was a breaker's yard, full of junk and reclaimed scrap. The iron walls were too high to see over or get over and as far as I knew there was no door. Coming here meant I was searching for something and would almost certainly end up lost. I never liked it and recognised it with irritation now: you see a magical fox and then you're back into this ordinary anxiety-dream shit?

My dream self went on with his mooching, poking at things, looking for a way out, much as usual. I felt that at least I knew it was a dream and therefore the boredom and the low-grade grinding sense of wrongness would soon be over, all I had to do was wait it out until it ended as it always did, with some catastrophe that swallowed me and I woke wondering if this was it, this time.

I was pulling out some box of parts to look inside when I noticed that among the masses of domestic machinery and droid debris a few electrostatic sparks were flying. Sometimes they ran on a bit in tiny jagged streams of white and blue light. That was new. I didn't want to touch them in case I got electrocuted. I once miswired a battery to one of Two's creations and got thrown four metres, knocked out and burned. The memory of the pain and the months it took for this strange electricity to stop riffling through my nerves was what stopped me now. The static light crawled around. Its movements as a whole looked purposeful, like it was searching too.

I heard footsteps and a familiar breath – then Two turned the corner in front of me and she was there, just like that. She was smaller than in life, a kid again, as was I. She was wearing brown rags that camouflaged her against the iron and mud of the Bayou Settling Ponds where we had lived for a while until the noise of the frogs and the unease of the overly still water below the power plants moved us on. It'd been our worst place.

'Nico!'

We were in each other's arms like guided missiles. Our bones hurt in the hug.

'Where are you?' the lucid part of me broke in to the happy moment. We stepped apart, nervously looking around for patrol droids.

'Chaontium. The jackworks. I was looking for parts for this Switch. I don't think it's gonna last long. It needs blood or something. It's living, somehow. But I can't make it out here. I'm gonna go back and see if Kasha Dann will protect me.'

'That's crazy.'

'I'm going to give her the Switch, tell her I took it from Tashin, and tell her we can make them for ourselves, cut out the offworld problem.'

Greed and profit, Dann might go for that. It was about the only thing I could imagine her buying. 'And can you?'

'No. But she won't know that until I've made other plans. I can't stay out here, Nic. The fucking Inquisition are everywhere and the cartels are shooting anything that moves.' She was shaking as if she was cold and wet. Her hunger was a visceral bite in my guts.

I took hold of her upper arms, trying to stall the fear with

274

my grip. I didn't want to tell her what had become of me so I told her only that I was in prison. 'Tell me what to do.'

'I don't know what you should do. But I know this. The Switch in you is not like this one, the one Tashin had.' She lifted her hand and I saw in it a dripping piece of meat. It couldn't be mistaken for fresh steak – it was disintegrating into dirty water. I hoped that was a dream effect. 'Yours is – bigger. It has about a billion more things.'

'Then how come she always has control? I can hardly use it.'

'I don't know. I guess she had some backdoor put in it so she always had a hold over us.' She faltered and looked down, shamefaced. 'I'm sorry, Nico. I was such a fool.' She looked up, fighting off tears. The sluggish piece of Tashin's brain in her hand dripped forlorn black water into the mud.

I thought about her having to hack it out of her beloved's head and then carry it around with her, trying to find a way to make it work as she realised how very deeply we'd been had. Pity for her felt like it was breaking me in two.

'There's a question I need answered,' I said. 'You're smart, you can do it.'

She grinned mirthlessly, sad eyes crying. 'You should've gone to college, you sonofabitch. But go on. What is it?'

'Why would you make someone to be an outcast?' Vague intimations of the expanse and setting of the real question leaked out of me, the memory too recent to be hidden. She caught it.

'Nic, what happened to you?'

'I'm fine,' I said. 'Just answer the question.' I thought I knew, but I wanted confirmation. What do you get when you put people in that position? What makes them different to the rest?'

'You mean me an' you,' she said, sniffing back a noseload of snot and trying to wipe it on the back of the hand holding the Switch. She frowned, breathing through her mouth a few times, her breath misting a bit as the air around her swirled with a sudden chill. 'I don't know, I guess we're always on the back foot, like you say. We want to belong and we can't so it turns us, like a key. We're always afraid somewhere, and it wears us out. We're watchful, not asleep like the rest, not quite as asleep. We know they could turn on us, if they wanted to, any time. It makes us something you can call in any time, use as you like for the fear of death hanging over you.' She chuckled, shivered, her teeth chattered a bit. 'Why are we in this yard, Nic?'

'Dunno, I guess the yard is what all that represents to me.'

'Yes, but why are we sharing your dream yard? Why is it so cold— Wait, seriously is that how it is, Nic? We were made this way just so that there's a reason to kill us any time? If that was needed?'

Which was the answer I'd come up with: test subject aborted. I held on to her, as if by doing that I could maintain a physical link with my own body as well as with her. 'Stay alive,' I said to her, willing it to happen. 'I'll get out of this and I'll get you out.'

She looked so desolate.

I remembered. '*She*'s still alive. I heard from her.' Two looked up, sullen but trying to find it in her to keep caring. To prove it I added, 'She told me to get the evidence if I wanted to get out.'

'That does sound like her.' She smiled faintly for a split second. She had the look of someone not quite with it, as though worldly concerns were of no consequence.

A crackle of white lightning snapped overhead between two ramshackle pylons.

'I think this yard is the ship,' I said.

Two nodded vaguely at me and then she sharpened up suddenly. 'What if Tashin's Switch isn't really a Switch at all but a Relay?' She shook her head like she used to when she had to dumb stuff down for the dim guy and said it again, a different way. 'Suppose what she's got is in the way, between you and whatever is out there? That's how she'd keep the controls to herself, by routing everything through her connections. But if she's talking to you now then she's got another one. Must have

276

another body or another – something. Somewhere. Fucking offworld *bitch*!' A strange exulting had come over her with the triumphal reasoning she'd managed, coupled with a fierce admiration for Tashin and another dose of self-recrimination. I couldn't tell if she was more admiring of Tashin or more angry.

Shame for the avatar's death coated me in a thin film of sweat. At least Two could still be a good guy.

'She told me it was crazy,' I said, scuffing the filthy ground with the toe of my boot. It was one I'd worn until the soles came off. I still remembered everything about it, down to the last stitch. It still hurt me where my foot had grown too big for it.

Around the spoil heaps the white and blue lightning crept up and down, oiling smoothly as if part of the scale pattern of a single enormous snake. As it explored the surface of a dead 'bot something came loose and a load of tiny components went skittering downhill to cascade over our feet. Two bent reflexively and grabbed one up, peered at it.

'Tygon Chip,' she said.

'What?'

She blinked. I'd never heard her use that name before. 'Offworld tech. Why would that be in *your* dreamscape?'

'Two, did you ever wonder why you're so good at fixing and breaking machines?'

'No.' She faded, about halfway to nothing, as if she were a ghost. Her mind was elsewhere. 'If this is a Relay, then I should be able to find the other connections, if there are any.'

I saw her about to go off into one of her genius fugues and shook her firmly to get her eyes back on me. 'That won't help. Only she can block the ship if that's what she's going to do.'

'It's getting away from her,' Two said, looking around. Her form flickered. 'I'm losing this Switch. Listen, if Dann goes for it I'll get back into some proper gear and maybe then I can get back into the mix. It'll take a couple of days, if I survive.'

I was about to agree when a tremor shook the ground. Then

another. The light began to dim and at the same moment the surges of electricity that had been creeping around us increased. A coil of lightning fibres crept together like vines, twining, building as they came out of the spoil heaps on either side. Without warning a single lash leapt out and snaked around Two's ankle.

With a shriek she looked down at her feet and then up at me, sudden surprise making her mouth and eyes into zeroes. She spoke as fast as she could, 'It's the ship. It found me! It's throwing me out! Nico, you need to wake up!' She cringed backwards in a whole-body flinch, the bloody chunk thrown from her fingers as if it'd bit her, and there she vanished.

I stumbled forwards, hands closing on thin air.

In her place a ripple of static licked the ground.

Before I had time to decide whether or not I believed that if you die in your dreams you die for real the colour of everything began to change. A red haze spread quickly like blood in water. The heaviness of my nightmare – that oppressive heat and pressure from above – closed in. On instinct I looked for somewhere to hide.

A sound like a sigh came over the wall – an *ahhh!* of recognition that something longed for is found at last. I heard and felt a heavy tread though it seemed to come from all over, as if I was surrounded on all sides by one thing. I knew I couldn't escape it here. This was not going to go well for me. I had no illusions. I was the sparrow.

The need to wake up became all-consuming. I felt my awareness falter, tried to cling to the sense that this was a dream but my conviction scattered. I was on the wrong hunting ground at the wrong moment. This place which had once been mine now belonged to him and I couldn't put two thoughts together anywhere on it now he had my scent.

'Who's that trip-trapping across my bridge?' said the dirt inside Two's bootprints.

The stalking sensation creeping on my skin hesitated, as if

my hunter listened. In that moment I sensed an open door and leapt for it. The electricity caught me effortlessly in mid-jump, rushing up from the ground into the holed soles of my shoes. It ran through me with a thrilling, overpowered rush, a pain so intense and physical, so rooted in my body that the fact of my connection to it and the world of the living could be in no doubt. I was sure it would kill me and so, like the sailing moment of freedom between the wall and the car, I did nothing but watch, amazed at how strange and beautiful everything was and had always been though I almost never noticed it until these two separated instants in which I could not hope to have any control at all. I had nothing. I had always had nothing.

It ended with me on my feet in the yard.

High on a spoil heap at the other end of the yard a malformed creature, part animal and part machine, squatted on its haunches. It looked stitched together, but effectively. It was huge, red-eyed and contemplative, this beast that the ship had made for a body. It was observing me as I stood in its demesne. Bloody red fuel oil dripped from its claws. It was like a dog, if a dog is like a dragon and that dragon has been assembled from the death of a minor world.

I was in my old sweatpants and my worst pair of trainers. My washed-until-it's-ruined T-shirt of a moonrise over old Earth was soft against my skin. The air was charged with anticipation.

The hunt was on.

Thirteen. Triskaidekaphobia can kiss my ass

My master used to speak of stalking. A warrior stalks himself. I didn't get that for years. Stalks himself. Like you didn't know where you were. But finally I got it. She meant stalking yourself inside, watching your mind think instead of being thought by it. You stalk yourself to see what you're making of the world, to make sure you're not constructing some harmful load of bullshit that gets in the way of being who you really are.

Now the ship and I were stalking each other. After that would come the showdown display. If that didn't get us a winner then there would be a real fight. Warping of reality or not, if you think you're hunting me down and killing me without some trouble you've backed the wrong horse.

When I looked hard at the creature on the heap I saw through it clearly. I saw beyond Harmony and its four-mile atmosphere, beyond its moon and the rings of satellites put up to keep sanity at bay with their constantly disrupting fuzz-work of interference. Far off in the deep ocean of space, where its leviathan physical body had once flicked a fin and launched a bird, the ship I'd come to call Beast lay at rest, wakeful and twitching in its Nico-tainted dreams. Right here. Right now.

Between us a barrier. We leaked around it like trickling blood.

I got the impression that Tashin was there, not in the Relay, but actually *out there*, aboard the ship. She wasn't alone either.

There were others, faint blobs of greyish energy floating around like motes of dust, all dwarfed by the enormous physical mass of the Beast's slumbering body. Even I grokked at that point – this is really a ship. This is *the* ship. This is the ship which I have the Switch for.

This is my *ship*.

This is *my* freaking ship!

The Beast on the spoil heap seemed to smile. The bay of its mouth opened to reveal row on row of white, gleaming fangs: a buried army on a red plain. Behind them smouldering fires flickered and glowed, casting shadows like the murky patterns on the surface of the sun.

I had to stop then, and hold my breath, and hide in plain sight by freezing so I wasn't noticed; the surge of excitement I'd sparked was all choked up inside me like a lit firework I'd just swallowed. But the fuse was burning.

The smell of psychic gunpowder was enough. The Beast twitched and stirred, rumbling in its scrapheap bed. It rose, an island of iron suddenly made liquid by animation, and on cats' careful paws began to silently descend to the ground. We were on.

Tashin came barrelling out of nowhere with the impact of a bullet. The creature and the entire landscape froze, quivering with resistance as she held it in stasis. It cost her a great effort.

Stop right there. Go back. You don't know what you're doing. You have no idea what you're dealing with. You'll ruin everything, for ever. I mean it. Stop!

I stayed put because there was real heartfelt appeal in her voice that was entirely new to me.

– Tell me what's going on here or I will wake it up.

You can't.

I started to open my dream-mouth with the intention of exposing the blue touchpaper and lighting all fuses. I was a dead man waiting in a gaol cell for someone to come and fuck me up any way they wanted. I really didn't put any store in promises about futures and cursed myself for ever having done so.

She knew I meant business.

Fine. Stop. I'll tell you.

I shut my mouth again.

There was a pause, a gathering of wits and resolve, a resignation, a commitment. I believed whatever she was about to say. Her bitter reluctance if nothing else made me think it would be some form of the truth.

This 'ship' is Forged Darkcaster Shoftiel the Judge of god.

– Hell of a name.

It didn't call itself that.It was intended to bring law and order to the wider reaches of the Diaspora but it has shunned all human convention: entirely rogue. Out in the wider systems it is the subject of various agencies' extreme measures actions—

– So who did you steal it from?

I rescued it from certain death. A thing like that could not be permitted to roam freely at its own incomprehensible whims. Plus the ship itself has an interest in the Exalted. I came here to find out the truth of Tecmaten's developments...

She paused and I felt omissions fleeing between us silently in an effort to escape. At the same time the dream juddered and the beast put a paw down, then snagged, frozen again.

– There's a personal reason too.

I met Bitna Valkyrian. This was years ago. On Harmony's closest waystation, where they do all their trading. Her story of what was going on here convinced me that SolSystems should immediately intervene and shut Harmony down on choice crimes, but we were under a black order not to interfere here. So I had to come here and get enough evidence to convict. I will make it public.

– So you're a rogue, with a stolen vessel. I don't think this could get any better. And choice theft? Seriously.

Ironic, I know. But choice theft is one of the primary crimes of the Diaspora. The imposition of a nonbeneficial state of being on another through physical, psychological or other means.

– Tell me about the ship. Why are you micromanaging the shit out of everything?

It, unfortunately, did not turn out as intended. That's why it was fitted with the Switch and assigned pilots who were to look after it and help it to manage itself. However it has rejected all its guardians to date. With some prejudice: there were eight of them, all are now dead. It is slated for termination due to having an unbalanced mind and an unstable personality inconcomitant with its capacity for extreme destruction. It has its own reasons for wanting to know about Exaltation and is here only on the promise that it would discover the truth. It's been under voluntary sedation and restraint in order to prevent it compromising the mission. The only reason it hasn't been hunted down yet is that there's nobody with the balls to come get it. But they'll make up an army for it in time. Until then as far as the System security is concerned I can do whatever I want with it as long as it's not their problem. They know I'm out here. They gave me the rope. They're waiting for me to hang myself.

Nico? Am I to understand that finally you have nothing to say?

Nico.

– Your drugs aren't working.

What are you talking about?

– I don't know what the technical term for it is but I am being hunted down right here and right now by this thing you claim is in a straitjacket. It's here. We've met.

Then it was her turn to be silent.

I don't know how that's possible. Everything on the control collars looks like it's working from here.

– And where's that?

283

I'm on board. Hibernation is ongoing. There's no significant activity anywhere. I don't understand it.

She sounded panicky. The Beast rippled with static and very slowly it began to resume its descent of the slope towards me, progressing one jerky centimetre at a time. This time in response to Tashin's command it only snarled. There was no pause.

– Did you use *it* when you shot the guards at my execution?

Of course, but only a very small subset of its capacities. It was only aware of the mission particulars, nothing else. When it was done there was no change in its status.

– Are you sure?

Of course I'm sure.

– If it didn't kill me then why would it now?

It always let them live for a while, testing them, trying them out.

– Why not just destroy it if it didn't work out?

We aren't in the business of killing what doesn't suit us. We had it made. Sometimes things are not as intended. We were responsible and we took that seriously.

There was a hesitation about her. I waited, and waited, wondering about this *we*. We. Suddenly she was an agent with a bunch of buddies again.

The Beast got its forefoot onto the ground. Now there were only a few steps between us.

The issue was always with the final decision-making process. We thought that the burden of destruction should always be shared so that whoever ordered the platform – the ship – to act was accountable, and so that it didn't have to take those decisions alone. The situations we face often require very fast, on-the-spot actions. There's no time for strategy, referrals, orders. Reaction must be instantaneous but also within the law. But somewhere in that process it started to make decisions about the pilots, the handlers, the support crews and various other places,

outposts, colonies. It made moral judgements alone, very quickly,
and that led to it drawing some unfortunate conclusions.

The Beast snarled again, leaving its lips curled up over its teeth. I knew it could hear every word.

– It didn't think any of you were worthy.

No.

– So you all figured that eventually it was going to judge you – prejudicially?

It said so itself.

– But it didn't do it?

No. But that was why it was slated for termination. The risk.

– Wow. Slated for termination. Bad kitty, huh? How come it hasn't killed you?

I promised to find it a suitable pilot, one that could help it to manage itself and all the things it doesn't understand because we never enabled it to.

And there we had it all, for what it was worth. The whole sad story.

The Beast was before me, one brief leap away.

I felt Tashin leave, the falling coin hitting the floor with a surprise note of being lost and not put down. It had been put down *for* her and her astonishment was the last thing that came over the connection. The Beast had allowed her to tell the tale and now it had cut her off, her usefulness completed. It had wanted me to know.

The time for our private reckoning had come.

I was at the edge of the reclamation yard, hands empty, in my old training sweats, ruined trainers. The Beast had dissipated suddenly from his giant form into a thousand shadows that flew out in all directions. They slipped and gathered, ran like water, briefly forming shapes that hunted around the surface of every object between us. They roosted in corners and fluttered across the edges of the wreckage.

It was hypnotic. I had to force myself to consider my exits.

There were none. Well that was typical. Gossamer strands of black silk leapt towards me, twining into threads, then cables, until it seemed every surface was splitting apart as whatever was inside demanded exit. The lines wrapped around me fast as whips and where they touched my skin felt like it had caught fire.

I knew it hadn't. I said no to fire and the burning stopped. The Beast sought to pour up every nerve ending and at every point I was a sure, cold *No*. I was through with merging and blending and co-operating and being taken over. *No*.

The intensity and speed of attack leapt up, the black smothering my face, my eyes and ears, nose, every entry, but as the moments passed my conviction increased. I could die here, but not in any physical way. This body was an illusion. This assault was a suggestion. I need do nothing. I was not moved.

The gates of the yard flew open, blown off their hinges right in front of me as the shadow weave withdrew itself. They opened onto a vision of incredible destructive power: fatal ignition in the hearts of stars, an expanding sheet of radiance encompassing planets within seconds. The view shifted to within the planets' atmospheres as they boiled away, stripped in seconds, oceans evaporating, cities and forests on fire, animals and people, everything living being torn to bits, turned to ash with the energy of their own bodies: men, women, children, babies, nothing and nobody was spared. I saw so many faces with a momentary inkling turning to look at me, wondering, and then there was nothing left of them but my memory. It was no hellfire with its promises of endless pain, it was ashfire: a total rendering from wonder to dirt.

I was the ship and although my rage consumed everything it showed me it could not consume me, though I wished it would if just to put an end to it all.

Then I was myself again and the ship was spewing at me. A barrage of violence followed that I struggle to depict. Imagine every soldier, every spy, every assassin, every torturer of all kinds deployed at once and for ever. Just and unjust, with cause and without, they flow with the ripple of igniting petrol vapour over the innocent and the guilty alike. The scenes were high speed, merciless and insistent. They searched me for an answer like a relentless scourge. I felt they demanded a response from me: here we are, what do you make of this?

That was easy. None of it was anything to do with me. 'Thanks for making me witness this shit. There's ten minutes of my life I won't get back.'

Everything stopped.

The yard morphed. One wall vanished, the mud and mess becoming wooden boards. It now opened onto my rooms at Ito. I walked out into them and it felt so real I could have doubted that it was a dream were it not for my memory of where my body really was being so sharp and clear in my mind.

I opened my bedside drawer and with that action I felt the strange conviction that there was another me, an avatar that was an exact replica, alive and acting far from the real me and here I was, both him and not him. Yes, the ship confirmed. Bodies from the air. Real enough. Objects of any kind, once imagined.

It had constructed a copy of me and was piloting it around in my absence – was that right? Yes, came the reply. Yes, that's what has happened.

The slight comfort of the dream shattered. I couldn't reach into the waking world. I could only witness what this ship was going to do with the new me it had made. I was along for the ride and I felt every move and every second.

With calm purpose and the knowledge of exactly what it was going to pick out my hand selected the heavy knife that I remembered from the apartment Two and I used to share. The inside of the drawer was our kitchen drawer and it felt unsurprising to find it here although part of me knew then that this was one more layer of trick. The knife was eight inches of steel with a pointed tip and it sat in perfect balance like every good knife should – a demon in material form, merely awaiting a mind weak enough to command.

I closed the drawer with my other hand as I left the room and walked silently across the laboratory to Isylon's quarters.

He was asleep on his daybed, a pillow cuddled in his arms and another under his head. Lines on his face and twitches revealed stress that wouldn't let go of him even when he was unconscious. He didn't hear me arrive and showed no sign of waking up. Outside the door two Confessors stood guard but they didn't notice me.

The ship queried silently: what will you do when I threaten what matters? If I make you do this thing, what will you do?

– If you do something it's *nothing* to do with me. Your choice.

I was barely aware of speaking and I didn't expect to be heard. It was for the record. For me.

I went to stand next to Isylon and watched the knife point take up a place one millimetre off the skin of his temple. A child could kill him from here with a good solid shove downwards. Then we waited. I felt expectancy, perhaps a threat from me would be forthcoming? Would there be pleading, tears, twisting on the uncertainty like a bug on a pin? There was a keen anticipation about it, a palpable breathlessness.

Do not engage. I don't even believe the sparrow tiger theory. How could you ever know which was which?

I did nothing. Life could go like this any time. Fate comes, you're powerless, there's no escape, that's it. Wasn't I already in the dungeon, incapacitated? What actually went through my mind was a streak of furious impatience.

– Really – is this all you've got?

I saw my hand on the knife hilt – my gaze was fixed to it. Beneath its point Isylon's unprotected head with its load of toffee-coloured hair was suddenly an innocence and a vulnerability too far. My contempt and impatience snapped out of control.

288

– Give me a fucking break. If he dies then you never get your answers. You're showing me your power? Cool. Now fucking do something worth doing, instead of this pissing contest.

I felt a grinding furious annoyance with myself that my last experience was going to be furious annoyance with myself. So much holding back, for so long, and now I had to let everything fall to pieces when it mattered the most?

I felt voluntary control entrusted back to me immediately and completely. At the same moment the avatar Nico shattered into dark dust, knife and all. The particles lifted up on the warmth of Isylon's breath and dissipated into the air as smoke.

We were back in the salvage yard and stood in the open gateway, shoulder to shoulder, I and the Beast.

Fourteen: at last, my lucky number

He was a jaguar, his shoulder as high as my waist, his fur mottled with shadows in the patterns of distant constellations. His breath came in steady rumbles, as deep and powerful as an engine. We walked out of the yard and into the lighting rigs and the arena, the cages and the dancing girl decks of Chaontium's underground, and though the crowds and the vendors were ghostly with unimportance my five dead opponents stood waiting for me in the ring.

The Beast looked up at me with green eyes like lamps. We might be talking now, but we weren't done. He wanted to know what I thought of this place and this killing. I made no move to enter the ring – fucked if I was going through that again, even as a showpiece.

He moved off and I followed him, watching the heavy beat of his tail wag slowly side to side as it balanced him. He sat down by the ringside. Slowly, as if they were watercolours being very weakly painted in, the shapes of other people began to appear in the ring, and other things too: animals, creatures I didn't have any names for. There were many of them. Eventually their pale, washed-out forms filled the ring up and began to spill out into the hotdog stalls, the TV cameras and the first rows of the audience. Over the raked stands a couple of gigantic shapes appeared, so indistinct I had no idea what they could be.

Eventually my dead stood next to his dead.

I looked at the faces. I could put their fight names to them, but not their real names. Two at least weren't my doing but I guess they were on my tab. Dying on the spot or later, what difference did that make? They looked at me expressionlessly; how would I know what they thought about it? I didn't feel much. I did ask to fight, but I'd meant in the fair way where both people walked out at the end. I didn't ask for this. Tashin, or the likeness of her, stood at the edge, flickering in and out of existence.

The jaguar sighed and lay down, head on his paws.

I guess I could've said no. Then I'd be a ghost in someone else's dream now. That's what *no* would have got me: a bullet and then the gutter. The cleanup droids would have picked me up and carted me off to the incinerator. I didn't know if I was meant to feel remorse. Whatever I felt I could tell it was going to seal the nature of what happened next. If I'd been guilty or ashamed I'd have been OK with that – you kill someone, you can expect it – but I didn't feel those things and I never had. I don't know why. I thought maybe because I didn't feel that much of anything most of the time. To care I'd have had to be connected to them and I wasn't because I'd spent most of my life being professionally disconnected; I didn't trust anyone except Two. These men were a part of the environment that required acting for my survival.

Did I think of them as people?

Of course. There but for the grace of fuck go I. People and equals. The situation was fucked up. Some of them were fuck-ups. Razorblade had threatened to drink my blood and I believe he meant it. But then I was a fuckup too, so I didn't hold that against him. I had nothing against any of them. I had nothing against me either. It was war, but not our war.

The jaguar looked up over its own silent host. There was no sound, but the air cleared as if a bell had been struck. A number of them faded away, a few, then many. But there were some left by the time the silent ringing had finished and these it looked at through narrowed eyes.

I felt a question in the air. These were the ship's dead and I knew nothing about them. I assumed the fact they were still there meant that the ship counted them unjustified deaths, accidental or in some other category where it had ended their lives for reasons of its own.

Without their stories I couldn't say anything.

From the stands a human girl stepped forwards. 'We didn't do anything. We were in the way.'

'I was too close to a missile strike meant for someone else.' Another one, a man this time, from further off.

Others with similar explanations moved closer to each other.

Then the largest remaining ghost, a creature I couldn't have named or speculated about, which was too large to fit in this arena but whose limb appeared here as a massive bulk stretching upwards into shadow, said, 'I opposed the creation of this entity. When my actions and words did not convince the council to deactivate the plans and the program for the making of a ship such as this one I took it upon myself to destroy the Pangaean oversystem responsible for the gestation, manufacture and teaching that gave rise to it. My actions ruined the Pangaea, but I failed to completely abort the ship and in return it destroyed me in an act of vengeance. Four thousand and some other lives were lost in the action: my crew, my staff and my Earth-allies.'

The other ghosts came closer, as though they were cold and searched for warmth and company from each other. Out of the blank tree trunks the forms of the additional dead flickered as Tashin did, imperfectly recalled, some no more than anonymous silhouettes.

I looked down at the jaguar which sat quite still. It was awaiting my judgement.

I didn't have a judgement to give. It was a sad story.

'Made wrong,' said the cat and hung its head.

'No,' I said. 'Merely not as intended. But that's their problem.'

There was a pause and gradually the rest of the dead faded away until only the ring and the lights were left. A faint smell of crushed onions and overcooked sausage made my stomach growl suddenly. The cat flicked an ear.

'Dat so?' the cat said. 'My mother dead because me.'

'Because of whoever that was,' I said, meaning the vast creature that had spoken. 'Not you.'

'Not finish being born,' the cat said and sighed. 'Tashlynnai promise care find me. Be finish need friend. Mother un-die, maybe?'

Oh, there it was. The bait that had led it here. And what if the bait is just a smell and there's nothing to eat?

I thought that and at the same time I experienced a horrible feeling I'd never felt before. The one I expected to feel if anything had happened to Two or Isylon. Of being crushed from within, like this, and willing to take a chance on the least likely story to make it stop, god, make it stop.

'Doc say no way un-die things. Harmony say maybe.'

I shrugged. 'I don't know.' I'd have said there should be a body to go back to, but I'd seen some bodies lately that made me think that wasn't the difficult part.

'Time go,' the cat said. 'We much do together now.' It stood up and the ring and the lights vanished.

Abruptly the dream was gone and I was awake and alone.

I lay on the stone bench in the cell, yellow salt light glowing. I could feel myself breathing. I moved my hand. It moved. I felt fine. I listened.

And I could hear more than twenty people. I could feel where they were in relation to me in the building and if I wanted to I could move in and see what they did, hear what they said, even know what they were thinking.

Fifteen – now we're cooking

A few metres away from me in another tiny confinement cell Isylon's father was being put to the question. Unlike my interrogation he was permitted to speak for himself, the Inquisitor merely a threatening focus and a protector for the Confessor. She was the woman from the car and it was from her viewpoint that I was able to see into the room.

Isylon's father was sweating, his robes in disarray as he sat with his head bowed, looking at the floor. 'Everything that went into the genesis of my son was undertaken with the strictest Alchemical principles.'

The Confessor was watching him closely. Her ability to empathise was extraordinary, though it was more as though she copied him exactly: his mental state, his body language, his energy. From that, once the copy was good enough she could reach further and decipher flickering hints of thoughts and memories. She copied him and then she read from her copy.

'You were a part of the Exaltation development since its inception,' the Inquisitor said, emotionlessly. There was no empathy in him, or if there was he wasn't using it. 'Bitna Valkyrian proved under test that her germline was adequate and it is almost an exact copy of the one used to generate Isylon. But I must ask you again to be very specific. Did you employ gene sequences or other materials from beyond the Harmony source?'

So now they didn't even know what was going on?

The Inquisitor frowned and Isylon's father put his head in his hands as if he felt pain or pressure bearing on him. 'The demands, the necessity to produce anything that could work... you don't understand. The enormity of the task, to prove a supposition that was possibly only the product of collective imagination... to make it true... He was going to have everyone killed. Forty years of work for nothing, wasted. He believes his own story – we're not even colleagues to him any more. Haven't been for years. You know this! He would erase all of us to start again. The idea of the golden grail, this eternal life, it isn't science, it's insanity.'

'Your heresy is not unexpected. However you still do not answer,' the Inquisitor said and then Isylon's father wailed and bent double and tried to protect his head with his arms.

'They used something – peculiar,' the Confessor whispered as he paused to draw breath. 'But I cannot identify it.' Her musing was interrupted by a breathless insistence from Isylon's father.

'You're hardly an expert! You know nothing of the Alchemy at these levels. It is a meta science, an art. We kept to the methodology. There was nothing—' but he had to break off as the Inquisitor silenced him with an accompanying gesture of dismissal to notify the Confessor that he had done so.

'Something came in from outworld,' the Confessor said, eyes closed now as she puzzled over the vague impressions she saw. She rapidly tried to match it with anything in her experience in order to identify it. 'It's no use. The material is so alien I have no way to say what it was. I keep seeing vials or maybe cell culture vessels, taken outside of – is it a wormhole? Some kind of spatial anomaly. There's a winged man who isn't what he seems floating in space. It's garbage. I think he's punking me.'

'Human?' insisted the Inquisitor, unmoved by the Confessor's continued speculations as the man in front of him sobbed silently through paralysed vocal cords.

The Confessor picked delicately at the fragments she could sense, combing them carefully for emotions and the threads that linked these to thoughts. 'Yes, and no machineries but...'

'Did you know the exact nature of this material?' The Inquisitor let go his hold suddenly and Isylon's father gasped and sat up, wheezing. His face bore no relation at all to that of his son. He was pale and almost grey with fatigue. He was older than I'd imagined, at least seventy if he was a day.

'No, I never knew the provenance. But of course it was human. How else could it ever have reacted as it should? Human in the broader sense, that is...'

'Who got it for you?'

'The cartels. They brought it in, in exchange for favours during the Purges. You've got to understand the pressure we were under. The years were passing, the—'

The Inquisitor cut him off again and turned to the Confessor, who nodded. 'Did you get the names?'

'I know who they are,' she said and I knew, knew beyond a shadow of a doubt that she was the go-between. She already knew everything. She'd be protecting herself now with her icy efficiency act. Who was going to read her anyway? 'I think we're done here. Let's report.' She stood up.

'It's not very satisfactory,' the Inquisitor said, but he stood too after a moment's thought. 'But we can always come back.'

They left without a backward glance.

So now I guess I had Tashin's proof of outside interference.

I rode with the Confessor, Daylus Chann, as she and her partner left the cell blocks. I watched the doors and the turns. The doors responded to touches, which I guessed meant coded DNA recognition. As I was borne into higher levels I recognised some of the halls. At one point they were passed by armed guards in Purge fatigues and behind them a tall, grim-faced woman in a commander's uniform. She was talking into a comm.

'I don't want excuses. Bring in Bitna Valkyrian. She has been seen in Chaontium, Drasser Blocks.'

Drasser Blocks was Kasha Dann's turf, barked right up against Harmony's border, including the same place that Two and I had first crossed over.

My host registered this news with interest. She turned to her colleague. 'Valkyrian is still on Harmony?'

'They're always saying things like that,' he said, dismissing it. 'Anyway she's hardly important now that there's another one. I've seen him Confess. He believes.'

A flicker of doubt, quickly crushed, flashed through Daylus' mind. Over it she re-stamped her commitments and convictions with feverish haste. I recognised the panic that doubt brought and the prayers it drove into her mind. You know if you're praying for the strength to keep on believing that you're already fucked. It amused me – though I was one step from prayer myself.

An announcement came over the public address system, halting everyone in their tracks and forcing them to stand like statues, hands folded, heads bowed in the posture of submission.

'The incident at the arboretum has been cleared. There has been no breach of Alchemical Quarantine. You are free to resume your duties.'

Then, on the heels of that, Tecmaten's angry hissing voice came clearly through Daylus' personal comm. 'Fetch Isylon Selamaa and bring him to interrogation room four. Bring the spy too.'

Her partner had heard too. They glanced at each other with a look that contained only the slightest revelation of disturbance at the agitation in that summons. It had had more than a taste of crazy about it, and they noted it, but their investment, their loyalties – they shored each other up as they both turned and began to retrace their steps.

I dropped out of the link and figured I had a few minutes

before I got company. I needed to get out of here but my plans all rested on the Beast's quasi-magical powers. What it had done and how – thinking about that made me queasy but I didn't have the luxury of time for it. Instead I prayed to the Beast. He answered, but only those who had come into contact with the shadow mist were within his reach. Alive they were useful informants. Dead they could be co-opted like Number One Fan. I felt a pang of guilt then and sat up before remembering I was supposed to be paraplegic right now. I assumed the pose they had left me in. The seconds passed so slowly. I wondered about Two and the Beast must have taken it as a command because in that instant I felt her back in the link.

She was in a cell too, only hers was much darker and larger. It contained basic gear – sling, hookups, droid workbench – and a commode. Shackles were on both her wrists.

'Dann didn't buy the Switch story,' she said, as soon as she was aware of me. Gladness for my presence struggled to get out against the focus and despair she was bringing to bear on the assembly of circuits in front of her, as if that was going to fix them. 'But she's happy to have me work for her. Where are you, Nic?'

'Don't worry about me, I'm coming for you,' I said.

'Nic.' She meant she knew I was lying. She sniffed and I felt my own throat constrict with the need to stop anything stupid like tears.

'I'm here,' I said finally, because it was all I could say and then I had to shut off the connection.

Inwardly I turned to the ship but it had seen and heard.

'I send something,' it said and then, more uncertainly. 'What I send?'

'Send a weapons package,' I said, adding mental images of lacquered boxes, gilt inlays, all the ceremonial gobbledeshit that cartel lords sucked up like premium whisky. 'Something impressive. From Two's friends. Something all surface and fabulous that will knock her socks off. Something full of yourself.'

'Blow socks off.'

Not literally. Not until I say.

We were in accord.

The door opened and Daylus came in, a doubtful pout on her face making her oddly pleasant as it almost humanised her rigour. Behind her the Inquisitor sighed and stared down at me. He ushered in two guards with a stretcher but then he had to awkwardly wriggle out as there wasn't enough room for all of them. They manhandled me onto the carrier, slamming my knuckles into the walls, trapping themselves in the cloth warps of my robes, but they must have done it many times because they tucked everything in with rapid precision once I was moved and then carried me without trouble.

We cleared the doorway and progressed along the corridor, the Inquisitor and Daylus going ahead. I wondered for a moment if I'd be able to reach them in time, but only for a moment. Caught was caught and I had to take my chances.

I bounced up from the stretcher crocodile style and used my hands on its edge for a brace, slamming my feet into the back of the front carrier. As shock and balance made him stagger I pushed off him, got my feet under me as the stretcher went sideways and launched my forehead straight into the face of the second guard. There was a moment of tumbling confusion as stretcher and myself met the floor in an uneven mess. At the same time I felt the first intimation of the pressure wave that would close my brain down and take me away, but there was resistance, as if it was a sled trying to force its way up a rocky hill. I heard the Inquisitor's murmur of surprise as I slammed headbutt guy's head into the wall to be sure and then turned to put my elbow in the face of foot guy who was fumbling his gun up into a reasonable position before my body got in the way of the barrel and knocked it sideways to the wall. Stinging blood got in my eyes – I must have gashed my brow – but I still saw well enough to punch him down. He took his gun with him on its strap, sadly, which left me facing the other two.

Daylus had her hands raised and was backing off but her partner was furiously focused on me, his brow pinched and lowered like a bull's before it launches a charge. I could feel his efforts slowing me down, filling me with lethargy. I felt drunk and as if we were underwater but I managed the first step, then another and another. He refused to back down, as though he were sure that with just one more second he'd have me, had to. He'd never lost against an ordinary human and he couldn't believe it was possible now. He was still not believing it when I grabbed his wrist and twisted his arm hard enough that we all heard a dull snap, like a hollow stick being trodden on. He screamed and his control vanished.

Daylus turned, picked up her robe skirts and started to make a run for it. I was delayed by knocking out her colleague but I'd still almost caught her when the door to a room just before us opened and I saw Isylon dragged into the corridor by an armed guard, closely followed by the skeletal figure of Tecmaten. He had a gun and kept it levelled at Isylon. The safety was off. I doubted he'd fire but he had a wild air about him that hadn't been there before. There was a faint smell of some kind of metal and hard liquor in the air, the kind I always associated with guys who were very crazy, high on their own supply, their pores leaking toxins as a natural warning.

I slowed down. Daylus carried on until she was safely beyond them before she stopped, turned, put her hand on the wall, panting and wide-eyed. 'But you ... he had you ...' She peered at me with the intense close-sightedness that characterised her use of her talent. 'But ... you ...' And blinked at what she was seeing, her mouth working and no sounds coming out.

Tecmaten didn't notice. He beckoned me. 'This way, Nico. You wouldn't leave without your lover, would you?' His smile stretched his lips too far. 'I don't think you're that kind of man. I think you want to know the truth before you go, hm? Don't you want to see if all the years and all the tears have finally pushed the human race one further step?'

Isylon was staring at me, wild of expression. Fear and the childlike vulnerability of someone torn into an unexpected world all made his face a curiously blank mask of shock. People didn't do this. They didn't behave like this. I read it so clearly in his eyes. He blinked as he watched me. I knew I was wearing a very different look on my face, one as familiar to me as a shabby old pair of shoes.

'Delighted, I'm sure,' I said to the old man. I wiped blood out of my eye, straightened my robes as I walked forwards to his humourless smile. I wasn't used to people so close to the end game, had only seen standoffs from a distance, guns in my hands, my attention on the minions and not the action. I wished I had Mr Gun right now. Not that I could have used him, but it would have been nice to have something solid to hang on to.

We all went into the interrogation room. The door was closed. The guard released Isylon at Tecmaten's command and stood, much more ready for anything than I liked. Of all the people in the building I could have surfed into, none of them were in here. My forehead ached where it was cut and I had to use the sleeve of my robe to mop it up. I felt that events were turning against me now, something closing in. I checked the space behind my left shoulder and out of the corner of my eye I saw a little girl in white. When I turned to look better the white wall looked back at me.

'Although your connection to this – invasion – is clearly there, its nature is deceiving, I think. Who sent you? Really?' He began to talk then, in a steady salesman's patter, about his work, the Alchemy, the pinnacle of his life, the building of something from nothing, all that crap and justification that he'd been constructing in his head for ever. I could have listened to it but that would have been too much like engaging and he didn't interest me other than as an opponent.

He didn't notice my lack of attention. He was fiddling with his gun, checking its settings with repeated twitches of his fingers as though he wasn't convinced it was displaying the right readings. Bad sign. Very bad sign.

I looked at Isylon. 'Sorry,' I said, shaking my head slowly as the babble about virtue and perfection carried on in the background.

He had calmed down now. His grey eyes were clear. He smiled a little with the corners of his mouth. 'It's OK,' he said. 'Not your fault.'

Tecmaten straightened suddenly, his hand on the grip of the weapon, testing it. 'Oh but it is your fault. All this rushing about. All this upheaval when we were so close. I suppose you want to steal it. Of course you do. And that is not acceptable to me. I doubt you are alone here. And that means that things have come to an unfortunate head. Yes. Unfortunate. But at least I will have my answers. I will have them. One way or another.'

With a speed surprising for the trembling fatigue he'd shown earlier he raised his hand and shot me. I saw Isy's face warp with horror. Then there were sparks – a cold fire across my sight – and I was falling. I saw everything sideways until my eye filled with blood. A dark purple rose that bloomed over the world and blotted it out and then I was no longer in my body but above it, in the corner of the room, looking down on everything.

Beside me was the little girl in white. Everything about her was white and shone faintly like distant moons. She put her finger to her lips in the sign for *shhh* and looked down, so I obeyed her and looked down too. In the distance I heard a wolf howl and then a bellow of rage. In the dark beyond the world a furious storm erupted, silently, but in this room Isylon fell to his knees, bent over me as the old man stood, wheezing, leaning on the stone bench weakly, the gun loosely held in icy fingers now.

I was dead.

A feeling filled me suddenly and overflowed, with nowhere to overflow to, without eyes to cry or a mouth to tell it. I'd felt it before when I was alive, but I'd never named it. It was the feeling of terrifying nights alone in the dark of the orphanage, of moments in the wild in the rubbish heaps listening to the scuff of droids, the sniff of dogs. It had wrenched me when Two and I parted. It had made it impossible to speak to my master. It had made me a silent idiot in the embrace of the man holding my body now and I thought it was fear, shame, embarrassment, hesitancy, something mortal and fatal. I thought it was loss and loneliness and pain but now I was without a voice or anything to show it I knew what it was at last.

Love.

I saw it in Isylon. I saw it in the guard, recovering from his surprise, bracing himself a bit with a grip on his weapon. I saw it in the lined and beautifully hideous face of Tecmaten and all his works. I loved it all. I had never been so in love. It was not possible to feel anything else. There was nothing else here but that and the people in the room below me were full of it, surrounded by it, swimming in it, and they didn't notice it. Feeling and knowing it was unbearably painful, with a pain that I never wanted to let go. I looked at the girl beside me, her face so indistinct she barely had one, but I saw her nod and smile at me. Yes. You are right, Nico.

Isylon looked up then, and saw me.

His face was wet with tears but determined and clear. He glanced sideways at the old man.

Tecmaten was muttering, almost to himself, 'But I had to prove it you see, you'll be grateful in the end that I've proved that you can work. You could bring him back. Probably. If the settings on this were reliable. I think it's possible but now that matters are slipping out of my grasp I find that it's really much more interesting to discover if you can keep him wherever he is

303

and give me his body instead. We did some tests with Valkyrian, you know, before she left us. And I do think that's possible. Of course I know you wouldn't do that for me, why should you? But to give you the incentive to try it I've had your family brought in. For every minute you delay I'm going to have them shot, starting with your father. It's a weak policy, a terrible gambit, I do realise that, I do, but there it is it can't be helped.'

'I am not giving Nico's body to you,' Isylon said, hoarse with emotion, his hands gripping my robe and arm.

'Well then we'll both have to watch them all die,' Tecmaten said and waved the gun feebly at the guard.

The wall dissolved into a clear observation panel which opened onto a secondary cell. Lined up against the wall were Isylon's father and the rest of his family, I supposed: a woman, a younger woman, two boys of about ten. Each of them was imprisoned by a security droid, held fast by shackles and the droids' flexible claspers. As I watched, the droid holding his father in its black, unyielding proboscis came forward. It moved out of that room and then opened a door and entered ours. The guard moved to the side to give it space.

'I'm sorry,' were the first words out of his father's mouth to Isylon. Fear sweat stood out on his forehead.

'Everybody's sorry,' Tecmaten said contemptuously. 'So sorry, so sorry. Because you were weak. You couldn't do what had to be done, could you? No vision. No follow through.' He turned his gaze, fatherly, towards Isylon. 'I hope you learn from this.' He flicked his gun hand in a gesture that wouldn't have crushed a fly and the droid's appendage moved to crush the back of Isylon's father's neck with a sickening crunch. He went limp immediately and hung from the machine's grasp, feet twitching.

A convulsion went through Isylon. His hands flexed, letting go of my collar and lifting up a few inches to hover palm down over my corpse. As he did so I saw an egg-like shape of light detach from his father's body and float upwards, losing definition and lustre as it rose. I heard his voice coming from nowhere, 'What's happening? Is this it? I need to explain.'

At the same moment a similar apparition rose from Isylon, only this one remained strongly attached by ropes of golden light to the midsection of Isy's body and it was much more humanoid. 'No need,' he said, as fast as he could, as if he knew what was happening. Before either of them could say any more an indistinct being that I perceived only as a shimmer in the air appeared beside his father's spirit and engulfed it completely. With the speed of a supersonic jet it launched them both upwards and outwards, away from us. He was gone in less than the blink of an eye.

I didn't think there was any coming back from that.

Isylon watched the space where he'd been and then looked at me.

'You stay, for now,' said the girl at my shoulder, with a nod. 'And know we have always been here. These matters are not for you to decide. Even though he –' part of her arm like a floating scarf gestured at Tecmaten '– believes it is possible to choose, no moment here is of his making.'

'Forgive me,' Isylon's golden ghost said to her from floor level as he closed his eyes and bent, seemingly in a quandary of shock and despair, unable to decide.

'You may see us,' she told him. 'You may do as you will. But even you may not reach or pass beyond the...' and I couldn't understand the word she said there. It had no human equivalent perhaps.

Behind the observation window the silent, ghoulish pantomime of Isylon's imprisoned family went on as they struggled with rage, grief and terror, each in the hell of their own isolation.

'Consider your actions carefully,' Tecmaten said. 'Anything happens to me and the droids are programmed to kill them all.'

'You shocked him too hard,' Isylon said, letting his hands drop in defeat. 'I can't do anything.' He stood up. A change had come over him. The softness, the sensitivity were there but hidden suddenly behind the huge shape, the cold and heavy outline of the armour he had copied from me.

'I don't believe you,' Tecmaten said and made his gun hand twitch again.

As the droids moved to change places I felt a sudden very powerful push from the girl and a pull from Isylon; both equally irresistible.

I was back in my body. It felt different. Lighter, less real, as if my immersion in it was incomplete. I felt the surprise of the Beast as the Switch came back up. It halted in its preparations for a personal slaughterhouse revenge, a metaphorical eyebrow raised. I felt Tashin's relief, which was almost heart-warming.

I got up from my deathbed, pushing Isy so that he stumbled backwards and fell, getting in the way of the droid coming in and blocking the guard's view. Tecmaten was raising the gun but shock made him much too slow. I grabbed his hand in both of mine and yanked it around, pushing his finger down on the trigger so that the electro-shot took the droid down; then I kept the trigger down until I was sure the guard had taken a dose of it as well. A second or so had passed. I heard the raspy breath intake for Tecmaten's command to do – whatever he wanted to do, and I let go with my right hand and elbowed him in the face.

Blood had started to drip sluggishly out of my cuts again. I watched the dark purplish drops fall off the tip of my nose to splatter on my hand. They landed like boulders, smashing apart, dust at their edges. I moved so that they fell on the exposed skin of the old man's wrist instead. By now he'd taken that breath and was moaning, held upright only because I was still using his arm as a weapon holder.

Beyond the room the Inquisitors had all, as one, moved to respond to his distress. The Beast had to go trip-trapping across a lot of bridges very fast to stop them. Those who had been infected with the plague dust were enough to stall the rest. The building and its inhabitants descended into a series of standoffs and paralysing confusions.

After a few moments the Beast in my blood had penetrated Tecmaten's skin and was flushed rapidly into his system. We were a slow poison, painless but unmerciful. He had time to see us coming. As I took the gun from his limp fingers I saw him peering at me over the shaking protection of his other hand, horror in his eyes.

I'd been ready for this moment all my life. I smiled. For a second I was tempted to... but no. Seriously, what more was there to say?

'See ya,' I said. 'Wouldn' wanna be ya.'

He reached out towards my face, spine slumping as he felt himself fatally slowed. 'You... were... the... one...' and then sensibility slid out of him and he collapsed backwards onto the bench with a sigh.

So annoying this 'the one' business. One. Who makes only one?

Isylon started and I knew that he could see what a dunderhead like me never would – the spirit leaving the body – which wasn't exactly dead, but it certainly wasn't alive any more. I made an imaginary salute to Number One Fan's memory. Then Isy was standing up himself, anger and determination on his face. His chin was down, grey eyes focused on something invisible.

– What do you know? I said to Tashin. – Looks like you've got yourself another avatar.

Tecmaten's body twitched.

Isylon's gaze became sharper, his attention more acute. I stood beside him, shoulder against his for support though as far as I could see we were alone in the room now, and I couldn't feel anything either though I tried. He reached out with his more powerful hand and made the slightest subtle motion of undoing.

Then he grabbed my arm and I had to catch him before his knees went out. I did it and kept him on his feet.

He looked up into my eyes. 'He really didn't want to go.'

'I can imagine,' I said and was nearly pulled over as Isylon jumped with shock.

Tecmaten was on the move. He rolled to his side, used his hands to push himself to a crabbed sitting position.

I held Isy back. He was staring at the spectre reassembling itself, prodding its broken upper mandible with rheumatic fingers, moaning with the pain. 'I have to say, Nico, this is an unexpected...' but the line was lost in wincing and wheezing. I was glad Two wasn't there to see what her squeeze had turned into this time.

'Payback's a bitch,' I said. 'Now sort this out and get us out of here. All of us.'

Tecmaten got to his feet and looked around. 'Return these people to their homes. Unharmed,' he said to the droids. Stooped and shuffling, far more decrepit an act than was really justified, I thought.

'What success,' he said as he reached the door and leaned on the panel to open it. 'I... um...' His gaze took in the droid that was in the hall, bereft of instructions, the heavy corpse still hanging in its tentacled grasp. 'Not appropriate to congratulate oneself in the circumstances, I suppose. I'm, uh – sorry for your loss.'

'We can get out by ourselves,' I said. 'I'm sure you can get your own evidence from here.'

'Right.' He turned the corner, straightening with a wince into the basic approximation of Tecmaten's entitled shuffle.

I turned to look at Isylon and found him staring at me as if I were a complete stranger. 'I don't understand,' he said. 'Was that your master?'

'It's complicated,' I said.

He studied me for a while and I wasn't sure what he was

seeing but eventually he nodded. I didn't let him go. 'What he wanted isn't possible, you know. You can give someone your life energy, but you can't change bodies like that.'

'We snatched the body with machines,' I said. 'It won't last long. Long enough for him to give some important instructions before he *dies* though.'

He kept his slight nod going, accepting it if not liking it. Then a twitch at the side of his mouth became an almost smile for an instant. 'You look like hell, but unmistakably you. I'd know you anywhere. Even dead. Definitely you.'

'Be sure of that,' I said and hugged him as tightly as I could.

'My ribs are sure.' He hugged me back.

In the end it was decided he would stay to oversee his family's safe return home and the recovery of his father's body.

'I'll be back in a few hours,' I said. 'Less than a day. Don't go far.'

He nodded, but he was looking at his father's body. 'Nowhere to go.'

Sixteen: two eights, which is getting very lucky

I walked out of the stolen car and into suddenly familiar streets with a sense of surprise that I had any deja vu left in me. There, one block away, was the grim diner Two said Bitna had come from, and around its corner was the wall and the empty lot where I'd – well, where whatever had happened with the car had happened. The roads here were strewn with rubbish, one municipal droid trundling along picking litter at a pace marginally faster than the heat death of the universe. A crew of kids hung around at the corner, edgy on what was still gang turf, looking out in all directions as they drank and ate from cartons stolen uptown. Good to see tradition upheld.

The diner was a quarter full. Nobody looked up when I came in. A safety screen cut the kitchen view off though there was still a wide walk through.

'Tea with lemon, no ice,' I said to the server, at which point every head went up because the cartels have certain phrases they use around the city which are there to tell everyone who's about, and that they're in business for something, so listen up and charge everything to the tab. By invoking tea, lemon, no ice I'd decided to charge Kasha Dann with my business and anyone wanting a bit of her favour could trade with me.

The server took my actual food order of noodles on a grimy notepad ready for cartel accounts, and possibly a description of

310

me in case there was going to be an argument about who I was later on. Meanwhile a man in gang fatigues slid into the seat next to me at a respectful but expectant distance. 'Help you?'

'I'm looking for someone,' I said, and described Bitna the best I could. I didn't turn my head to look at him. We were never going to make eye contact.

'Most of the priests that hung around here been rounded up already,' he said, meaning the Inquisition had taken them back.

'Premium rates apply,' I added as my nuked noodle soup arrived.

'Then you're in luck,' he murmured as he lit up a reefer so strong the first draw nearly knocked me out from a metre away. 'Little kids in the Ashcan got a protector lady. Live out of a container stack. Droid guard. Rounds up every stray this side of Nexi. She was a priest so they say.'

'Where's it at?'

He sighed a full sigh of greenish smoke. The server coughed. 'What you want with her?'

It was brassy of him to ask. They must want to protect her very badly.

'Just to talk about old times.'

'Mmm, she's friendly with a lot of people, a good lady. I can pass a message. Tell her where to find you.' He took another drag. I would, flirting with a cartel agent like this.

'Tell her her son's back from the dead.'

He coughed a little, wiped his nose as it began to run. 'What?'

'Are you fucking deaf?' I did look at him, the kind of look that won't forget a single nose hair.

'No, sir.' He got off his chair and was out the door faster than I would've betted he could move.

I ate the soup. It was hot enough to kill anything and it took a long time.

I heard the door go a few more times in the next ten minutes. The last was the entry of a pair of Inquisition patrollers. They took a free drink and left without checking anyone. I watched them go through the reflections in the filthy mirror that backed the bar's pitiful alcohol selection. In the distance the wall of the orphanage was just visible where the old trees had been removed. As the guards passed the gang of kids re-formed on their corner, a few less than before.

I waited another hour, and another, and had a second bowl of soup. It was starting to get dark by the time someone came and sat on the seat beside mine and the owner of the diner went outside to drag down the metal shutters though they were staying open and the lights stayed on.

Under the rattle and bang of the activity a female voice said, 'Well, this is new.'

I turned and there she was right next to me, taller than I'd thought: white hair, brown skin, clever eyes narrowed. 'Bitna?'

'Don't go by that name,' she said. 'Dersala. And you are?'

'A kid you helped up after an accident fifteen years ago.'

'Do you have a name?'

'Not one I'd use here.'

She smiled. 'Smart kid. But under the Dann banner. So, not that smart maybe. What do you want?'

'Can't tell you here.'

'Here is the only place I'll be.' She folded her arms.

I looked at the server until he changed his mind about listening in and went round the back. 'I met a guy the other day, the next one in line to the title of Exalted.'

She got to her feet. 'Can't help you.' She was moving off, leaving. On reflex I reached out and grabbed her upper arm, not hard. Then several things happened at once.

A surge of energy shot across the gap between my hand and Bitna's arm as if it had lain in wait for the right connection. At the same time we heard the churn and drive of droid transport engines in the street outside and whooping commotion from the people there. As that rose in volume the remaining customers in the diner either got up to rush the door and see what was going on or scarpered around the counter and bar heading for the back rooms and presumably all exits.

Bitna beat me to the punchline, making no effort to detach my grip. 'Let's go!'

She took the counter route into the kitchen which was empty of people but full of smoke and steam in a way that suggested it was regularly used as an escape route. Bitna was used to it; she avoided the obvious door out and dragged me through the refrigerator and out its half-height kicktrap into the alley at the side of the building. We came out behind a carefully positioned dumpster, crossed and were through an unmarked door into the next building before I figured out the route. In a pitch-black room full of dead air my feet crunched and rustled in litter, then there were other doors and turns in an unlit labyrinth before we emerged into a windowless room lit by battery LEDs.

'You can let go now,' she said as the door closed and locked itself.

I did. 'Where is this?'

'It's one of my places.' She gestured to a plastic chair with a tattered cushion on it. 'Make yourself at home.'

There were a few long-life food containers, a desk, an otto-man and, on the counter that lined the back wall, what looked like a cheaper and more primitive version of the lab gear at Ito.

'You've got an Alembic?'

'Not a full one.' She paused to listen and switched on a device at the desk, waiting to see its screen. 'Hm, nobody coming so far. Hold out your hand.'

I did and she came over and without any hesitation or announcement jabbed a pin into my finger and slid the blood onto a slide.

'Ow!'

'Let's see who you really are.' She took the slide, wary of me now as if I might suddenly change my mind, and sidled to her counter where she droppered a solution onto the slide and shoved it into one of the gizmos. As it started to work the lights dimmed into a sulky twilight.

'Couldn't give up the research?' I didn't understand the point of it, but if you kept your own lab there had to be some reason.

She turned and leaned against the counter, scrutinising me with disapproval. 'I keep an eye on who's getting thrown out where.'

I decided to up my game a bit. 'I thought you would have gone offworld after splitting with the faith. The Inquisition must know you're here. But they didn't make you go back?'

She narrowed her eyes and stared me down. 'Bitna the runaway. I remember the story. But it wasn't like that.' She glanced at her machinery, humming to itself. 'I am here with their permission, doing my work. What did you think? There is some organisation that could protect me from them or I was just very clever? Perhaps that I am a wizard, hm?'

I was used to being mocked. It was almost like old times, but however long that machine took to pick out my identity it wasn't going to outpace the cartel hounds that my flash use of Dann's name had brought howling down on us. I didn't have time for a relationship. 'I'll trade you my story for yours.'

As I told the abbreviated and slightly adjusted for effect tale of my life since the orphanage I watched her listen and fuss with her instruments; the machine popped out the slide and began to scroll information onto the wall. Bitna read it easily. I recognised my own ID code from my institution days and the fake one that VanSant had given me after we were picked off the streets. I trusted that whatever it said and what I was saying added up to something.

I finished before she turned from studying the output. She sat in thought, then decoupled the power. 'So, it is you.'

The lights came up a bit. She took out the slide and threw

it on the floor before stamping it to dust with her boot heel. It wouldn't stop any good investigation but the gesture was nice.

'I was a full Cardinal when I left the Alchemy,' she said, composing her hands, fixing me with a watchful gaze. 'I was a believer, with a little scepticism of course, but I had hopes because there was a group of progressive thinkers who seemed to be working on the real disjoints between the science and the theology. In fact as I got higher and more advanced in my research I realised that there is no such thing as simple building-block genetics. But the Alchemy insists there must be. So I was faced with the issue so many of us are faced with...'

'That the Alchemy is clearly a pile of shit.'

One side of her face smoothed, the other wrinkled as if she'd bit on acid but then she grinned and snorted that kind of laugh that says it's funny now but it wasn't funny sometime in the past. 'Yes. And then after you accept that, you magically become the agent of a theocratic oligarchy with no justification what-soever behind anything it stands for, anything it has done and said and claimed.' A cold, hard and bitter expression replaced the smile and when she looked up she was every inch a tiger I would not cross. 'And then time runs out, because your doubt is obvious. They treat you as a test subject. You discover you can see the dying leave. You can perhaps pull them back, if it is timely. You see the bodiless ones. You think you had enough a long time ago.'

'But,' I supplied, wondering if *and* would be better.

'But,' she said. 'But then you have to figure out how you can get out, if you can. And what will you do?'

'Plenty of people would stay and enjoy the hay,' I said, shrugging. Like I didn't know lots of them. Some right now, searching hard for me, not a hundred metres from our location.

She nodded. 'Those are the ones in charge. And a few who insist on the primacy of the Alchemy and the feebleness of the human intellect in misunderstanding it. Greed and Vanity.'

315

I could see why she'd gone into the priesthood. Ideas were people to her, in their way, and they had her loyalty and her friendship. She'd derail onto them if I didn't keep her going. 'But you did get out.'

'I ran away because I couldn't think of any other solution,' she said. 'I reached Chaontium and paid a huge sum of money to the Black Feather cartel group for a passage offworld. I took the freighter and I came to a place called Skyline Orbital which is just next door, in system terms. It's a trading post and a rest stop. I saw Harmony from the outside. I saw Harmony from the shop of the same name in the orbital station. I saw the catalogues and I browsed the create-your-own suite. I sat through the very beautiful educational presentation about how easy it is to tailor human beings to their perfect forms and to combine that with a basic but powerfully rewarding game-tweaked socioreligious structure to create a peaceful and productive world in which every foible – their words – was directed to the best interests of the individual and the society and in which every virtue was rewarded or, if you preferred, every mistake punished. And for there to be good there must be evil, yes? This is balance. So you can have your scapegoats to make sure that the virtuous understand the rightness of their calling. Everything exists in its opposite, and only there.' She was nodding again, lips pouted and braced like a fighter about to deliver a knockout punch. She looked at me, slyly, teasing. 'Do you know what this place really is?'

'A dump with no way out full of criminals?' I made a shrugging apology twist with my shoulders and held up my hands as she glared at me because I felt like I was offending her though I'd stick by the statement.

She nodded because yes, it was blinding obviousness. 'It's a storefront display.'

You see it coming and still you get hit. That's the speed of the real pro. Yes. Catalogue, sales pitch, promises – the only thing missing was the shop. A real-time example of what you could make if you put your mind to it. You could actually make a whole world run, tweak it here and there, amuse yourself with it no end.

Everything that I had lived in as absolute reality was a lie.

I've said this before but there's no end to how often this bastard can get up and hit you again, even after you think you've walked out of the ring. I grinned at Bitna, wild, white, semi-madman and all laughter at the sheer extent to which I'd been played for a fool. 'It's the triviality that hurts most, right?' It made me smile. Some part of me thought it was funny now although I was pretty sure it was the triviality of it that fucking killed with its stone dark stare. I really was an action toy, and nothing else. 'When you see what it really is and you know you're just another moron? Agree with me. That's a sweet moment. Even you didn't see it coming.'

'You're right.' She made a diving motion with her hand – from high to crashed in one swoop. Then she continued, low and quiet. 'So, I'm a store dummy and I have enough cash to get maybe somewhere else but I don't know anywhere else and Skyline is full of things which I can only describe as *things* but they're people or aliens or something and it was all so much to take in.'

'Nowhere to go and nothing to live for.'

'No,' she corrected me firmly. 'In all Harmony's promotions they make a lot about using only natural source material. Even up there in the shop. It's their big thing. Organic, natural, first primary source... whatever marketing crap that is. But I had the healing touch.' She held out both her hands, cupped loosely in the air.

'And no way that came out of the genome by itself, am I right?'

'Yes.'

'So you never heard of Inceptor.'

She blinked. I could see by her reaction that she hadn't. 'Inceptor? What is that?'

'I don't know, but it's the golden key to getting out of here. Something that's not organic. The magic ingredient.'

The bafflement I'd assumed was my default face was now hers. 'Are you telling me that there actually is alien material in us?'

Alien. That I had not considered until this very second. 'I don't know. Whatever it is, though, it's in you. I don't know if it's in me. I wondered if that was the thing that let you do your mojo. Your faith healing goes beyond the usual *they did it themselves with my prompt* kind of thing, doesn't it?'

'I—' She looked around, shaking her head. 'I always thought it was as Tecmaten said. Forced evolution. I don't... No. Is it?'

At least she was honest. I trusted her and felt my insides check me. Can't trust anyone. 'Was I really dead?'

Bitna sighed. 'Maybe. There wasn't time to be sure, really. I used my gift, you got up. I didn't know who you were.'

I didn't ask about that though, did I? So why mention it now? Why be there, at that moment, on that day? I didn't know if I believed her now.

I skipped it. 'Why did you make me?'

'I was trying to make strong people. I mean, the kind who don't follow everything like a sheep. But there was some idea that the Exalted could heal better on people who were more receptive than the ordinary, too. I remember trying to figure out how that worked. It was a long time ago.'

We both sat up, alert, as a crashing noise came from the direction of the most external door. I was first to my feet. Bitna hurried to pull the plugs on the devices and then put her hand to a panel which opened another door, obviously ready to go.

I jumped across the gap between us and got her arm twisted up behind her back.

She squealed in pain and surprise. 'What the hell are you doing?'

'Shh, I'm an evil spy demanding information you're not giving,' I said as fast as I could. My adrenaline spiked and Bitna squeaked with agony. I relaxed a bit. 'Otherwise they'll have you in too.'

More crashing and fumbling sounds indicated the search party making progress in our direction.

'Is this what you wanted?' she gasped.

'I came to see you, to let you know that it's over. Tecmaten's dead and there'll be some new management soon. But before I go I need to get my friend out and she's one of Kasha Dann's favourite guests right now. So it's two for the price of one.' I kissed her on the ear as the door caved in and added, 'Thank you.'

Thank you for my life, I guess. Sure, why not? Thank you.

Six guys in black Dann-styled fatigues jumped me. I got a gun butt behind the ear fairly quickly and it was hard to tell what happened in the next few minutes. I was truss-tied like a chicken and I heard them talking to Bitna, but she seemed OK. I wanted to pass out honestly because my head hurt like fucking hell but a surging fury in my body wouldn't let it happen. I could feel the Beast searching through my nerves like it was bin-diving, shredding things left, right and centre in its insistence to see and to know. I tried to convey that we should be grateful to be alive and in transit to our next destination – plans going pretty well all things considered – but I didn't feel we were communicating all that well. It kept working my arms against the restraints and filling me with a crushing disappointment.

By the time I was more like my old conscious self in the back-seat of the Dann sedan I gathered that Bitna was well respected in their group and that explained the rest of my aches and pains: they'd decided I should get a good kicking before Dann passed sentence. I felt almost happy though. Cartel hierarchy was working out for me at last. Not dead. Soon to find out where Two was. It was mostly pluses in spite of how it seemed.

The Beast sulked, unconvinced. After the shooting it had taken a dim view of anything that threatened my survival. At times I felt that it was covering up a kind of embarrassment at having revealed itself so thoroughly when it believed that I'd died – preparing to zombie convert half the population to wreak vengeance on the other half. Damned if it wasn't good to have someone show up so intently on my side, though.

It signalled that I was a pain in the ass and then briefly replaced my little painful existence in the car with a vast and mighty sense of bulk surrounded by huge starscapes, a planet not far away, jewel bright in its daylight, the atmosphere a halo of white.

We'd always been using tricky frequencies to escape detection but finally our orbital-to-ground activities had been noticed. From the far side of the world the bright motes of incoming ships were visible. My attention zoomed in. They were big.

Yes, confirmed the Beast. They were bad business, but it was OK, because we were all about taking care of business. Predatory satisfaction filled us to the brim. I counselled patience and strategy. The Beast growled faintly and cut me off.

And then I was back in the car on my own and we were pulling up high and far from the streets at the entrance to the penthouse suites where Dann held court. I was dragged out, face down on the carpeting that inconveniently protected me from a concrete shave, then made to get up at gunpoint and limp inside. Did I mention how much the cartel loves a drama? I think if it had been up to me I would have done this al fresco on the roof overlooking the sunset city, but Dann had a thing about air pollution so inside it was.

I was almost sick with gratitude when I saw that Two was actually going to be in the room with us. She was a shrinking figure, leaning on a second woman who reminded me a little of Juliette with her calm, assured presence. The resemblance ended there. Her skin was a shade of black rarely seen in Harmony humans, so dark it verged on blue, her eyes helpfully highlighted by a startling strip of white paint across them which looked like it had been daubed on by a three-year-old. Her hair was a shade of red that made everything else in the room look green by contrast, weighted with metal beads and all collected in a ponytail that obviously doubled as a blinding whip. Her clothing seemed to be made entirely of white ribbons and these hung in festoons from her wrists, floating on nonexistent breezes in a way that was unnerving. There were three white slashes on her cheek by which I knew her instantly: the hallmarks of the Beast. So, this was what he'd sent Two as a weapons cache: the personification of a ceremonial sword, a katana – interesting interpretation but Two was still alive so it hadn't been that bad a choice.

A brief but fragrant distance away Dann herself sat comfortably in one of her power seats and we prisoners crept towards her through the valleys of her soft furnishings and the mazes of ornamental planting. I was put a few metres short of her.

'Well, well,' Dann said, staring intently at my face. She came forwards and examined me, much as if I was a specimen under a microscope. Her perfume was elegant and understated. I wondered where she'd got this touch of class from and how much it'd cost.

I heard the hum of a heatknife and felt my utilitarian monk overalls and my underclothes part under it silently over my right leg. She tugged open the fabric and looked at the tattoo. 'I didn't believe it, but damned if it isn't Test Subject Number One.' She tossed the knife onto the nearest table and came to stand in front of me with her arms crossed. 'Which brings us to the thorny problem of where you've been, since you weren't atomised.'

I felt this was rhetorical.

'Perhaps your associate here will help us.' She beckoned Two forwards but also gestured to my side and Bitna was pushed a few steps up into the spotlight too.

Associate can mean anything in this situation, from coerced kidnap victim to godmother. I looked over at Two for the first time properly and met her gaze. At her side the katana moved with assurance, supporting her arm as she kept a cool observance on everything going on, exactly like a bodyguard.

Dann didn't look at anyone except me. 'Now, Bitna. What's so special about Test Flower here? Why is he back? He clearly knows you, for some reason.'

'You should be thanking me,' I objected. 'With Dashein out of the way there's nobody left to oppose you on that orbital trade queendom.'

'I suppose you have been quite useful,' she said. Then she waited and there must have been a long association between her and Bitna for Bitna to respond with such confident timing to the silent suggestion it was her turn to speak.

'Nico Perseid was a successful reanimate of mine.'

Two ogled me with a look that said 'What the hell is this shit?' I spared a glance at her and felt shock and rage hit me inside. Two looked gaunt. Her face was bruised and she was thinner even than when we lived on the rats' leavings.

'And what does that mean?' Kasha was going to get it spelled out.

'It means that he was killed but could be returned to normal function via goldlight intervention.'

'Exaltation,' Kasha looked at me with great interest. 'Sanctuary's great new innovation. Worth a fortune. What a pity it doesn't work on everybody. I think out of a hundred people tested only one or two ever responded with the exact tuning required for a full resurrection. Certainly the healing was reasonable but not enough to create a buzz. Not enough to create paladins for the Alchemy to prove its universal power. Just imagine if absolutely anyone could be cured with a single gesture from a great healer. Imagine if they could sustain lives indefinitely.'

Somebody had been injecting the marketing juice all right. Dann was so high I could smell the future wealth from where I was standing.

Bitna looked deeply uncomfortable. She met my gaze but with a grim return that said she didn't like any of this. There was a resignation though: this was part of her story – she relied on Dann's mercies because she had to.

'Nobody would know it only works on those prepared to receive it. But preparing those to dispense it was also a great trial. Vast expense. Risk. And with the bottom dropping out of human gengineering, what to do? Fashion is so cruel.'

From my swollen left eye I glanced at Bitna during this speech. She looked like she'd swallowed poison. Dann was pleased with her big reveal.

'So, you're in league with Ito Sanctuary,' I said to keep her on line.

'They need me to maintain their offworld supplies and keep their cover.'

'Hmm, I guess things would be a bit ruined if everyone found out they were toys in a research factory,' I agreed. 'So what was the Exaltation plan? If it didn't work out...'

'Reputation is everything. Tecmaten is as mad as a box of frogs, all focused on this being the proof of the Alchemy, gods on Earth, that kind of thing. But nobody stops him. It will be good business. But I rather think Tecmaten will mismanage it. Too much mystic hocus pocus, not enough business foresight. Now, given your rather special status I think I can offer you a good deal – give me your ship and I'll let you and Twostar go. Perhaps you might consider working for me running supplies and products. Under contract of course.'

I looked at Two – seriously?

'Don't blame her,' Kasha said with silky pleasure. 'She had to tell me when her associates at the ship sent this droid.' She flicked her polished fingertips at the katana. 'I was very mean.' She made a catlike scratching gesture and I saw Two's expression go from miserable to crushed.

'I'm glad you found it acceptable,' I said, looking at the black redhead who returned my glance with serenity and a nod which could have easily looked like it was simply agreeing with me.

'Indeed. Technology far better than we could dream of making. It is capable of as much as entire teams of comms workers. And so pretty! Which is why I think it's best that I keep it.'

It was cruel, stringing her along like this, although the amount of firepower in the room aimed in my general direction made me a bit nervous. 'And if I say no?'

'No? Well then you'll leave me no alternative but to blow it up. You will be returned to the Inquisition. I understand the Alchemical Archives would be interested in revisiting you. How grateful Dashein was when Bitna told him you would definitely survive the ship implant.'

I looked at Bitna. She shrugged. It was true. I sighed. I guess we were all deep in other people's pockets and at the end of their guns. I didn't blame her and anyway, it might have done me a favour after all.

Behind Kasha's shoulder Two opened her eyes slightly wider – she was waiting for me to call the shots. I checked my restraints but they were solid. Behind me the four or five armed guards that had brought me here were still present and still armed. There were four more I could see in the room in front of me at various vantage points, and a few I couldn't if standard practice was in operation. I'd have to guess where they were.

'The ship's just a souped-up freighter but it still won't run without me,' I said to Kasha. I didn't know what she thought

324

it was but her expression didn't alter much. At least Tashin had managed to conceal something.

'Which is why you get to work for me. And I'm sure that other pilots can be found however essential you imagine you are. But I know you. We have an established working relationship. I'd make you captain of the fleet, reporting only to me. So, what do you say?'

So, she didn't know what the ship was and she was confident of destroying it – surely with the craft I'd seen on approach while I was in the car. I felt disappointed that the notions I had fondly held of enmity between state and criminal were so thoroughly wrong. The knowledge that we were all scum on the same pond offended me on a deep level I didn't know I had.

'I say . . .' I hesitated.

I looked at Two. Kasha looked between us.

'Really? Still asking your girlfriend for instructions, Nico?'

As she was focused on Two I gave the sad nod of defeat that indicated to Two that we were going to play Bait and Switch.

'. . . all right.'

'Of course I will be keeping Twostar as my guest for the foreseeable future as insurance against your good behaviour.'

'I was really hoping we could be together,' I said, trying for whiny and getting it pretty good.

'Surely you will have to be aboard the ship? You can meet. Once a month there can be some – what do they call it, furlough?'

I gave a resigned nod, feeling saliva rush into my mouth and working to hide it from her because you didn't get to miss big tells like that if you wanted to be in charge. 'Now that we have a deal, get this crap off my hands.'

'Of course.' She motioned for someone to deal with it and I felt myself freed. I rubbed my sore wrists. Given the way I'd felt when I was chewing the carpet earlier I was in a lot better shape than I expected.

'But I don't want you getting any silly ideas,' Dann said. 'Whatever you've been telling each other behind my back is obviously more than endearments,' and with that she turned and shot me in the legs with a gun I hadn't even seen she had.

The shock was bad. The pain was worse. I collapsed, screaming, in a red haze. I thought my vision must be ruined too because from the floor I saw the Beast's katana break up into hundreds of small, infinitely black shards which exploded in all directions as if she was glass that had shattered to the pitch of a scream: mine.

The ship is being threatened. It wants to kill everything but it says you said no? Nico. What's going on?

– Exit strategy. Bring it right now.

We're coming.

The pain stopped. My hazed vision resolved. I saw Bitna's hands over me and realised the room was eerily quiet. All of the armed guards lay dead, precision stabbed through the heart. The Beast's avatar looked coldly pleased as she picked her way through them, collecting up their hardware as though it weighed nothing; the guns and ammo on their belts clanked and clunked all over her like an ugly metal coat. Two was busy with the heatknife, slicing something out of her arm – a tracking device of some kind. She flung it away with a snarl as I watched.

At the same moment far out in space two missiles struck their targets and whatever ships had been sent to intercept Tashin's ride became silent flowers of grey matter.

I tested my legs. They still hurt but they worked. There was no catastrophic collapse as I got to my feet, cautiously, but without any trouble. Bitna backed off, her hands held up in a gesture that reminded me instantly of Isylon – the healing hands raised to ward, to show no threat. Her face had a greenish sheen and she looked like only cussedness was preventing her from fainting.

Dann was frozen as though she would vanish if she could only stay still enough. The whites of her eyes showed all the way around. The technology of the katana was way outside her experience. I was about to say something but before I could Twostar stepped up beside her with the heatknife and cut through the back of her neck. She was dead before she hit the floor. Two flicked the knife off and threw it onto the body, fixed me with a hard look.

'There,' she said. 'I fight too. One each. We're even.'

We were in each other's arms in a heartbeat, gripped tight. Over Two's shoulder I saw Bitna bending down to Dann's body, an uncertain look on her face between compassion and confusion.

The katana looked around dispassionately, satisfied that nothing else but the plants was left alive in the room. She eased a shoulder under her arsenal. 'People are coming.'

Two and I let go at the same moment. I looked at Bitna, met her eye as she rolled Dann over onto her back. The body had the same scared expression as before. Bitna passed her hand over the terrified eyes and closed them gently.

'We're leaving,' I said. 'You can come if you want to.'

Bitna shook her head slowly. I guess that decision was made long ago.

'How about just out of the building?'

'I should...' She paused again. Dann was no prize but I could see that the killing didn't sit right with her. The way her face was falling apart in expression I thought she might collapse if there was no intervention.

'Let's go.' I reached down and hauled her up by the collar, reaching out for Two's hand at the same time.

We took Dann's personal car. Katana flew it while the three of us sat in the back. Two raided the bar for snacks, ripping open packs and cartons, shoving food into her mouth with bloody, filthy fingers. Bitna looked blankly at me, the lines in her face strong, her eyes dulled in aftershock.

'Thanks,' I said to her, loading a gun I'd taken from Katana's stockpile and checking it. I kept going with the rest, safety on for now. My legs felt weak, but they were fine.

She nodded and spoke weakly in her exhaustion. 'I have to stay and look after the children,' she said. 'I should have tried to help her too, but...'

I let her not finish it. But. I knew that but. But I didn't want to *enough*.

Abruptly Bitna got up and busied herself at the bar beside Two. She popped the top off a brandy shot and took it in a gulp.

We soared at medium altitude, maximum speed, faultless piloting.

The Beast narrowcasted to me the gist of what was happening. We were pursued, of course, but at the same time the Inquisition and the cartels had broken into open warfare over the loss of their ships. There was chaos. It would be a perfect time for a revolution but I said no, leave it, if there's going to be one it belongs to the people, not you and me, leave it.

'If you're going to get out, it has to be now,' I told Bitna, signalling for a descent to a safe spot. 'I'm not coming back.'

She nodded and made her way to the car's door, ready. Then she looked at me. 'When I was on the trading outpost I met someone. We became friends. She was very ideological, passionately opposed to everything Tecmaten had made on humanitarian grounds. She introduced me to the wider world, opened my eyes to everything, good and bad, that exists beyond Harmony.'

The car slid through alleys, descending, changing its means of passage from airborne to wheeled with only the merest hiss of adaptation. We rolled to a halt and the windows cleared briefly enough to see we were just off a popular street in a safe area, if there is such a thing in Chaontium. Bitna popped the door and

I thought that was it but as she stuck her foot out she looked back at me.

'I stayed here because of her. She said she would find a way to help from the outside but she needed a little help on the ground too, that I could do more good here. Part of me wants to go with you, to get out of Chaontium and to see what happens, but I can't. I trust you, Nico, because I trusted Tashin, and she came back. I didn't make you. That was only a design. But I found you for her, and here you are. Be good. And if you can't be good, then be lucky.'

Before I could take a breath she was out and had slammed the door closed.

'Evasive action,' Katana said calmly and we were thrown to the thickly carpeted floor, beer and chips flying as the car heaved itself skywards with a screaming shudder.

Seventeen – You Gotta Be Fucking Kidding Me, already

With Bitna's words ringing in my ears I felt like my sanity was going to fall to bits. I was onto Tashin before a second thought escaped me –

– Why the hell couldn't you have got that evidence the first time around, Tashin? Infection tech, possession avatars ... why me?

I wasn't looking for it then. I was looking for a reason to get my agency involved in prosecuting Tecmaten and liberating Harmony's population. I didn't know there was any alienware involvement until much later, after I'd done more research into the trades going through Skyline.

– So you had no fucking clue that Bitna was iffy?

I don't know if she is, as you say, iffy. I'm sure that the codes of the Exalted program are technospliced though not necessarily with alien gear.

– And if it is alien then we're supposed to blast it out of existence?

That depends on what alien we're talking about.

– You knew Bitna. You could have just asked her.

I didn't want you to go after Bitna. She'd risked everything. She'd done enough. I promised I'd never involve her in it.

– You're a bad cop, Tash. A very bad cop.

You can tell me that in person when we're done. If it's still true then.

'Are you talking to Tashin?' Two asked gingerly, tugging on my sleeve and nearly getting a rifle barrel in the knee. 'You've got that expression of a dog chasing its tail.'

'Yeah,' I said. 'She's been super helpful.' I hoped my sarcasm didn't melt the silver and gold finish on the car's interior.

Two, mouth fixed around the straw on a juice cocktail, snickered at me. 'I still kinda like her.'

I rolled my eyes at her.

'Where are we going now?'

'We're approaching Harmony airspace at Ito,' Katana said from the driver's compartment. 'Entry to the Sanctuary deck in one minute six seconds.'

I got up, shoving some of the fallen chips into my mouth and eating them because that was pragmatic. Two did the same with a cake bar, pushing it into her face with both hands. We were soaked in sticky spilled juice and brandy.

'Nic. What's the game here?' Two spluttered through cake. She looked around the car and got up onto the seat. She shivered and patted about for stray chips in the deep fur of the covers.

For a moment I felt thirteen again – food was opportunist stuff, vital. Plans were sketchy. There was always a survival game afoot. We gave them silly names to make them doable instead of fucking terrifying and impossible.

'The game is Rip the Rugs. You're going to steal the whole of the Sanctuary's Alembic database; that's your rug. I'm going to break this guy out of gaol; that's my rug. Then Katana's gonna make sure we escape in this fine car.' I looked through Katana's eyes at the Beast. She was a spectacular avatar. He/she nodded at me in assent.

'Nico.' Two looked at me, licking chips out of her teeth. 'That's a shit plan. We're never going to make it. We're already inside the Inquisition right here. There's two – three of us and a sedan.' She didn't seem upset, only depressed by my obvious stupidity.

'I'm open to suggestions.'

Two groped around behind her for the brandy and took a swig.

I could feel us approaching the mountain as if it had a tidal pull on me. I waited, watching her.

She scratched vigorously among her dreadlocks. 'We need an army.'

Katana spoke into the silence. 'I am army.' And with that she made an elegant move of her hands. We were now headed directly towards the carved summit of Sanctuary itself. 'Please take seat, put on belt, hold tight. Crash landing. Very safe. No worry.' She used one hand to pull her own safety harness together and clip it shut.

Two and I scrabbled to find anything resembling a harness anywhere in the sofas and cushions. We found one and huddled together with it round both of us, feet braced against the doors.

'What the hell was her arrival like?' I asked Two, jerking my head at the driver's position.

'She came in a box marked *fragile*,' Two grunted, heaving on the belt's short end in an effort to tighten it further and break my pelvis. 'She had an *on* switch and she pretended to be like some dumb robot in a movie who only answered to me. She also brought a bunch of ship manifests and stuff that convinced Dann the ship is a star freighter running out to the system edge and back all the time – enough cargo value to buy a much bigger landmass than shitbag Mars North or whatever this piece of it is called— Aieeee!'

The last part was a scream of terror to be fair, although I decided that if I did buy a planet one day I would call it *Aiee!*

We had a great view through the windscreen as the Katana Beast angled us at a huge panoramic viewport set into the side of the tree-scaped magnificence of the groves of academe.

Inside my skin I could feel the whole thing as a bizarre set of sensations mapping themselves across my mind. I knew we were going to be all right – a billion calculations done effortlessly soared through me like wings soaring in an empty sky. We hit the wall, precisely at the angle required to break it and preserve our capsule, allowing us to barge through and into the interior, sliding and breaking minor structures inside until we came to a jarring halt at the lift shafts which controlled the centre of the structure. Maths. Physics. Should have done college after all.

Two unclipped us and we fell forward. The car was still upright and the windows crazed but intact. Katana was already with us in the main compartment, crouched, her head moving like a little blackbird's as she peered through at the room beyond and whoever was doing whatever in it. I thought she looked happy, and maybe like she was salivating.

'Now,' she said, opening the door.

We got out into a smoky fug, icy breeze cutting it up like knives. An alarm was sounding and there were shouts. The body of the crashed car hid us for the time being as the Beast smiled and then changed form. Two started back into me, nearly knocking me over. Where the girl had been a second ago a copy of me now stood, complete with mad hair and filthy overalls. I looked way more wasted than I liked.

'I give you keys now,' the Beast said through my mouth. 'You drive.' She meant drive the action. She meant keys to everything that she could do. The moment passed so quickly I didn't get to hesitate but I wanted to. This was all I had ever wanted and it was the end of my life because I had nothing that came after that. I never believed.

She also handed me the keys to the car. 'Move car around by time I get back. Quick exit best.'

As the keycards touched my hand my mind exploded. My body became vast. What I used to be was gone. It was profound, but as usual only glib stupidities came to mind.

'Nico?' Two asked, holding my arm. 'You all right?'

I staggered, half man, half galactic-destruction monster, briefly confused as to which by the sudden surge of activity in the Switch as the Beast made its calculations. We were no longer distinct but a fuzzy entity, stretched over multiple bodies in multiple places. I asked it, 'Is that Earth technology?'

'Forged technology,' the Katana Beast said, grinning my grin, and rushed off into the smoky dark and the strobe of damaged emergency lighting.

I couldn't focus in more than one place at once, so we divided the chores. The Beast made a second avatar by splitting itself in two. This became an Inquisition guard. We pretended that it had arrested Two and was marching her to the Alembic under pretence of taking her to Tecmaten's emergency command centre within the summit. That was the way to get Two to the data.

The other, 'original', Katana made its own Cardinal's robes and replicated my body underneath that complete concealment. It/we descended rapidly through the disaster area where the personnel were still fumbling around, too busy with medical attentions and the prevention of fire to wonder at anyone looking familiar. It went straight to the level where Isylon and his family were waiting.

In the time that took I removed the overalls I was wearing, throwing them aside so I could do the grunt work that was all I was fit for. In my wandering priest outfit I yanked debris out of the way and pushed the car around so the nose faced the gaping hole we'd made on the way in. I didn't see any bodies but it was hard to tell and I didn't look too hard. We all moved as fast as we were able. Events took on an accelerated pace that gave them an unreal quality, no time for reflection anywhere.

A word to the wise, Captain, but the shooting up here has attracted the attention of System state law units in the area. I can see a Hunter Tracker class decelerating in.

– What does that mean, Tash? Your friends catching up with you for nicking the ship at last?

That's exactly what it means. The Tracker will merely identify targets and confirm locations and the situation, but given the nature and extent of my behavioural divergence from accepted norms I expect that it will dispatch a Judgement Class executor in order to retrieve or destroy said property.

– Wait, what?

Do you know the phrase 'Wanted: Dead or Alive'?

I cut her off. One outlaw at a time.

Two had located a working Alembic very close to Tecmaten's seat of office. I could feel where she was, the Inquisition Beast covering the entrances for me. There were relatively few guards on the upper levels, and fewer now they were occupied with managing the casualties. At my position they were still looking for attackers. A guard came to investigate the wreckage, guns drawn, and peered all around nervously, constantly looking over her shoulder and twisting around as if things were hiding in the shadows, which they were.

I moved around quietly, kept the car between us. After a few minutes she steeled herself to enter it. I admired her but I don't think I'd have bothered risking my lone neck in the circumstances. She left herself vulnerable as she stepped aboard and found nobody.

I was so close outside the car door that I heard her comms insisting she search for explosives. She obeyed. I could feel her dread but finally she said, 'There's an arsenal here, but it's untouched.' She sounded puzzled. Surely if you were coming to kill everyone you wouldn't leave all your guns behind? 'I guess it's just a crazy extremist thing inspired by the bird or something.'

Some people will believe anything, especially when it's convenient.

They advised her to get out and she left so fast she didn't notice me even though she passed within a metre of me and nobody could call the remaining dust clouds thick. I let her go and went back to prep the car, doors open, engine reactivated. I watched my hands working on these simple things while my attention drifted far away, riding with the Nico avatar as I searched for Isylon. I couldn't let the Beast do the talking, he wasn't up to it, so I talked to agitated guards and calmed them with plausible explanations and false reports of arrests. I heard from their comms the summons from Tecmaten that wanted Isylon taken up for questioning, so I sped towards his cell door, the avatar body transformed into Inquisition Nico, complete with his own standard issue firearms and his heavy purple uniform that hung like a skirt in panels.

Congrats, Nic. Now you are Number One Fan.

Isy did a double take of epic proportions as I entered his cell and held up my hand for silence, giving the head shake that suggested collusion. He put up the hood of his robe and went before me, my gun at his back. Better to pretend you're their kind when you're in their contested territory. I put my own hood over my head. It had a veil so that whoever wore it could look like a spectacularly impersonal Hand of Fate – which was really a massive security oversight but you get what you pay for.

Meanwhile up at the Alembic Two had been brought before Tecmaten to answer for her gatecrashing crime in person. With my focus in the Katana clone there I cleared the room of spare idiots and then stood back and watched the weirdness as Two and the decrepit creature tentatively hugged one another and started to cry. I was glad I wasn't keeping pictures of it for posterity, though. I wanted my guy in his original chocolate wrapper and only maggot-fodder cute when time had made him that way all on its own. For Two's sake I hoped Tashin's original form wasn't something in a tank with mandibles.

Around them bleats and alarms kept going off, of comms

336

wanting instructions in the sudden absence of a spacefleet. After a minute more Two detached herself with only the faintest of shudders and sat down. She gave Tashin instructions and let the DNA of Tecmaten's hands do the rest of the talking. I downloaded the Alembic direct to the Beast while the two of them set about locking Harmony down into a safe mode to protect those few of the population who weren't in on the cash-for-avatars dealership and to pave the start of the way for an incursion of space invaders, or System cops as they were known to the wider world.

Tecmaten looked up at me as the download finished. 'Time's up.'

The Hunter Tracker has us on a sight mark. You've got about five minutes before something else gets within range.

Isylon arrived at the same moment that the corpse of Tecmaten finally went limp and slumped over his Alembic for the last time. After a glance around Isy moved forward to check for a pulse as if he were a triage doctor. We all looked at him, Two and I, and he shook his head slowly.

'You're not seriously going to save him, are you?' Two was asking, having figured out who he was and what he could do on the instant.

Isy glanced at Inquisitor me and then at her with a blank look. He was still in shock. His hand was shaking.

'This man made you for profit,' Two objected, still in a misunderstanding. She thought he was going to show mercy.

'Oh, don't worry,' Isylon said quietly, withdrawing his hands into his sleeves. 'I killed him earlier. I was just checking, for my own satisfaction really. I haven't seen the dead walk before.'

'More than he deserved,' Two spat, adjusting her expression and awkwardly giving Isylon a pat on the shoulder like he was a rookie gang pup who'd done well.

'How can you make jokes about it?' he said. He looked ill.

'Been on the receiving end too long,' Two said. She looked around the room. 'What're we waiting for?'

'Nothing,' I said, putting my veil in place and checking the gun in my sleeve. 'Lead the way.'

'No, wait.' Isylon held his hand up. 'This isn't right. You two are acting like...'

'Criminals?' I suggested to speed matters up a bit.

'Wanted criminals,' Two said. 'With a hostage. Move your ass.' She was giving him a look that said she wasn't in the mood for sympathising so he'd better man up. 'I'm guessing Nic won't leave without you but I'm damned if I'll be shot because of your heartbreaking ethical crisis, or whatever this is. Move it.'

He looked at me with real hurt, eyes slow-blinking in an attempt to process what was happening. He looked around the room and then shook his head, covering his face with his hair and flipping up his hood.

We returned to the car, passing a few groups of assembling guards on the way although none close enough to the car to stop us in time. Katana returned to her usual form as Two and Isy got in the back and I hit the controls for getting the hell out of there. Two tried explaining things to Isy as I pushed the drive as hard as it would go. Shots rang off the bodywork and a window smashed as we ground slowly into motion, hampered by the remains of whatever very expensive and tasteful stuff had been in the room.

'They'll execute my family when they know I've gone,' Isylon said, the pure misery of his tone cutting through the shattering hail of gunfire as our plan was thoroughly discovered.

'It's unlikely,' I said. 'Most of the officers are straitjacketed. But I guess there'll be some very pissed off morons who might go for it. Where are they?' I asked as the car began to accelerate, the last of the obstacles in its way slithering aside.

'You have to be fucking joking,' Two said.

'I stay keep safety,' Katana said without a hesitation, opened the car door and got out, slamming it behind her.

We crashed into the remains of the window a moment later and were out, falling into the deep blue frozen night air. The car struggled – some fan was cutting out in the front – but it made horizontal and then began to fly well enough on its overcharged, underused engines. We cleared the capital centre city before serious pursuit began.

Droids from Ito and pursuit cars from the city had no trouble finding us in the otherwise empty air thanks to the traffic ban they'd imposed after the bird had struck. The sedan was top spec but it had been damaged in the crash and there was no way I could outrun them for more than a minute or two.

I could feel the approach of an intercept craft – mine – coming out of the neutral space beyond Harmony's border where it had been loitering for a couple of days now, but it wouldn't get here in time. I didn't fancy betting against a machine targeting system. I pushed the wheel and headed for the forest and the ground. No sooner had I made the decision than I felt the cool putter of a missile launch a couple of kilometres behind us.

In the car Two was fighting to get the lone harness fitted on Isy. As we started our deathslide descent she slid away and tumbled against the drinks cabinet, thoughtfully stocked with crystal. Bottles chinked and she swore. Isy clung to the webbing of the harness and saved himself the same trip.

'I'm going to put us down in the woods. We'll have to run for it.'

'Run?' Two's contempt was nearly visible.

'It's that or get shot out of the sky and turned into pot-roast.'

A few shots spattered the back end and then the missile hit the engine bay. It was only a tiny thing, meant for stopping people not vehicles, and it was at the limit of its range but it smacked into us and exploded with a sharp bang and an impact that slammed us all into the nearest hard, unyielding object.

A whining, unhappy noise started in the fan housing and our drop became erratic. I fought to keep us flat, hoping we could break our fall using the underside as a shield to surf through the trees. I had already planned to slow down but the dying engine determined when that was going to happen.

'I knew I hated this plan,' Two snarled, wedging herself against the seats, giving Isy's seatbelt one more yank. 'Pot Roast Fiasco. Shit, I don't want to die now. We've nearly made it!'

I could hear her voice cracking with emotion. It made me hesitate. 'We already made it. Harmony won't be the same.'

'Oh fuck, yeah. Well now you say it that makes everything all right!'

Nothing made anything all right, but it wasn't the moment to say it, I was too busy pulling at controls that no longer wanted to react. What happened next wasn't up to me.

'I'm sorry, Isy!' I yelled over the screaming sound of the fans grinding themselves up. 'I did my best.' I felt he'd had the worst deal. Two and I always knew the odds were shitty, but he'd been on the winning side for a long time. I don't know why that was worse, but it was.

He said something which I thought was, 'If you hadn't come...' but I missed it because we hit the trees at the wrong angle, on a bad slope and the car flipped. I was knocked around violently, a jumble of dark seizures. I got a sudden view from outside and saw the car tumble once before it struck a huge old pine on the edge of a ridge and lost most of its momentum, leaving just enough for it to fall down and tip end over end into a steep, narrow ravine. I heard water rushing and felt a bitter cold. In the sky a bird stooped like an arrow on its prey. I saw it come for us but I never saw it land.

Eighteen – You Got Me

Nico.

– I'm guessing this is bad news.

I could only hear Tashin's voice; everything else was, well, there was nothing else.

Ah, you're all right.

– Where is *we*? What happened?

We're aboard the ship. That is, myself, Twostar and Isylon Selamaa.

I didn't like the sound of this.

– Where am I?

Mmn, there's no easy way to say this. Nico, you didn't make it out of the car crash in a wholesome state.

– I'm dead AGAIN?

No, no, of course not. If you were dead we'd hardly be having this conversation. Do keep up. Isylon is working on fixing you but it's not an easy job. Wait, Twostar wants to say something to you...

'Nico, can you hear me?' That was Two, supremely excited. I could hear her because Tashin could hear her. The Beast made a voice for me from some speaker somewhere so that we could talk.

– Yes. Is Isylon all right? What's happening?

'He's great. You're going to be fine. Better than fine. The

Judgement Class Whatever that's been arresting us is even going to let you off pending some deposition formality thing but that's not the point. Listen to me, Nico, you're free. We're free. We did it! And there's more, it's better than that.'

– Better? I searched hard then, for any signs of a lie, but I couldn't find a thing. Sight returned slowly – I saw her with Isylon, standing over a clear plasglas shield under which a very battered-looking me was lying with all kinds of tubes and bandages everywhere.

'Yeah,' Isylon said softly, his hand stretched out over the glass. Two joined him, bouncing up and down and unable to help herself so that they spoke together, even the swearing.

'Nico, you have the fucking ship!'

It was all a bit fast for me.

– Wait, where's Tashin? Is she an octopus or something?

'I'm here.' A short, powerfully built woman in some kind of engineer's flightsuit came from behind the camera's viewing angle and waved to it. She was mature, dark hair, soft, glamorous and with a face that was much more empathic than her voice had ever been. Her skin was silvered with machine tattoos.

– And this isn't a—

'Nico!' Two shrieked in an objection to my stubbornness, hammering the glass with her open hand until Isy stopped her gently.

'No, this isn't a prank. You and the ship – the Beast, as you call it – are now integrated. Partners. You can speak to each other whenever you like. There's nobody else in the mix. Nobody at all. You're still getting Tashin because the Beast is relaying her for you. But she hasn't got any connection directly to you.'

I felt my waking up had a way to go. I looked harder.

Space was around us, its bitter cold a refreshing draught against my sides, the Beast a quiet presence far in the back left of my awareness, glad to see me. I so wanted to be able to hug them all. I wanted to tell them, in some way that didn't sound sappy, about the time I was dead and realised that even the worst of my hatreds was only a stupid form of love. Only the sense that I could get to do that one day kept me quiet about it. These things are hard to do unless you're stupendously drunk.

Then something else occurred to me.

– Isn't there something you need to say to me, Miss Tashlyn-nai?

She waited and I knew she could feel the dig through the link perfectly well. She composed herself for a moment. 'Permission to stay aboard, sir.'

– Airlock's right over there.

'Nico!' Two said, horrified. Even Isylon looked worried, biting his lower lip – and me with no way to kiss it.

I let her stew for a moment.

– Permission granted.

With Tecmaten dead and unable to make any further returns on his investments and with a score of the old guard infiltrated by the Beast the incident was soon cleared away and business restored to the usual. There was limited fuss about finding a successor to the great man who had developed the Alchemy and saved humanity from the degradation and dilution going on everywhere else in the known universe. That bought us a few weeks to get our acts together and, more importantly, gave the Judgement Class *Avenging Deity in the Absence of Democracy* a chance to examine all the evidence about our varying cases before deciding what it was going to do, if anything, with regard to applying some System Law. Since I allowed it to send a droid unit of its own with us, it was fine with our idea of taking a short restorative break to visit the Orbital.

I spent most of the time in suspended consciousness recovering. By the time the weeks of waiting had passed I was back up and back to normal. The worst part of the return was the discovery that we all had to wear whatever we could fit into from Tashin's wardrobe – she'd been the only human to come aboard before us and she hadn't brought much with her. I wound up in a grey jumpsuit whose arm and leg sections came two thirds of the way down my limbs and which bit me in the crotch every time I sat down. I wore it for twenty seconds before making its destruction my first priority.

'I doesn't have crew,' the Beast said firmly, making its position clear on responsibility re garments. It spoke directly to me through the Switch, voice rough and somehow chewy as though it was always devouring something.

'It's not your fault,' I said. 'But with all this technology couldn't you make something?'

'I doesn't do outfitting,' the Beast replied with a happy contempt for all beings that required clothing or any form of accessories.

'What about armour?'

A grudging pause. 'Maybe do that.' It went off into its private aether to do whatever it took to get that underway. I got off my sickbed and walked out of the medical bay, service droids scattering before me. The ship corridors were a neutral clay ochre, functional, a little more like a burrow than I'd expected. Everyone else aboard was asleep, except Tashin but I didn't alert her. I went by myself to look around my quarters. Unusual and beautiful objects were everywhere: rugs, plants, art things – and the furniture looked handcrafted, whatever it was. Someone had taken great trouble over it all. It was luxurious but not with the cartel's bombastic aesthetic. It was gentle. I sensed Isylon's touch and searched for him. He was in the second bedroom. I didn't go in, not yet, I wanted to see the ship for myself. As I made my rounds I felt the Beast watching me, but not like before; this time it was only following me out of curiosity.

Because of the human scale and the organic, earthy feel of the interior, when I came to the viewing deck to look out I didn't understand at all what I was seeing. A huge expanse of black, starlit space opened out, cut through by what seemed to be the bottom of a strange hourglass through which sand poured in a fine stream down to create a perfect hill with a broad base and shallow sides. It was marked at intervals with lines. Large, bright objects hovered to either side of it, big near the base and tiny where they clustered close to the sand fall.

In trying to make out what it was my curiosity itself adjusted the light filtering and I realised that what I'd thought was flat was three-dimensional. It wasn't sand falling into a hill, it was a strip like a huge ribbon of road that ran out from our right side and swept off and into the distance before arching up and up, becoming so fine that it was a thread and then was lost to my visibility. I sat down on one of the command chairs that had been placed there and, given the dust, never used. 'What is that?'

'That the Orbital,' the Beast said, pleased to be of use. 'The Pericarp, where all are made or born and most live if they land animal.'

I looked around for nearby planets but the closest one was Earth itself, barely visible it was so far off. I understood that the Orbital was orbiting it, a gossamer hoop over four million k in diameter. The lines were the edges of the sections it was made of, each like a tray thousands of kilometres per side and of a depth that permitted each its own land, sea and atmosphere or whatever it was meant to contain. My guts closed hard and I felt an icy wash run down my body, a shooting electricity in my shins and calves so that if I hadn't already been sitting I would have fallen on the floor.

There below us, sand in a box, was Harmony. It was one of thousands. Not even a planet. Not even a real world.

Was all this other stuff here all the time? Was that the iron wall? No, couldn't be, it was too small.

'The wall you saw is generator, create sky, block sight of

345

endwalls, take out visible line of Orbital so that Harmony look natural, like planet.'

'A wall that hides a wall?'

'Heh, yes, is funny.' The Beast chuckled, something I didn't hear but I did feel, like a flutter in my chest.

'But...' Well, that mostly covered it. Let's leave it at *but*. Only, 'How come nobody found you if everyone is here?' Fuck me, it was all here all the time. In my mind the Diaspora, hope, life had been beyond the back of the furthest stars.

'I got shadow coat. Can't be seen, heard. Stealthy. Sneak up on things.'

I looked some more. 'Are we in hiding now?'

'Can't tell?'

Yes, I could tell. We were hiding. We were—

'You're over six kilometres long!'

'For now. Easier for coat. Can be other shapes. Modular.'

What the hell was in that six kilometres? It was... it was...

I was sitting on an arsenal big enough to conduct a war in its own right from the soldiers on the ground to the intelligence units, the tactical systems, the navy, the air command... not to mention the space combat. 'Who were you meant to be fighting?'

'Aliens. Yes, yes. And some rogue states, some pirates, little pilfer tinkers, bit organise crime. Not here. Out. Way out. Rebels, stuff.'

'I can see why they didn't want to lose you.'

'Mmn. Judgement Class want me to come back, do job, be good worker. Police.'

But the Beast could not work for them because they'd killed his mother. 'We'll think of something,' I said. 'There's good money in protection.' I was still looking at Harmony. Twinkle twinkle little star: it really was a fucking tea-tray in the sky. 'Are each of those sections separate?'

'Yes, all different factories. Your friends very keen you go shop. They wait very impatient.'

'Is there a clothes shop?'

'All thing shop.'

Fine. We would go shop. But first I had to sit and look at this for a few more hours or maybe centuries.

The jumpsuit defeated the view in the end. I went to find Tashin. She was sitting in a small room, surrounded by a huge amount of gear which I realised after a minute was nearly all different kinds of droids, but packed up in hibernation. She looked comfortable in her pale blue shirt and trousers. I made the door chime sound though I was damned if I was waiting to be asked in.

She looked up in surprise and then her mouth twisted in a snicker as she saw what I was wearing. 'Nico, you look very well.'

'Give me something else to wear.'

'What, not even a thank you for my lovely overalls?'

'Thank you for the ball ache. And I mean that metaphorically, in fact, in every way. Give me something else.'

'All right all right.' She left what she was reading and went to a wardrobe.

As she was rooting about in there I examined her machines. 'Friends of yours?'

'Tools of the trade. None of them are sentient.' Oh that voice and how I disbelieved it.

'They're not mine. I want them off here.'

'Which is why I'm packing them for return to the department. Here we go...' She returned to me with a pair of white cotton trousers and a blue pullover in some kind of very large arty-looking knit. 'I rather like these but sadly I don't think anything else will fit you.' She handed them over. They smelled of her subtle perfume. I stripped off the overalls and put them on. Tashin turned her face away.

'Yeah, modesty suits you,' I said, kicking the shredded overalls

347

back towards her. 'So what are your plans now that Tecmaten's been disposed of? Personal justice crusade ended?'

She sighed. 'Didn't you just get everything you wanted? Am I never going to be, I don't know – forgiven, I suppose, let off the hook?'

'I might forgive you but I'll never forget.'

She shrugged with an expression that said OK. 'I should be grateful, I suppose.'

I wanted to say a whole lot more about it, ask her whether all her unsuspecting victims were graciously understanding, but abruptly I remembered: Do Not Engage. It was time to disengage with this. It had nowhere to go that was any good, so I gave myself a moment to imagine her grisly death and then I let it go and got out.

While I waited for the ship's internal *night* cycle to end and for the sleepers to wake I toured the huge interior of the living areas, but like a moth to a candle I kept going back to the viewing ports or looking from my mind's eye at that extraordinary sight of the ribbon of my world. Harmony was over three hundred thousand kilometres distant now – I could have blotted it out with my finger. Eventually I had to stop and close the ports. I'd started to feel too exposed out here in this massive expanse, and to think with longing of the dojo. Until now I didn't know that it was home.

Isylon found me sitting in my room and started slightly, as he'd clearly come in thinking I was still in the medical bay. I got up from my silent slump and went to greet him. We hugged fast and hard, then moved back to examine one another. I felt suddenly awkward. Looking at him here was different. He was wearing a cleaned but ragged version of his robes, but without the sense of imminent death and upheaval it was almost as if we were strangers. He must have had longer to get used to it because he gave me a wry smile, 'Second thoughts?'

I shook my head slowly. I could feel myself connecting up slowly to the parts of me that liked him, and the longer I looked at him the stronger the connections became. 'I'm not so much a thoughts person,' I said to cover up. 'How are you doing?' It was easier to be concerned about him than me. He'd lost a father, a family, a life – what had I lost? Not much.

He made an equivocal shrug and shook his head. 'I have bad times and good times. It's all so new. Hasn't sunk in yet. And I'm not sure what's going on in Harmony so it's hard to put things straight in my mind. I'm waiting to see.' His hands on my arms were stable but I felt his reluctance to let go. 'It's difficult to imagine – I mean, being on this ship, and what Harmony really is. I feel my mind accept it but the rest of me...' He shook his head again, that repeated *No, No*.

I got it. I kissed him because I wanted to see if that spark was still there. When we surfaced that question was answered but I felt too raw and off balance to take things any further at that moment. 'What have you been doing while I was out of it?'

'Aside from going crazy? We, I mean Two and Tashin and I, we all went down to the Orbital Convention Point. It's just an hour from here. We looked around at all the uh... store fronts. And we saw... people... who.' He stopped; words had failed him.

'Who?'

'They're people but they don't look like us. At all. Although I did see some definite Harmony um, natives are they? Around. But they were...'

I kissed him again because I didn't care what they were. 'You can still go back, if you want to. Any time.'

Isylon put his hand to my forehead. 'It's all right, Nic. Everything is all right. You don't have to do any more. You don't have to save everyone and protect everything. We can all do it ourselves. You've done so much. Just be for now. Walk around, take your time, look at things. We'll figure it out. It doesn't have to be today.'

The touch and his words lifted the ton of lead blankets that had descended on me over the last... I was going to say days but really it was longer than that. It was much longer. For ever, perhaps. The Beast prowled in the back of my mind, anxious but at the same time eager to please in its own way. I felt its presence react to Isylon too. It relaxed.

'Are you using juju on me?' I asked, grinning, well, trying to grin but finding it difficult because my face wanted to collapse and cry.

'Nothing special,' he said and smiled. Then the sun came out.

'Um... we'll wait for Two to get up and then we'll go and see this shopping thing, the Orbital. How do we get there anyway?'

'Oh, you've got a car,' he said, grinning at me with his extra knowledge. 'Several actually.'

'Is it safe there for us?'

'Tashin says yes, absolutely, but we took a Katana anyway, left it there to keep an eye on things for us.'

A Katana. I had Katanas. And cars. I was a cartel.

My immediate reaction was rejection. I had no interest in being that kind of bastard. But I looked at Isylon and he was giving me his gentle, patient look that said *Not Today, Bro.* So, we could figure out what to be later. My moment of fury subsided.

'Sometimes you look as if you should have horns,' he said, hugging me closely. He had a very warm embrace, not sexy but very sweet and kind. I lingered.

'They're invisible.'

'Well that explains it.'

We were interrupted by a screech like a scalded cat, 'AAAAAAhhh, Niii-co!' It was Two. She hit us at speed and knocked us sideways, a human hug missile of skinny, intent grip. Since Isylon was in the way he got included. It was the best I'd felt in so long I found it hard to let go even after a minute. After two.

A while later we had sorted ourselves out and left for the Orbital. On the way I learned about the shape of the Beast's ship body, how it maintained areas of interior gravity, some greater and some lesser, how it rearranged itself as needed so that we didn't have to travel to a distant garage to find a dropship, one was brought round for us. The entire hangar bay could be brought round.

At the door the duty Katana brought me my armour and I put it on. Inside its flexible skin I felt much as I had when suiting up for a job – suddenly able, powerful. There were no skirts, no fancy swords, no guns. It was practical, blue-grey and matt. I looked like I was about to start work on something manual and a bit messy. I was perfectly anonymous. The boots were heavy but that felt good, grounding me on the deck. I thanked the Beast and it glowed inwardly with pride.

Sitting in the car's comfortable interior with nothing to do but look at Isy was one of the most surreal experiences of my life. Two and Tashin sat beside one another, kind of close but not too close: they'd come to a truce. There was no more romance at the moment, but there was something. I couldn't get over how much Tashin did and didn't resemble her Harmony avatar.

'So how come you're the only person that cared to invade?' I asked her, putting my feet up on the table that was between us. 'I mean, of all the people that it must take to run the System. Why no Judgement Class interest?'

Tashin put her head to the side and did the kind of thing with her mouth that gave the impression she was trying hard to put something into words. She glanced around and saw every eye on her and went through a few more expressions as she kept changing her mind about what to say or how to say it or

351

both. Finally she threw her hands up in the air and let them fall empty into her lap. 'Nico, I don't know how to say this to you, darling. Or any of you. Or you, dear Two ...' She put a hand out automatically to touch Two who let her, a little sadness in her face. 'I *am* the Judgement Class, for want of a better way to put it. But not all of it. I am only a part of its totality.'

'Another avatar?'

'No, a body, but not like before. This is me. This is the piece of me that you can see here.'

'You said your superiors didn't want you to intervene,' Two said, objecting to a lot more than that, her voice outraged.

'No, they didn't. System wanted Harmony to run to see what Tecmaten could really make with the Alchemy. It was against the law, of course, but they felt that people like Isylon were worth suspending action for. It was – it is true that the genetic research and development done was of a higher quality than any other. And I had met Bitna and seen that she was different. Genuinely odd. There is an enormous beauty and quality, an enormous reverence everywhere in the System for the new and the odd.'

'Then why didn't they want the Beast?' I said.

'They were afraid it would do terrible damage and they couldn't find a way to stop it. But now they have. And now I have intervened and ... from now on the fate of Harmony is something I will have to hand over to System Operatives. But I would like you to speak for it, Isylon, if you're willing.'

Isylon nodded slowly.

I felt something subtle close around me. 'I'm not working for you.'

She looked at me and I was taken aback by her directness and calm. 'I would never expect you to. You and the Beast are free to do as you wish. I will always be here to act as your defender, as long as you don't break the law. In that event maybe you can contact me indirectly.' She sighed and looked down at her hands.

'You're leaving,' Two said, having watched her closely this entire time.

'Yes, I won't come back with you from the Orbital,' Tashin said. 'I think it's better if you all have time to adjust to what has happened and, if you want to, you can stay in touch with me.'

'In touch,' Two said, making a motion with her hand of dismissal. 'Is that it?'

'I...' Tashin began.

'No,' Two said. 'I'm tired of being taken care of and shipped around and told what to do. I'm going with you. I want to see this System and everything for myself. I think you owe me that.' She looked at me, a fearful, daring, scared, hopeful look.

I smiled at her. 'If it sucks you can always come back. Come and go as you like.'

She grinned at me, relieved.

Tashin agreed silently, with a nod, a lean in Two's direction which I suddenly saw as gladness.

We arrived and decanted into the Orbital port and busied ourselves out of our serious mood with customs and other activity, the Katana bringing up the rear patiently.

'Nic,' Isylon said softly, at my arm, 'there's something you should see...' But I was already seeing. I couldn't do anything but see strange people, and stranger things, everywhere I looked, and there, in the distance, moving slowly through the crowds on the boulevards that spread out and out I saw a tall figure, stooping to smell a frond of palm on his way past it – a bull-headed man, a real minotaur, massively and spectacularly real, his torso crisscrossed with belts that held his possessions, a kind of insect flying around his head. It settled on one of his horns as he was talking to it and they both seemed to pause for a laugh at something. He was one of hundreds of variants on human I saw in that moment. Had he been here all along, while I was in that orphanage and its walls, so close as this? As real as this?

I was overwhelmed. Everything passed in a blur: people, shopfronts, bazaars, gathering places full of new smells, new shapes and even the most simple objects strange in their designs.

'It's much too much,' Two said, at my other arm. Had she been there long? I wasn't sure. I was constantly observing everywhere and I felt that everywhere there was something to notice, to consider in the generation of a speedy and safe exit. And then it hit me. I had no need to leave. Nobody cared about me, either to kill me or to act the fan. Nobody knew me at all and there was nothing about me to single me out as worthy of remark, let alone arrest.

We stopped.

'This is it,' Two whispered. She was cuddled close against my side, Isylon calmly centred on the other.

A foyer, a lounge, a huge banner display of holographs. We were at the Harmony shop. The walls were made of a fantastic landscape of light in which the Alchemy's particular view of genetics was visually laid out, moulded, used, developed into people.

Balance is Everything.

All three of us were transfixed like kids.

Two tugged my hand. We passed into a lounge, attended by people wearing some kind of skin paint so that their features seemed to change constantly but slowly in the eternal round of what was possible. Their skin, their faces, the colours of their eyes – all that didn't change was their build. A nifty little pattern of symbols would run over them like water now and again, lest you forget it was a spell of engineering that made them. We avoided the assistants and Two stood me at a terminal, one she'd obviously seen before by the way her hands flashed over its commands.

'Here,' she said. 'You can design your own.'

Isylon took in a deep breath and blew it out carefully through his mouth.

'Or,' Two said, as I hesitated, 'you can buy one from a pre-designed template.' Her hands flashed again and suddenly I was looking in a mirror. Above my face it said, '#Perseid – model still under test'. Beneath my picture a standard disclaimer read: 'Variations in longevity, intelligence and temperament are uncontrollable beyond basic conditioning and cannot be guaranteed.'

Her hand moved and I was looking at her. '#Fae'

Again and I was looking at Isylon. '#Selamaa variant 2: this model is for display and presentation purposes only and is not for sale.'

There were details I didn't read. We sat through a presentation which told us clearly that every aspect of the culture of Harmony had been engineered to prove some point or other about the influence of nurture, personal and environmental factors on genetic potentials. The darker aspects of its regime were deliberately engineered to prove that any personality type could be persuaded to conform. It was all about the right pressure to the right person at the right moment. They made it sound as if you could order a recipe from them, take it away and then follow the baking instructions until you got exactly what you asked for twenty years later. They included a warm speech about Tecmaten's devotion to exacting techniques and the brilliance of his social and religious insights into the power of control of the mind.

I got up after a while and walked out. It's not that I hadn't known what Harmony was but seeing the cheesy, marketed version of it was more than I could stand. Was this it, then? Business as usual. It didn't seem right that we could go through all that for this. Cut off the head, the body hardly notices.

Two joined me, leaning on a balcony rail and looking down into a sunlit plaza where cafés, bars and game arenas jostled for space. There was some hubbub and a general air of fun and leisure. 'I've got to get away from here,' she said.

'Don't want to change it?'

'How? How the hell would we change it? What would we do? Take away the Alchemy and all the filth will step into the gap and impose another kind of bad order. Change the religion and you won't change the underlying nature of the people, will you? Different, sure. Better?' She snorted and crossed her arms on the rail, rested her forehead on them for a minute, bent double as if the weight on her back was too much to carry.

She was right. I didn't have a clue what would help. I wanted to blow up the bad bits, but they were all hidden down the back of people's cerebella. It was pretty rare you got a whole person bad enough to shoot. 'Escape was enough before. Why isn't it now?'

'Because you got power, Nic, and you think that means you should do something with it.'

'Shouldn't I?'

Isylon and Tashin returned, Katana keeping a polite distance.

Maybe keeping harm out of the way was already enough. I could be a lot of harm, and I'd done a lot of it. Bottom line was I didn't know what to do now I had nothing to fight, so I was picking a fight – or trying to – only I couldn't find the person who needed the slap. I should do something. I should be something. How can I be here, free, powerful and not know what to do?

We stayed on the Orbital for a few days, I can call it that now I know it is one. The Beast covered the finances, or Tashin did, I'm not sure which. They said not to worry about money so I guess they had a lot of it. The hotels we stopped at were gorgeous, their settings breathtaking. It was a great relief; but equally a constant sense of waiting for the other shoe to drop prevented me enjoying it wholeheartedly. My heart wasn't whole, about anything.

I bought some baggy, shapeless hobo clothes and I felt a bit better. We filled our time telling the stories of our lives to each other, bit by bit, mostly just the three of us without Tashin who was carefully keeping at range. At last we ran out of things to say and there was a calm.

'Fucking Harmony,' I said to Isy as we stayed up late drinking wine and watching inexplicable vids from other parts of the System. 'Can't live in it, can't nuke it from orbit. Can't forget about it.'

'Why would you want to forget it?' He rested his head against my shoulder and twirled his glass against the light.

'How can we sit here and leave them all there?' and by *them* I meant everyone like us who was outlawed for no fault of their own.

'You have to trust that the System won't be so corrupt they will allow it to go on for ever. They've got expertise in mass social intervention. They'll find the best way for everyone.'

'That feels like a cop-out.'

'Your alternative is to create Nico world. Or Beastworld, whatever. Is that better?'

No kidding it was not better. Even we didn't want to live in it. 'It's a lot worse. We're scrappy and bad tempered.'

'So, let others have a chance. You lived there for more than twenty-five years. They can do the same. You don't have to be god.'

'Says the resurrectionist.'

'I don't really know that's what I am. But even if I was, is there a point to it? I mean, I don't mind showing a path for the dying but I'm damned if I'm forcing people to live on and there's no way I'm acting like a transporter for avatar transfer which is, I think, where I was headed. I wonder what that part of the Alchemy story would have been like?'

'The progression of the divine through many incarnations...' I began.

'Don't,' he said and winced. 'It's too close to the truth.' He hesitated. 'Won't you miss Two?'

357

'Yeah,' I said. 'But everything's got to grow and change. And she and I aren't really into the same things now we don't have a mutual enemy. She's all smart and stuff and I'm—' I wasn't sure what I was.

'You're a Beast,' Isylon said with satisfaction. 'Someone should put you in a labyrinth.'

'It's all right, I have my own priest to exorcise me,' I said and a mote of happiness like a sunlit fragment of dust turned and shone in my chest.

'Zzzzt,' Isylon said, pretending to shoot lightning or holy fire at me with his fingertips.

I felt the Beast itself, quiet and sad although it was peaceful. I felt that way too, like coming to rest after a long fall, safe and back on the ground.

The Judgement Class main body, a massive ship that dwarfed the Beast, was departing for the other side of the Orbital. Two was aboard it, and Tashin. We watched it go and I felt my eyes water and my face become wet. We were really free, as you can be, given everything, you know, and at that moment I felt myself so clearly reach the end of something that it was a dying.

'Zzzzt,' said Isylon again, drunkenly giving me another dose of imaginary magic.

'Yeah, yeah,' I said. 'I'm not that easy to kill.'

Acknowledgements

Thanks for the origin conditions for this story to Gergo Vizeli – you really set me up! Although it was a fun adventure to try to fulfil the brief. Maybe it's not the last time I'll take someone up on a difficult challenge because otherwise I'd never have written this. I hope that the results don't go too wide of the mark.

For their constant support in every way thanks to my family, especially my mother and Laszlo. You have made my writing life possible in every way.

For advice, insight and feedback on the working script a heartfelt round of applause to Kelley Eskridge – you rock.

And for spiritual and emotional bolstering and inspiration thanks to Tricia Sullivan, Freda Warrington, Adrian and Annie Tchaikovsky and Stephanie Burgis. I love you all.

Grateful thanks to my previous editor, Simon Spanton, who has always been a rock. It was great working with you for the last six books. I wish you every good fortune in what life brings next.

Last but not least thanks to my new editor, Gillian Redfearn: hail, fellow, well met by sunlight! Your instinct for good story-telling and your fine taste in authors has not gone unnoticed here. I'm so glad to be working with you again. Her accomplice Rachel Winterbottom also had a hand in the final draft edit and provided many helpful suggestions – thanks to you too!

Finally, a note. To those of you familiar with the work of Iain Banks you will see that the ship names here are somewhat reminiscent of his Culture ship names and that Harmony exists on an Orbital of the type pioneered in his stories. So much of his work has such an influence on my imagination of a spacefaring world that it was impossible not to include them. They are what his work made of my mind and they are here as everything else is here, from someone else, going under and rising up as stories recreate themselves anew. All things have been imagined and spoken of before but some of them are worth replicating quite closely because they're so fantastic.

Errors, poor timing and other mistakes of all kinds are mine alone.